THE PEARL OF HONG KONG

HENRY KWUN CHEN

MINERVA PRESS

LONDON
MIAMI   DELHI   SYDNEY

THE PEARL OF HONG KONG
Copyright © Henry Kwun Chen 2000

ISBN 0 75410 799 X

First Published 2000 by
MINERVA PRESS
315–317 Regent Street
London W1R 7YB

Printed in Great Britain for Minerva Press

THE PEARL OF
HONG KONG

Part One

Chapter One

After classes ended one warm autumn afternoon, the girls scattered from the front gate of the school onto Robinson Road. Most of the girls were Chinese; a few were Eurasian. Carrying book satchels over their shoulders with a strap, they wore sky-blue uniforms, long-sleeved blouses and pleated skirts that fell below their knees; a red tie complemented their white stockings and black shoes.

A yellow wooden tablet that hung above the gate read: 'St Mary's Anglo-Chinese Secondary School'. Below the tablet, a white banner announced: School Exhibition, 8th October, 1940.

With its playgrounds and two-storey, Western-style buildings on several levels, the school stood high on the hill opposite to the harbour side of the road. Located in the Mid-Levels District of Mount Victoria on Hong Kong Island, it commanded a spectacular view of the extensive Victoria Harbour, far below to the north.

With no public transportation available on that part of the island, some of the girls were driven home in private cars while most of them walked. The bulk of those who walked descended by winding paths to the bustling downtown Central District, where they boarded trams, buses or ferries to complete their travels home. About two scores of the rest headed east or west from the gate by way of Robinson Road.

With only a few pedestrians on this road, many of them were attracted to one girl walking westward with a group of her schoolmates. Two middle-aged, wide-eyed women wearing glasses turned to each other and smiled.

One remarked, 'She is like a red flower that catches one's eye in the midst of thick, green foliage!' Nodding her head, the other replied, 'Oh my! What an apt simile.'

At the same time, a few feet away, a young man elbowed another and said, 'When I look at her sweet face, I feel like my eyes are tasting ice cream.' Both laughed.

This 'red flower', taller than the average Chinese girl for her age, had wide, sparkling mahogany eyes, dark crescent-shaped eyebrows and naturally curled eyelashes. Her ebony hair contrasted with her soft pink and white complexion.

The girls reached the cable-tram station, from which they would take either an upward or a downward tram to get to their homes situated at different levels on Mount Victoria.

One of the girls handed 'the red flower' an envelope and said, 'Li-ling, this get-well card is for your mother. The fifteen of us wish her a speedy recovery.'

'Thank you so much,' said Li-ling. Then she put it in her satchel. 'I've seen my mother every night for more than three weeks. And it's only these past two or three days that she seems to have been getting better. I heartily thank all of you again on my mother's behalf.'

'By the way,' said another girl, 'are your papa and second mama coming to the exhibition tomorrow?'

'No,' said Li-ling. 'They're too busy.'

'I know, some parents can't come because tomorrow is a workday,' said a third girl.

Then all the girls waved goodbye to Li-ling. She smiled faintly, exposing her dimples, and waved back.

Alone now, she resumed her journey westward. On two sides of the road stood sparsely scattered single houses which were in general two-storeyed, each with a garden. Throughout the vast space in between them on the harbour side, she leisurely watched gulls perform a ballet above the ripping sea in a sky of ever-changing colours, with the red round sun peeping behind the horizon as a background. What a lovely world! she felt.

Looking down to the harbour on occasions, she saw the flowing traffic of barges, sailing junks and sampans. There were a few gray warships, too, each with a fluttering Union Jack, rusty merchantmen and steamers from various countries flying their different flags. From her vantage point, all the vessels appeared to be toys bobbing in a bathtub, and the houses across the harbour on the Kowloon Peninsula looked like matchboxes.

As Hong Kong was not a large city, she imagined from her position that the whole of Hong Kong was under her feet, including Hong Kong Island, the Kowloon Peninsula and the New Territories bordering the southernmost part, then occupied by the Japanese, of Kwangtung Province of Mainland China.

As Li-ling continued walking, she came to a green three-storeyed apartment building, then a blue one called the Green and Blue Mansions, side by side on the hill side, which showed an exception to this district of two-storeyed single houses. Either building had a path that sloped down one hundred feet from the main entrance to the road.

These once grand buildings were now neglected. Their exteriors needed painting; plaster cracks marred their peeling surfaces. At one time, some professionals such as doctors and lawyers lived here. Now only school teachers, senior clerks, and secretaries dwelled in them. Yet, in Li-ling's mind, the mansions still maintained their original dignity.

About a half-minute walk from the mansions on the hill side of the road, there stood an old magnificent Chinese banyan tree. Its large, wide-spreading evergreen halo bore many slender supporting trunks, each with its own crown of dense foliage.

As Li-ling approached the tree, a tall young man in his late teens stepped out from behind. He was powerfully built, with Western features, and was handsome in a rugged sort of way. His white shirt hung over a pair of dark-blue slacks. His dark chestnut hair, somewhat messy, flopped over his large brown eyes. But it was his strange lopsided grin that frightened her. As he stood in the way, she instinctively tried to avoid him by crossing the road, but he stretched out his arms to stop her.

'Hello, Miss So,' he said.

'I don't know you. How do you know my name?'

'Why are you so pretty?' he asked, grimacing.

'Please, get out of my way.'

'Hold on. My name is Mike. I just want a date.'

Li-ling stepped back and bit the inside of her lip. 'Please let me pass.' She tried to cross the road again, but he blocked her with his body.

The young man pinched his chin and studied her face. 'This Saturday afternoon there's a party. There'll be all kinds of games. You'll enjoy yourself, and I'll treat you like a princess. Come on, don't act like a shy, old-fashioned Chinese girl. I can see you're part Western. We have something in common.'

Li-ling was aware of the panic growing inside her. 'Please, leave me alone.'

He looked at her with a wry smile and said, 'You know, you're even prettier when you're scared. Don't worry. Just promise me.'

Catching sight of two men talking a block away, she forced a cry from her parched, constricted throat, 'Help! Help me… please!' But no one responded.

Just then, an old Standard automobile pulled up to the kerb near the banyan tree. Looking at Li-ling and the man blocking her way, the white driver called out, 'Hey, Mike, what are you doing? Who's that, a friend of yours?'

Mike turned to him. 'Umm, Steve, what brings you here?'

Turning to Steve, Li-ling hollered, 'Please, help me. I don't know this man. I just want to go home.'

The driver, in his late twenties, dressed in an old brown suit, stepped out. He was strongly built like the harasser, but not quite as tall. He wore his rather short, light-brown hair combed straight back. He stared at Mike and a slight frown creased his otherwise smooth, sun-bronzed forehead. Then he turned his gaze to Li-ling.

'You look familiar, a St Mary's girl from this neighbourhood?'

Clasping her hands in front of her in a pleading gesture, she looked straight into her rescuer's blue eyes. 'Please, tell him to stop bothering me.'

With his eyebrows raised, the shorter man turned to Mike. 'Come on, leave her alone.'

Dropping his hands to his side, Mike turned to Steve. 'All I want is a date – just a date.'

Steve shrugged. 'The young lady doesn't seem interested. You can't force her.'

Mike's eyes turned to fire. 'This is none of your business, Steve. Besides, she's only a half-breed.'

Li-ling tried to walk away, but Mike grabbed her arm. Steve ran up and pulled her free.

Throwing a quick punch that caught Steve off guard, Mike knocked him to the ground and snapped, 'Damn you!'

Rising swiftly, Steve swung and connected squarely with Mike's jaw. Now the two men were locked in a fierce fight. Fists, feet and elbows exchanged quickly, bruises and abrasions in their faces.

Her heart still pounding, Li-ling half ran and half walked quite a distance before she turned to look back. She saw that the evil man seemed to be winning. She went on until she reached the gate of her house. Safe now, she tugged at the bell and waited.

A manservant, dressed in a Chinese jacket and pants of gray coarse cloth, soon opened the gate for her. Out of breath, she hurried past him without saying a word. Still panting slightly, she walked along the tree-lined drive through the middle of the garden toward the Western-style, two-storey house which overlooked the harbour below.

After lingering a moment at the entrance to the living room to catch her breath, she walked on the rich Peking carpet past the blackwood tables and chairs scattered around the room. A few sofas were arranged against the wall, which had an elegant balance of Chinese landscape paintings and scrolls of Chinese calligraphy hanging on it.

She moved up the flight of stairs to her room and shut the door behind her. Leaning against it for several seconds, she heaved a long sigh.

Mrs Chen, the short, middle-aged maid, knitted her brows and followed. Dressed in a jacket and pants of gray coarse cloth, she wore a chignon. Entering the room after gently rapping on the door, she found Li-ling reclining on the bed with her head resting on the palms of her locked hands, face still flushed.

With pleading eyes, Li-ling asked before Chen Ma had a chance to open her mouth, 'Chen Ma, do I look somewhat Western?'

'Why, yes, Young Mistress,' said Chen Ma, 'but Master looks much more.'

Nodding her head slightly, Li-ling said, 'I think Papa and I must have some Western blood in us. But Grandpa So and Grandma So appear completely Chinese in the portraits on the ancestral altar. I've asked Mama about this matter, but every time she ignored my questions.'

Chen Ma shrugged.

Looking up, Li-ling put her forefinger to her cheek. 'It's very strange that Papa never speaks of his parents, and neither does Mama, to say nothing of Second Mama, who's been with us for only six years. And Papa's so against Western customs.'

Chen Ma sat down on the side of the bed. 'I know very little of your father's parents, though I've worked for the So family almost twenty years. Since Master and Mistress never even mention the matter, I keep quiet. What's the matter with you? Why are you suddenly interested in this now?'

Li-ling propped herself up on both elbows and looked at Chen Ma. 'A Western boy who stopped me on my way home said I have Western blood.'

Chen Ma drew closer. 'Who was he?'

Li-ling related the incident.

Chen Ma opened her eyes and mouth wide. 'Have you told the police?'

Li-ling dropped back down onto the bed. 'No, of course not! I don't want a scandal. And I don't want Papa and Mama to worry about me walking to and from school.'

Chen Ma pointed her finger at Li-ling. 'You must be cautious. Beware of that boy.'

Li-ling smiled and put her hand on Chen Ma's lap.

'Don't worry. In broad daylight there are always some pedestrians on the road. I don't know why no one was around today. I guess that's why that villain had the audacity to harass me.'

'Why don't you let Ah Lai drive you home from school?'

'Because I'd rather enjoy the scenery while I'm walking.'

Chen Ma said nothing but smiled.

Li-ling sat up suddenly. 'Chen Ma, the man who saved me must have been hurt. He challenged a bigger man for my sake, a stranger. He was so brave and just, and I left him behind without so much as a word of thanks. But I couldn't. I didn't have a chance.'

Chen Ma got up from the bed and faced Li-ling. 'Remember to thank him if you see him again.'

'I will, Chen Ma.'

'I've bought a bouquet of flowers for Mistress. I can't see her because of my household work.'

'I'll take it to Mama tonight. She'll be so happy.'

Then Chen Ma left.

Alone, Li-ling lay on the bed again. She thought of Steve, her brave rescuer.

How handsome he is! she thought.

She had been too frightened to pay attention to his looks. But now her heart beat a little faster when she drifted back to the time when his tender blue eyes had gazed at her with such concern. She could not help hoping that she would some day see him again.

She imagined that one day they might take an evening stroll, hand in hand, in a beautiful garden. There they would see a pair of butterflies flying freely and a pair of larks singing merrily.

'Oh, this is only fantasy,' she murmured to herself. But in spite of this, he would always be the young gallant hero in her mind.

Chapter Two

One week later, four ladies sat at a square table playing mahjong at a corner of the So family's living room. Their ankle-length cheongsams with expert tailoring declared the wealth of their individual households. The high mandarin collars and long sleeves were set off by imported high-heeled shoes and a glittering array of expensive jewellery. Beside the table stood a large cabinet with a glass front which housed priceless treasures such as a ceremonial jade of the Chou dynasty, a bronze Buddha from the Tang dynasty and a glazed vase of the Ming dynasty. At the rear of the cabinet was the wall which held a large photograph of the former highest-ranking officers of the Nationalist Government of China. Many of them, including Li-ling's father, wore traditional Chinese gowns; some appeared in Western suits and others in military uniform. They all served as a background commensurate to the status of the ladies.

At the end of the first game, the players turned the tiles marked in suits, resembling dominoes, face down on the table. Then they shuffled the tiles by swirling them in a circular motion, making clicking sounds.

'How is your son, Mrs So? Still attending Mr Leung's traditional school?' asked one of the ladies.

Before the addressee could answer, another lady broke in.

'Mrs Luk, why do you call her "Mrs So"? Mrs So is still recuperating in a sanitarium. The title of our delightful hostess is *Second* Mrs So.'

When the Second Mrs So heard the emphasis on the word 'second', her flawless, yellow-ivory complexion blushed beneath her jade-pinned chignon. But she kept silent. The only continual sound was the mahjong tiles striking one another.

She was in her late twenties, slender and petite in comparison to her more matronly companions. Her finest feature, the one that she felt captivated Mr So, was her eyes, keen and sparkling with ebony hues.

Second Mrs So often played mahjong for long hours with these ladies, sometimes at their houses. However, they were not close to her, for they were simply the principal wives of her husband's wealthy friends. That's why being addressed as Second Mrs So served as an irritating reminder that she was not on the same honoured level as her gambling companions.

After shuffling the tiles, the ladies stacked them to make four 'walls' and then pushed the completed 'walls' to the centre of the table to form a square for another game. The question about Second Mrs So's son remained unanswered throughout the day though conversation about other topics continued as usual.

Later that night, Second Mrs So had a dream. All of these women came to her and one by one, called to her, 'Second Mrs So!' When she heard this appellation, she felt as if a bunch of needles had pricked her eardrums.

In the dining room during the family supper the following evening, she broached the subject. In fact, during recent years she had dropped hints at least three or four times. But each time, Mr So had delicately side-stepped the issue. This time, she stared right into his deep-set eyes from across the table. 'I must be promoted from concubine to co-wife as soon as possible!'

Mr So ran his hands slowly through his dark brown hair, lightly flecked with gray at the temples. As he shook his head, she noticed a blank expression settle on his light-yellow face with its conspicuous Roman nose.

'Can't you wait until Mistress recovers?' he asked.

With a fiery look in her eyes, Second Mrs So retorted, 'So far, she's taken to her bed for a whole month. What if she remains ill for the rest of her life?'

Her husband placed both hands on the table and leaned toward her. 'How do you know she won't recover soon? I'll consult her when she does.'

With a pouting look, Second Mrs So persisted. 'Why must we consult her?'

Now, sitting straight up, he said, 'Whether we consult her or not is not the issue. The important thing is that she, as the principal wife, must be present at the banquet for the promotion. It would go against etiquette, not to mention that she would lose face.'

Second Mrs So threw her chopsticks onto the table with a crash and sat pinched-faced throughout the rest of the meal.

After the family finished their supper in silence, Chen Ma began to clear the dishes away.

'Chen Ma,' said Second Mrs So, 'bring my bedding, pyjamas and slippers downstairs to the family room!'

Chen Ma continued her chores, giving no response to her order.

'Chen Ma!' shouted Second Mrs So, 'go upstairs right now!'

Hurriedly, Chen Ma left.

Staring at his second wife, Mr So said nothing. Then he stood up and left. Li-ling and Chi-ching, her five-year-old half-brother, held each other's hands tightly under the table.

For two nights, Mr So faced quiet solitude. His concubine stubbornly remained in the family room on the ground floor, sleeping on the overstuffed couch. Throughout the 'cold war', neither spoke to the other.

On the third morning at the breakfast table, Mr So said to his 'small wife' in front of his two children, 'I'm sorry. I'll invite relatives and friends here for a promotion dinner as soon as possible. Are you happy now?'

Then she smiled for the first time in two days.

★

Ten days later, the promotion banquet was a splendid affair. Polished windows and scrubbed floors gleamed; the servants brought out the best china, crystal and gold utensils; every room was aglow with the brightness of the electrical fixtures.

Mr So, wearing a long felt gown, and the new, young Mrs So, dressed in a green velvet cheongsam with an intricate phoenix pattern representing nobility, stood at the entrance to the house, greeting the guests as they arrived.

'Congratulations to you both, Mr So and Young Mrs So,' said each guest upon entering. The new Mrs So listened to the words as if they were music to her ears.

Never again will I have to hang my head in embarrassment, she thought. Never again will I be plagued by that horrible dream. She smiled.

In the living room, several ladies, all dressed in cheongsams with floral patterns, wearing bracelets and necklaces, and a number of gentlemen, either garbed in Western attire or in Chinese fashion, talked, sipped tea or cracked the shells of melon seeds to extract the meat before nibbling it. Dinner would not be served until the last of the guests had arrived.

Dressed in a long-sleeved cheongsam of white velvet with deep green piping, liberally embroidered with colourful flowers, Li-ling approached her parents.

'Papa, since the family has already paid respect to our ancestors upstairs, may I go to the sanitarium now to see Old Mama? I'll be back in an hour. I was unable to do so earlier, because I was so busy helping to prepare for the banquet.'

Her father smiled. 'All right, then. Tell your mother I'll see her early tomorrow morning. Let Ah Mok drive the Morris for you because Ah Lai's very ill.'

'Goodbye, Papa,' said Li-ling when a gentleman pulled Mr So aside for a talk.

Li-ling then turned to the new Mrs So. 'Goodbye, Second Mama.'

Grabbing Li-ling's tender upper arm roughly, the new Mrs So hissed, 'Li-ling, do you intend to sneer at me?'

Li-ling's face went blank. 'Oh, Young Mama, please forgive me… I've called you "Second Mama" for so long… It won't happen again.'

Tears began to form in Li-ling's eyes as she left the house.

*

Three weeks after the banquet, Old Mrs So came home from the sanitarium in the evening.

She looked up at her daughter from the bed, her pale but still beautiful face showing fatigue.

'Li-ling, I've been treated by many famous herbalist doctors and acupuncturists for weak kidneys for more than two months now. In the fourth week I felt much better. But since the fifth week, I have gradually become worse and worse. My health has not improved. It seems there is no hope.'

Li-ling bent down and looked steadily into her eyes. 'Mama, there is always hope.'

'No.' The old Mrs So shook her head. 'Yesterday, I decided to come home so I could see more of my beloved family before I die.'

Li-ling caressed her mother's face. 'We pleaded with you to stay home before, but you refused.'

'Because I didn't want to be a burden to anyone.'

In the afternoon, Mr So had sent two bouquets of chrysanthemums to his principal wife from his office. The flowers, in two white china vases, were placed on the table beside her bed. But the cheerful bright yellow flowers and their pleasant scent did not seem to cheer up her spirits.

As tears welled up in her lovely daughter's eyes, the middle-aged woman said softly, 'Don't cry, my darling. We can't change destiny. Now there is much I must tell you, so listen to me carefully. I feel sorry for the So family, for I've failed to give birth to a son all these years. It was at my insistence and on the repeated advice of Sir William that your father finally consented to take a concubine, your second mother. She was twenty and you were only ten then.'

Li-ling dropped her gaze to her lap, not wanting her mother to see her tears. 'Mama, you always treat Young Mama like your own sister and her son as your own.'

Patting Li-ling's forearm tenderly, Old Mrs So said, 'Frankly, I treat him better than I do you, my own child. During the first year I thought that Second Mama was a virtuous woman and pitied her because she had lost her parents as a child and been under the custody of her late poor aunt. But she's become arrogant to us since she gave birth to Chi-ching. She speaks ill of us to Papa, too. Beware. Exercise patience and never, ever, offend her. Otherwise you will suffer more by her hand after I die. Papa is a good man. Since he loves her, try to love her for Papa's sake, my filial daughter. You are the joy of my life. And don't forget to call her "Young Mama".'

Struggling to hold her tears back, Li-ling said, 'Mama, I'll never forget your instructions. I'll be seventeen and graduating in a few months. Please don't worry about me.'

Her mother's breathing became laboured and soon she closed her eyes.

Within a few days of her return home, the elder Mrs So passed away. For two weeks the family was busy with the funeral service and the burial. Mr So, Li-ling, Chi-ching and Chen Ma cried often, but none was in more turmoil than Li-ling, whose face appeared wan. Even Mr So's co-wife looked sad, but only in the presence of her husband.

★

One morning as they all sat at breakfast, Mr So's co-wife said to her husband, 'It's been a month since your principal wife died. In three months' time, I want you to make me your principal wife. So let's start to make arrangements now for a big ceremony.'

Mr So's face went almost colourless. 'No, no! We can't do it so soon. I wouldn't be able to face her underground if I did such a thing to her now.'

The co-wife's lips tensed. 'You love a dead woman more than you love me!' she shouted, pounding the table several times.

He countered, 'People will criticize us. According to etiquette, one year is the minimum period for mourning.'

His co-wife abruptly rose from her chair, knocking it over. She threw herself on the floor and rolled about, crying hysterically. Li-ling felt as if the ceiling had been cracking.

She knelt before her father and pleaded in tears with him to accept her young mother's demand.

Mr So instantly left the room, and slammed the door.

That night when he came home after dining with friends at a restaurant, Li-ling told him that her stepmother had eaten neither lunch nor supper.

'What shall I do, Li-ling?' asked Mr So.

'Papa, please, for the sake of peace and harmony of the family…'

★

One afternoon, about four months after the death of Li-ling's birth mother, a band of musicians dressed in flame-red costumes started from the home of Second Mrs So's late aunt to march through the downtown streets, then up the sloping roads into the Mid-Level district, playing on Chinese clarinets, gongs and cymbals. A beautifully decorated bridal palanquin carried by eight bearers followed, attracting the attention of a lot of pedestrians. Finally, welcomed by noisy firecrackers, the procession came to a halt in Mr So's garden.

Stepping out of the palanquin with the help of a middle-aged woman, Mr So's co-wife was the picture of beauty and elegance. She wore a traditional wedding outfit of floral-embroidered, shimmering pink satin, with a gorgeous jacket that fell quite gracefully over a long pleated skirt, accentuating her petite form to perfection. Shielding her face from view, strings of beads danced from a colourful headdress as she walked. The middle-aged woman, called a *tai kum*, was hired to serve the bride on the wedding day only. Her coarse brown silk jacket and pants appeared conspicuously plain beside the bride's costume.

Handsomely dressed in a long, blue, silk-padded gown, covered by a black satin waistcoat, Mr So gave a tight smile and welcomed his happy bride at the entrance of the house.

In the living room, the guests applauded the bride and groom. Then the couple walked up the stairway to the ancestral worship room.

After the *tai kum* had removed the bride's headdress, the couple knelt down on the cushions three times, each time making three kowtows before the altar table. Above it hung a tablet which read: 'The Ancestors of the So Family'. Li-ling and her brother also paid the same respect of kowtowing nine times. The altar table held a censer of burning joss sticks, dishes of fruit and chicken, cups of wine and two lighted red candles along with the photos of Li-ling's grandparents, all arranged in proper order according to custom.

Following the ceremony, the family descended to the living room and joined the guests, who were chatting in groups, sipping tea or nibbling melon seeds.

A young man, who stood in the centre of the living room, shouted an announcement:

'Honoured guests, may I have your attention? Sir William Wen, the wedding witness, is about to speak.'

A short, middle-aged man with a great domed head, dressed in a floor-length blue, silk-padded gown, stood up. After clearing his throat, he said, 'Gentlemen and ladies, I have the honour of presenting to you Mr So and his new principal wife. This wedding will consolidate their long-time deep-rooted love. I wish their love to last one hundred years. Our beautiful Mrs So has a slim waist which is admired by all except one person – her husband. Mr So, on the other hand, wants her to have a big waist every year so that he may have many sons to come.'

Sir William paused while the whole room erupted in laughter.

'May Heaven bless our couple with many sons and countless grandsons to come,' he concluded.

All the guests applauded and soon surrounded the couple to offer their congratulations.

As Li-ling circulated about the room, she overheard one woman whisper to another, 'And the ex-principal wife's corpse hasn't even turned cold yet.'

Chapter Three

Several days after the marriage ceremony, Li-ling entered the dining room while Chen Ma was serving supper. As her young mistress walked in wearing a body-fitting, knee-length cheongsam, Chen Ma spilled a good portion of the soup onto the floor. She quickly bent down to clean up the mess.

'Papa, after supper I'm going to the seven-thirty show at the King's Theatre...' Li-ling stopped abruptly when she noticed her stepmother draw her lips tight and her father turn red.

Her stepmother, the only Mrs So in the family after the death of Li-ling's birth mother, turned a grim gaze upon Li-ling. 'Is it another Hollywood film with lots of hugging and kissing?' she asked. 'Such films infect people's eyes, which should be cleaned with a strong disinfectant to remove the filth.'

'What is the title of this film you feel you must see?' asked Mr So.

'*Romeo and Juliet*.'

Shaking her head, Mrs So interjected, 'It is a licentious film, encouraging young people to make love before marriage. Mr Leung told us so.'

'A film about the greatness of love is not licentious,' said Li-ling calmly.

Mrs So's voice rose. 'And I am saying that this film is very bad.'

'It is definitely a breach of morality. It is unsuitable for young people,' said Li-ling's father.

'My final examination will contain questions based upon this classic English play,' said Li-ling.

'And why are you dressed in that shameful cheongsam?' Mrs So scanned Li-ling from top to toe. 'Are you seeing a boyfriend this evening?'

Looking squarely at her stepmother, she answered, 'No, no, Young Mama. I'll be going with Miss Susan Silva, our respectable teacher of English. She invited me. I'm going to pick her up at the Green Mansion.'

'Those modern educators not only don't behave themselves,' snorted Mrs So, 'but they even teach and encourage their students to make love. How can our young people concentrate on their studies?'

'It is wise,' said Mr So, 'to learn what is good of Western science and technology, but not their loose and free ways and their immoral behaviour.'

'Nor the Western practices of revealing the body in public,' added Mrs So.

Li-ling found herself growing red under their full and weighty gaze. She could not trust herself to speak at that moment, afraid that a heated retort might further anger her parents.

Throwing her arms in the air, Mrs So turned to Li-ling.

'Just look at your shamefully short, tight dress. It displays your knees and bosom.' She shook her head before she continued. 'This is the result of Western education! We will not allow you to bring disgrace to our family.'

'Dinner is served,' said Chen Ma softly.

'Li-ling, what are you waiting for? Change that disgusting dress immediately,' sneered Mrs So, 'before we lose our appetites.'

'Yes, Young Mama,' replied Li-ling.

Once in the privacy of her room, Li-ling shed the fashionable cheongsam. She had laboured so hard on it, using the fine needlework she had learned recently in a sewing class. Tears filled her eyes as she gently straightened the blue woollen flower of mourning inserted in her hair while she looked at her birth mother's picture on her desk. She picked it up and held it against her heart.

'Oh, Mama,' she said, 'I remember your words. You wanted me to exercise patience.'

Wiping away the tears and taking a deep breath to steady her emotions, she chose from the armoire a looser cheongsam which fell well below the knees.

Downstairs, Mrs So continued her tirade. 'Why did you promise to let her attend university after she finished her secondary education?'

'Because it is the modern trend,' said Mr So.

'You listen too much to Sir William's foolish advice. You saw the photos of what they call "social functions" at Hong Kong University. Didn't you see how proud those shameless girls looked, held tightly about the waist by those boys? Some of the pairs even danced cheek to cheek. How horrible! I can't believe that you, Li-ling's own father, promised to send her to that place to be trained as a whore. Furthermore, those Western-style Chinese even say that daughters should take equal shares with sons of the family's property when their father dies. How absurd!'

'That reminds me, where's my dear son?' he enquired of Chen Ma.

'Young Master will be coming very soon, but you should start eating now, Master, before the food gets cold.'

'No. We will wait for him.'

Chapter Four

In early June every year, graduation day at St Mary's Anglo-Chinese Secondary School was a grand occasion, with everybody wearing a smile. All the students, dressed neatly in their school uniforms, assembled in the school's spacious hall. The first five rows were reserved for special guests and staff while the graduating class sat in the rows directly behind.

As each guest arrived at the entrance to the building, he or she was given a programme and a copy of the school's annual report before climbing the flight of stairs to the hall entrance. Junior staff members ushered in special guests, who were wearing silk badges, to the designated section.

'Look! Winnie, your parents just came in. Smile,' said Irene, a girl in the graduating class to her friend.

Winnie grinned.

'Why's your father so short and your mother so tall?' snickered Irene.

'Grandpa and Grandma wanted tall children,' giggled Winnie.

'I bet your father has no guts to get a concubine,' said Irene kidding.

'How do you know?'

'Look how much attention he's paying to your mother. He's definitely henpecked.'

The other girls burst into laughter.

Another classmate, whose eyes were hidden behind heavy glasses, said excitedly, 'My father's here!'

Her friends turned to see the man she indicated. He too wore thick glasses, and sported a moustache, à la Charlie Chaplin. He nearly tripped on his long Chinese gown as he anxiously searched for his daughter. Though she waved at him, he did not seem to see her.

'Oh, Diana, your father is so funny!' said a girl sitting next to Li-ling.

'Yes, he is. We children love to play practical jokes on him.'

'Doesn't he ever get upset with you?'

'Never, Fong-in,' responded Diana beamingly.

'I wish I had such a father,' said Fong-in. 'My father always looks so stern, and seldom talks to us.'

'Is he coming today?' asked Diana.

'How can he? He's much too busy.'

'With his work? Even on a Saturday afternoon?'

'Yes.' Fong-in's face turned red.

Fong-in had told Li-ling about her father. He had three concubines and numerous mistresses at the cabarets and brothels he frequented, but he cared nothing for his wife or for his children. Li-ling squeezed Fong-in's hand.

'Oh, look! Miss Silva has brought a gentleman friend with her. What a handsome man!' said a girl, seated near Li-ling.

They all strained their necks to catch a glimpse of the Western man as he whispered something into Miss Silva's ear.

Miss Silva was a fairly tall Portuguese, her olive complexion complemented nicely by the dark cap and gown she wore, and her hair a lustrous shade of brown. Finally noticing the man beside Miss Silva, Li-ling felt there was something oddly familiar about him. An instant later, she recognised him as her gallant hero named Steve, who had saved her some eight months before. And here he was, with her teacher, at her school, on her graduation day. Her heart pounded as she saw Miss Silva show her friend a seat in the special guests section.

'I wonder if they're close friends,' said Li-ling, once her composure had returned.

'I don't know,' replied one of the girls. 'Although Miss Silva isn't really beautiful, I've seen her out with this handsome man at least twice.'

Li-ling began to squirm. Then a hush fell over the gathering as the principal, a British lady, dressed in cap and gown, entered the hall. Leading a procession of teachers and honoured guests, both Chinese and Western, some in cap and gown, including Miss Silva, the lady headed for the dais, which was decked out with flowers on the floor in front of it. Once everyone was seated, the principal spoke into the microphone at the centre of the dais and a female teacher acted as interpreter at the other microphone by the side.

'There is no need for me to read the 1940–1941 Report on the activities and academic results of our pupils during this past year, for you all have received a copy. I would, however, like to express my thanks once more for the advice of the education department. Our teachers have employed modern methods in an effort to encourage our students to hold free discussions, especially in the field of the humanities during the learning and teaching process. Thought-provoking questions rather than fact-finding ones have been incorporated into the examinations, especially for the upper classes over the past few years. The purpose of this new teaching method is to prepare pupils to deal independently with challenges which they may one day encounter in a changing world.

'I would like now to introduce Mrs Helen Au, chairman of the Hong Kong Chinese Women's Association. She is not only one of the foremost leaders in the cause for women's liberation, but also an active civic leader.'

As polite applause rose from the audience, Mrs Au, a pert, middle-aged woman, dressed in a Western-style, light-brown suit, stepped forward. Though still distracted, Li-ling turned her attention to her. She spoke in English.

'Women all over the world have been regarded as inferior to men for a long time. In the past few thousand years in China, marriage was pre-arranged by parents. Even now, this custom has not yet been completely abolished. Thus women have suffered while men have been able to take concubines as freely as one buys pigs in the market.'

Some of the older men and women turned wide-eyed to one another. Li-ling was fascinated; the words absorbed her completely.

'To make matters worse,' continued Mrs Au, 'girls were seldom allowed to study in schools. They were merely taught at home the rules of morality and etiquette in general, and those concerning women in particular, such as obedience to their fathers- and mothers-in-law, and lifelong devotion to their husbands. In the countryside, even today, many girls are still deprived of education in traditional schools, to mention nothing of modern schools. You girls are fortunate. You are receiving the same academic, moral and physical education as boys in modern schools.

'I sincerely hope that after graduation, no matter whether you enter into society or further your studies at a university, the least that you should do is something substantial – to show the world that women are equal to men in ability, judgement and courage. Only when men and women are equal and cooperate with one another in a congenial atmosphere can substantial progress in civilization be made.'

As she bowed slightly at the conclusion of her speech, the elderly and more conservative adults barely clapped while the rest of the audience, including the students, gave hearty applause.

One old, portly gentleman seated in the first row turned and gave the graduates an annoyed look. But the girls who saw him continued to clap long after the applause had died down. The angrier he looked, the happier they became; the redder his face, the louder their applause.

Then Mrs Au handed prizes to the students one by one.

When all the stages of the graduation ceremony were completed, the guests, staff and graduates enjoyed a party held in an adjoining room. Tea, coffee, cakes and sandwiches were set out on several long tables.

Congratulating her classmates on their success and receiving congratulations in return, Li-ling held her graduation certificate and first prize awards in Chinese, English and Modern History, and a special first prize in good conduct. Her awards consisted of a fountain pen, Chinese and English books and stationery.

At times, Li-ling scanned the room until she saw Miss Silva and her guest. They were engaged in a quiet and seemingly intimate discourse.

Li-ling tried to analyze the strange emotion she was experiencing. I respect Miss Silva too much to be jealous of her. Steve is her best friend, and someone with whom I'm not even acquainted. How could I possibly be jealous? Should I take the initiative to thank him for his brave deed? He must have been hurt.

She edged slowly toward them through the crowd, hoping that he would greet her first.

Still some distance away, Li-ling hesitated to go any closer. Twice, when their eyes made fleeting contact, she thought that Steve seemed to pull his gaze away. At that point, she could not fathom what her feelings were.

Is he purposely avoiding me? she thought. Maybe he doesn't recognise me. Yet I distinctly remember him saying that I looked familiar when he first met me only eight months earlier. I was even dressed in the same school uniform as I am now. If I don't take this opportunity to speak to him, I may never get another chance.

Lost in the turmoil of her thoughts, Li-ling suddenly heard her name. Miss Silva called to her from the crowd and was approaching, her friend following. Li-ling's heartbeat quickened once again as a wave of heat swept her face. After sipping some tea in an attempt to compose herself, she put the cup on the table next to her.

'Congratulations, Li-ling,' said Miss Silva, shaking her pupil's hand warmly, though Li-ling was more aware of the man behind her teacher than her teacher's words.

'Ah, thank you, Miss Silva. Any success… I may have… is due to the guidance of my teachers.'

'Steve, this is Miss Li-ling So, one of my best students. And, Li-ling, I'd like you to meet a friend of mine, Mr Stephen Jones.'

'How do you do?' he said softly.

The coolness in his blue eyes is matched only by the tone of his voice, she thought, but the sympathetic look I remember is not there today.

Li-ling curtsied. 'How do you do?'

How can he be so indifferent? she asked herself. Maybe he's angry that I didn't express any gratitude and hurried away. Still, he should give me a chance to explain. There must be some special reason.

However, she decided not to mention the incident unless he did so first.

'Li-ling, where are your parents?' asked Miss Silva. 'They must be very proud of you.'

Li-ling forced a smile. 'Ah… They couldn't come.'

'Oh, I'm sorry to hear that.'

A heavy silence fell over them for some time, during which Stephen seemed preoccupied, his eyes looking elsewhere. Finally he made an excuse to leave. Miss Silva left with him after they had exchanged goodbyes with Li-ling.

Li-ling walked away and joined a group of her fellow students, but she was unable to match their light-hearted mood.

'Congratulations, Maisy, on your sports prizes,' she said to a tall, masculine-looking Eurasian girl.

'The same to you!' said Maisy. 'By the way, I saw you talking to Miss Silva and Mr Jones.'

'Oh, do you know Miss Silva's friend?' asked Li-ling. 'She just introduced me.'

'Not really, but two years ago, I went to see my uncle at a construction site. Mr Jones was there giving directions to the workmen. That's all I ever saw of him. He was a senior engineer at the prestigious Hong Kong Land Company, and my uncle was his assistant. According to my uncle, Mr Jones resigned six months later despite his bright future with the company.'

'He came alone. Is he single?'

'Oh, no. He is a divorcee. He came here from England to forget his past, so they say. He lives alone in an apartment in the mansion next to Miss Silva's. For some reason, I guess she felt sorry for him and looked after him.'

'Does she treat him like a brother?' asked Li-ling.

Maisy shrugged. 'Perhaps.'

'Maybe Miss Silva really thinks of him as a prospective husband. After all, she must be thinking of getting married some day soon.'

'Don't know. What I do know is that he's in his late twenties and she's about seven or eight years older.'

Cutting into their conversation, a male voice called out for Maisy.

'Oh! That's my daddy. He must have finished his conversation with the chemistry teacher. Bye-bye, Li-ling.'

Li-ling stood surrounded by people, yet she felt utterly alone. All of her classmates had parents or relatives with them on what should have been their most joyous day. Not even the knowledge of the age difference between Miss Silva and her friend could comfort her.

Not until most of the people had dispersed did she finally decide to leave. She did not want to be seen walking home alone on such a grand occasion; she refused to be pitied.

Suddenly, Maisy's large frame came looming toward her. 'Li-ling,' Maisy called out, 'your father's been injured! His chauffeur's waiting for you outside. Hurry!'

Li-ling's legs wobbled as she left the hall and ran down the stairs and out of the building.

'What happened, Ah Mok?' she gasped.

'Master's at a clinic!' The chauffeur rushed her into the back seat of the Daimler, closed the door and jumped in behind the wheel. He started the engine and then panted, 'Master arrived at the building when the ceremony began. When he saw your name along with all your awards on the programme, he became so excited that he tripped on his way up the concrete stairs. The pain in his ankle was so acute… He returned to the car. I quickly drove him to Dr Fan, the herbalist-chiropractor.'

'Poor Papa,' she cried.

*

Throughout the two following months, Li-ling attentively administered her father's treatment. The chiropractor had prescribed massages with a sort of liquor mixed with a herbal powder. Since the younger Mrs So was so 'allergic' to the odious concoction, Li-ling was more than happy to apply the salve and massage her father's swollen ankle. She repeated the process several times at each treatment, and did two treatments every day.

When alone, she sometimes pondered the confusing situation in which she had found herself with Miss Silva and Mr Jones. Guilt assailed her, for she had not been able to express her gratitude to him. And she could now admit to herself the feeling she had had when she saw him and Miss Silva together.

Call it jealousy, pure and simple, she thought. Could I possibly be in love with Stephen Jones, a total stranger?

The thought plagued her. She had never before experienced such a tumultuous but wonderful obsession.

Chapter Five

Though the bedroom was somewhat darkened by draperies, sunlight filtered in around the edges, softening the scene.

Having tossed her blonde hair to one side, the woman sat up, bent over and whispered to her bedmate, 'My dearest, last night you made me very happy!'

The man did not move, his face covered by a pillow.

'Do you know how mad I am about you?' she continued, gently pulling away the sheet that kept the corded muscles of his strong body from her view. She began raining tiny kisses across his hairy chest and up along the curve of his arms.

From beneath the pillow he chuckled as he tried to evade her feathery kisses.

'Please stop. I'm ticklish there,' came the muffled voice.

'I want to swallow you up,' she said, 'so no other woman can ever make love to you.'

'You're crazy.'

'I guess you could say that – crazy about you. Say you love me.' She pushed the pillow away, letting it fall to the floor, and gazed into his blue eyes. They belonged to Stephen Jones. She laid her head against his chest.

'Please, Steve, say the words that will make me a happy woman.' Tears welled up in her eyes and one fell into the hollow of his throat.

Stephen hesitated for a moment before he breathed, 'I love you, Eliza.' He kissed her forehead lightly.

'Then let's get married!' she said. 'You don't have to be afraid. Most marriages have happy endings. They don't all have to end up like your first one.'

Stephen was silent as he recalled a scene in London.

★

Like many nights in London, it was cold and foggy. Stephen took a taxi to a residential district on the outskirts of the city. As he stepped out of the vehicle, he looked up at the large Victorian mansion, set apart from the thoroughfare. Pristine grounds surrounded the stately building, soft lighting spilling from the foyer transom and edging the drapery of an upper-floor window.

He rang the bell and waited, announcing himself as Sir Reginald Grantham to a stiff, white-haired butler before the massive gate swung open.

The butler looked stunned. 'Mr Jones!' he said.

Stephen grimaced. 'Sorry,' he said, as he brushed past the butler. 'That's the only way I could get in.'

Then the servant followed him down a tree-lined path in the garden leading to the house.

'Has Lord Kirkwood retired yet?' asked Stephen as he stepped into the foyer.

'I don't know. Perhaps he's asleep,' said the butler.

'I just want to have a short talk with him.'

'Please wait in the drawing room.'

Stephen looked into the drawing room beyond, with its walnut panelling, and all its trappings of wealth, the impeccable taste that money could buy, along with family tradition. But he decided not to enter. Instead, he waited for the old man to climb the stairs, then followed at a discreet distance, keeping close to the portrait-filled wall. He saw the butler rap at a particular door.

'What is it, Leslie?' asked a middle-aged man, dressed in artistically patterned satin pyjamas as he opened the door. His partially gray hair was tousled, but his moustache was well trimmed.

The butler, standing at the half-opened door, said, 'Lord Kirkwood, Mr Stephen Jones is waiting in the drawing room.'

Surprised, the lord asked, 'Why did you let him in?'

'Sir, he posed as Sir Reginald Grantham, your cousin.'

Lord Kirkwood's eyes became cold. 'Tell him I'm asleep and ask him to leave at once. And next time, don't open the gate for him.'

Before the butler could reply, Stephen stormed past him into the room.

'Jimmy,' said Stephen to the lord, 'I don't want any trouble. I just want to get my wife back.'

A shriek came from a woman crouching on the bed further inside this large room. She arose, her flimsy nightgown revealing her rounded bosom. Visibly shaken, she walked toward them and spoke, her voice sounding strident.

'Steve, get out of here! Why should you come?'

'Linda, I should ask you the same question,' rasped Stephen. 'You are my wife, yet you've hidden here and refused to see me for weeks.'

She broke into laughter, which sounded like an electric shot into his ears.

Stephen's forehead wrinkled. 'Since I became broke a few months ago,' he said, 'I've been unhappy here. I'm going to Hong Kong to work for a few years and pay off all my debts – with my creditors' approval, of course. Then we'll start from scratch there again.'

She laughed out loud. 'And you want me to come back with you. There's no way. I didn't marry you to suffer. It was all your fault.'

Stephen walked up to her and pulled her by the sleeve. 'You're my wife, not a damned whore. You're coming home with me!'

Throwing a knock that caught Stephen off guard, Lord Kirkwood thrust him a few paces back and snapped, 'Damn you!'

Stephen righted himself and swung a left, connecting squarely with the lord's jaw. The two men grappled on the luxurious carpet, rolling and punching, each one drawing grunts and groans from the other. The butler raised an alarm in no time. Though the lord was Steve's senior by a number of years, he fended off the younger man's harsh blows and delivered a few of his own. But soon the battle turned in Stephen's favour, for anger drove him with a fiercer determination.

As the fight progressed, more and more of the household staff ran in and quickly subdued the raging young man. Blood dripping down his face and clothes, Lord Kirkwood straightened himself up and gave a slight nod to his men. They roughly dragged Stephen down the steps and outside the house to the garden.

Just before his men threw him into the foggy London night, Lord Kirkwood said, 'I suggest you be a good chap and stay away from my home and Linda, or next time I will call a bobby and have you jailed.'

After the foyer light was extinguished, Stephen stood there, shivering with rage, his face and clothes stained with blood. Angry tears obscured his vision.

★

The harsh sound of Elizabeth's voice brought him back to the reality of the bedroom once again. 'Winning as well as losing a fortune in such a short time as you did in the London Commodity Exchange is a pure speculation,' she said. 'Forget your past and think about the future. Why not let us get married? And you could go back to London with all the respect you deserve. What are you worried about?'

Stephen grinned humourlessly, his eyes an icy hue as he looked at her squarely. 'Don't you see?' he asked. 'I wouldn't be Stephen Jones any longer. I'd be known as the husband of Lady McDonnall, former wife of the late Sir Henry McDonnall, ex-chairman of the board of directors of the Hong Kong and Shanghai Banking Corporation.'

Eliza shook her head, her full lips stretched into a taut smile.

The clock struck noon. Both of them arose and each put on a robe. As he drew back the drapes, a flood of light spilled into the exquisitely furnished room. Walking together to the brocade-upholstered divan, they sat down and Stephen lit a cigarette.

Bathed as she was in sunlight now, he took in the not so tiny lines that creased the corners of her mouth and large hazel eyes. He could not help but notice the heavy application of make-up that helped mask many of her flaws.

'Cheer up, darling,' she said. 'What is it you propose to do?'

'As long as the Sino-Japanese War is going on in China, an ever-increasing number of wealthy Chinese will keep coming to Hong Kong. I want to build large custom-made houses for them. And luckily, at present no construction company is interested in such a project. Since there's no competition, it would bring in large profits.' He hesitated before adding, 'I need a million dollars!'

She paused, then said, 'I'll try to secure such a large loan for you and have it to you within, say, a couple of months. Are you happy now?'

Steve took a deep drag of his cigarette and then exhaled in relief. He became so exhilarated that he extinguished it immediately and kissed her warmly several times. He felt as if he were an unknown actor who had just landed the leading role in a great film.

'The loan, hefty as it may be, could be repaid in no time.'

'No one can guarantee the success of a business, but you have a great idea, and the timing sounds right.'

'If I fail and go into debt,' he declared, his eyes rolling to the left, 'I'll work for your hotels for the rest of my life, and you can deduct the debt from my salary. That's all I can guarantee.'

'Silly boy, don't think about failure. Think about success. You'll become rich. By the way, when your enterprise is successful, what will you give me as a reward?'

'How about twenty-five per cent of the net profits?' offered Stephen.

'Are you crazy?' shouted Elizabeth. 'Only twenty-five per cent?'

He kept silent.

She laughed. 'I was only joking. By that time, we'll get married and then I'll get double the twenty-five per cent and one hundred per cent of you, sweetheart!' She pinched his cheek.

Chapter Six

At night Li-ling tossed and turned in bed, thinking of Stephen long before she could fall asleep.

Why am I so interested in Mr Jones? He is a stranger, a foreigner. He was aloof at the graduation ceremony. So what if he saved me from being harassed? All I owe him is an apology.

And then there were other thoughts about Miss Silva.

She is a few years older than Mr Jones, and she isn't even beautiful. Is he really in love with her? But many things, especially matters concerning love, happen without reason. After all, both of them are Westerners. He is divorced and alone. She has a kind heart and is well educated. Being neighbours, they see each other often. Affection often grows out of such relationships.

Then a new idea entered her mind. Why should I bother myself with such a trivial matter? Since 1931, Japan has been invading my country, and we patiently did not offer resistance until 1937 when we were better prepared. That is what should be important to me. Many of my former classmates are planning to go to Free China to help further the war effort. And despite Papa's objections, I'll join them for this great cause. I will do something useful and show the world that women are as capable as men. But before I leave Hong Kong, I must see Mr Jones.

On a public holiday two weeks later, after some hesitation, Li-ling went to the Blue Mansion where he lived. She paced for several minutes before stopping at the door of a first-floor apartment and stared at a plate which read, 'Stephen Jones'. Then she heard footsteps coming up the stairs.

'Oh! Mr Jones, good morning... I mean, good afternoon,' she said.

'Oh, it's you! Good afternoon, Miss... So, how... do you do?' His eyes were glassy and his breath smelled of alcohol.

'I... have come to see you,' she said, a warm flush sweeping across her face.

'Come in, please, Miss So,' he said as he opened the door, the key making clattering sounds in the lock. She followed him into the apartment.

'Please sit down and wait... a minute.' He went straight to the bathroom.

In the living room, Li-ling sat on a rickety wooden chair which creaked as she leaned back. The leather surfaces of the sofas were slightly cracked and torn. The other furniture was somewhat worn and shabby. The decorations were few and the walls bare. She was surprised that a man of his social status would live in such a place.

However, at least everything is reasonably clean, she thought.

After splashing water onto his face, Stephen came out of the bathroom. Wiping his face with a towel, he said, 'Sorry to keep you waiting. By the way, how did you know my place?'

'Maisy Diaz, a former classmate of mine,' said Li-ling, 'has an uncle who was once your assistant. Two weeks ago, at the graduation, she saw me talking to you and Miss Silva and told me you lived in the mansion next to Miss Silva's.'

'Oh, yeah, Douglas was a good colleague of mine.'

'Mr Jones,' she asked with a smile, 'do you mind answering a question?'

'Not at all.'

'About eight months ago, didn't you defend me against a harasser?'

He nodded.

Li-ling bowed slightly. 'I've come here to apologise for not thanking you.'

A smile brightened his face.

'Chinese girls avoid scandals at all costs,' she continued. 'That's why I didn't report the incident to the police.'

'Yes, yes. I understand that much,' he said, nodding his head.

'We Chinese are taught to be patient with people. We have a proverb that goes, "Grave matters should be met as if they were trifling; trifles as if they were nothing." In this way, we keep away from daily annoyances and achieve peace of mind.'

Stephen scratched his head. 'What a strange way of looking at life!'

'Mr Jones, who was that big boy? Was he a friend of yours?'

'No… just a casual acquaintance.'

'Did you get hurt?'

'Only a black eye and few bruises and abrasions in the face.'

'I'm very sorry. But thank you very much. By the way, why did you pretend that we hadn't met each other before when Miss Silva introduced us at my graduation?'

'Well, I thought that since you ran away, you might not want people to know about the incident, like many conservative Chinese girls. Like I said, I know that much about your culture.'

'That was very thoughtful of you.'

'I was feeling depressed that morning. Miss Silva invited me to the ceremony to cheer me up. She said it might remind me of my schooldays. I used to tell her that my childhood was wonderful when my friends were naive and innocent.' He stood up. 'I could brew some tea. Would you like some?'

'With pleasure.'

Stephen went into the kitchen and in a short time returned with a cup of tea for Li-ling and one with sugar and cream for himself. 'Most Chinese drink plain tea, don't they?'

'Yes. Mr Jones, you seem to know some Chinese customs, but you don't know that even in this age many so-called modern Chinese still consider it immoral for a girl to be alone with a man, a greater sin if he is a Westerner. My father won't even let me work with men in his business.' She took a sip of tea.

He shook his head and said, 'But I hear that... educated Chinese are more liberal than the uneducated.' Then he stirred his tea.

'Yes, but there are many semi-liberals like my father. For instance, they advocate science and democracy in general, but they prefer Chinese herbal medicine to the more scientific Western one. And they strongly object to too much liberation, especially for women.'

After Stephen took a few sips of tea, he said, 'Chinese and Westerners are different in many ways. I've noticed that many Chinese living in wooden shacks look rather content.'

'Yes. Most Chinese are content with their lot and can be quite happy living simple lives. That's why there are so few psychopaths and suicide victims compared to the West. Do you feel content with life as it is?'

'No, I'm not so content, especially with the way life turned out for me.'

'Is that why you drink?'

He paused before answering. 'I don't usually drink. But when I think of my past, I buy a bottle of gin to take the sting out of my memories. You see, when I lived in London, I was quite wealthy. In those days, I had everyone's respect.

Then I lost my money and everyone turned his back on me. Even my wife, Linda, deserted me. As a result, I could no longer live in London. Therefore I came to Hong Kong three years ago. I worked very hard and lived thriftily. By the end of the second year, I had paid off all the debts I owed in London.'

Li-ling smiled. 'Congratulations to you. Now you don't have to be so frugal.'

Stephen looked directly into her eyes. 'But I have to save as much as possible, for I've planned to begin a new business venture which requires a lot of money.

'Listen, Miss So, since I went broke, I have lost confidence in mankind and I don't like being with people. I am a loner. But the Silva family is an exception. Mrs Silva, your teacher's stepmother, treats me like a son. She cleans my house. And Miss Silva treats me like her brother.'

All of a sudden, the answer Li-ling had hoped for came, but she tried to hide her exultation. Then she asked, 'Mr Jones, how do you spend your weekends?'

'Well, once in a while I go out with the woman I work for. I need her help to finance my business in the future.'

After clearing his throat, Stephen continued. 'In Hong Kong I'll take any job that offers the best pay. Now I am the manager of two hotels. I no longer work as an engineer. I'd like to return to London some day a rich man, and again command respect from everyone there.'

'Did you have peace of mind when you were rich?'

'Are you kidding? I spent all of my time engrossed in investments, or rather, speculation. In those days, one wise decision made would bring me a fortune while one miscalculation could result in my ruin. Rather, I should say, I spent most of my time walking a tightrope.'

Li-ling took another sip of tea. 'Since your business was so risky and your life so nerve-racking, why didn't you wind it up after you earned enough money?'

'As far as money is concerned,' said Stephen with a smile, 'the adjective "enough" is never applied to the word "money" in the minds of businessmen.'

Smiling, she asked, 'Mr Jones, how come you are so ambitious?'

'I wasn't born that way. When I was a child, I couldn't concentrate on anything, especially my studies.'

'What was wrong with you?'

'The doctors said it was an attention span deficiency. I did poorly in school and my fellow pupils taunted me calling me "retarded".'

'You must have been very unhappy.'

'Of course I was. I suffered from an inferiority complex, but at the same time I developed strong self-assertion tendencies. According to psychologists, these two emotional attitudes go hand in hand. Though I tried my best to focus my attention on learning, I still got low test scores.'

'You must have been frustrated.'

'Yes, but luckily my father got a therapist to treat me during my first two years in secondary school. As my problem with my attention span gradually subsided, my scores went up. In the last two years of secondary school and my third and fourth years in the university, I came first in the examinations. I could not tolerate second place. After my graduation, I got a high salary as an engineer for one year. When I learned that two of my fellow university graduates who had a business of their own had become very rich, I quit my job as an employee and engaged in a get-rich-quick speculation in the London Commodity Exchange. I made a lot of money in the first year, but later I lost all I had earned and was heavily in debt.'

Li-ling continued to look at him. 'It seems that your ambition drove you to emulate people who were richer than you.'

'Probably so,' he remarked.

'But then there is no way you could gain peace of mind. The Chinese have a proverb: "Even if a mountain is very high, there is always another mountain higher; even if a man is very powerful, there is always another man more powerful!"'

'But tell me, if the Chinese are not ambitious as you say, why do they work so hard?'

'Only the poor work hard for old age or against a rainy day. Not for fame, position, luxury and wealth. They think these factors disturb peace of mind and peace of mind is the main source of happiness. On the whole, Chinese usually retire at an early age.'

Li-ling stopped for a while.

'Go on, go on,' he said with a smile. 'I'm learning about the Chinese mind.'

'The wealthy are not as enterprising as those in the West. If they can keep their existing fortunes, they feel content.'

After a pause, Stephen asked with a smile, 'Miss So, may I ask how come you can express your opinions so fluently in a foreign language?'

She gave a slight nod. 'Thank you, but I don't deserve your praise. It is rather due to the guidance of our teachers who encouraged us to hold free discussions on many subjects and to take part in debates and speech contests in English.'

As Stephen's eyes looked into Li-ling's, holding her spellbound, she felt his gaze drawing her in. The way he studied her quickened her heartbeat. Suddenly she felt an impulse to flee his apartment, but something in his stare compelled her to stay. Blushing, she tore her eyes from him. 'I must go, Mr Jones.'

He caught her hand. 'Miss So.'

By now, she was so embarrassed that her breathing had become laboured.

'Will you go to dinner with me on Saturday night?' he asked.

Her heart raced at the thought of going out with him.

'Yes!' she exclaimed at once without thinking and then sighed, 'I mean – no, I can't.'

He continued to hold her hand, and now looked deep into her eyes. 'Why not?'

Li-ling looked away. 'Although my father has some European blood in him, he is prejudiced against Western people and cultures. I don't know why. He would be upset if he knew I was going out with a Westerner.'

Stephen's voice softened; 'How do you feel about Westerners?'

She looked back again. 'I don't discriminate against them.'

'Please promise me, Miss So. See me on Saturday.'

She felt thrilled and terrified at the same time. His gaze continued to hypnotise her, and she could not speak, but stared back mutely into his fascinating blue eyes.

Finally she said, 'All right, Mr Jones.'

Chapter Seven

That Saturday night Li-ling met Stephen. From that time on, when her parents were out, she often took the risk of leaving home to be with him. The two of them would sometimes travel to the New Territories and stroll in the countryside. Once when they entered a village hand in hand, they saw a marching band of musicians dressed in flame-red jackets and pants, playing Chinese clarinets, gongs and cymbals. A beautifully decorated enclosed bridal palanquin carried by four bearers followed.

'This is part of a traditional wedding ceremony,' explained Li-ling. 'That's how my mother was carried from her home to my father's house on their wedding day in Canton long ago, and my second mother not so long ago. The richer families hire bigger palanquins which require eight bearers.'

'What about marrying a concubine?' asked Stephen.

'No, and not for marrying a co-wife either. The marriage of a concubine or a co-wife is not regarded as a formal marriage. The bride does not dress in traditional bridal clothing, and there is no need to hire an attendant, called *tai kum*.'

The procession stopped at the open entrance of a large hut. Firecrackers exploded, welcoming the bride. When the young girl stepped out of the palanquin, both Li-ling and Stephen saw that she was wearing a gorgeous dress and a colourful headdress with strands of beads hanging over her face. A crowd gathered around as the *tai kum* helped the bride into the hut. From the entrance Li-ling and Stephen saw many guests, all dressed in their new clothing, looking very happy.

An easel holding a plaque, which bore the photo of a young man, stood beside the bride. She kowtowed before the altar table of the bridegroom's ancestors, on which dishes of meat and fruit and a censer with burning joss sticks were properly set. Throughout the ritual, monks chanted and chimed small bells beside the altar. Later, when an old couple took their seats in front of the altar, the bride kowtowed to them as well.

'Who's this couple?' asked Stephen.

'Must be the groom's parents,' said Li-ling.

'Where's the groom?'

'He's dead. The plaque which bears the photo of the groom stands for him. This is a ghost wedding.'

'What on earth are you talking about?' he asked in a puzzled tone, eyes popping out. She put her hand on his arm to calm him down.

An old man in the crowd spoke to them in English. 'Country people are very much superstitious than city people... Months ago boy and girl engage to marry. He die one month before. She very sad and want kill herself... Both parents arrange this wedding. This way, she show life-long love.'

'Suppose this girl falls in love with another man some day,' asked Stephen, 'could she marry him?'

'No marry,' said the man, shaking his head vigorously when Stephen frowned. 'Who dare to marry wife of ghost? Ghost husband become jealous,' he snickered.

Li-ling and Stephen looked at each other and then burst into laughter. She laughed so hard that she fell into his arms. The next instant they saw people gazing at them, so they separated. She blushed and Stephen avoided their stares by looking at the ground.

After a few moments, he sighed, 'She can never marry again. What a tragedy!'

The old man turned to Stephen again. 'This single ghost wedding... Double ghost wedding bridegroom and bride are both die. Long time before, such ceremony two, three times every month in this country place, but now not many...'

'Is such a wedding costly?' asked Stephen.

'Yes,' answered the old man. 'Chinese think marriage and... funeral most important. Poor people spend all their money on these things.'

After saying goodbye to the old man, Li-ling and Stephen continued with their walk. They entered a cemetery enclosed by a short wall. Inside they saw people offering meat and fruit as sacrifices to the dead, lighting joss sticks and kowtowing before tombstones. Some of them burned paper representations of clothes, houses, radios, motor cars, and servants, as well as notes printed in denominations of one million dollars issued by 'The Bank of Hades', as presents to their loved ones in the other world.

'Do all Westernised Chinese also believe in ghosts?' Stephen asked Li-ling as people dressed in Western clothing kowtowed before the graves.

'Since the existence of ghosts has never been disproved, most Chinese continue to observe this Confucian ritual regularly, no matter what religion they believe in. Besides, this is the only way they can show love and respect for their ancestors and seek peace of mind. This practice also promotes filial piety.'

'What's that?'

'Filial piety implies not only love for one's family, especially one's parents, but also observance of all rules of ethics, no matter what, in order not to sully the family name.'

'Look, Li-ling, many people are eating the offerings.'

'Wouldn't it be a waste if they didn't?'

He smiled. 'I guess it's the same with Westerners, who place flowers at their loved ones' graves as a sign of love though the dead can't smell the fragrance.'

She nodded.

'I see the Chinese are a religious people?' he said as they continued their walk through the cemetery.

'No,' she said, 'not on the whole. Chinese culture is a strange blend of three schools of thought: Confucianism, Taoism and Buddhism.'

'What are these schools about?'

'Do you really want to know about my culture?'

'Of course I do. Besides, I love to hear your sweet voice and watch your rosy lips move as you speak.'

Li-ling blushed and tried her best to continue. 'Confucianism is not a religion because Confucians are interested in this world rather than the next. Since many educated Chinese are Confucians, they seldom worship gods. Taoism and Buddhism are religions, but Taoists and Buddhists are few in proportion to the vast population. However, next to Confucianism, both these religions have a great influence on Chinese life. On the other hand, many Chinese, especially the uneducated, worship different gods at different times or even at the same time.'

Obsessed with his deep azure eyes inquisitively staring at her, Li-ling could not concentrate long enough to discuss this subject until she had recuperated after a minute or so.

'According to my teacher,' she continued, 'despite the basic differences of the three schools, their common view of life is peace of mind.'

'How do they attain it?'

'Through patience,' she answered, 'though with different shades of meaning. The Confucians patiently observe rules of morality so that they may live a life with a clear conscience. The Taoists patiently avoid emulation and quarrels so that they may live a life of tranquillity. The Buddhists patiently subdue all worldly temptations so that they may live a life free of all disturbing emotions.' She paused, ashamed that she had talked for so long.

He smiled. 'Please, go on. I want to know more about this "peace of mind".'

'They all believe in varying degrees that everything is predestined. The Confucians laugh at poverty and failure. The Taoists go further by looking upon injury or insult with a grin. The Buddhists go still further by regarding afflictions with a smile.'

Li-ling relaxed, content in musing that because of his interest in her, Stephen had become interested in her culture.

★

Li-ling could not go out as often as she wished. Of course, she could go out alone for a walk in the quiet neighbourhood for half an hour or so in the evening. She could go out downtown for three or four hours at the most in the daytime without raising her parents' suspicions. But if she stayed out too long, especially at night, her parents would ask questions.

Li-ling could only see Stephen secretly two or three times a week. One of their activities was motor boating; Stephen taught her how to take the helm. He also taught her to swim in private pools and to drive a car in the countryside of the New Territories. They would dance at parties. They made the most of their outings, even though she thought that each date never lasted long enough.

In downtown areas they seldom walked together, but they never lost each other. She thought it was because their souls were inseparable.

In planning their dates, to guard against discovery, Li-ling would go to a nearby restaurant and use the phone. Stephen would ask Maisy Diaz to arrange their appointments. Sometimes Li-ling called Chen Ma to find out if her parents would be home early at night. If so, she would leave Stephen immediately.

Once in a while Stephen lost his patience with this 'life of illusion' as he called it.

One and a half months after their first date, Li-ling discovered a place where they could see each other more often. To reach it she had to walk up a long flight of stone steps located a few houses west of her residence. This led to a Chinese-style light-green pavilion on the edge of Conduit Road on the harbour side. Like Robinson Road, this road was one of the few winding roads which hugged Mount Victoria.

The pavilion was an open-air, concrete structure situated on a meadow. It had an umbrella-like canopy with a centre pole supporting it. Surrounding this pole was a round table with a matching curved bench. A low wall separate from the canopy formed the outside of the pavilion. In the daytime hikers rested there; at night there was no one.

Around the pavilion grew a few native orchid trees with long spreading branches bearing rounded, double-lobed leaves with fragrant, purplish-red flowers which bloomed from early August to the end of March.

Since this discovery, after Li-ling finished her supper at about 6.20 p.m., she would half run and half walk to the pavilion to meet Steve at 6.30 p.m. There they were together for only twenty minutes before she had to be home by 7 p.m. But too often her parents kept her talking after the meal, which made it impossible for her to get away. On these occasions Stephen would wait in vain for her and eventually return home.

During their first few trysts at the pavilion, they enjoyed a platonic relationship. At their fourth meeting, they strolled hand in hand in the meadow, enjoying the orchid trees abloom with their exquisite flowers as a pair of butterflies fluttered about freely and two larks sang merrily. She smiled when this reminded her of a similar scene that she had imagined on the day of their first meeting ten months before.

'Steve,' she said, 'I wonder if we human beings are freer and happier than these creatures?'

'And yet,' he said with a shrug, 'we claim we are the wisest of all animals.'

At a later meeting he chased after her and caught hold of her. He turned her around and she melted into his kisses. She felt as if every drop of blood in her body was waltzing. Her legs would have given way had not Stephen's strong embrace held her steady. From then on, they kissed when they were alone. However, each of these rendezvous lasted but briefly, like the night-blooming cereus.

One day when Li-ling and Stephen were together in the pavilion, two boys in their mid-teens engaged in conversation walked up Conduit Road, passing close by. Suddenly Stephen turned red and dropped Li-ling's hand. Then he rose quickly to his feet, ran after them and grabbed one of them by the arm. Li-ling heard him hollering and saw him raise his fist at them. Then all of a sudden Stephen dropped his fist and said something. The boys then turned and ran away. Stephen came back to Li-ling.

Eyes wide open, he said, 'When they passed here, I heard one of them mention *fain gwai*. I asked him if he referred to me. He only said that Chinese should not marry *fain gwai*. I wanted him to apologise for insulting us non-Chinese, but he refused. So I raised my fist to hit him. Then I suddenly remembered the Chinese saying about trifles being regarded as nothing. I let him go.'

'Steve, I also heard him say these words. Since the Opium War in 1839, the great powers have politically and economically exploited China. We Chinese used to call these nationals "foreign devils", but nowadays we seldom use this term even in our conversation. At present foreigners are not offended when they occasionally overhear these words spoken by Chinese. They understand that we entertain no bad intentions. Early this year the Westerners organised a team to enter the race during the Dragon Boat Festival and called it the "Foreign Devil Team".'

Stephen squinted his eyes. 'I still think that it's wrong. I feel hurt when we are called *fain gwai.*'

'If you fume over daily trifles, you can never be happy.'

Chapter Eight

One month later, when Li-ling came home, the manservant who had opened the gate for her told her that a foreign lady had come to pay her a visit. She wondered who it could be. She saw a Rolls Royce with an Indian chauffeur parked in front of the house. After she entered the living room, a middle-aged European lady in a gorgeous dress, wearing a big diamond ring and a platinum necklace mounted with emeralds, stood up from a chair beside a side table with a cup of hot tea on it. Li-ling bit her lower lip.

'Good afternoon, madam,' said Li-ling.

'Good afternoon, Miss So,' said the lady with a smile.

Li-ling noticed that the woman's heavy make-up could not hide the wrinkles at the corner of her eyes. Even so, thought Li-ling, she is a lady with refined manners and charming poise.

After motioning her guest to sit down, Li-ling asked, 'How did you know my name?' She sat beside her.

'How I knew isn't important. I've come here about Mr Stephen Jones.'

Li-ling was uneasy at the mention of Stephen's name.

'To speak frankly,' continued the lady, 'Mr Jones and I have been… well, like husband and wife.'

'No! No!' said Li-ling, her face turning red. 'I know that he was married once, but he's divorced now.'

'What I meant,' went on the lady, her red, spiked finger-nails flashing, 'is that we've… slept together regularly for the past two years though we're not yet married.'

'I don't believe you,' said Li-ling. Inwardly she was flabbergasted by the woman's lack of modesty in disclosing her sexual relationship, whether true or not, to a stranger. This destroyed the good image of the lady in her mind.

'Perhaps you don't believe me. Here's a photo I took in my bedroom.'

She handed Li-ling a large photo of Stephen, dressed in pyjamas with an unshaven face and dishevelled hair, sitting in a double bed with a well-decorated wall in the background on which a picture of the lady hung.

'Please take a look at the calendar on the side table next to the bed.' The lady pointed at the calendar as her red nail scraped the surface of the photo.

Li-ling studied it closely. Sure enough, the date on the calendar indicated 20th September, 1941, only ten days before. She felt such a pressure in her chest that she could hardly breathe. She then returned the photo.

'I'm very sorry. I didn't know he's still involved with someone else.' She fought for control. 'Are you his boss?'

'Yes. And I am his lover, too.'

'I never thought that you had gone any further than an employer–employee relationship. Mr Jones only told me that he went out with his boss on business once in a while.'

'Yes. I am sure that is all he told you,' smirked the lady. After she cleared her throat, she took a sip of tea. 'But I must know: does he tell you that he loves you?'

'Well… yes.'

'He tells me the same thing. Well, there you are. He is in love…' the lady paused for a second, raised her eyebrows and then continued, 'with two women or more at the same time.' Then she placed her cup on the side table and sighed.

Li-ling's head swam and her stomach churned.

'Miss So, I've made up my mind to break up with him. If you don't mind his erratic romantic character, you can have him. Perhaps he won't desert you.'

'Oh, no! If he has cast you aside like a "fan in autumn", he'll do the same thing to me sooner or later. Thank you for being so frank with me.'

'As you know, he is extremely ambitious. Even at university after he failed to be re-elected as president of the student union, he suffered insomnia for weeks. It's clear that without great success in life, he'll never be happy, and if you were married to him, you'd probably ruin his prospects.'

'Why do you say that?'

'Of course I don't have any prejudice against you Chinese. But if you become his wife, he'd have less chance of making friends with the elite in the Western community. Without their connections it wouldn't be easy for him to achieve anything in his career in Hong Kong.' She rose, waving one of her taloned hands. 'Well, I must go.'

'Why did you come here to tell me about his double dealings?'

'We are both in the same boat. I've been cheated. I want to keep others from suffering.'

'Thank you very much. May I know your name?'

'Mrs McDonnall. My husband passed away ten years ago.'

Then Li-ling walked her to the Rolls-Royce and they shook hands.

'Goodbye, Mrs McDonnall.'

'Goodbye, Miss So. Please don't tell Stephen about my visit. It'll just upset him.'

Li-ling returned to the house as Chen Ma came out of the dining room.

'Young Mistress, no one else is at home now, but lunch is ready.'

'I'm not hungry,' she said and then fled upstairs into her bedroom while Chen Ma stood still, elbows bent and palms up in the air.

Li-ling sat in her chair, staring at the ceiling all after-noon. During the evening meal she made the excuse of having a headache and went to bed early. Throughout the night she tossed and turned.

I gave Steve my whole soul, she thought, but he cheated me. All the time, I felt love was sweet, but now I taste its bitterness.

Why should I think of him? I'll forget him and never fall in love again. To stay in Hong Kong would be an endless nightmare. I'll go to Free China for a great cause and join my ex-schoolmates who left only two days ago.

What about Papa? I'll miss him, but it can't be helped. The saying is true: 'How can families exist if the country does not?'

After tossing and turning in her bed the whole night, Li-ling arose early the next morning. With her tear-streaked face twisted in anguish, she wrote a letter:

My Dearest Papa,
You have given me life and brought me up with sweat and care. I am very much indebted to you.

When you read this letter, I shall be on my way to Free China to join a group of my former schoolmates to work for our country against Japan.

You have shown your sense of responsibility for our ancestral homeland by contributing generous sums toward the war efforts, and I will show mine by participating in them first-hand.

I shall for ever feel deep regret to think that during my absence from Hong Kong I cannot wait upon you and Young Mama. I am sorry also that I won't be able to say goodbye to you before I leave lest you should forbid me to go. I hope you'll take good care of yourself as well as Young Mama and Chi-ching.

As soon as we win the war against Japan and recover our lost territories, I'll return home for a reunion with all of you. I'm looking forward to that day. Do not worry about me. I'll take care of myself.
May you be healthy.
Your loving daughter,
Li-ling

She placed the tear-stained letter under her pillow, and then filled a leather bag with clothing and daily necessities.

At about 9.30 a.m., after her father left for his office and her stepmother went back to bed, Li-ling departed quietly even without Chen Ma's knowledge.

Chapter Nine

Knowing that Stephen was at work in his office, Li-ling went to his apartment before starting her journey to Free China. As soon as she entered the living room, she saw the depression on the sofa which Stephen had made with her sitting on his lap on many amorous occasions.

Li-ling then saw a photo on the desk of the two of them dancing at a party. She remembered that night they had happily whirled to the tune of Richard Rodger's 'Love'. At the end of the music, Stephen had held her in his arms and they had kissed.

Li-ling could picture the two of them watching *The Great Waltz* at the cinema. Towards the end, the great music composer and the prima donna sadly parted for good as *The Blue Danube* was played. She and Stephen had been moved to tears.

Li-ling turned and looked at the bunch of lilies with their white trumpet-shaped flowers settled in a large white china vase inlaid with colourful, artistic patterns on the mantelpiece. The bouquet had been fresh and bright when Li-ling had sent it to Stephen a few days before. She always regarded the lily as a symbol of purity and honesty. But now the bouquet looked wilted and devoid of life, just like their love. She took it out of the vase and threw it in the waste-paper basket.

With tears dripping onto the paper, Li-ling scribbled a note and left it on the desk. Then she put Stephen's key on top of it.

After she had looked around the room where she had tasted the sweet obsession of her first love for the last time, she wiped away her tears and prepared to leave. When she reached the door, she heard Stephen and his woman boss talking in the corridor, so she turned around to head for the back door. As she passed the kitchen, she suddenly went back to the living room to fetch her handbag before hurrying away.

'Have a seat, please,' said Stephen after he and Lady McDonnall entered the living room. 'Eliza, what's so important that you have to tell me here instead of in my office?' He took off his coat.

'Honey, I have successfully made arrangements for getting you a one-million-dollar loan within a week – with my guarantee, of course,' said the lady.

He rushed to her and kissed her face feverishly. 'Thank you! Oh, thank you, dear Eliza. I'm sure I can repay the loan plus interest in four years.'

'I am not interested in the money.' She grinned and took a seat. 'I want you to set a wedding date right away.'

'Right now?'

'Yes. You always tell me that you love me, but you never promise to marry me.'

Squinting, he answered, 'You know very well that each time we meet, you want me to tell you so.'

'All right, then. Since you've slept with me, why don't you marry me?'

'Because it's you who always strips off your clothes first and then asks me to follow.'

'Yes,' she said calmly. 'Take it for granted that you are under no obligation to marry me, but you shouldn't go out with another woman as long as we remain intimate friends.'

'And why not?'

'Well, you could at least have told me that you were seeing another woman.'

He walked to the window and looked outside. 'I have no obligation to tell you everything about my private life.'

'A lady friend of mine saw you walking with an attractive Chinese girl in the New Territories. How ungrateful you are! I made you general manager of my two hotels, despite strong objections from some board members because you had no previous experience in this business.'

He walked back to her. 'But haven't I done my duties to the satisfaction of all of you?'

'Yes, we know very well you've improved the service of the hotels, and that other first-class hotels have lost some of their customers to us. I admit, my dear Steve, that you are clever, and I love you all the more. Since I can help you with a large loan, you'll be able to carry out your construction project smoothly. Can't you see yourself returning to London, successful in your own right, not just the husband of the former Lady McDonnall?'

Lifting his head and looking straight at Lady McDonnall, he said, 'I love this Chinese girl and will marry her. You and I could still be friends, and perhaps...' Just then he saw the key resting on the note. He grabbed them.

Dear Steve,
I must say goodbye. I'm leaving Hong Kong to join a group of my ex-schoolmates on their way to Free China.

Sorry I can't see you before I leave. Thank you for your friendship, but my country needs young people. The Chinese have a saying: 'Everyone should be held responsible for the rise and fall of his country.' I'm going to Free China for a great cause. Wish you success. Goodbye!
Li-ling

'She's gone,' he sighed, his face turning red. 'I feel the earth shaking beneath me.'

'What's the matter?' asked Lady McDonnall.

He handed her the shaking note and slumped into a chair.

As she read, she relaxed.

'Steve,' she said after reading it, 'don't take it to heart. I doubt either of you would be happy if you were married. You have entirely different cultural backgrounds. Besides, she might jeopardise your social position.'

'What made Li-ling so resolute?' asked Stephen aloud. 'There's something fishy about this.'

'Why do you say that?'

'She once mentioned going to Free China, asserting that she couldn't go because of her love for me and her father. Besides, she would never leave without talking to me about it first.'

'She might have been afraid that if she'd consulted you, you would have stopped her.' The lady shifted from one foot to the other.

'Who else is so concerned about the relationship between her and me? You must have seen her after your friend, or should I say your detective, got her name and address somehow. You might as well admit it because sooner or later, when I find it out, our friendship will be over for ever!' Stephen wiped his wet forehead.

'If I do admit it, all I've done is prove that I love you very much. Even though she's gone, I won't press you to marry me. Let's just be good friends as usual and you'll forget her as time goes by. And with my help, you'll become a rich man again.'

His muscles bulged beneath his shirt. 'No, Lady McDonnall, I'll resign from my jobs as of this second, and I will not accept a loan from you, ever.'

She stood straight from the chair. 'Then your ambition will never be realized.'

'Lady McDonnall, I've lost my love; I don't care about money or position any more. You know very well that I've never loved you. Why did you interfere with my relationship with Miss So? Please go now.'

Lady McDonnall darted to the mantelpiece, seized the large white vase with both hands and smashed it against the hardwood floor with a bang. As the shattered pieces settled, she shouted, 'You have a poor man's blood: you don't deserve this valuable present of mine!' Then she slammed the door as she left.

Stephen felt as if his heart were so light that he could fly freely. But on second thoughts, he could not do so happily without Li-ling. Then his heart became heavy again and he sank deeper into his chair.

'Linda slept with Lord Kirkwood for gain,' he shouted, 'and I called her a whore. Now I've slept with Lady McDonnall for the same reason. Am I any better than Linda – any better than a whore?'

He walked to the window and looked up to the sky, his eyes veiled with tears.

'My dearest Li-ling,' he cried aloud, 'I am a gigolo! I am contemptible and despicable. I don't deserve you, but I still love you. Where are you? Where are you? How can I find you?' He hit his chest with his fists.

'My dearest Steve,' said a voice behind his back, 'I love you, too, and I always will.'

'Could it be…?' He turned around, tears running down his cheeks.

Li-ling stood there right in front of him. 'Steve, when I was ready to leave, you arrived with… Lady McDonnall, so I rushed to the back door. When I got there, I suddenly feared that I would make a noise, opening and shutting the door. I turned around and saw the pantry with its partly open door which is opposite the kitchen. I slipped in and hid inside. I'm very sorry that I overheard your conversation.'

They embraced, kissing over and over again.

In the afternoon, Li-ling went home. Not even Chen Ma was aware that she had almost left Hong Kong for good. In her bedroom, Li-ling removed the letter to her father from underneath her pillow and threw it into the waste-paper basket.

Now Stephen gave up his two jobs as hotel manager and returned to his former profession as an engineer. Now he was not as busy as before and had more time to see her. He dressed better. He had his apartment repainted, bought new furniture and even purchased a brand-new Standard automobile. With Lady McDonnall out of the way, they were very happy, but still they had to keep their dates secret. Even this 'sweet-sour life', as Stephen termed it, did not last long.

Chapter Ten

Colourful birds sang outside Li-ling's bedroom window while she knitted. As the birds' songs accompanied the rhythmic clicking of her wooden needles, each stitch reminded her of a musical note which seemed to be flying into the air. She smiled, realizing that it was her love for Stephen that made everything so wonderful. This was a gift of her love, a sweater made specially for him with all her heart. She knitted it carefully, making sure it was just right.

'I'll surprise him on his birthday two days before Christmas,' she said to herself.

Suddenly a knock on the door startled her. She hurriedly put the sweater, the two needles and the ball of yarn into her wardrobe before she opened the door. Chen Ma stood patiently outside, holding a letter. Silently, Li-ling took the envelope from her and scanned the handwriting. It did not look familiar. After she closed the door, she read the letter.

Miss Li-ling So,
Sorry I was so rude when I saw you last. I'll never be that way again. I want to make it up to you and invite you to a birthday party of a friend on Wednesday, 26th November. Please meet me at 6.30 p.m. under the big banyan where we first met. Only last month did I find out you had a very strict father.

I know you've been seeing Stephen secretly and that he'll be away at a special camp in the New Territories on week-

days for another three weeks, training new gunners of the Hong Kong Volunteer Defence Corps.

Now that you have free time, you don't have any excuse to turn me down. Don't worry, I won't tell him about our date. You must be grateful to me for keeping your secret dates from your father, and also for not having another confrontation with Steve. He is no match for me.

If you can go out with him so often, you can go out with me this once. After all, you should thank me, for without me you'd have never known him in the first place. You are a clever girl. Make a wise decision.

Waiting to meet you,
Michael Young

As she read this note, Li-ling's faced turned blue. After consideration she thought it advisable to decline the invitation politely by mail, but as there was no return address given in the letter, she could not. Her only alternative was to send Chen Ma to hand-carry her reply to Michael Young at the appointed time and place. But Chen Ma was unable to do so because she would have to serve the family supper at that time. Li-ling was afraid that the blackmailer would not give up that easily. She thought of him as a ghost, haunting her everywhere, giving her soul no rest. Over the following days she ate and slept little, expecting the villain to make further trouble for her.

Early on Saturday afternoon a few days later, a quivering Chen Ma entered Li-ling's room.

'Young Mistress,' she said, 'Master and Mistress want you in their bedroom. They are furious.'

After Li-ling motioned her maid to leave, she remained frozen for a few moments. She tried to conquer her fears by drawing a few deep breaths before she reluctantly went to see her parents.

When she entered the room, she saw that their faces seemed shrouded in dark clouds. Mr So, dressed in silk pyjamas, sat on a blackwood chair looking like a mandarin magistrate trying a criminal while Mrs So, wearing a satin dressing gown, stood like the prosecuting attorney next to him.

'Li-ling, what have you done in the past six months since your graduation, besides teaching your brother Chinese and going to a sewing and embroidery school twice a week?' asked Mr So.

'We've received a letter written in English by a man called Young addressed to your father,' said Mrs So. 'It says you have had many secret dates with an Englishman, called Jones, who lives in the Blue Mansion. Tell us everything, you unfilial daughter.'

Her head drooping, Li-ling remained silent.

'Look at Papa,' said her stepmother. 'He's suffering from heart trouble. If you keep silent, he will die from rage.'

'How did you come to know him?' asked Mr So.

'A little more than a year ago,' said Li-ling, 'this Michael Young, a Westerner, stopped me on Robinson Road and tried to force his attentions on me. But Mr Jones happened to pass by and saved me from harassment.'

'Then you've been going out with this stranger since then?' asked her father.

'Not until about eight and a half months later when I went to his home to thank him for rescuing me.'

'All you needed to do was to write him a letter of thanks,' said Mr So. 'How could a family girl like you visit a stranger alone at his home, especially a Western man?'

'This is what comes of a Western education,' said her stepmother with a sneer.

'How many times have you seen him?' he queried.

'About sixty.'

'Sixty times!' he shouted, the veins in his temple protruding.

'There you are,' said Mrs So. 'You are nothing but an indecent girl! Only bar girls go out with Western men.'

'You must look like a whore to our friends and relatives,' said her father, shaking his head. 'Young men from decent families will never marry girls who mix with men freely, let alone Western men.'

'How about your short meetings at the pavilion nearby as mentioned in the letter?' asked Mrs So. 'You may not be afraid of neighbours' gossip, but we are. Li-ling, you are allowed neither to go outside the house nor to make or receive telephone calls without our knowledge until further notice.'

'Chen Ma,' added Mrs So, 'you too. You always take sides with Li-ling. As the foreign devil is living nearby, you are forbidden to deliver notes for her.'

'Yes, Mistress.'

'Li-ling,' said her father, 'as I have told you before, on your initiation day at Mr Leung's traditional school, Sir William talked me into sending you to a modern school after a few years' study there. If I had ignored his advice and kept you at Mr Leung's school, you wouldn't have committed such disgraceful acts.'

Li-ling had promised to see Stephen at his home at 7 p.m. Now, she knew that her parents would not let her go out no matter how good her excuse might be.

He will be waiting for me anxiously for hours tonight, she worried.

'Have you ever given yourself to him?' asked Mrs So.

Li-ling shook her head.

'You shall be sent to a woman doctor for examination,' said Mrs So.

'No! No!' protested Li-ling.

Pointing a finger at her, her stepmother said, 'There you are. You are no longer a virgin.'

Li-ling said after a pause, 'All right. Since you don't believe me, I will offer myself for examination to clear up your suspicion.'

'But people would gossip and we would lose face,' said her father.

'I can never believe in her chastity after so many dates with a Western man,' said Mrs So. 'In the future, if we marry her off to a respectable family, wouldn't she be sent back to us the following day in disgrace once the previous loss of her virginity is discovered on the wedding night? Wouldn't we lose more face then? Li-ling, you know about the Sun family. Two years ago Mr Sun disowned his daughter because she married a Westerner.'

'By the way, where's this Jones working?' asked Mr So.

'He's an engineer for a big company,' replied Li-ling.

'What is its name?'

She did not answer.

'What is its name?' shouted Mr So.

'Papa, you're not going to make trouble for him, are you? He is a good man.' She fell to her knees.

'She is in love with him,' sneered Mrs So, 'otherwise she wouldn't be so concerned about him.'

'No, I won't bother with Jones, who has nothing to do with me, but I'm going to teach you a lesson.' Mr So's entire body trembled as he pushed himself up from his chair. Then he looked around the room for something. Chen Ma grabbed a stick in the corner. But when she began to slip out of the room with it, Mr So ordered, 'Chen Ma, give me that.'

'Please don't,' pleaded Chen Ma.

Jumping to his feet, Mr So barked, 'Give me that stick!'

She handed it to her master, her teeth clattering rapidly.

He beat his daughter on the back with the stick three times. Though she did not utter a groan, tears streamed down her cheeks.

'If your date were a Chinese, I might not have hit you, but...' He staggered back to his chair and sobbed.

Before Chen Ma helped Li-ling leave the room, he said, 'Chen Ma, go to my bathroom and get the bottle of the leftover medicated liquor for Young Mistress.'

'Master, do you mean the same medication, with which Young Mistress massaged your sprained ankle for two whole months?' asked Chen Ma loudly.

Mr So did not reply. Chen Ma helped her young mistress to her bedroom before she went to Mr So's bathroom for the medication.

★

In her bedroom Li-ling lay on her stomach while Chen Ma kneaded her bruised back gently with the herbal liquor. Afterwards Li-ling continued to lie face down, and did not put on clothing so that nothing came in contact with her bruises to cause additional pain.

In the evening after Chen Ma had served her master and mistress at the supper table, she went to Li-ling's room.

'Young Mistress, are you hungry? I'll bring supper up for you.'

'No, I can't eat anything tonight.'

'Young Mistress, I've got good news for you.'

'What good news?'

'At six o'clock I went to Master and Mistress's bedroom to ask them to come downstairs for supper. When I got near the door I heard them talking about you. So I waited and listened. Mistress said that you must be sent to the doctor for examination, but Master said that you wouldn't have been that bad because of your early education at Mr Leung's school.'

'I'm glad Papa still trusts me. Chen Ma, you always eavesdrop. That's very underhand.'

'I only do so to get information from Mistress,' protested Chen Ma.

As Li-ling coughed, Chen Ma hurried to get a cup of water for her from the thermos bottle on the table.

'Young Mistress, I beg you, as a girl from a decent family, don't go out with that Westerner any more. And you know that Master doesn't like Westerners. As a faithful daughter, you shouldn't make him mad.'

'Chen Ma, have you ever been in love?'

'Yes, of course.'

'With whom?' Li-ling took a few sips of water.

'With you, of course. I have no child of my own.'

'No, no, I don't mean that sort of love,' said Li-ling a little impatiently. 'Did you love your husband?'

'I... I really don't know. When I was young I was, like all girls, forbidden to come into contact with boys. When I was fifteen my parents married me to a stranger. Then I lived with him and his elderly parents in a village. I did all the household chores. My husband spoke little to me. He hardly ever slept with me. He used to stay out overnight in gambling houses and brothels in town. His parents never cared as long as he gave us enough money for our family expenses. But also they didn't like me because I didn't bear them any grandsons or even granddaughters.'

'That might not have been your fault,' said Li-ling.

'But people always blame the women.' The maidservant took the cup of water from Li-ling and put it back on the table. 'In the sixth year of my marriage, my in-laws died one after the other. In the seventh year, my husband left me and never returned. Since then, I've never missed him.'

'Chen Ma, if Papa and Mama try to force me to marry another man, I would rather become a Buddhist nun for life.'

'I didn't realize until now that you loved this man so much. I had no love at all in my marriage. Now I sympathize with you all the more.'

'Thank you, Chen Ma. You must be tired. Goodnight.'

'Goodnight, Mistress.'

Lying in bed, Li-ling wept for a long time before falling asleep.

Chapter Eleven

That very night while young Mrs So was asleep beside him, Mr So lay wide awake. He recalled a scene.

★

'Mr So,' said a short gentleman with a great domed head, wearing a Chinese long gown, 'congratulations. This morning you have placed your five-year-old daughter, Li-ling under the good care of Mr Leung.' He inhaled smoke through the water in a Chinese tobacco pipe, and puffed.

'Sir William, I'd like her to study in Mr Leung's traditional school as long as possible.'

They were now talking in the Honourable Sir William Wen's Chinese-style living room, a room adorned with gorgeous blackwood furniture, dragon and phoenix upholstery, framed Chinese landscapes and scrolls of Chinese calligraphy on the walls. A photograph of Dr Sun Yat-sen hung over the mantelpiece.

Mr So often consulted Sir William about important business and personal matters. A child's initiation at school was very important to Mr So, as was generally the case with most Chinese.

Sir William smiled at Mr So. 'Do you mean that your daughter will never go to a Western-style, modern school with a complete curriculum, which includes a variety of subjects, such as mathematics, geography, and English besides Chinese?'

'Yes, I mean it.'

'We always think of our own generation. But you must remember that she belongs to the present generation – a new generation of our children. They are studying in modern schools where modern ideas are taught.'

'But virtue and morality are not emphasised. The rate of juvenile delinquency is very high in the West. Hong Kong will follow the footsteps of the West before long,' sighed Mr So.

'Although we have a very old civilization, morality-wise, we have been defeated at war by the great powers including the Westernised Little Japan since the Opium War broke out one century ago. They are powerful, so we have to learn from them in order to become powerful again.'

Sir William paused for a moment. After he had inhaled deeply from his water pipe, he began to speak louder. 'Mr So, it has been ten years since the May Fourth Movement was launched in 1919 under the leadership of American-educated Dr Hu Shih, Chen Took-Shiu and Tsai Yuen-Pei. This movement advocated a radical introduction of science and democracy through education from the West in order to make China strong. Now most families send their children to study in modern schools rather than traditional schools, where only Chinese subjects, especially Confucianism, are taught. More wealthy families send their sons and even daughters abroad for further studies. You can't change the tide of the times, good or bad. We must adjust to change. After all, civil service examinations on Confucianism have been abolished since 1901 even before the establishment of the Chinese Republic in 1911.'

Mr So leaned forward in his seat. 'But sir, I simply want my daughter to become the virtuous wife of a young man from a decent family and bring up half a dozen children. Is there any need for her, a mere girl, to learn a foreign culture, including science and those rebellious modern ideas of woman's liberation?'

His friend snapped his fingers. 'That's just it! Likely she will marry a member of a new generation, heart and soul. What son of a decent family will marry her if she is ignorant of modern ideas? Think of your daughter's future. She should have the opportunity to be educated in a modern school after a few years of studying with Mr Leung.'

Mr So nodded.

'How is Mrs So?' Sir William puffed on his water pipe.

'She's now praying to the son-bestowing goddess, Kwanyin, in a Buddhist temple. She has done so for some years, but in vain. She has urged me to take a concubine.'

'If I were you, I'd take a few concubines in order to beget a number of sons. Confucius, I'm sorry, Mencius, the great successor of Confucius, said, "Of three things against filial piety, lack of a son is the greatest." That's why I married my second concubine hurriedly before I became a Christian two years ago.'

'My wife is a lovely woman with traditional virtues,' said Mr So. 'I love her dearly. What do I need another woman for?' He was serious, though the connection between taking a concubine and having sons was not entirely lost on him.

After a short while, Mr So rose to leave. He passed the entrance of the adjacent Western-designed room, full of sofas and Western drawings, where he caught a glimpse of the photograph of King George V hanging on the wall.

★

Finally, Mr So turned over on his side and fell asleep.

Chapter Twelve

The next day as Li-ling's injuries confined her to bed, Chen Ma brought her meals to her bedroom.

That evening after Mr So came home from office, he asked Chen Ma, 'How is Young Mistress doing?'

'She's all right.'

'Are you sure? If her condition worsens, tell me and I'll send for Dr Fan.'

When Chen Ma told her young mistress of her father's concern, Li-ling felt some consolation, though it bothered her that neither her father nor her stepmother came to see her.

Another day later Li-ling's condition improved greatly. She felt less pain, and needed less treatment. Still she left her back uncovered to ensure earlier recovery. Then she remembered a childhood scene.

*

When she was four years old, she refused to drink a bowl of medicated soup and vented her anger on an expensive china vase by smashing it. At first, her father was infuriated. But before he started to scold her, he noticed that her hand was bleeding. He examined it and quickly but carefully removed the splinters of china from the cuts. He applied iodine to the wounds as Li-ling cried aloud in pain. His anger had turned into compassion.

*

Lost in her recollection, Li-ling was startled by the unexpected appearance of the smiling face of her stepmother, who held a bowl of hot soup.

'Li-ling, I know you've eaten little in the past two days,' said Mrs So in a soothing tone. 'Drink this ginseng to give you nourishment. Papa beat you because he cared for you. In fact he felt more pain than you. Poor Li-ling, how's your back?'

'Much better now, Young Mama. Thank you very much.' Li-ling turned slowly, barely covering her naked breast with a towel before she sat up. She then sipped the soup.

'Li-ling, you are not a child any more,' said Mrs So, sitting on the edge of the bed. 'You should get married. Papa and I love you and want you to have a happy life.'

'Young Mama, I don't want to marry just yet.'

'Silly girl, if you don't marry when you are young, when will you? Now get up and dress.'

'Why?'

'A young man's waiting downstairs. Papa and I have met him a couple of times and we like him very much. He is very good at Chinese calligraphy and poetry. He's good looking, too.'

'Young Mama, I'm not completely well yet, I can't see him today—'

'Li-ling, listen to me. If you don't see him now, Papa will suspect that you're still in love with that Westerner. For Papa's sake, meet the young man. I'll entertain him for the moment. I expect you to go downstairs in fifteen minutes.'

After her stepmother left, Li-ling could not help crying. Later she wiped away her tears and put on a white velvet cheongsam embroidered with artistic patterns.

Downstairs, she entered the living room. A young man stood up and bowed to her. She returned his greeting, feeling some pain on her tender back.

Mrs So's description was right. His face was white, his skin smooth and his lips like cherries. Smartly dressed in Western clothing, he looked delicate and was of a somewhat smallish build. Li-ling's first impression was that he looked like a teenage girl disguised as a boy.

'This is Mr Hung Mor-li,' said Mrs So. 'His father is a good friend of Papa's. This is my daughter, Li-ling.'

'Is your given name Mor-li, the name of a flower?' asked Li-ling after the usual preliminaries.

'Yes,' said Mr Hung in a soft voice, his head drooping. A thin red blush came over his face as he explained, 'My father gave me this... feminine name because he was afraid that many evil spirits were jealous of his having a son and might take me from him as they had taken my two elder brothers when they were young. He continued to fool the spirits by dressing me and treating me... like a daughter until I was fifteen or so. Of course this was sheer superstition. In order not to displease him, I've kept this name.'

'Mr Hung, you are a filial son,' complimented Mrs So. 'By the way, both you and Li-ling were Mr Leung's pupils at different times.'

'When were you there?' asked Li-ling.

'Oh, I've never been to his school. He was my private tutor some twenty years ago when I was seven.'

'Then you're much older than you look,' said Li-ling.

'Mr Hung, I'm very sorry. What she meant is that you look younger than you are,' said Mrs So.

He produced a small embroidered handkerchief and dabbed his slightly wet forehead with it.

'Li-ling,' went on Mrs So, 'I invited Mr Hung here when I happened to meet him in the street. I promised not to keep him long because he had an appointment with a business friend at the Hermits' Club.'

'What sort of club is that?' asked Li-ling.

'It's famous for its opium-smoking service,' explained Mr Hung. 'People who smoke opium feel as if they are hermits living in a secluded world, free from worry and anxiety. Hence the name.'

'Mr Hung, isn't opium smoking harmful to health?' asked Li-ling.

Mrs So leaned forward until she perched on the edge of the chair. She quickly said, 'on the other hand, such a club is healthy because it is an ideal recreation spot for businessmen. Now say goodbye to Mr Hung. Let me see him off. You stay here.'

'Goodbye,' said Li-ling, bowing slightly to him, again feeling some pain.

'Goodbye, Miss So,' said Mr Hung, bowing too. 'Some day my father will invite all of you to our humble home for a Peking duck dinner.'

At the front door, Mrs So asked, 'How do you like my daughter?'

'As soon as you introduced her to me, I felt as if a princess had emerged from a fairy tale. My soul flew into the sky and feeling inferior I dared not hold up my head to look her in the face for some time.' Mr Hung stood before the small mirror hanging beside the door, appreciating his young face.

'No wonder you are known as a poet.' Mrs So smiled. 'But why didn't you tell her personally how you felt about her?'

He only blushed before he said goodbye.

After Mrs So came back to the living room, she said cheerfully, 'Li-ling, you are a lucky girl. Any girl would like to marry this young man – the only son of a multimillionaire. I am sure he is infatuated with your beauty. Am I not a good matchmaker? Li-ling, you'll be grateful to me all your life. On Sunday, we'll meet the senior Mr Hung at Sir William's birthday party, and talk with him about your marriage to his son.'

Li-ling stiffened.

Mrs So looked triumphant. 'You see, Li-ling, the junior Mr Hung is courteous and modest, unlike those haughty European boys. Papa once said that he still lives up to the traditional rules of morality, though he has studied in the West for a few years.'

'But young Mama, he smokes opium.'

'Many rich and famous people do so.'

'But as a well-educated man with modern ideas, why?'

'Oh, it is his father's idea. When young Mr Hung came back from England, he had a lot of new ideas. His father was afraid that his son might engage in some ventures that could ruin the family's steady business in real estate. If he was addicted to opium, he'd lie on his couch, smoking all the time, and be content with his lot. This was the safest way of keeping the family's vast fortune for ever.'

'I don't understand, Mama. Don't you like ambitious young men?'

'Yes, I do. But the junior Mr Hung is already very rich. Why does he need to be ambitious? There is a saying: "The higher a tree grows, the harder the wind blows".'

Li-ling went back to her bedroom, took off her clothing and lay on her stomach again. She asked Chen Ma to treat her bruises once more.

After Chen Ma left, Li-ling cried again.

Should I part with Steve once and for all? she thought.

Since he fell in love with me, he has broken off with Lady McDonnall. He's given up his desire of pursuing wealth, prestige and position, and has sought peace of mind as the source of real happiness. Now he has never been happier.

If I leave him, what about his confidence in mankind? What about our love? Will he go back to Lady McDonnall?

I cannot leave him. He is the only man I will ever love.

Li-ling thought about her love again and again until she fell asleep late that night.

Chapter Thirteen

One afternoon a few days later, Chen Ma knocked on Li-ling's bedroom door. As soon as she entered the room, she locked the door and took a letter from her pocket.

'Young Mistress,' she said, 'when I collected the mail from our post box today, I saw this letter written in a foreign language. I thought it might be another letter addressed to Master from the same evil man. Therefore I saved it for you so Master wouldn't be able to receive it. But suddenly, I remembered that last night Mistress ordered me not to collect the mail any more. So I dropped the others back to let Mistress collect them herself.'

Li-ling was relieved by the familiar handwriting on the envelope. She opened it and read:

Hong Kong Volunteer Defence Corps.
Fanling, the New Territories,
Fifth Artillery,
No. 1 Battery,
Fanling Barracks,
4th Dec., 1941

My Dearest Li-ling,
Ten days ago we had a battle with the enemy. My men and I were holding a position with a howitzer on the top of a hill when the enemy forces attacked us wave by wave. We opened fire with grapeshot and killed many of them, but they threw

grenades at us. I was wounded, and two of my fellow volunteers were killed.

Fortunately, it was only a mock battle. My dear Li-ling, I thought to myself, if I die in real combat, what will become of you? I can hardly imagine.

Last week we agreed that you'd come to my home for a long Saturday night under the pretext of attending a girl-friend's birthday party. I came home and waited until midnight. I kept looking out the window. Each time I saw the shadows of the branches waving in the moonlight, I wondered if you were coming. When I heard the leaves flutter, I suspected they were your footsteps. Every time the breeze wafted up the fragrance of flowers, I guessed that you were approaching. But alas! You never came! Imagine my disappointment!

I had a hunch that something went wrong. Otherwise you would have told me in time that you couldn't keep our engagement. I could've had Maisy phone you, but I didn't think it advisable. I was afraid that it might have aroused your parents' suspicion. I waited all day long on Sunday, disappointed, and early Monday morning I returned by train to the New Territories for duty. The only prudent thing I could do was wait for your letter.

Thank Heaven, the day before yesterday I received one. You told me that your parents had learned about our rendez-vous, and that they'd kept you virtually a prisoner at home. My hunch was right! How could your parents do that to you? After all, you are grown up and the two of us have done nothing wrong.

I am more indignant to learn from your second letter received today that your parents have suddenly become kind to you, and that they are planning to marry you off to some rich man. You must break away from your parents' hold and stand on your own feet, like women in the West. This is the only way!

You told me that your parents will leave home at about 6 p.m. on Sunday, 7th December and won't be back from Sir William's dinner party until midnight. And you're coming to see me at 7 p.m. I will wait for you then.

But I have to tell you that we're also giving a farewell party in honour of Major Simpson, the head of our Volunteer Corps, at 5 p.m. that day at the Kowloon YMCA. As it is a formal party, all Volunteers will wear uniforms. Anyway, I'll try my best to get back home on time.

I understand how you must feel about being a prisoner, because I would rather die than be one myself.

With all my love,
For ever yours,
Stephen

That Sunday evening Stephen Jones, dressed in his military uniform, met Li-ling at the door of his apartment. She jumped into his outstretched arms. She felt as if he had come back to her alive from battle. She thought he must have felt as if she had escaped from prison to see him.

As he held her in his strong embrace, they kissed again and again. She had so much to talk about, but she did not know where to begin. Stephen did not say a word either. Although a number of people passed them in the corridor, the lovers did not stop kissing.

Li-ling broke the long silence. 'Oh, Steve, I'm very sorry I failed to come that evening. My parents learned about our meetings and my mother warned Chen Ma not to deliver notes for me.'

'Li-ling, I suspect that it was Mike who told your father about us.'

'No. It was a friend of my father's,' lied Li-ling. She was afraid that if she told Stephen about Michael's malicious behaviour, Stephen would have another fight with him, and

Michael might write more slanderous letters to her father. She also kept her father's beating a secret from Stephen.

Hand in hand, they entered his apartment. 'Steve, my stepmother has selected a husband for me with my father's full support. What can we do?'

For some time they looked at each other in silence.

Finally, he said, 'After my wife left me, I made up my mind not to fall in love again. But then I met you. Now I will never love anyone else. Li-ling, will you... elope with me?'

'I... I... well...'

'We must make our decision now. We will either go away together or part for ever.'

'Steve, I... I...'

'Some time ago I told Major Simpson of our love. Last week he was assigned to Singapore. He said that if we agreed to elope, he'd have me transferred there under him. Then I'd leave Hong Kong by air in two or three weeks and you could take a ship to Singapore. At today's farewell party he reassured me of his help.'

Tears collected in Li-ling's eyes. 'Steve, I cannot. My father would never forgive me.'

He took her by the shoulders and looked into her eyes and spoke in an agitated voice. 'I understand your love for your father – but what about us? Are we to give up our love for the sake of your Chinese principles?'

'The Chinese say, "Lack of patience ruins great plans." I love you both.'

He was silent for a long time. At last he said softly, 'We are human beings and yet when we're together, we're afraid of being seen by people, like rats and roaches. We are law-abiding citizens, and yet we act like burglars. I've had enough of this sneaking around.'

'Surely with patience, things will be all right.'

He turned away, shaking his head, saying, 'No! No! Please, go back to your father, Li-ling. It's better to part now than to go on in this awful, underhand way, concealing our love when we should be proudly showing it to everyone.'

Sobbing, she said, 'Oh Steve, I will never marry anyone else. I will wait for you always. But I just can't elope right now.'

'You are free to do as you like. You'd better leave now before we hurt each other any more.'

He drank a glass of whisky and then poured another. She tried to stop him, but to no avail.

A few minutes of silence engulfed the room when both of them lowered their heads. She felt as though each minute was a day.

Stephen took another drink, and looked up. 'Li-ling, leave now! You have no right to interfere in my life any more. You Chinese, especially women, are too submissive to authority.'

Her eyes widened, but she remained silent.

Smelling of whisky, he said, 'My car's still in the garage for repair. I'll call you a taxi.'

He phoned many taxi companies, but in vain. All the lines were busy.

'I'll walk you home,' he finally said.

'No need. The walk would take us twelve minutes. We could easily be seen by neighbours. Do you want them to report back to my father?'

He exploded. 'Father! Father! You are always afraid of your father.' He gulped down two more mouthfuls of whisky.

'It's still early.' She looked at her watch. 'Only 9.25. I can walk home alone safely. Besides, you are too drunk. Don't worry about me.'

His face flushed, Stephen opened the door and then walked back to take a seat on the sofa. He rested his elbows on his knees and covered his eyes with his hands.

'Goodbye. Take good care of yourself, Steve.' But he did not respond. For a few moments the distraught Li-ling took a look at the chairs, the table, the desk, the ceiling and the floor – things she had come to love and cherish because of Stephen.

'Get out! I don't want to see you any more!'

Frightened, she departed in a hurry, leaving the door ajar. He did not even raise his head.

Outside, Li-ling looked at the corridor, the stairs, and then the Blue Mansion, which were like old friends. In her heart she said goodbye to each one. As she walked down the sloping path in the dim light of the crescent moon towards Robinson Road, her whole body trembled.

Why must Heaven be so cruel as to force me to make an instant decision to give up either Papa or Steve? she thought.

Images of Mr Leung, the old teacher of Confucianism, and Papa argued heatedly with those of Mrs Au, the speaker on women's liberation and Steve.

'Oh, have mercy on me! Leave me alone!' cried out Li-ling. All the images disappeared.

Near the bottom of the sloping path, suddenly she turned and ran back to the mansion breathlessly.

I can never love anyone but him, she thought.

In the living room, Stephen was switching the radio from station to station, shouting, 'The damned music!' when Li-ling pushed open the door. As he was about to turn the radio off, she rushed into his arms. Her tears bathed his cheeks as they kissed.

'At last you've made up your mind,' he said. 'I am the happiest man in the world.'

'I am the happiest girl, too,' she gasped. 'For the first time together we'll fly freely like butterflies and sing merrily like larks. Oh Steve, I love you so much!'

'Oh, Li-ling, I love you so much too, but... what about your father?'

'I love him all the more. I hope that time will soften his racial prejudice and we'll all be together.'

'Oh, Li-ling, I hope so.'

'Imagine – as soon as I arrive in Singapore, we'll be married—'

'And we'll live happily ever after.'

The music from the radio suddenly stopped. The broadcast announced: 'Attention! Attention! All members of the British Military Forces and Volunteers of Hong Kong: owing to the exceptional military activity of a certain nation, near the northern border of Hong Kong, Sir Mark Young, Governor and Commander-in-Chief of Hong Kong, hereby orders all regular troops on day passes to report back to their units and all Volunteers to report to their duty assignments immediately. This is our third announcement from IBW.'

Both Li-ling and Stephen froze, clinging to each other tightly. Li-ling hoped it was all a dream, a radio fiction, anything but the truth.

The telephone rang and Stephen answered.

'Mobilisation,' he barked after he hung up. 'Li-ling, Japanese troops in Kwangtung are mustering near the Hong Kong border! A military truck is coming here right now to pick me up. Let me get a taxi for you.'

He called company after company, but the lines were still busy. It took him ten minutes before he finally got through to a manager, who told him that all the motor vehicles in Hong Kong, including taxis, had been commandeered by the Government.

Hands clenched in fists, she whispered, 'Is the situation really that serious?'

Stephen gently raised her chin with his hand. 'Li-ling, don't worry. They said that according to intelligence reports, the Japanese might not be foolish enough to attack Great Britain and the United States, and that this may be just another large-scale exercise. If there is no war, I'll be back here to meet you in a week and we can discuss our plans further.'

'My parents will try their best to separate us. Maisy has called me many times, so they recognise her voice. Let's get someone else to make arrangements for us.'

'I'll ask Mrs Wei, the clerk at our artillery unit. She can pose as your former teacher.'

When they heard a few honks from Robinson Road, they hurriedly left the apartment. After they stepped out of the Blue Mansion, they kissed again and again.

'Hurry! Lieutenant Jones!' shouted one of the officers from a military truck which had just parked beside the kerb. Stephen then ran down the sloping path.

'Steve, I'll wait for you. We'll be together again soon,' she shouted.

He jumped onto the truck and it sped eastward.

Suddenly she had a feeling that Hong Kong was like a small boat drifting in the sea, being blown against a rocky shore at the mercy of a storm. She felt as though she was a passenger who could do nothing, but wait helplessly for the inevitable.

Chapter Fourteen

As the noise of the military truck faded into the night, Li-ling walked down the sloping path. What if war breaks out? she thought. Not only are we unable to leave Hong Kong, but Steve may die. She dared not think any further.

She stepped onto the pavement on the hill side of Robinson Road. After walking some distance westward, she sensed that someone was following her. Instinctively, she turned her head. Aghast at the sight of a big man, she quickened her pace, but he soon caught up with her. It was Michael! Her nostrils flared and her breathing froze.

'Unhappy?' he asked.

She could not speak.

'I'll make you happy,' he said with that strange lopsided grin.

She started to run, but he grabbed her around the waist and dragged her across the road to the pavement on the harbour side. Li-ling scratched and kicked and hit.

'Help! Help!' she screamed.

'Quiet!' he ordered, twisting her left wrist and holding his hand over her mouth.

He pulled her down the slope into the bushes. He tightened his grip over her mouth, his fingers digging into the soft flesh of her face. Her head thrashed back and forth. 'I just wanna talk,' he said. 'That's all. Why so afraid? Damn it! You ain't afraid of that Englishman.'

'M-mmfff...'

'Promise not to scream; I'll take my hand off.' She nodded.

'Please,' she pleaded, 'let me go.'

'I like to see you beg... you look prettier,' he jeered. 'Now, if you try to run, I'll follow you home. Tell your old man you sneaked out to meet Steve again today. How about that, eh?' He kept his arms locked around her from the back, and kissed the side of her neck. Li-ling flinched as if struck by a hot cinder. 'I watched you two kiss in front of a whole truckload of soldiers. Don't pretend to be decent. You must have enjoyed yourselves for a long time.'

'You beast,' she spat.

'If he can, I can too,' he said, slapping her face. 'And I'm better than him at playing these pleasure games. I'm stronger and will last longer, too. Ha ha!'

He turned her around. His hands passed behind her buttocks and pulled her in to him, forcing her to feel his desire throbbing against her abdomen.

She tried to twist free. 'Help! Help!' she cried, but her voice vanished into the darkness of the night.

'Stop shouting!' With his free arm he slapped her face several times.

She paled and dared not say a word.

Michael pulled out a knife and held the blade close to Li-ling's throat. She began to shake and broke into heaving sobs.

'You little whore,' he uttered in a guttural tone, 'you're gonna give me what I've wanted from you for a long time or I'll kill you! Ten days ago, I was waiting at the big banyan at six. I whistled popular tunes to welcome you. But you didn't show. Now you're gonna make up for it.' Staring at her with a crazy look in his eyes, he demanded, 'Take off your clothes. Don't get them wrinkled. You wouldn't want your parents to notice, would you?'

Suddenly she pushed him, but before she could turn and run, he socked her squarely on the chin. She fell and hit the back of her head against a rock. Stunned, she lay there, blood dripping from her nape. Everything was swimming in her head. For the moment she could only lie still. He unbuttoned her cheongsam and took everything off her except her stockings before he quickly stripped himself to the skin. Naked, he rolled over onto her. She felt the full weight of his body crushing her. Roughly he kissed her face again and again, his breath reeking of liquor before he moved his lips to her breast, sucking and biting mercilessly. In agony and fear, strengthless Li-ling could only gasp for air.

A moment later, he forced his legs between hers. She felt pressure against the core of her femininity. She sobbed again as her abductor thrust his way inside. Red hot pain, like a searing iron, tore, burned, and stung as he ripped his way into her. His thrusts were tearing her insides. Finally, he pulsed, pulled and relaxed. 'OOO-ooh!' he moaned.

Her insides squirmed. He dressed quietly and quickly, then disappeared into the night.

Still unclothed, Li-ling curled up into a tight little ball, sobbing. Her entire body ached with fevered agony; a tearing pain burned in her groin. Blood trickled down her nape and also down the lower part of her body. Exhausted, she trembled and her teeth chattered. She began to cough and sneeze severely.

To her surprise, she found her handbag and all of her clothing placed in a pile beside her. She quickly put on her panties and bra. She took her handkerchief and tissue out of her purse. She used them to wipe away the blood, some whitish fluid and sticky earth from her body and dress. Then she beat the dust from all her clothing. She tried to make herself appear clean but in vain, for she could not find water. After she got to her feet, she mournfully put on her slip and cheongsam.

She glanced at her watch and was upset that both hands were on twelve. She knew that by midnight her parents would have already returned from Sir William's party. She wondered where she could go now. She envisioned the horrible scenes that might follow.

*

'Look at yourself. You must have been raped,' Mrs So would stare at her stepdaughter with wide eyes as if she had screamed.

'Get out of my house, you black sheep of the family,' Mr So would shake his fist as if he had howled.

'Li-ling, you're no longer an intact pearl,' Stephen would pucker up his brows as if he had muttered.

'To avoid scandal, we don't accept a raped girl as a nun,' the Buddhist abbess would squint at Li-ling as if she had grumbled.

*

Caught up in her imagination, tears in her eyes, Li-ling reeled aimlessly through the bushes, like a wild goose separated from its formation, or a battered kite with a broken tail.

Looking up at the full moon against the expanse of the inky sky studded with many little stars, she became overwhelmed by the infinity of the universe.

My life is so insignificant, she thought, to end it will be like dissolving a grain of sand in the ocean. She wiped away her tears with the back of her hand.

She looked over the harbour, where the moonlight showed a million reflections from the little waves, among which the warships, steamers, merchantmen, barges, junks and sampans bobbed at anchor.

In the distance, she could see the edge of a cliff and the shimmer of the horizon beyond. A half smile flashed across her face the way lightning splits the sky. No longer dragging her feet, she rushed toward the cliff, as if running to an oasis on the desert.

Just before reaching its brink, she tripped. Down she went, sprawling on all fours. Dust and earth splattered her face and clothing. Numb, she was unaware of the bleeding, the bruises and the pain from the fall. She managed to pull herself up, but halfway she collapsed again, suffering the final stages of exhaustion. Finally, she dozed off...

Chapter Fifteen

Lying face down on the ground, Li-ling awoke from a half sleep. Her entire body aching, she slowly turned over and pulled herself up. Bloodstains on her nape, face and hands, and across her torn cheongsam, she managed to stand up, her eyes full of tears.

Only a few hours ago, she thought, I made Steve the happiest man in the world. Now, haven't I made him the saddest? I always tell him to be patient; but now, I lack the patience to live on. They say that the Chinese seldom commit suicide no matter how terrible their situation may be, so long as there is a glimmer of hope.

If I die, she wondered, will Steve ever regain his faith in mankind? Will he go insane? Contemplate suicide? And Papa? He'll surely grieve himself to death. And Mr Leung will shake his head in disappointment if the pupil he regards as one of his best turns out to be a daughter with so little filial piety. We learn from Confucius: 'One's body originated from one's parents and should be kept uninjured.' Besides, an autopsy will reveal my rape and suicide. People will more likely think that I secretly left home at night to meet Stephen, and that after he raped me, I felt ashamed and committed suicide. No! I must save not only my own honour, but my family's and Steve's.

Looking up at the moon and the stars against the grand expanse of the dark sky, Li-ling was once more fascinated with the greatness of the universe.

The fate of a human being is so insignificant that there's no reason to take it seriously, she thought.

She shuddered at the possibility that she would have for ever separated herself from both Steve and Papa if she hadn't fallen down and dozed off.

Li-ling combed her dishevelled hair. She beat as much of the dust from her body and cheongsam as she could and tried to rub away the bloodstains and sticky earth with her handkerchief. She knew that she must return home, no matter how indecent she looked. She walked down from the cliff.

Papa and Mama might not have learned of my absence from home, thought Li-ling, because Chen Ma might have covered it up. However, she must be anxiously waiting for me, for it's well after midnight.

Did King Edward VIII not abdicate his throne only a few years earlier for the love of a twice-divorced woman? Perhaps Steve is not as concerned about virginity as a Chinese.

Life is worth living as long as I have Steve, she reasoned. Maybe there won't be a war here, at least not for the time being. I will go to Singapore to be with Steve; then we'll have a happy life. She felt her heart grow lighter when she thought of Stephen.

As she neared her house, she saw a figure emerge from the darkness and approach her. For a moment her heart jumped into her throat.

'Where have you been all this time?' asked a stunned Chen Ma. 'Why are your face and your torn cheongsam covered with dirt and blood stains? I've been worried to death. It's half past one now. Master and Mistress returned home much earlier because they heard that the Japanese are coming. They discussed plans in case of war and have now just gone to bed. I told them you were asleep. Now let's walk quietly to your room.'

After they entered the house through the back door and climbed the stairs, they went into Li-ling's bedroom. As soon as Chen Ma closed the door, Li-ling burst into tears.

'I w-w-was r-r-raped,' Li-ling managed to choke out.

Chen Ma eyes widened. 'What?'

Li-ling told her briefly what had happened since she left home to see Stephen. Chen Ma wept.

Li-ling then shed her dirty clothes and took a bath. Afterwards, Chen Ma applied iodine to the cuts on Li-ling's nape.

'Young Mistress, you are very tired. Go to bed. I won't wash your clothing now; it's too late. But don't worry, we'll cover up everything to avoid suspicion.' Chen Ma left with the laundry. 'Goodnight,' she said.

Li-ling felt unwell, wetting the pillow case as dark turned to dawn.

★

The next day, about 8 a.m., Japanese soldiers crossed the Shumchun River on the Hong Kong border with China into the New Territories, and their aeroplanes and warships started bombing and shelling Hong Kong. Everywhere there were explosions, piercing every nerve and striking every soul. Instantly, trails of black smoke bellowed and fires broke out, killing and wounding innocent people and reducing buildings and houses to rubble. Sirens blaring, fire engines and ambulances speeded in the streets with lights flashing. Frequently, air raid warnings sounded and people scurried to air raid shelters. British troops were on the move. Policemen with loaded pistols patrolled the streets.

The newspaper headlines read: 'Japan Declares War on Great Britain and United States.'

The Pacific War broke out on this very day – Monday, 8th December, 1941, Hong Kong time.

Shops, banks, offices and schools closed. Terrifying rumours spread quickly throughout Hong Kong started by treacherous Chinese fifth columnist members of the Koa Kikan: Major Gray and his Punjabis had been annihilated on the China–Hong Kong border; all the reservoirs in Kowloon had been bombed; the Alhambra Theatre had burned down. Each rumour created a new infectious tension. As the Japanese attacked from the north, thousands of people moved hurriedly, many with children, southwards from the New Territories and Kowloon to Hong Kong Island with their light luggage.

The possibility of an imminent Japanese siege caused panic. There was an immediate scramble for food. As a result, prices skyrocketed. Often rice could not be bought even at any price. Robberies, thefts and murders became common despite the fact that many criminals and some innocent suspects were shot or executed on the spot by squads of armed policemen. There were no more friendly exchanges of smiles among people.

Eleven days later, the New Territories and Kowloon fell to the Japanese. Hong Kong Island continued its resistance for another week before surrendering on Christmas Day.

During the eighteen-day Battle of Hong Kong, some Japanese soldiers killed innocent civilians and bedridden soldiers. They even raped old women.

For the first few weeks in occupied Hong Kong, terror reigned day and night. Japanese soldiers searched people in the streets and raided homes for weapons; some even took money and precious stones. Chinese looters did the same, especially at night when the lack of electricity made their work easier.

As a temporary emergency measure to check inflation in the early period of occupation, banknotes of fifty-dollar denominations and above were declared invalid by the Japanese authorities. Only small amounts of money were allowed to be withdrawn from banks. As a result, poor people became destitute and the wealthy became poor.

During this period, people visited their better-off relatives and friends on the pretence of inquiring about their health. As a matter of course, they often stayed for meals and ate more than in peacetime though they were not welcome.

As victims of this exploitive practice began to see the excessive drain on their limited resources, they put up notices at their doors saying things like: 'This is not a charitable organisation.'

At that time, very few Europeans were seen on the streets. Any Englishman or American was imprisoned. A few nationals of Japan's allies, Germany and Italy, and those of neutral countries, such as Portugal and Spain, were the only exceptions.

★

The morning the War broke out, Li-ling felt very ill. Mr So sent for an herbalist doctor; but he could not come due to the chaotic situation until two days later. He said it was a severe cold and confined her to bed for a week more.

During this time she ached for her Steve. Is he wounded in a hospital or taken prisoner? If he is dead, is his head being soaked in the rain? His body beaten by the wind? His bones bleached by the sun? His flesh eaten by birds and insects?

On top of all this, Li-ling had another worry when she missed her period. She did not know if pregnancy could be caused by rape. But Chen Ma told her so.

'Chen Ma, if I'm pregnant, I'll never let people, especially Papa and Mama, know about it. I'll run away to Free China to have the baby. I'll get a job with the Chinese Government to support it.'

'Young Mistress, how about your foreign friend? If he's still alive, he'll undoubtedly look for you when the war's over.'

'Then I'll come back to Hong Kong and tell him the truth. Whether he'll continue to love me or not will rest with fate. At any rate I want to bring up this innocent child properly.'

Li-ling read a few books on childbirth in her bedroom late at night, and was especially interested in the sections that discussed symptoms of pregnancy. It bothered her whenever she felt like eating sour foods. She became nervous whenever she felt dizzy; got suspicious whenever she felt tired. In the streets, her heart froze at the sight of women with big stomachs, whether pregnant or not; she turned away from lovely babies which she would have eagerly cuddled in ordinary times. She ate and slept little. She had to wear a mask of normality before her parents, especially her stepmother. This went on for several weeks. Right before Chen Ma was ready to make arrangements with a medical laboratory for a pregnancy test, Li-ling's period came.

Li-ling learned from an ex-schoolmate whose relative was working with the Japanese Government that her Steve was imprisoned in The Shamshuipo Prisoner-of-War Camp in Kowloon. She felt her heart soar. She ate and slept more. She went to the camp several times but could not contact Stephen. Communicating with prisoners was strictly forbidden. However, in all outward respects, her life returned to normal as long as she knew her Steve was alive.

In spite of this, before long, she felt heart-sick when she heard rumours that in the Japanese Gendarmerie Main Headquarters at the former Supreme Court building, then known as the 'Centre of Torture', the most horrifying treatment was administered to people suspected of anti-Japanese activities. She also heard that in prisoner-of-war camps similar acts of brutality were also performed for even the slightest infringement of the rules.

Li-ling dreamed that in the POW camp, after Stephen was accused of using a short-wave radio to pick up Allied broadcasts, a sheet of red-hot metal was placed on his back. He screamed until he fainted, as the flesh of his back burned away.

And then, when Steve was caught stealing food, the Japanese threw him into a compound where savage dogs attacked him. He defended himself with his feet, legs, and bare hands until he collapsed, bleeding from wounds all over his body.

Li-ling was still shaken when she awoke from those horrible nightmares about her beloved, each one brought about by the rumour she had heard. The dreams caused her to lose sleep again. She grew thinner and paler day by day.

For some time, Li-ling also worried that she would be forced to marry the junior Mr Hung. But one day, Chen Ma told her otherwise.

Chen Ma had overheard Mrs So saying to her husband, 'This is wartime. It is a good reason to turn down any proposal. Besides, the Hung family has become poor, for many Hung buildings were burned down during the Battle of Hong Kong and the price of real estate has taken a dive.'

Even two months after the Battle of Hong Kong, life did not seem to improve. Prices of rice and wheat further skyrocketed. Vegetables, as well as fish, chicken, beef and pork were out of reach of the masses. Many people exchanged their cats, dogs and other pets for food. As business remained at a standstill, even the wealthy had little or no income. When they could no longer draw enough money from the bank, the Sos, like the other rich, had to sell jewellery to get money for food from time to time. People leaving Hong Kong also did so in order to get money to meet travelling expenses. As a result, the price of jewels dropped sharply for some time.

Chapter Sixteen

One morning, two and a half months after the surrender of Hong Kong, members of the Chinese Intelligence Section, attached to the Japanese Gendarmerie Main Headquarters, along with a few gendarmes, raided Mr So's house. The Chinese were dressed in civilian clothes and wore yellow armbands. Although the raiders ransacked the house, they failed to find any anti-Japanese evidence. When they found money, jewels or small curios, they slipped those items into their pockets. At noon when the raiding party left, they took Mr So away in a military van while his family wept bitterly.

'I told Papa to leave Hong Kong with us for Macao a month ago,' said Young Mrs So, 'but he didn't listen.'

'Young Mama,' said Li-ling, 'you know he wouldn't leave until he has made full severance payments to all his employees.'

'Your stubborn father is always kind to people at his own expense. That's why he has so much trouble.'

'Young Mama, perhaps Sir William could help us.'

'How?'

'He accepted the Japanese governor's offer to serve on the Chinese Representative and Chinese Cooperative Councils.'

On that very afternoon Li-ling took a cable tram from the Mid-Levels District to the Peak District and walked for fifteen minutes to get to Sir William's old, magnificent residence.

After she answered the gatekeeper's questions, he showed her through a beautiful garden into a Chinese-style living room on the ground floor. Although her father had once told her that a photograph of Dr Sun Yat-sen hung on the wall of this room, she did not see it.

Sir William entered the room and greeted Li-ling warmly.

'Why have you come without your father?'

'Sir William, the Chinese Intelligence Section and Japanese gendarmes arrested him,' she said abruptly. 'They accused him of collaborating with the Chungking Government. He's now in custody at the Japanese Gendarmerie Main Headquarters.'

He puffed thoughtfully at his water pipe, then said, 'I think I know why. He worked with the National Government a long time ago.'

'But you know very well he hasn't taken part in any political activities since he came to Hong Kong.'

'Yes. That's true.'

'Could you please use your influence with the Japanese authorities to get him released?'

'Do you think I have influence with the Japanese? I myself had to accept appointments from them lest I should get into trouble. As I am merely a figurehead, my duties are to rubber-stamp certain orders of the Japanese governor. That's all.' He shook his head. 'Your father shouldn't have ignored my advice to serve on the two Chinese councils. Otherwise he wouldn't be in trouble now.'

'Please, Sir William, help him.'

'Well, I do value your father's friendship. I'll see Chief Wong, Head of the Chinese Intelligence Section, tomorrow morning first thing. I have an important engagement this afternoon.'

'Thank you very much. We are greatly indebted to you.'

After they left the room, they passed the open entrance to his adjacent Western-style living room. As Li-ling took a glimpse at a photo of Japan's Emperor Hirohito instead of that of King George V hanging on the wall, Sir William said with a slight blush, 'Oh… this room is now for Japanese guests.'

★

Late that afternoon, at the Gendarmerie Main Head-quarters, Mr So looked exhausted but still dignified as two guards brought him handcuffed for trial before Chief Wong. Chief Wong wore a blue Western suit made of an expensive English woollen material and a bright tie. He was in his late fifties, tall and strong, with his hair cropped short. There were those who said that his sharp eyes, bushy eyebrows and thick moustache gave him a rather sinister appearance. Seated, he was flanked by several Chinese assistants and Japanese gendarme officers, each with a pistol.

'Mr So Wing-on,' the chief said in Chinese. 'You've served as a high-ranking civil officer with the Nationalist Government.'

'Yes, I have,' Mr So said calmly, 'but I broke with my former colleagues twenty years ago because of differing opinions on political matters before I moved to Hong Kong as a political refugee. Since then I have lived here as a merchant, having no connections with them whatsoever.'

'Mr Tang, show him the letter,' Chief Wong ordered one of his assistants, a middle-aged, bald-headed man, who had a long strand of hair growing out of a big dark mole on his chin.

'Have you received such a letter from General Yu, Chungking's commander of their Seventh Military Zone?' asked Mr Tang. 'This is only a copy.'

After reading it, Mr So admitted that he had received the letter four months earlier. 'How did you get a copy of my letter?' he asked after handing it back to Mr Tang.

'That was the brilliant work of the Koa Kikan, our predecessor, under the leadership of the Japanese before the Pacific War,' responded Chief Wong, this time in Japanese, throwing a sideward glance at the Japanese officers, who nodded.

'Mr So,' said Mr Tang, 'at least you must have had an intention of serving with the Chungking Government. Otherwise General Yu wouldn't have written you such a letter.'

'In this letter General Yu merely said that as Hong Kong might be in immediate danger of war, I should go back to live in the interior of Free China. He was one of my colleagues twenty years ago. The letter had nothing to do with politics.'

'You contributed large sums of money toward the build-up of the Chinese Air Force in 1932 and in 1937 on the birthday of Dr Sun Yat-sen, and a third handsome sum toward the so-called National Defence Campaign in 1941,' said Mr Tang, looking at the documents he held in his hand. 'These were all anti-Japanese.'

Cries of agony emanated from one of the torture cubicles erected on the verandas of the building. After Chief Wong nodded to his assistant, Mr Tang threatened, 'Now if you don't admit that you are a Chungking agent, you shall be given the same treatment.'

Mr So shook his head firmly.

'Mr So,' said Chief Wong, 'whether you admit it or not, you will be charged with collaborating with Chungking. But...' Chief Wong paused before softly continuing, 'if you're clever enough to cooperate with us, you'll be awarded a high position in the Japanese Hong Kong Government instead.'

'No!' said Mr So.

'If you don't want to work as an officer in this government,' said Mr Tang more softly than Chief Wong, 'why not serve on the two Chinese councils? You would have only nominal duties.'

'No!' replied Mr So loudly.

'We don't force people to cooperate with the Japanese Government,' said Mr Tang, his voice now almost a whisper. 'We just want to give you a chance for amnesty – that's all.'

'No!' cried Mr So.

'You Chungking pig!' said Chief Wong in a strong booming voice. 'You have twenty-four hours to reconsider. Take him away.'

The guards dragged Mr So away, and the Japanese gendarme officers withdrew from the meeting.

'Chief Wong,' said an assistant with white hair, 'it's evident that this man will never cooperate with us. As we have no substantial evidence against him, shall we make some up?'

Chief Wong puckered his lips and then said. 'That's not necessary, Mr Ma. Lieutenant Colonel Soken has invested complete power in me to handle such cases. I can acquit or convict any anti-Japanese elements as I please. Who will dare protest?'

'Yes, Chief Wong, you are right,' said Mr Tang. 'Everybody knows that you are a favourite with Colonel Tamura – excuse me, now General Tamura. Without your information, his troops couldn't have succeeded so easily in landing on Hong Kong Island. Anyone who offends you offends General Tamura. No one will dare protest.'

★

The next afternoon only members of the Chinese Intelligence Section gathered for a meeting. When Chief Wong entered the room a few minutes later with a cigarette dangling from his lips, they all rose.

After they were seated, the old assistant said, 'Chief Wong, Sir William Wen came to visit you this morning when you were out.'

'Mr Ma, you shouldn't address him as "Sir William", a British title and a British name. Have you forgotten that the Japanese have ordered the eradication of such vestiges of British colonial rule?'

Mr Ma blushed a little and quickly said, 'I'm terribly sorry, Chief Wong. This morning I interviewed – Mr Wen on your behalf.'

'What did he want?'

'He assured So's innocence and requested that you release him; he says they're good friends.'

'Fuck his mother! This is a Japanese city, not a British colony. He still thinks he has some influence because of his British knighthood. Your Majisdei, His Majisdei, Your Excelliensei, His...' Chief Wong mimicked in English, puckering his nose. He then reverted to Chinese. 'All this rubbish should go to hell with the British Empire!' As he slammed his fist on the table, all of his subordinates clapped.

'Then I told... Mr Wen,' said Mr Ma, 'that he couldn't help So because we had substantial evidence of his anti-Japanese activities. Only if Mr So would cooperate with the Japanese as a sign of repentance would he be granted amnesty.'

'That's fine. How did So respond?'

'Even after Mr Wen talked with him alone for almost an hour, he still insisted he'd rather be tortured or even executed than cooperate with the Japanese.'

'So he is tough, eh?' Chief Wong shook his fist in the air.

A guard came in at that moment and presented a small, beautifully embroidered linen pouch to Chief Wong. He said, 'Chief Wong, Mrs So and her daughter have requested an interview with you.'

As he felt the contents through the pouch, Chief Wong's eyes brightened. He placed it unopened on the table.

'Colleagues, the meeting is adjourned,' he said. Then he turned to Mr Tang. 'Stay behind.' The rest left.

Chief Wong opened the pouch and took out a large glittering diamond ring and a card. His face grew more radiant. The card read:

To Honourable Chief Wong,
Presented by Mrs So Wing-on.

Chief Wong put the ring on his finger, and smiled. 'Mrs So will certainly ask for leniency for her husband,' he said. 'Last night Colonel Yoshida, the new head of the Japanese gendarmerie, told me to try my best to win So Wing-on over because he is one of the highest ranking among all the present and former officers of the Chinese Government now residing in Hong Kong. If he cooperates with us, the other officers will follow suit. Mr Tang, threaten So's wife and daughter with his life so they'll exert pressure on him to yield.'

'Yes, Chief Wong,' said Mr Tang. 'But there are other people in the waiting room.'

'Then use this room and tell the ladies I'm out.' Chief Wong went through a door in the wooden partition to a small adjoining room and closed the door behind him.

Chapter Seventeen

Two guards ushered in the two ladies.

'My name is Tang. I'm Chief Wong's assistant. What can I do for you?'

'We'd like to see Chief Wong,' said Mrs So.

'You can leave your message with me.'

'This is confidential. We must talk to him in person now,' said Li-ling.

'He won't be back for some time. Come back again, say, this time tomorrow.'

'Please, Mr Tang,' pleaded Li-ling. 'Time is running out. My father's life is in danger. Sir William told us so this morning.'

'What Sir William?' said Mr Tang in a scornful tone. 'British titles are rubbish.'

The two ladies started to cry.

'This is no place for you to make a scene! You should leave.'

'But can't we see my father first?'

'All right,' he said after a pause, 'but you'd better persuade him to cooperate with the Japanese. Otherwise, he will be tortured today and executed tomorrow. This will be his last chance.' Mr Tang turned to the guards and ordered them to bring in So Wing-on.

After a while, Mr So, still handcuffed and looking pale, was brought in. The women started to cry again.

'Husband,' said Mrs So, 'please follow Sir William's, no, Mr Wen's advice: "Trim the sail according to the direction of the wind." Accept a post in the Japanese Government.'

'No! I am not afraid of death.'

'Even if you are not, how could you stand the torture? Why are you so dumb and stubborn?'

'I'll never betray my country.' Mr So straightened with an air of majesty. 'I learned from Mencius that a gentleman will not hesitate to die in defence of truth and righteousness.'

Li-ling had never been so full of admiration for her father. In her eyes he was a national hero, no less great than those recorded in Chinese history, such as Wun Tien-hsien who refused to surrender to the Mongolians.

Mr Tang bent over closely to Mrs So. 'Mrs So,' he threatened, 'your husband's head will be chopped off.'

'His head?' she whispered, her voice choked with emotion. 'Husband, how could you take our offerings before your altar and tomb after you die?'

'Don't worry. My body may be torn apart, but my soul will never be!'

'And, Mr So,' added Mr Tang, 'all your property shall be confiscated.'

'Husband, please think of our children – to say nothing of me – they will suffer from hunger.'

'For our country, every one of us should make sacrifices, especially during a national crisis,' said Mr So.

'Li-ling, why don't you say something to Papa, or he'll surely die?' pleaded Mrs So.

'Li-ling,' said Mr So, 'I know you understand me because you are well educated in the Confucian classics. Talk to your mother and make her understand. Goodbye to you all, and take care of yourselves. My spirit will be with you always.'

Li-ling raised her chin. 'Papa is patriotic and I am proud of him.' Then she added, 'Mama, don't worry, I will work hard to support you and Chi-ching.'

Mr So nodded.

'Li-ling,' shrieked Mrs So, 'you lack filial piety! Do you want to kill Papa and us too?'

'Take him away!' Mr Tang ordered the guards.

Li-ling burst into tears. 'Papa, Goodbye.'

Mrs So darted to her husband and grabbed his arm. The two guards yanked her away and pushed her to the floor. She cried hysterically. Li-ling quickly helped her to her feet.

As soon as Mr So was dragged away, a series of knocks sounded from the partition of the adjoining room. Mr Tang immediately went into the room and closed the door behind him.

'Mama,' said Li-ling, 'as a patriotic revolutionary, Papa struggled many years against those treacherous warlords, especially the powerful Yuan Shih-kai, the first president of the Chinese Republic, the one who betrayed China to seek help from Japan for a throne. How could Papa give up all he believed and fought for in the past by selling out his country now?'

Poking a trembling finger at her stepdaughter's nose, Mrs So yelled, 'You unfilial daughter! You unfilial daughter!'

★

'Chief Wong,' said Mr Tang in the adjoining room, 'So Wing-on is a hard egg to crack. May I make a suggestion? Although he's not afraid of death, we still can milk his wife for money, but not for small money. Nowadays, the former rich have not much cash on hand. And no withdrawal of large amounts of money is permitted, at least for some time. Besides, Mr So will have to sell his stocks at very low prices in order to make final severance payments to his scores of employees. But we aim at big money – very big money.'

'How?' Chief Wong tapped his finger to his forehead.

'Three years ago,' said Mr Tang, spittle dribbling from his chin, 'an international art exhibition was held in Hong Kong. Mr So lent the well known picture of *The Seven Fairies* drawn by the great artist Taung Jen of the Ming dynasty for display at the exhibition. A merchant offered three hundred thousand dollars in good money for it, but Mr So flatly refused. He keeps it in a safety deposit box in a bank. No one can afford to buy it now, but when life returns to normal, it can be sold even though the price skyrockets.'

Chief Wong stripped the diamond ring off and handed it to Mr Tang, who looked amazed. Chief Wong leaned over to Mr Tang and whispered for quite a while. As he listened, he nodded his head several times and grinned.

'It will all depend on your eloquence,' concluded Chief Wong. 'I saw you confer with the So family, but I couldn't hear you talk. This time keep the door open.'

Contemplating Chief Wong's plan, Mr Tang twisted his long strand of hair as if he were trying to squeeze eloquence from his big dark mole. Then he left the adjoining room without closing the door.

'That is a beautiful girl in tears – just like a dewy water lily,' sighed Chief Wong, his eyes falling on the gorgeous young lady through the small transparent spot in the opaque glass beside him on the partition. A smile came to his face and he licked his lips.

*

'Now let's hold a discussion and see how I can help you,' Mr Tang said after he came back. To Li-ling and her stepmother, this was like a reprieve.

'Thank you very, very much,' said her stepmother, with tears still in her eyes. 'We'll repay your kindness.'

'Don't talk about reward. I'm trying to help you out of sympathy.' He came to a pause and then went on, 'But I first want to make one point clear. This is a very serious case. The Japanese officers present at the trial yesterday told us to impose a death sentence on Mr So unless he would consent to work with them. Even if I could persuade my Chief to be lenient, the Japanese won't be. That's the core of the question.'

'You'd like to help my father? How?' asked Li-ling.

'So Wing-on's head must definitely be chopped off.'

The ladies shuddered.

Li-ling stammered, 'Then... what... do... you... mean by helping him?'

'Another man could be named after your father and "shortened by a few inches" – in his place.' He grinned.

The ladies looked all the more bewildered.

'Miss So, we could substitute one of those numerous convicts now in prison, already sentenced to death, for your father at the execution. He must, of course, look more or less the same age as your father so that the Japanese will not detect the replacement.'

'Since you are so powerful, couldn't you change the verdict? You have no substantial evidence against my father,' said Li-ling.

'It would be too difficult to overturn a death sentence in so short a time,' drawled Mr Tang. 'During wartime our policy is to execute any person even slightly suspected of engaging in anti-Japanese activity. Anyway, at present we want to save your father's life by whatever means possible. But if the Japanese find out, what would become of Chief Wong?' He paused before continuing, 'His head would be chopped off, too!'

'If he's willing to help us, we can never thank him enough,' said Mrs So.

'Therefore, I'd like to put a few questions to you, Mrs So. First of all, are you Chief Wong's friends?' asked the assistant.

'No, of course not.'

'Are you his relatives?'

'Certainly not.'

'Chief Wong is kind-hearted, but could he help all the convicts in this way?'

The ladies shook their heads.

'Since you are neither his friends nor his relatives, how could I persuade Chief Wong to help you?'

Mrs So leaned forward in her chair. 'What would you recommend?'

'It's very difficult for me to speak frankly. Now, what would you suggest in order to become his relatives so that he may help you?'

'What do you mean?'

'Well, he has a wife, sons, even grandchildren. He is powerful, you see.'

'Do you mean…?'

'Yes, marry off your daughter to him.'

'As a concubine?'

'Of course. Then you will become his relatives.'

'How old is he?'

'He's fifty-eight, but he looks a few years younger.'

Silence filled the room and fear clutched Li-ling's heart as Mrs So wrung her hands.

'Then Mr So and you'd be related to Chief Wong,' said Mr Tang with a smile. 'That'd be a happy ending for everybody. How could a person refuse to save his father-in-law's life according to our moral tradition? This marriage would guarantee Mr So's life.'

Saying nothing, stepmother and stepdaughter faced each other for some time.

Finally, Mrs So broke the silence. 'Li-ling, what do you think?'

Li-ling did not reply. Her eyes filled with tears. She recalled what Stephen had said to her: 'Go back to your father, Li-ling. We'll find our own way.'

'Li-ling,' said Mrs So gently, 'It is you who encouraged Papa to die rather than yield to the Japanese. Now it is your turn to save his life by giving yourself to Chief Wong.'

At that, Mr Tang handed the diamond ring back to Mrs So and said, 'I'm very sorry, Chief Wong can't accept your present.'

'Please keep it for Chief Wong,' begged Mrs So. Then she turned to Li-ling.

'Our whole family is at your mercy.'

For a moment Li-ling was overcome by the image of her beloved Steve. The thought of losing him and marrying a man she did not know tied her stomach into knots so tightly that she nearly doubled over and cried out. Steve, my very life, my very breath, is being removed from me for ever!

'You must decide now,' pressed Mr Tang.

Li-ling was too caught up in her thoughts to hear him. If I miss this last chance to save my father's life, I will never forgive myself and all accusing fingers will point at me. But if I save my father's life, I'll never be able to face Steve.

While Li-ling was wavering, Mrs So hit her own chest continuously with her clenched fists, crying, 'Heaven, I don't know what serious crimes we committed in our former lives to cause such suffering in our present ones.'

According to Confucius, thought Li-ling, filial piety is the first and foremost of all virtues. How can I care about my personal interests and let Papa die? Steve, I'm sorry. I have no alternative.

Then she plucked up courage and said, 'Young Mama, please, calm down.' Li-ling held on to her stepmother's arms. 'I'll never desert you.' She turned to Mr Tang.

'If I consent, will my father be released right away?'

'I'm glad you're getting wiser. But your father will not be released until you've married Chief Wong.'

'Why?' cried Li-ling.

'He'll be denied knowledge of the marriage for the time being because we expect your father to make a *de facto* acknowledgement afterwards. If you want your father to be cleared early, you should marry Chief Wong as soon as possible. Otherwise, he may change his mind, or circumstances may change. Since you'll become Chief Wong's relatives, there's no reason for him to accept your valuable present.' He again handed the ring to Mrs So, who accepted it this time.

Mrs So wiped off her tears before she smiled for the first time that day.

*

'My head may be cut off for helping So Wing-on – what an ingenious lie!' Chief Wong applauded Mr Tang, chuckling after the two ladies had left.

'So they should feel grateful to you,' said Mr Tang with a wink, 'especially the beautiful Miss So.'

Chapter Eighteen

A week later, a ceremony and a banquet took place at Chief Wong's house.

His home was a large three-storey house located in the lower part of the Mid-Levels District, just above the Central District's police station. Li-ling learned that Chief Wong had chosen this residence for security reasons. It had been once inhabited by a rich Chinese banker who had connections with Chungking, but who had been lucky enough to leave Hong Kong before the outbreak of the Pacific War. To add to security Chief Wong had also hired two young men as nightwatchmen.

In the lavishly decorated living room, small groups of guests, either seated or standing, chatted, sipped tea or nibbled the meat of melon seeds.

Chief Wong smiled as he stood among his guests. He wore a long blue, silk gown with a black, silk waistcoat. The fifty-year-old Mrs Wong wore a brown silk cheongsam with floral patterns. Although her complexion was dark, she had powdered it heavily for this occasion, which created an inharmonious mixture of conflicting colours.

'The bride is coming!' announced a young woman.

All eyes turned toward the stairs; the guests held their breath. A blushing Li-ling, her head modestly bent, walked slowly down the stairs toward Mr and Mrs Wong. Escorted by Chen Ma, she wore a beautiful white satin cheongsam with intricate floral patterns. Many guests praised Li-ling's beauty.

'Master Wong and Mistress Wong,' said Chen Ma, 'the bride has paid proper respects to the Wong ancestors upstairs. Please be seated so that she may pay her respects to you.'

Mr and Mrs Wong sat down on the satin-covered chairs, which flanked a small square, blackwood table. Chen Ma placed a cushion in front of the host and hostess.

The bride knelt on the cushion. After Chen Ma handed her two cups of tea, she offered them to the old couple.

'Master and Mistress, please drink tea,' said Li-ling.

After they each took a sip of tea, they put the cups on the table.

'Good luck to you,' said Mr and Mrs Wong, each handing the concubine bride a red paper packet containing banknotes.

'Thank you, Master and Mistress,' she said, realising she was now officially a member of the household.

My second mama was once the central figure in such a ceremony, thought Li-ling. Now it's my turn. Time has passed so quickly. How unpredictable life is! How strange fate is! Am I dreaming? Or am I in Chief Wong's dream? Is the concubine in the dream another girl who looks like me? Another girl who bears my name?

Sad at heart, and with an empty expression, Li-ling rose to her feet. Chen Ma positioned a chair for Li-ling to sit beside Mrs Wong.

When a man in his late thirties and a woman six or seven years younger approached Li-ling, she stood up immediately. Chief Wong introduced them. 'This is my eldest son, Sik-kai, and daughter-in-law, Lai-tsing.'

'Second Mama,' chorused the couple as they bowed slightly to her. Li-ling responded with a moderate bow, saying, 'Young Master and Young Mistress,' her face flushing red.

'This is Ah Mei, my daughter, and Ah Tat, my youngest son,' continued Chief Wong. The girl in her late teens and the boy a bit younger bowed moderately and addressed her as 'Second Mama'.

Li-ling returned their courtesy with the same respect and said, 'Young Master, Young Mistress.'

Later Chief Wong appropriately introduced Mrs So and her son, Chi-ching, to all the members of his family.

★

Just before dawn the next morning Chief Wong, dressed in his silk pyjamas, stormed around like a raging bull in his bedroom. As Li-ling sobbed in the king-size bed, he panted out, 'I've been cheated! You took me for a fool. You are not a virgin! Who did this to you? Who is he? Where is he?'

'As a matter of fact I was raped by a Westerner on the eve of Japan's attack on Hong Kong.'

'How can I believe such a hybrid as you?' sneered Chief Wong.

Li-ling cried even harder.

After a while, he said in a soft voice, 'If you give the name of the rapist, we'll easily learn the truth. Then you'll be cleared.'

I must not, thought Li-ling. If Wong questions Michael Young, he'll definitely deny it and instead attribute my loss of virginity to Steve. Wong is so jealous and vengeful. Who knows, he might bribe some Chinese such as a cook working in Shamshuipo Camp to poison my Steve.

'I don't know his name,' replied Li-ling. 'After I was raped, I went home. My face and clothes were still dirty with bloodstains and sticky earth. I haven't told anyone about the incident except Chen Ma.'

'Give me a clear description of his face and features.'

'I can't. It was so dark, I couldn't see very well.'

'It's an excuse. You must have a secret Chinese lover and be afraid I'll cause him trouble.' Chief Wong fumed.

'I have no Chinese lover.'

'You're clever, but I'm not so foolish.' Chief Wong pressed the bell button. Before long, someone knocked on the door. He called out, 'Send for Chen Ma!'

Then he turned to Li-ling, saying, 'I'll find out the truth from her. I'm glad she's staying here for a few days to help you get settled.'

In a few minutes, Chen Ma arrived.

'Did you know your mistress was not a virgin before she came here?' bellowed Chief Wong. 'And don't take sides with your young mistress by withholding the truth.'

'No!' Chen Ma blurted out, trembling.

'You liar!' Chief Wong howled and slapped Li-ling's face.

Li-ling cried. 'Chen Ma, speak the truth,' she ordered as she nursed the red marks made by the blow.

'On the eve of the Japanese attack on Hong Kong,' stammered Chen Ma, 'Young Mistress came home late with her face and cheongsam dirty with bloodstains and sticky earth—'

'What did she tell you?' interrupted Chief Wong.

'She said that she'd been raped.'

'By a Chinese?'

'No. By a Westerner.'

'Did she report it to the police?'

'No.'

'Did she tell your master and mistress about it?'

'No.'

'You can go now.'

Chen Ma left, looking back several times at her young mistress.

'Li-ling, I'm very sorry,' said Chief Wong. 'I was too impetuous. But I'm certain you must have at least a few Chinese boyfriends.'

She shook her head.

'Not even one?'

She shook her head again.

'Perhaps you have had no boyfriends because you were given a traditional Chinese education when you were a child.'

Chief Wong grinned for the first time since his discovery of the loss of her virginity.

Part Two

Chapter One

Two days later, Mr So was released.

One afternoon a couple of weeks later, Chief Wong's family gathered together in the family room to eat a big egg cake. With the cut portions placed in dishes, his daughter-in-law served him first. Li-ling, who was working on her embroidery, blushed when he handed her the dish. She took it after putting aside her work. With both hands, she offered the dish to Mrs Wong. 'Mistress, take it first.'

'How can I be the first to eat? It is you who should eat first,' Mrs Wong replied as she still held her two-year-old grandson in her arms.

'What does it matter who eats first? Li-ling, eat,' ordered Chief Wong.

She complied though it was against propriety.

'Ah Mei,' he said to his teenage daughter, who was also embroidering, 'you ought to learn embroidery from Second Mama. She's very intelligent. Look at her work. How beautiful it is!'

'No, not at all,' said Li-ling, blushing.

'Yes, very beautiful indeed!' said Ah Mei.

'Now I'm going to the hospital to see a sick Japanese officer,' said Chief Wong, rising.

As soon as Chief Wong was gone, Li-ling looked at Ah Mei's work, and, out of curiosity, asked, 'Young Mistress, how did you make that beautiful design?'

'Why should you ask me?' snorted Ah Mei. 'You're always first to eat and first in intelligence.'

Everyone laughed. Soon after they left the room, leaving Li-ling behind.

In the big family I have only one ally, Chief Wong, she thought. Among the rest, I am all alone.

One day when Li-ling sat alone feeling unhappy in the living room, someone patted her on the shoulder.

'Second Mama, please don't feel sad,' said Chief Wong's daughter-in-law.

'I can't help it,' said Li-ling.

'In a big family like this, I have to be discreet. Otherwise, they won't like me and will regard me as an outsider, too.'

As time went on, Chief Wong showered Li-ling with more and more affection. Still she was not happy in his house. When he was out, she would go back to her birth home by cable tram and teach Chi-ching Chinese in order to make up for the schooling he had missed since Mr Leung had retired and many teachers had left Hong Kong.

★

Chief Wong earned his fortune by collecting so-called 'protection fees' from brothels, gambling halls, opium dens, theatres and big restaurants. He also blackmailed rich people who were even slightly suspected of pro-British activities or connections with Chungking.

Chief Wong wanted to give valuable presents to Li-ling and her family. As she and her father declined his presents many times, he turned to Mrs So. He used to invite the So family to dinner with various excuses, including the celebrations of his grandson's recovery from pneumonia, the repainting of his house and the rearranging of the positions of his furniture for better luck, as suggested by a professional *feng shui* master. As a rule, Mr So did not attend such dinners while Mrs So was glad to bring her son along.

Chief Wong gave Chi-ching many 'small presents' – a jade Buddha, a platinum pendant, a silver flower vase, and a gold piggy bank. All of these regained their value as life and business returned to normal, now some five or six months after the fall of Hong Kong. Once he gave Mrs So a genuine two-carat diamond which he described as 'only an imitation and not worth much'.

Chief Wong arranged mahjong parties for Mrs So at his house, where she always won a lot of money from the other players, all wives of Wong's friends. He would refund what they had been told to lose, along with appropriate remunerations. As a result, she spoke well of her son-in-law in front of Mr So.

For some time after Li-ling was married, Mrs So spoke well of her. But not long afterwards, as Mrs So received more and more presents from Chief Wong, Li-ling could sense that her stepmother was becoming annoyed at her ever-increasing visits home.

Mrs So reminded her husband one day. 'Li-ling is not a member of the So family now. She belongs to the Wong family. It is against etiquette for a married woman to come back so often to her birth home.'

'Then what about Chi-ching's Chinese lessons?' he asked.

'There's no need for Li-ling to give Chi-ching any tutoring hereafter. This morning I was lucky enough to meet our new neighbour, Mr Deng. He said his uncle had recently come to live in his house. He's a retired teacher of Chinese, and would be glad to tutor Chi-ching for free as a pastime.'

During the next visit, Mrs So told Li-ling she was not welcome, which made her even more unhappy. As her loneliness increased, so did her love for Stephen. She missed him more each day and cried while she was alone. She came more and more to hate the Wong House. She especially dreaded bedtime, when the insatiable Chief Wong would make love to her.

Chief Wong told Li-ling she must learn Japanese. He criticised her, stating, 'In front of my many friends, you look like a deaf and dumb woman.'

As she was unhappy, she passed her time studying Japanese at a tutorial school, run by an old Japanese woman. Li-ling worked very hard, and before long, could speak Japanese fairly well.

Chapter Two

In 1931, the Japanese army annexed Manchuria, the northernmost part of China, with little or no resistance from the Chinese army. Shortly thereafter, the population of Hong Kong increased from three quarters of a million to a million people due to a steady stream of refugees. Following the outbreak of the Sino-Japanese War in 1937, the Japanese occupied additional territory, and more and more Chinese fled to Hong Kong. By the end of 1941, just before the Pacific War broke out, the population had soared to one and a half million.

By that time, Japan had taken a great deal of Chinese territory: many provinces in addition to Manchuria. Japan had also occupied part of Kwangtung, the southernmost province, including its capital, Canton. The rest of the territory, including all the west of China, was still in Chinese hands, with Chungking in Szechuan Province as the provisional capital of Free China. The Chinese regular army had inferior weapons but bravely put up resistance everywhere to check Japanese advances. Ill-equipped guerrillas, some Nationalist, but mostly Communist, spread throughout the countryside within the occupied areas and surprised the Japanese armies, seizing munitions and destroying military installations.

During the first few months of the Hong Kong occupation, Japanese authorities encouraged a mass exodus from Hong Kong to the nearest Kwangtung Province and the rest of the mainland, whether occupied or not. Now the population dwindled in a few months to less than a million people.

In spite of this, the food shortage still remained a serious concern. Hong Kong had little farmland and no ample foodstuffs could be imported because of the war. Though the people drew rice rations from the Japanese Government of Hong Kong, they were so meagre that the poor still had to gather grass roots for food from the countryside. Normal business was at a standstill. Only a small minority of affluent people could afford expensive restaurants, the opera, theatres, and the horse races later restored at Happy Valley Racecourse. This community included corrupt officials working with the Japanese Government of Hong Kong; people who ran gambling halls, brothels and opium dens; unscrupulous merchants who hoarded goods for fabulous profits.

Early in the afternoon, two months after her marriage, Li-ling took tea and dim sum as a treat with her father, stepmother and half-brother in a large restaurant located in the Western District of the busy downtown Hong Kong Island. Sir William and his second concubine, a beautiful woman in her mid-thirties, happened to come in and joined the So family at their table.

'Mr So,' said Sir William, 'I do envy you for having a daughter who was willing to make such a sacrifice for you. Her education in Mr Leung's school has borne its fruit.'

As Sir William served Li-ling some spare ribs prepared in black bean sauce, she instantly stood up and said, 'Thank you very much.'

'Sir William,' said Mrs So, 'my husband is very unhappy since the Japanese came. Moreover, as his corporation is closed, he has nothing to keep himself busy. Please advise him.'

Sir William turned to Mr So. 'Although I do admire Confucius as you, I take life easy. At forty-five, I handed my business over to my eldest son; at fifty, I resigned as the number one unofficial member of the Executive Council. Since then I've lived a leisurely life for over ten years. Mr So, you do adhere to Confucius's moral principles so firmly. Now you, like me, must learn from the Taoists to adapt yourself happily to an intolerable environment, and from the Buddhists to feel at ease under any adverse circumstance. Then you'll gain peace of mind.'

'Husband,' said the young Mrs So, 'look at Sir William. Now you know why he looks at least ten years younger.'

Sir William stood up and bowed slightly to her with a smile.

Then he sat down and stuttered in a hushed voice, 'Mr So, the Axis advances have been slowed down. The tide of the war will run in favour of the Allies, so why worry?'

'Sir William,' said Mr So, 'I'd rather die than live under Japanese rule here where I can do nothing to serve my country. My reason for continuing to live is to wait for the day when I can see with my own eyes all Japanese expelled from our country and all traitors executed.'

'Now, now, don't talk too loud here,' said Sir William, looking around. "If you keep calm, you feel cool even in hot weather", as the proverb goes.'

All of a sudden the noise in the restaurant stilled. All attention was drawn to a short, middle-aged man with a well-trimmed moustache, dressed in Western clothing. He was escorted by some Japanese civil and military officers. The party was cordially shown by the manager and a few waitresses to a specially reserved partitioned room.

'Mr So, please do excuse me.' Sir William got up. 'That is Mr Tomio Tobikomi, chief political adviser to the governor.' He and his concubine quickly went to the room. They bowed deeply in Japanese style to Mr Tobikomi, who did the same in return and invited them to join him.

After Sir William and his concubine had left, Mrs So said to her husband, 'The King of England interviewed Sir William at his palace years ago. Maybe one day the Emperor of Japan will follow suit, too. He's like a rubber ball bouncing in any direction while you are like a rock, heavy and stationary.'

Li-ling kept quiet, for she knew it would be futile to argue with her stepmother about such matters, while Mr So just smiled what seemed to be a bitter smile.

Shortly thereafter Li-ling paid the bill and left her family.

Chief Wong's personal attendant and bodyguard waited for her at the restaurant entrance. He was a short, stocky Chinese, dressed in a uniform like that of a big hotel doorman, wearing a blazer with copper buttons and creased pants. He escorted her to a limousine that boasted a Japanese pennant. The car had been specifically awarded to Chief Wong by the Japanese governor of Hong Kong for his contributions to the Japanese army in the Battle of Hong Kong. A small crowd soon gathered near the car and stared at Li-ling curiously, some of them curling their lips. The attendant opened the door for her, then took his seat beside the chauffeur. The car started its journey eastward.

The tram service, limited to the few flat and level roads on Hong Kong Island since its establishment, still remained in operation, but bus and taxi services were suspended due to a shortage of gasoline.

As motor cars, trams, rickshaws, and even bicycles could no longer be imported, there was little vehicular traffic, and people on foot mostly filled the streets. The British Hong Kong Government commandeered all motor vehicles just prior to the start of the Pacific War; the Japanese confiscated them after the occupation. The best cars were assigned for high- and middle-ranking officers and their chief Chinese lackeys, such as Chief Wong. These cars each carried a Japanese pennant whereas all the other cars, especially the older ones, were used for errands, and featured no pennants.

The limousine continued from the Western District eastward along one of the busiest streets in Hong Kong – Queen's Road, where the buildings were three- and four-storeys high. As the car approached the Central District, Li-ling noticed many peddlers occupying the roadsides as well as the pavements with goods: rice, flour, meat, milk, cigarettes, soap, toothpaste, towels and other daily necessities offered at exorbitant prices. Pedestrians had to use what limited space was left of the roads. When a truck, motor car, pedicab, rickshaw, or even a bicycle approached, pedestrians moved aside to allow its passage. The limousine proceeded very slowly.

In addition, starving people walked about the streets, begging for food and money. But few pedestrians could afford to be charitable. After eating a banana, a man threw the peel onto the ground and all the children around scrambled for it. The lucky child who grabbed it stuffed it into his mouth, dust and all, before it could be seized by a stronger hand. Women carrying young children slung on their backs searched garbage bins for leftovers. When a man vomited, people scrambled to scoop it up from the ground with their hands. Many people, young and old died in the streets, their skeletons barely covered with thin layers of skin. Other people just stepped over the bodies before they were carried away in government trucks.

Witnessing all this, Li-ling cringed and gave out a long sigh.

Now the limousine halted before a crowd. There one Japanese gendarme slapped the face of a thin old man who had tried to seize a woman's food parcel.

The attendant hastily alighted from the limousine and rushed toward the man. He struck him fiercely several times until he dropped to the ground with his face bleeding.

The attendant dragged him to the gutter and ordered the crowd to disperse so the limousine could pass. As the Japanese gendarme put up his thumb to show appreciation, the attendant bowed deeply with a smile to him in return. While Li-ling noticed, a mixture of anger and contempt on the faces of many onlookers, she shuddered at the attendant's cruelty and humility.

It took all of her self-control to keep herself from losing her temper. She got out of the car and handed the old man some Japanese military notes, the legal tender in Hong Kong.

Both the attendant and Li-ling returned to the limousine, which then continued on its way.

'That old man was very hungry, yet to him you were more cruel than the Japanese gendarme. Ah Fook, are you actually a Chinese?' Li-ling pursed up her nose.

Ah Fook paused before he stammered, 'Yes, Second Mrs Wong.'

'I thought you were a Japanese,' she said with a cold laugh.

'I wish… I were!' he sounded unabashed.

'How could you say that?' she shrieked. 'How could you?'

'The Japanese race is… superior to the Chinese,' he answered. 'We can never govern ourselves… properly and make… progress toward prosperity unless Japan takes the lead. Why not let the Japanese govern and lead us? Don't you understand that if the Japanese hadn't come to the… rescue, China would have been… exterminated by the whites?'

'In other words, we ought to be grateful to the Japanese?'

'Yes. Though the Japanese and the Chinese are of the same… yellow race, the Chinese in Hong Kong who are… poisoned with English education don't understand the policy of the... Co-Prosperity... Sphere of Greater East Asia.'

'Ah Fook, I'll have you fired.'

'Very well, go ahead,' he said nonchalantly.

Her stomach knotted in disgust.

The limousine moved on past a magnificent building with two large bronze lions, glowing in the sunlight like a pair of armour-clad knights guarding both sides of the entrance. Above hung a sign which read: 'The Hong Kong and Shanghai Banking Corporation.'

The car then reached the sloping Garden Road and climbed south. Finally after she arrived at Chief Wong's house, Li-ling was greeted by her husband at the living room entrance.

'What's the matter, Li-ling?'

'I have to talk to you in private.' She entered the room, followed by Chief Wong. 'I want you to fire Ah Fook.'

She then related how Ah Fook had struck an innocent old man and insulted the Chinese in general.

'He was a most obedient servant of Emperor Hirohito,' he laughed. 'He is an expert in kung fu and knows a little Japanese. For two years he served as the bodyguard and personal attendant of Lieutenant Colonel Soken, the Japanese top intelligence officer in Japanese-held Nanking. One week after Japan took Hong Kong, Soken flew here with Ah Fook and assumed the directorship of the Gendarmerie Intelligence Department. Soken worked here for about three months before he was back to Tokyo for a post in the Ministry of War. As my ex-boss, he recommended Ah Fook to me. How could I dismiss him?'

After Chief Wong left, she shook her fists and shrieked.

From that time on, she and Ah Fook did not greet each other. To her, he was even worse than her husband because he looked down upon his fellow citizens while at least Chief Wong did not. Whenever the attendant and Li-ling met, he curled his lips. She regarded this gesture as an unspoken 'So what?'

One evening half a month later when Li-ling was getting undressed for a bath, she heard a knock at the door.

'Who is it?' she asked. But the knocking persisted. 'Who is there?' she yelled. There was still no response.

Irritated, she hastily put on a robe and opened the door. A gun barrel appeared right in front of her nose.

Chapter Three

'Keep quiet! Keep quiet, or I'll kill you,' a man's voice said as he slipped in and quickly shut the door.

Backing up, Li-ling gasped, 'Ah Fook! What's this? And why did you come back without my husband?'

'It's now 7.40. Chief Wong's having an... emergency meeting and luckily Mrs Wong and all her children are attending a Cantonese opera at the... Koshing Theatre.'

'So?'

'So, this is a rare chance to deal with you – alone.'

Her eyes reddened. 'How dare you come in here and threaten me?'

'Don't speak so loud or I'll have to... shoot you!'

Despite her anger, she asked in a quieter tone, 'What do you want?'

'You are a Chungking spy. I am... authorised by the Japanese to search your possessions for evidence.'

'I won't let you. We must wait for my husband to return.'

'Ha! Ha! Who is the boss, the Japanese or your husband?'

'Anyway, you'll be punished.'

'If I find... evidence against you, I'll be rewarded and you'll be severely tortured,' sneered Ah Fook.

'While I am not a Chungking spy, I don't approve of the treacherous acts you commit against your own country,' she reproved.

'Does this mean you don't approve of your own husband?' he asked grinningly.

'As a Chinese, I don't. If I had to be a spy, I'd rather work for the devil than for the Japanese.'

'Second Mrs Wong, I want you to be my friend.' He replaced his pistol in his waist holster. Then he took a pack of cigarettes out of his pocket and lit one.

Her eyes widened. 'Are you mad? Why did you point your pistol at me in the first place?' Her face showed both anger and surprise.

'I'm very sorry,' he said softly. 'I was afraid you'd shout for help. I've been a member of the National Intelligence Bureau of the Government of Free China in Chungking – the same organisation of which Chief Wong was a member. Before, we worked underground at different places: I was in occupied Nanking and he in Hong Kong before it was taken. At the beginning of the Pacific War, he sold out six of his fellow underground workers including his immediate superior, the former head of the Hong Kong branch of the National Intelligence Bureau. In this way, he gained his present position in the Japanese gendarmerie. Later, all six of the men were beheaded.'

'This isn't news. I heard it before,' she said with a taut smile.

'Second Mrs Wong, after I worked for Chief Wong for one month, I was appointed head of the newly organised Hong Kong branch of the National Intelligence Bureau.'

'So?'

'As "Every citizen should be held responsible for the rise and fall of his nation", I request your cooperation,' he said as he suddenly fell on his knees before Li-ling.

Taking a step back, she asked, 'How do you know you can trust me?'

'Last month I struck an old man in order to put you to a test. I figured I could trust you in case of an emergency.'

Ah Fook is one hundred per cent pro-Japanese, thought Li-ling. But now he claims he's a Chungking spy. What are his intentions? How can I trust him?

Then she replied, 'But I am Chief Wong's concubine.'

'You were forced to marry him. I don't think you can feel at peace as long as you remain a traitor's wife.'

'Get out or I'll tell my husband. I don't want to be dragged into all of this.'

'Go ahead and tell your husband. I'm not leaving until you promise to help me. I'm ready to sacrifice myself for our country at any time.'

'Why pick me? I have to take care of my parents and brother.'

'This is an emergency. I need your help right now because time is running out. I can't trust anyone in this house except you. If you don't help, sixteen or more underground workers will die and our mission in Hong Kong will suffer a severe blow.'

As Li-ling was torn between patriotism and family love, Ah Fook suddenly pulled up his left sleeve and pressed the burning end of his cigarette against his inside forearm again and again.

Wide-eyed, she tried to grab his arm. 'What are you doing?' she asked. 'Are you crazy?'

But he kept on.

'This can hardly compare with the ordeal the underground workers would suffer at the hands of the Japanese if they get caught.' Although tears continued to drip down his cheeks, he did not utter a sound.

Finally, Li-ling seized the cigarette from his hand, extinguished it in the ashtray on the desk and helped him to his feet. Then she darted into the bathroom to fetch a bottle of gentian violet and a piece of cotton and applied the medicine to the wound.

Why shouldn't I do something for my country if I have a chance? she thought. Why should I enjoy life, shirking my responsibilities to my country while millions of my fellow countrymen are suffering and millions of soldiers are shedding their blood? How ashamed I should be standing before such a patriot – the soul of Free China. I feel I have to trust him.

'All right,' Li-ling summoned up courage to speak. 'How can I help you?'

'Listen carefully. Tomorrow morning at one-thirty, heads of sixteen underground units in Hong Kong will hold an emergency meeting at a secret place in the small city of Shekwuhui, a few miles north of Fanling.'

'Oh yes, I know Fanling, where the barracks for British soldiers were situated. It is one of the cities in the New Territories on the Canton-Kowloon Railway line. The newspapers say that several parts of the tracks are under repair for damage caused by Typhoon Alice two days ago.'

'Yes, that's true. It's unlucky that train service is still in suspension.'

'As there are no trains running, how can your men get there to meet, so far away?'

'They'll cycle there.'

Li-ling nodded.

'The information concerning the meeting of the underground must have leaked out a short time ago,' said Ah Fook. 'Chief Wong will lead a party to make a surprise raid on the meeting place at about 2 a.m. tomorrow. Two cars will come here at midnight to pick up Chief Wong and me.'

Li-ling bit the inside of her lip.

'Second Mrs Wong, at first I didn't intend to seek your help,' he went on. 'But one of my two underground assistants responsible for carrying messages for me was seriously injured in a traffic accident three days ago. The other is the night watchman of a two-storey inn situated in

Fanling. His other duty is to be on standby... ready throughout the night for any emergency. Now I can't contact him by phone, because two and a half hours ago the Japanese gendarmerie ordered the telephone company to shut down all the phones in the New Territories until 4 a.m. Since the telephones are constantly on and off in Hong Kong, and even more so in the New Territories because of lack of supplies of equipment replacements, the underground will never suspect that the shut-off is intended for them.'

'Has Chief Wong sent some of his men to keep the secret meeting place under surveillance?'

'No, of course not. Chief Wong only trusts a few of his subordinates: Mr Tang, old Mr Ma, me and Miss Kwan, his confidential secretary. He wouldn't let other subordinates know about any raid beforehand.'

'Can anyone cycle to Shekwuhui to tip off the underground workers?'

'No. Too late.' Ah Fook shook his head. 'It takes seven or eight hours to cycle even from Kowloon to Shekwuhui.'

'What shall we do?'

Before Ah Fook could reply, they heard a knock at the door. They kept silent. Li-ling pointed to the door of the adjoining bathroom. He quietly picked up the bottle of gentian violet antiseptic, the piece of cotton and the ashtray from the desk.

'The smell of smoke still remains,' he said, wrinkling his nose before entering the bathroom.

'Let me turn on the ceiling fan,' she said and then asked the knocker at the door, 'Who is it?'

'Ping-tsai,' said a voice. 'The hot-water thermos has been filled.'

'Wait a minute,' said Li-ling.

Only after the smell was gone did she open the door for the young maid. As soon as the servant put the thermos on the desk, she turned around and walked straight towards the bathroom.

'Ping-tsai,' called Li-ling loudly.

'What's the matter?' asked the maid, stopping just short of the bathroom door. 'I'm going to pick up your underwear for laundering.'

'Oh, I haven't taken my bath yet. Come and get it tomorrow morning. Go to bed early.'

'Thank you, Second Mistress. Goodnight.' The maid left the bedroom and closed the door.

Ah Fook then flushed the piece of cotton, the cigarette and the match down the toilet. After he cleaned the ashtray, he came out of the bathroom and put it back on the desk.

'Now the only resort is for you to change the address of the underground workers' meeting place written in Chief Wong's notebook,' said Ah Fook.

Li-ling's mouth opened wide. 'How?'

'His notebook is in the inner right pocket of his coat. Where does Chief Wong keep his coat?'

'In the wardrobe.'

'Tonight while he's sleeping or taking a bath, try to change the number of Ching Wah Road in Shekwuhui in the notebook from 185 to 985 – just change the digit 1 to 9. You must take out Chief Wong's Waterman fountain pen from the top outer left pocket. Then write the digit 9 the way he wrote it on the other pages.'

'It'd be more risky to do the job when he's asleep. He could wake up any moment.'

'Then carry out the task when he's taking a bath. And remember: don't leave any fingerprints on the notebook!'

'In case I'm caught, will I have to kill myself to avoid being questioned?'

'Yes. We'd kill ourselves on the spot rather than be tortured and risk the security of the underground.'

Ah Fook handed her a capsule. 'This is cyanide.'

Li-ling's heart tightened as she took a close look at the white, crystalline substance through the semi-transparent capsule. She turned it over and over in her hands.

To be a patriot, I must be ready to die for my country, she thought.

Suddenly they heard a series of loud knocks at the door. Ah Fook went into the bathroom again.

Her heart beat fast. Then she took a deep breath.

'Who is it?' she asked casually.

'Yin-gall,' answered a male voice, 'the new nightwatchman.'

'What?'

'Three drunken, low-ranking Japanese gendarme officers, all with red faces, are in the living room.' Yin-gall's voice sounded urgent. 'Two of them are stretching out on the sofas...'

Li-ling trembled, her face turning pale. 'Why have they come at this hour?'

'Who knows? The third officer was comparatively sober. He took a seat in a chair. He asked me in broken Chinese where Chief Wong is. I told him that he isn't home yet.'

'Since Chief Wong isn't in, did you request the officer to leave with the others?'

'I did, but he said they'd wait for Chief Wong to come home.'

'Yin-gall, tell Ping-tsai to serve them tea and dim sum. Keep them occupied until Chief Wong returns.'

'Yes, Second Mrs Wong. Goodnight.'

Once Yin-gall had left, Li-ling opened the bathroom door.

'Ah Fook,' she asked, 'did you hear our conversation?'

'Yes.'

'Since you left in the midst of the emergency meeting, won't they suspect that you are a spy?'

'In that case, the gendarmes would've come here to arrest me instead of staying in the living room, waiting for Chief Wong.'

'But the Japanese seem to be looking for trouble.'

'Second Mrs Wong, no trouble at all.'

'Why are you so sure?'

'Because the gendarmes are drunk.'

'Drunk?'

'When they're on official business, they won't drink or they'll be court-martialled.'

Li-ling sighed with relief. 'In other words, they aren't on any official duty. Then why did they come here?'

'I know that on occasion some low-level gendarme officers secretly "borrow" money from Chief Wong.'

'Does he lend them money?'

'Yes. But they never return it. They're well aware that Chief Wong gets a lot of dirty money. As they don't get valuable presents from him as their superiors do, they want to share his loot. Second Mrs Wong, we'll go on with our business and let Chief Wong deal with them later.' Ah Fook cleared his throat before he continued.

'I got the information about the raiding plan at the 7 p.m. emergency meeting with Chief Wong, his two top assistants and Miss Kwan. Five minutes after the meeting began, Miss Kwan showed Chief Wong the address of the underground workers' meeting place when I stepped forward "by chance" to offer him a cigarette and give him a light. Then I saw the right address. I swiftly took a few steps back in order to avoid suspicion. After he took out his fountain pen, she whispered the address to him, which he copied into his notebook. Afterwards, discussion began. Fifteen minutes later, I faked a severe stomach-ache and Chief Wong ordered Ah Kung to drive me home. I pretended to refuse, but he insisted.'

'You must be a good actor.' She smiled.

'Thank you. If you succeed in changing the number, please wave goodbye to us with your right hand from your bedroom window when we are leaving tomorrow morning. If you fail to change the number, please wave with your left.'

'But If I'm caught on the spot,' Li-ling said firmly, 'I wont hesitate to take the cyanide.'

'I wish you success. Have you any questions?'

'May I ask why the meeting is to be held so late?'

'Two old Japanese judo instructors have recently moved to a house opposite our meeting place. Their students practise until midnight even on weekends and holidays.'

Li-ling and her new partner heard the limousine entering the garden. Ah Fook glanced at his watch, and noted that it was 8.40.

'Second Mrs Wong, act with confidence,' he breathed. 'I wish you the best of luck. Goodnight. Long live Free China!'

'Goodnight. Long live Free China!'

She opened the door, then motioned that it was safe for him to leave.

After closing the door, she took a deep breath. How mistaken I was in judging Ah Fook! she thought.

Chapter Four

Eventually Chief Wong returned home from the emergency meeting. He met the Japanese officers in the living room.

Ten minutes later he went upstairs to the bedroom, whistling a Cantonese song. As he hung his coat in the wardrobe, he muttered, 'I'll crush those Chungking men.'

'What did you say, Master,' asked Li-ling.

'Ah… Oh, nothing.'

'Did you see those Japanese downstairs?'

'Yes. They're gone.'

'So soon?'

'As soon as I gave them a cheque, they left. They're going to drink and see their girlfriends in "consolation houses".' Li-ling shuddered at the thought of women being forced to serve Japanese troops in those field brothels.

'I'll go to bed right now,' said Chief Wong. 'I'm getting up in two and a half hours at 11.30, and my men will pick me up at midnight for an important mission.'

She wanted to ask what mission it was, but she stopped herself. 'Are you going to take a bath now, Master?'

'No, I'd rather go to sleep early.'

'It's only nine now. How could you fall asleep at this hour?'

'Then get me half a glass of port wine and let my mind relax before I go to bed.'

Li-ling did as ordered, and Chief Wong drank it in one gulp.

He set the alarm clock on the desk for 11.30 p.m. and synchronized it with his pocket watch before he went to bed with her.

After he had been asleep for some time, she uttered two or three muffled cries as if she were having a bad dream. When he did not stir, she decided to begin her assignment. Before she was ready, he suddenly awakened, so she pretended to remain asleep.

'What's wrong?' he asked, gently shaking her.

She opened her eyes. 'I had a nightmare.'

'What about?'

'The rape.'

'Poor Li-ling! How that horrible memory always grips your mind!' sighed Chief Wong. 'Now relax,' he said, and then drifted back to sleep.

With her eyes closed, Li-ling worried about how she would deal with Ah Fook if she failed to do her mission.

'Ah Fook, I'm terribly sorry,' she would say when they were alone. 'I uttered muffled cries as if having a nightmare. If Chief Wong had remained asleep, I would have accomplished my assignment. But unfortunately, he awoke. It would have aroused his suspicion if I'd used the same trick twice. I racked my brain for another, but couldn't think of any.'

If I carry out the assignment, I may be caught and eventually beheaded, she kept thinking. I don't mind dying for my country, but Papa and Steve will grieve to death. How foolish I was to have fallen in with Ah Fook's plan on impulse! Even if people suspect that I had no intentions of taking the risk to help the underground workers, they'd sympathize with me for being concerned about my parents and brother.

After all, millions of soldiers and civilians have already died in this war. What difference will sixteen or more of these underground workers make anyhow?

I'd rather survive and wait until the war is over, so I can be with Steve.

Second by second, minute by minute, she tossed and turned for what seemed like hours. She finally got up, switched on the light, and took one of the last two sleeping pills left in the bottle. Before she was ready to turn off the light and go back to bed, she glanced at the clock. 11.25! She remembered what her father had said in the Japanese Gendarmerie Headquarters.

'I can never become a traitor to my country,' he had said with an air of majesty befitting a great hero. 'I've learned from Mencius that a gentleman will not hesitate to die in defence of truth and righteousness.'

What did I learn from the sages? she thought. Papa would rather die than collaborate with the Japanese. If I die for a great cause, he'll sympathize with me. Steve, too, for like Papa, he is patriotic. Within a few precious minutes if I don't take the risk, many patriots will die.

She looked at the clock again. Only four minutes were left. Chief Wong seems asleep, but I can't be sure, she thought.

Her heart beat wildly as she reached under the bed for the gloves she had hidden earlier. She put them on and opened the wardrobe. Silently, she withdrew the notebook and the fountain pen from Chief Wong's clothing, closed the wardrobe and went into the bathroom.

Having quickly looked up the address recorded in the book, she carefully changed the digit "1" in the house number to "9", being sure to match the style in which it was written on another page. She returned to the bedroom with the book still opened because the amount of ink in the digit "9" was somewhat overflowing.

Chief Wong began to snore.

Is he pretending so as to trap me? she wondered. No time to worry about it now.

She looked for the blotting paper, usually placed beside the inkstand on the desk. After she failed to find it, she quickly looked in the drawer and on the floor under the desk, the table and the chairs, but her search was in vain.

How about tissue or a handkerchief? she thought. No, either would spread the wet ink onto the page.

She had no alternative but to fan the air above the ink with a writing pad, waiting for it to dry. In the meantime, she kept a watchful eye on Chief Wong.

She had seen the small blotting paper beside the inkstand before they went to bed.

But where is it now? This worthless piece of paper holds the key to the lives of at least sixteen patriots. Doesn't Heaven want to save their lives? To save China? Does Heaven want me to die and my family and Steve to suffer? Why would Heaven be so cruel as to hide that worthless piece of paper?

With only forty seconds to go before the mechanism would ring its death toll, she suddenly felt relieved. I can set the clock back a few minutes, she thought. Then a feeling of despair immediately overwhelmed her. Chief Wong makes sure that the clock and his watch coincide to the second every night before he retires and every morning when he gets up. How can I set the clock back without setting his watch back too? His watch? It's lying beside his pillow!

She felt like a helpless ant in a pan which grows hotter and hotter as it sits over a fire. Each tick of the clock pierced her heart like an arrow as the long hand on the dial relentlessly approached the numeral six!

The ink did not appear quite dry, but with only a moment to go, she quickly opened the wardrobe, closed the notebook and returned it and the pen to their proper places. She shut the wardrobe. Just as she was about to take off her gloves, the alarm rang!

'Why are you up?' Chief Wong rubbed his bleary eyes. She swiftly placed her gloved hands behind her back.

'After you woke me, I couldn't get back to sleep. I just got up and took one of the last two sleeping pills.' She turned her head in the direction of the glass bottle on the table with only one pill remaining. 'We went to bed so early,' she added.

As soon as Chief Wong jumped out of bed, he checked his watch and clock to see if they coincided. Once he entered the bathroom, Li-ling took off her gloves.

A while later a horn sounded outside and the watchman opened the gate. She glanced at the clock which indicated 11.50. From the window, she saw Ah Fook running along the garden path toward two motor cars which had just halted outside the gate. She noted that they were old and did not carry pennants.

Chief Wong dressed quickly and left the house. Ah Fook opened the car door for his boss. Chief Wong got in the car, with his two assistants, Mr Ma and Mr Tang inside. Four Japanese gendarme officers occupied the other car.

When Ah Fook looked up, Li-ling waved her right hand from her first-floor bedroom window.

Suddenly a breeze blew in, bringing the lost blotting paper to her feet. She shook her head.

Chapter Five

About midnight Chief Wong's party started its journey to Shekwuhui. They went to Queen's Pier in the Central District, where they boarded a speed boat and crossed the harbour. Fifteen minutes later, they disembarked at a pier in Kowloon. Two old cars, without pennants, parked along the roadside, waited for them. As soon as Chief Wong's party boarded, they sped northwards. Chief Wong and his Chinese subordinates rode in the lead car and the gendarme officers followed in the other. Five minutes later two large enclosed vans emerged from a side street and joined them.

★

At 1.30 in the morning heads of the sixteen underground units of Hong Kong assembled in the living room of the house at 185 Ching Wah Road, Shekwuhui. It was a medium-sized, two-storey house with a garden in front and in the rear, all surrounded by a light yellow, six-foot wall. The fourteen men and two women sat in the dark living room and spoke in hushed tones. The crescent moon filtered light into the room through the thin curtains. A bald-headed man in his mid-fifties and his young co-workers were seated in a circle.

'My fellow patriots,' he said, 'owing to its centrally located position, Hong Kong has been serving as a depot for the supply of fuel, munitions and military equipment for the Japanese forces operating in Southeast Asia. The Allies are determined to deal a blow to occupied Hong Kong in order to impede the Japanese war effort.

'There are four items on today's agenda we'll discuss. First, latest instructions and guidelines from Chungking. Second, obtaining and transmitting accurate information swiftly on Japanese political policies, economic measures, military tactics and the various objectives in the Allies' future air raids. Third, division and coordination of our work. Fourth, expanded coordination with the British Army Aid Group.'

★

At 1.50 a.m., while Chief Wong's motorcade approached an old two-storey inn in Fanling, a white-haired watchman made his rounds on the first floor. When he heard the rumbling, he looked out the window. As the motorcade passed, a cigarette pack was thrown out of the lead car onto the pavement right in front of the ground floor of the inn.

The motorcade continued its journey. Twelve minutes later when they approached Shekwuhui, Chief Wong produced his notebook. He gazed at the address of the underground's meeting place while Ah Fook slowly positioned his hand under his jacket by his bolstered pistol.

If Chief Wong suddenly recalls the correct number, he thought, I'll fire at the whole carload of people in order to keep their mouths shut.

The closer the motorcade approached 185, the harder Ah Fook bit his lip.

He clung to one hope. He remembered that since last June when the Japanese had suffered a tremendous loss in the air and sea battles at Midway Island, the shadow of Japanese final defeat had loomed bigger and bigger in Chief Wong's mind, making him quite absent-minded. Ah Fook prayed silently again and again that his boss could not recall the number of the house.

★

The underground workers' meeting continued. A few minutes past two they heard the low rumbling of motor vehicles. The bald-headed man went to the windows facing the road and spoke quickly.

'Friends, I believe a motorcade is coming. Strange at such a late hour. We must prepare for the worst.'

Five underground workers, each armed with a pistol, came forward and bent down on one knee by the windows. The rest squatted behind chairs.

'Agent 159, ring up Agent 376,' the bald-headed man ordered a squat man. 'Find out what he knows about this motorcade.'

'Yes, 242.' Then 159 hurried to the telephone in a corner of the room.

The bald-headed man, Agent 242, and the five armed men looked out the windows through the curtains.

'The motorcade's coming closer,' he said as the rumbling became louder. 'If it stops in front of the gate and the raiders enter the garden, you five will open fire on them to cover our escape through the back door. If we fail to escape, we must set fire to the important documents and then resort to our cyanide before getting caught. Long live China!'

'Agent 242,' said 159 as he hurried back from the telephone, 'phone's down; I can't reach 376.'

As the bald-headed man announced that the motorcade was passing by the house at full speed, all his co-workers heaved a sigh of relief.

'Who were riding in those old cars without pennants?' asked one armed underground worker. 'Minor officials or low-ranking military officers?'

'Why were two vans following? Carrying munitions?' speculated another.

'Where were they heading? On what mission?' queried a third.

'We can't answer any of these questions yet,' said 242. 'But until we find out, we must be alert.'

★

After the motorcade passed the house, Chief Wong put his notebook back into his pocket and Ah Fook withdrew his hand. But his reprieve was short-lived. Twenty seconds later, Chief Wong turned his head and looked back.

'Stop!' he yelled.

The chauffeur promptly obeyed. The other vehicles followed suit.

'I seem to remember the house number as 185,' Chief Wong said, 'not 985 as recorded in my book. I think we ought to…'

Ah Fook reached for his gun again. While Chief Wong hesitated, no one responded.

At last the chief shook his head. 'I admit my memory has failed me lately, but never mind. Chauffeur, proceed to 985!'

Ah Fook breathed steadily again.

A few minutes later the motorcade pulled up three houses from 985 Ching Wah Road. Chief Wong, his two assistants, Ah Fook and four Japanese officers got out of the cars while ten other members of the Chinese Intelligence Section, also clad in plain clothes, but each with a yellow armband, and twenty Chinese uniformed policemen emerged from the back of the vans. The whole party walked quietly to the iron gate of number 985. After two CIS men climbed over the gate and opened the locks from inside, the raiders silently but swiftly entered the garden.

Meanwhile, in a room on the upper floor, a beautiful woman lay naked in bed while a bare middle-aged man bent over her. As a commander explores for weak spots in the enemy lines before a major attack, the man kissed four or five places of her smooth, white body that he deemed would be the most sensitive, sometimes like an affectionate tigress licking her baby and sometimes like a starved lion pounding a goat. From time to time he also employed psychological warfare to induce his enemy to surrender by whispering sweet words to her.

The woman was in her mid-thirties, but looked ten years younger. She was one of the few well known beauties among society women in Hong Kong. For some years before the Pacific War she had been the wife of a wealthy playboy until he died of chronic alcoholism. After his death her brother-in-law cheated her of her rightful inheritance. As a result, she became a high-class prostitute to maintain her luxurious life style. As she was one of the few Chinese women who could speak Japanese, she had friends among the highest-ranking officers in both the civil and military services in occupied Hong Kong. She did not go to bed with ordinary men – only very few rich and influential men.

Colonel Fujino first met this lady a few months before at a private party. Many nights since then the colonel had dreamed of being with her in bed. He tried very hard to make friends with her, but in vain.

The previous month he learned that her nephew was working as a senior clerk in the Food Bureau. There, like all the government units, most of the employees were Chinese, but a handful of Japanese held the highest positions. Through the colonel's influence, her nephew was promoted to Vice Director of the Rice Ration Department.

Because food was expensive, second only to jewellery, any Chinese officers of the Japanese Hong Kong Government would scramble for this high position which, through corruption, was extremely lucrative. Through these manoeuvrings Colonel Fujino gained her favour and thus obtained, one month in advance, this rare appointment for one night only.

It was common knowledge that Colonel Fujino was picky with women. That was the reason he remained single though he was in his early forties. People said he did not like whores or bar girls in general because 'they sleep with hundreds.' He told his friends that he seldom bedded women unless they were beautiful, 'family women'.

People also said that he was conscientious, not only as a soldier, but also as a lover. Before he launched any battle, he planned his preparations to ensure victory. Therefore, during the past month he read books of pornography as well as an anthology of love poems. He also saw to it that a dentist cured his teeth of decay to rid his mouth of bad breath. He bought a bottle of French 4711 cologne to enchant the woman and obtained a bottle of 'Indian Mysterious Oil' from a Chinese friend to sustain his virility in this battle of sex. He did everything possible in order to emerge the conqueror of this beauty he had longed for.

★

Some forty men of Chief Wong's party now surrounded the house at 985 Ching Wah Road. Some of them carried light machine-guns. Mr Tang stood in the middle of the garden and spoke into a microphone:

'Brothers and sisters, this is the CIS. You may still labour under the ignorant dream of Allied superiority, but it is time to awake now. You are completely surrounded by one hundred of our men. You can never escape.

'If you're willing to cooperate,' he paused, twisting the strand of hair from the dark mole on his chin, 'we will offer you a handsome cash award and posts with high salaries in the Japanese Government of Hong Kong. You'll be able to enjoy life with your families.

'Unlike cats who have nine lives, we have only one treasurable life to live. Why be so foolish by parting with your beloved ones for ever? Make a wise decision now. Hold up your hands and come out one by one.'

As Colonel Fujino reached the crucial point of launching an assault, body perspiring and blood bubbling, the microphone blared. He bitterly halted his attack. His enthusiasm dropped from the boiling to below freezing. Eyes nearly popping, he jumped out of bed and stared out the window. He caught a glimpse of many Chinese with rifles and pistols trained on the house. He reached out for his clothes and hastily put on his shorts back to front.

Receiving no response, Chief Wong ordered his men to break open the door. As soon as the first man stepped inside, he was ambushed in the darkness and his pistol forced out of his hand. Then he was forcefully thrown out of the house. He fell flat on the concrete path two yards away from the door, followed by a torrent of loud, angry Japanese words.

'Hold your fire!' shouted Chief Wong. 'Must be a VIP.'

When the beams of torchlights centred on the open door, a figure appeared, resembling an enraged rhino ready to stampede. When Chief Wong saw a short, stout, barefoot man with a big shaven head and a flat nose, wearing only a pair of white shorts, standing at the door with arms akimbo and legs apart, his expression froze.

Chief Wong quickly stepped forward and saluted. All the gendarmes, members of the CIS and Chinese policemen snapped to attention.

'Colonel Fujino, I'm very sorry, very sorry,' he exclaimed in Japanese. As he apologised, Colonel Fujino's eyes still blazed.

'How dare you disturb me at this hour? This is a private villa. You are all *bagayarou!*' Chief Wong winced when he heard this officer call him and his men stupid pigs.

Just then an attractive Chinese lady in a pink nightdress came into sight at the window on the upper floor, looking both puzzled and annoyed.

'All of you shall stand at attention for thirty minutes!' ordered the colonel. He then turned around and slammed the door.

Chief Wong and his party stood as crestfallen roosters while the colonel ate dim sum and drank brandy with his lady friend inside the house.

Chapter Six

The same white-haired watchman at the inn rode his cycle at full speed to Shekwuhui. Breathing heavily and dripping with perspiration, the old man reached Ching Wah Road. He hid the cycle two houses away from number 185 and continued on foot. He staggered as he approached the house. 'Let me in, please,' he slurred as he knocked on the door. 'Ma wife drue me out. I need shomwhere to schtay.'

The door opened and the old man swayed back and forth.

The bald-headed man smiled and said, 'Sober up, 376. Everything's fine here.'

After the old man said, 'Urgent, 242,' he handed a note to the bald-headed man. 'Agent 109 dropped it in a cigarette pack in front of my post forty minutes ago while he travelled with Chief Wong's motorcade. I couldn't ring you, so I came as fast as I could.'

The bald-headed man quickly read the note aloud:

24/10/42
2230 hrs.

From 109
242 and all unit heads:

Wong planned raid on 185 Ching Wah Rd at 0200, 25/10/42. Even if I succeed in changing address in his note-book to 985, and cause a delay, they may be back. If I fail, will kill Wong and men instantly, then destroy notebook in time for your escape.

Rest of raiding party won't know address until phone communications restored at 4 a.m.

If can't get away with important documents, burn them.

No one communicates for one week.

242, stay at 376's place until further notice. If you don't hear from me in ten days, take over command of Hong Kong branch.

Long live China!

After the bald-headed man had finished reading the note, the underground workers stared at one another. Then he struck a match to burn it.

'When did the motorcade pass?' asked the old watchman.

'Half an hour ago,' replied the bald-headed man. 'We've just adjourned. Three of us are going to leave soon and the rest intend to stay here until dawn.' Then he turned to his co-workers and said, 'Wong and his men may be back. We must leave as fast as we can.'

'You,' he ordered immediately, pointing to one of the two female associates, 'go and watch. If you hear the motorcade, shout!'

'You,' he commanded, pointing to the other woman, 'chain the three carts to three bikes in the courtyard.'

He also gave instructions to all his man co-workers:

'You three, go upstairs and bring here all the sheets from the beds and the twine from the table.

'You, three, neglect the packs of anti-Japanese handbills and the stationery, but bind the confidential documents into bundles with twine and wrap them in the sheets. Put them on one cart chained to a bike.

'You alone, ride the cycle and deliver the documents home.

'You, four, carry the radio transmitter, the receiving set, the four cameras, the film and the printing machine to the backyard. Cover them with sheets and put them on the two carts.

'You, two brothers, ride on the cycles to your hideout with all the equipment.'

The underground workers acted swiftly. Agent 242 and the old watchman each put on a pair of gloves, took a towel and wiped the fingerprints from the cups, dishes, door-knobs and other surfaces.

★

In front of the house at 985 Ching Wah Road, the forty men continued to stand at attention, shivering in the cold. One of Chief Wong's men said to another, 'We are like urchins being punished by a strict teacher.'

The other forced a smile.

After a few minutes past the prescribed time, Chief Wong, his men and the gendarmes returned to their vehicles.

The prostrate man was carried piggyback when someone said, 'Colonel Fujino is a well known judo expert.'

'Go back to number 185 house straight away,' ordered Chief Wong before entering the car. 'Chungking agents may still know nothing about this.'

After the raiding party came back, they re-enacted the same scene as at the number 985 house, but without a 'Colonel Fujino' appearing at the entrance. Finally, Chief Wong and his men broke open the door and entered the house while the gendarme officers stood guard outside.

Chief Wong turned red when they found no people in the house. The living room was a mess. Cups, either empty or partly filled with lukewarm water, were scattered across the tables. The floor was covered with sheets of blank paper and handbills.

Mr Tang picked up a handbill and saw that it contained a drawing of a wolf dressed in a kimono with two dogs, dressed in Chinese clothing, on a leash. The caption read: 'Traitors, Running Dogs.' He ordered two of his men to collect the handbills and burn them in the backyard.

'Who in the devil leaked the news?' blustered Chief Wong. He spat phlegm onto the floor before continuing, 'We had all the telephones shut down in the New Territories and we rode in old cars without pennants in order to avoid attention.'

'Chief Wong,' said old Mr Ma, 'when we passed by here, the rumbling of our vehicles must have alerted the Chungking agents. Can we still catch them?'

'If Colonel Fujino had not detained us,' said Mr Tang, 'we could have returned earlier and caught at least a few of them because there was no train service.'

'I'll fuck the bloody arse of that Fujino,' said Chief Wong through clenched teeth. 'He just wanted to flaunt his authority in order to impress his lady.'

After he left the house, Chief Wong thanked the whole raiding party, first in Japanese, then in Chinese. With heads hung low, they all returned to their vehicles.

'I'm hungry. It's been a gruelling night,' said Chief Wong to his assistants.

'There's a small restaurant in Shartin which opens at 3 a.m.,' said the old Mr Ma. 'It caters to farmers who bring their produce to the markets in Kowloon and Hong Kong Island very early in the morning.'

'Let's go,' said Chief Wong.

Thirty minutes later they arrived at the small restaurant.

Recognising the famous Chief Wong, the manager cordially led him and his assistants to two tables: the smaller one for him and his two right-hand men and the larger one for his CIS men, Ah Fook and the chauffeur. Chief Wong ordered a score of dishes of dim sum for both tables.

When they got up to leave, the waiter gave no bill to Chief Wong, and the manager saw them off at the door.

'Chief Wong,' he said, 'was the food to your satisfaction?'

Chief Wong nodded only once, and did not smile. He picked at his teeth with a toothpick. After he spat it on the ground, he got into the car with his men.

'Thank you very much for your visit. Please come again.'

The manager bowed to them, but they just drove off.

Later, after crossing the harbour back to Hong Kong Island, they returned to their office in the Gendarmerie Main Headquarters at 9 a.m. Chief Wong then went upstairs to report to his immediate superior, Lieutenant Colonel Mariko.

★

After Chief Wong and his party left at midnight, Li-ling lay in bed, unable to sleep though she had taken a pill earlier. Will Wong discover the address change? If so, will he arrest or kill all the underground workers on the spot? Will he be suspicious of Ah Fook and me? Will we have to take cyanide? or will we be caught and tortured to death? What about Papa and Steve?

After a restless night, she got up at 7 a.m. as usual. She tried to appear normal so she wouldn't arouse suspicion in the household.

'Why did Master leave so early?' asked Mrs Wong at the breakfast table.

'He said that he was going on an important mission,' replied Li-ling.

'What mission?'

'He didn't say.'

Although Li-ling ate as much as usual, she ate very slowly.

As she dared not phone Ah Fook, all day long she had to wait patiently for Chief Wong to come home and to face whatever consequences awaited her.

★

That afternoon, as soon as Chief Wong left his office, a short thin woman also left and hurried upstairs. She opened the door to the main office of the Intelligence Department. She passed through this large room where a group of men and a few women were working at their desks. Knocking at the door of a medium-sized, self-contained room which read 'Director's office', she waited until ordered to enter.

'Good afternoon, Lieutenant Colonel Mariko,' she said, bowing deeply to a tall, middle-aged officer with a moustache, a weasel face and a hooked nose.

'Miss Kwan,' said the lieutenant colonel, staring blankly at her, 'what do you want to see me for? It's almost five o'clock. Where's Chief Wong?' Mariko had risen to leave, but returned to his seat. He motioned her to be seated in front of his large desk.

'Chief Wong just left. Lieutenant Colonel Mariko, you know all about our abortive raids on the underground workers early this morning?'

'Yes, Chief Wong has already reported to me.'

'He blamed me for the failure of those raids,' sobbed the woman.

'Stop crying!' shouted the lieutenant colonel, striking the desk with his fist.

Miss Kwan stiffened, but obeyed the order.

'I hate to see people, even children, crying,' he said. 'I torture suspected spies more severely if they cry.'

She nodded before she said, 'Chief Wong accused me of telling him the wrong house number of the underground workers' meeting place.' She wiped her eyes with a handkerchief.

'Maybe he didn't hear the number clearly,' said Mariko. 'You know, he did place most of the blame on Colonel Fujino.'

'When I whispered the address to Chief Wong last night, I showed it to him too. Ah Fook then came forward and lit a cigarette for him before Chief Wong wrote 1–8–5 in his notebook, which I witnessed. But when Chief Wong showed the address to me this morning, it read 9–8–5. Second Mrs Wong must be the culprit. She is the only person who had access to Chief Wong's notebook.'

The officer did not reply. He lighted a cigarette.

'Ah Fook must have collaborated with her,' said Miss Kwan. 'He left the meeting early last night on the pretext of a severe stomach-ache—'

'Ah Fook?' interrupted Mariko, unwittingly dropping his cigarette on the desk. He picked it up and said, 'What other proof do you have?'

'As soon as Chief Wong copied the address, I pressed it carefully with a piece of blotting paper. Naturally, there shouldn't have been any ink stain left on the facing page. Strangely enough, this morning I discovered an ink stain there, directly opposite the digit 9. It couldn't just be a coincidence.'

'That is very serious indeed,' shrieked Mariko. 'Did you tell Chief Wong?'

'Of course. I even asked him to have his notebook examined for fingerprints at once, but he flatly refused. He said that Ah Fook and his second wife were not on good terms. That's why I appeal to you directly. Please investigate the matter.'

'Certainly. But Chief Wong's gone now. Tell him I want to see him first tomorrow morning.'

'Thank you very much.' Miss Kwan bowed deeply before taking leave. After she left, a large smile spread across her face.

Chapter Seven

After Chief Wong left the Gendarmerie Main Headquarters, he told his chauffeur to take him to the Good
Luck Bar instead of driving home. Next to the bar was the
four-storey Luk King Hotel. In front of the two buildings
rickshaws and pedicabs were parked under their flashing
neon lights; the coolies walked around looking for
customers. A middle-aged woman with heavy make-up,
wearing a glittering cheongsam, smiled broadly at Chief
Wong as she opened the gate to the bar for him.

'Welcome, Chief Wong, haven't seen you for quite some
time. Please be seated.'

'Mrs See, that's why I've been having bad luck,' he said
with a blank expression.

'If you come here more often, good luck will come to
you,' she teased. 'Let me get you a beautiful girl named
Tim-tim.'

Chief Wong nodded.

A young girl, lightly made up, smiled as she approached
him. Dressed in a tight Western-style blouse and skirt, she
sat on his lap. He smiled as he put his hand on her
stockinged knee.

A middle-aged woman devoid of make-up, wearing a
Chinese jacket and pants of coarse black silk, put a shot of
whisky and a glass of beer on the table. Chief Wong gulped
down his whisky and ordered another. The girl sipped her
beer.

After he emptied his second shot, he told her to come with him next door.

'So early?' asked the girl. 'Why don't we have a few more drinks?'

'I want to screw you. Now!' he said with a smile.

'What's the hurry?' she asked.

'When I'm unhappy, my nerves are paralyzed. I need stimulants to excite and rejuvenate my mind.'

They left the bar and walked next door to the hotel. A middle-aged man dressed in a European suit bowed to Chief Wong and led them to the lift, which they took to the top floor. He showed them a room recently painted pink with new Western furniture and colourful curtains.

Chief Wong looked around and smiled.

After the girl closed the door, he lost no time in removing his clothes and stripping off hers. Soon they were both in bed under a large blue blanket. For half an hour the bed resembled a rough sea with heaving billows wave upon wave.

When the sea finally calmed, Chief Wong got up and retrieved his underwear. He reached into his coat pocket, pulled out a fistful of Japanese military notes and put them on the table.

'Tim-tim,' he said, 'get out of bed, and tell Mrs See to get me another girl here as soon as possible.'

'Chief Wong, ain't I beautiful and good in bed?'

'But I want variety, too. That's why I like Cantonese cuisine,' he said laughing. He put on a robe furnished by the hotel and lighted a cigarette.

The girl dressed, took the money from the table, and thanked him before she left.

★

Since Chief Wong had left, Li-ling had been anxious to know the results of the raid. Though it was late now and she was very tired, she did not go to bed, but waited for him to come back.

Shortly after midnight he came home. He smelled of alcohol and staggered into the bedroom. She took his coat. Without hesitation he slurred, 'Li-ling, you and Ah Fook will be beheaded.'

The coat fell to the floor.

'Why?' she asked.

'You and Ah Fook were accused of... collaborating in changing the house number of the underground workers' meeting place recorded in my notebook. Therefore, we raided the... wrong house, then the right one, but we found all the underground workers were gone.'

'Who accused us?' she asked as she picked up his coat and hung it in the wardrobe.

'Miss Kwan.'

Li-ling felt her palms become moist. 'Your secretary whose mother is Japanese? Why? Is she crazy?'

He laughed.

'My dear Li-ling, don't worry. How could I trust her? She gave me the wrong house number. She'd rather accuse you and Ah Fook of treachery than admit her own mistake. To make matters worse, Colonel Fujino delayed our mission by more than half an hour. As a result, all the underground workers escaped. What a... disgrace for me!'

She raised her eyes. Thank Heaven, she thought.

'Who was this... colonel?' she asked.

'I'm too tired to tell you about him now. Perhaps tomorrow morning.'

Chief Wong took a quick bath before he and Li-ling went to bed. He checked his watch with the clock. He quickly fell asleep, but she lay awake, worried that Miss

Kwan would report her suspicion to Lieutenant Colonel Mariko. Eventually fatigue overtook her and she fell asleep.

★

Later, loud noises from the living room awakened Chief Wong and Li-ling. Flying into a rage, Wong hastily went downstairs in his pyjamas. In a moment Li-ling suddenly saw the young night watchman standing in the doorway, shivering.

'Second Mrs Wong,' he gasped, 'a few Japanese gendarmes are here. Chief Wong wants you and Ah Fook to come to the living room immediately.' Li-ling ground her teeth.

'Yin-gall, what do the Japanese want?'

'How do I know? I don't understand Japanese.'

She quickly got up and put on her cheongsam and shoes.

When she entered the living room, she saw that Ah Fook had already arrived.

The Japanese officer declared, 'So Li-ling, second wife of Chief Wong, and Liu Kwong-ming, nicknamed Ah Fook, you both are under arrest by order of Lieutenant Colonel Mariko on charges of aiding and abetting the underground workers' escape. You'll be taken to the Gendarmerie Main Headquarters for interrogation.'

As a gendarme tried to handcuff him, Ah Fook suddenly dropped to the floor. The gendarme squatted, felt his pulse, and shook his head to confirm his death. Li-ling stepped back with her mouth wide open. She regretted not bringing her handbag with her.

Another gendarme attempted to handcuff her.

'Lieutenant Yoshinaka, please don't,' said Chief Wong to the officer in Japanese. 'I guarantee she won't escape.'

The officer ordered the gendarme not to handcuff her.

Suddenly, to her surprise, Li-ling saw her handbag right in front of her feet. She seized it, opened it and fished out her cyanide capsule. But before she could swallow it, the gendarme grabbed her arm and slapped her face with a loud smack. The capsule dropped to the floor.

When Li-ling awoke, she found that she was still in bed with Chief Wong. Relieved, she got up and went into the bathroom to change because she was soaked with perspiration. And still, she felt the sting of the slap on her face.

★

The following day about 1.30 p.m., Chief Wong's limousine stopped at the Nathan Restaurant in Kowloon. Ah Fook got out first and opened the door for his boss and Li-ling. Chief Wong held her hand and led the way toward the entrance to the restaurant, Ah Fook following.

All of a sudden a young man rushed from behind, grabbed the back of Chief Wong's collar and tried to stab him in the neck with a dagger. In the nick of time, bang! A pistol was fired! The assailant dropped his dagger and fell, his back soaked with blood. Chief Wong's face turned ashen while Li-ling trembled. The man who fired was Ah Fook!

Chapter Eight

'Down with all traitors! Kill... all the Japs! Long live... Free China!' the young man gasped.

A crowd quickly gathered; a few men hissed at Ah Fook.

'Who ordered you to assassinate me?' asked Chief Wong, his voice quivering with rage.

'Patriotism!' screamed the young man.

'Who are you?' asked Ah Fook.

'Never mind who... I want... to kill all of you, running dogs of the Japs, especially the traitor Wong, for my country and my—' the would-be assassin stopped short, lying in a pool of blood.

Ah Fook squatted, felt the man's pulse and dropped his limp arm.

The death of the youth triggered a series of shouts from the crowd. Suddenly, three husky young men came at Ah Fook and Chief Wong. Ah Fook exchanged blows with them when Chief Wong quickly turned around and pulled Li-ling through the rotating glass doors into the safety of the restaurant.

The manager ordered the doorman to lock the doors and a waiter to ring the police station. Chief Wong and Li-ling watched the mêlée through the doors.

Outside, the crowd cheered the youths on. Ah Fook jumped forward and kicked the chest of the youth in front, knocking him down. After Ah Fook had warded off a blow from the second one, he whirled in a half circle from the rear with a heel kick to the head of the third youth, who crumpled to the ground. The second one grappled with Ah-Fook while the other two struggled to their feet. The three assailants and Ah Fook lashed each other with fists, feet and elbows.

Ah Fook's expertise in kung fu was all that saved him, though his three opponents were also trained in the martial arts. He was as agile as a monkey, leaping here and there, swerving from blows and kicks, and delivering his share to them. However, he could not dodge all of the blows. They blackened his eye and gave him several abrasions with blood on his face and bruises on his body. The three young men were also badly hurt, blood oozing from their noses and ears.

The violent confrontation ended when someone in the crowd cried, 'Police!' At the same time, the sirens of the police cars and an ambulance could be heard racing toward the scene. The three young men swiftly blended in with the crowd and dispersed with it.

The Chinese police and Japanese gendarmes got out of their cars. Ah Fook picked up the dagger and handed it to a police officer. Chief Wong came out of the restaurant.

Recognising him, the gendarmes and the police saluted. He related what had happened, first in Japanese, then in Chinese. In the meantime, two orderlies carried the dead body to the ambulance. Two policemen were temporarily posted at the entrance to the restaurant for the protection of Chief Wong.

Upon entering the restaurant, Chief Wong invited Ah Fook to sit next to him. He pulled out a chair for his bodyguard and wiped the blood from Ah Fook's face with his own handkerchief.

'Ah Fook,' said Chief Wong, 'yesterday I didn't tell you about Miss Kwan's accusation of both you and Li-ling. She said you had collaborated to defeat our raid on the underground workers.'

Ah Fook opened his mouth, but his tongue would not move.

'Now that you have saved my life,' went on Chief Wong, 'it doesn't matter what she thinks. Thank you very much.'

Ah Fook inhaled deeply through his nose.

'I was supposed to see Lieutenant Colonel Mariko this morning,' continued Chief Wong, 'but, unexpectedly, the governor summoned him for an emergency meeting for the whole Saturday morning.' Chief Wong took his seat. 'I'm going to see Mariko to raise your pay on Monday morning. In addition, I'll give you five taels of gold from my own pocket.'

'Chief Wong,' said Ah Fook, 'it is my... duty to protect you. How can I accept your reward?'

'Ah Fook,' said Chief Wong with a smile, 'it is an order.'

Ah Fook rose swiftly from his seat and bowed low to his boss. Li-ling forced herself to smile at him.

As Chief Wong's bodyguard as well as attendant, Ah Fook took hold of the teapot and filled his boss's cup, then Li-ling's, spilling tea on her clothing. She pushed back her chair, stood up and displayed the wet spots on her dress.

'Li-ling,' said Chief Wong, 'don't get angry with Ah Fook for this trifle. He's always clumsy, but in executing his main duty as a bodyguard, he is sure-footed. Today, you should thank him for saving you from the grief of becoming a widow.'

Chief Wong grinned, but Li-ling said nothing, wiping the tea from her clothing with her handkerchief.

★

Although they lived in the same house, Li-ling on the first floor and Ah Fook on the ground floor, they never met alone. Besides, whenever she saw him, she would turn her gaze away.

How could he kill a patriot to save the life of a notorious traitor who has killed so many of his fellow citizens? And not long ago, he persuaded me to save the lives of the underground workers by burning his forearm with a cigarette. How could an angel change into a devil in so short a time? Is he a double agent, cashing in on both sides? Are those so-called underground workers double agents, too? They have no sense of morality and no idea of right and wrong. What a fool I was risking my life to save theirs! I won't get involved with them again.

Li-ling felt that she was beginning to lose her faith in mankind, just as Stephen had once done.

★

On Sunday morning, three weeks after the assassination attempt, Li-ling still harboured the anger she felt for Ah Fook. Chief Wong knelt in his living room, patiently picking fleas from the furry body of his favourite Alsatian, Bella, and crushing them to death between his fingernails. In the garden, Li-ling watered a number of small camel's foot trees with their light rose flowers that bordered the path leading from the main gate to the entrance to the house.

A middle-aged servant mowed the grass near the gate. Ah Fook came along, handed him some money and said, 'Tom-shoak, will you buy me two packs of Double Seven cigarettes?'

Tom-shoak took the money, headed for the gate and left. Ah Fook took over the lawnmower and turned around. As he operated it, he sang a Cantonese song. Continuing to water the plants alongside the middle of the path, Li-ling had a hunch that he would come close to talk to her, but she still pretended not to notice him.

I wonder how he'll try to explain his treacherous act, and what new assignment he may attempt to induce me to undertake, she thought, as he approached. This time I'll be firm, not impulsive.

'Thank you very much for saving my life and the lives of the underground workers,' said Ah Fook quickly after he stopped singing.

Li-ling had to concentrate to hear him over the noise of the lawnmower.

'You must have heard from Wong about the unsuccessful raids,' he continued. 'Wong didn't know that before the motorcade reached Shekwuhui, I'd thrown a note about changing the house number in front of an inn in Fanling so that the nightwatchman there would promptly deliver it to the underground workers.

'In the last analysis, three elements contributed to our success: your changing the address, Colonel Fujino's delay and our man's tip-off. But you deserve the most credit.

'Whether you waved with your right or left hand, in an emergency I wouldn't have hesitated to fire at the whole carload, killing Wong, his assistants and the chauffeur so that our underground workers might escape safely.'

Ah Fook then walked away from Li-ling toward the house, singing again.

Ah Fook, no need to explain how the underground workers escaped, she thought. What I want is your explanation of why you killed a patriot to save a traitor's life.

After Ah Fook reached the house, he turned around, pushed the mower in the direction of the gate and continued singing.

When he came close to Li-ling again, he said, 'When I first started working with Chief Wong, I happened to transmit a piece of important military information to Free China I'd overheard during a high-ranking Japanese officer's conversation with Chief Wong. The Chungking bureau then switched its policy of assassinating him to that of protecting his life so that my unique relationship with him could be maintained. This accounts for my act of saving the life of the leading traitor in exchange for that of a patriot.'

Ah Fook left Li-ling and headed toward the gate. Chief Wong had just come to the window. When he saw Ah Fook, he smiled at Mrs Wong, who was carrying her two-year-old grandson.

'Look,' he said, 'Ah Fook is like a child playing with a big toy and singing happily.'

Mrs Wong smiled back.

After Ah Fook turned around at the gate, he headed back in Li-ling's direction. He stopped singing before he said to Li-ling: 'Chief Wong is popular among Japanese officers. He gives them presents and treats them to dinner. When they get drunk, they reveal valuable secrets. Since I saved his life, he trusts me all the more. I understand your feelings, and also admire the bravery of the three young patriots who attacked me. During the fight I had several chances to shoot them, but I didn't do so.'

Li-ling thought back to the time of the fight and confirmed that he was right.

Now Chief Wong stepped into the garden, his dog accompanying him. Ah Fook spoke more quickly before leaving Li-ling for the house.

'I learned later that the young man's father was one of the six former colleagues Wong betrayed. The young hero attempted to avenge his country as well as his father all on his own. And yet it is I who had to kill him. What irony! Miss So… please, remember: this is war!'

She was deeply impressed with Ah Fook. She held back her tears and tried to appear normal.

Tom-shoak returned with the cigarettes. After taking them, Ah Fook refused to give up the mower and went on with his work.

Chief Wong shook his head with a smile and continued to take a stroll with Bella.

Li-ling went back into the house. As soon as she entered the bathroom, she burst into tears. How could she doubt Ah Fook's and the underground workers' integrity?

★

One month later, sirens sounded throughout Hong Kong. Soon, about forty Allied aeroplanes appeared in the sky. People scrambled to nearby air raid shelters. This was the largest air raid on Hong Kong since the outbreak of the War. The Kaitak Airport, the warships, the docks, the barracks, the gasoline and coal depots, the munition magazines, the military installations, government offices and Japanese officers' residences were all heavily bombed. Inevitably, some non-military targets also were reduced to rubble or otherwise demolished, and some civilians were wounded or killed. But many people cheered the raid despite fear for their own lives.

Though Li-ling knew very well that she had indirectly contributed to the success of this air raid, she did not feel proud. Instead, she felt sorry for the innocent people who had been wounded or killed.

'This is war!' Ah Fook's words still echoed in her ears.

Chapter Nine

In a first-floor room of Chief Wong's house stood three altar tables lined up in a row against the wall opposite the door. Behind the middle table hung a portrait of the God of Wealth with a square face and big ears, dressed in the clothing of a high-ranking civil official at the royal court in ancient China. On the table at the left was a small stone statue of Buddha in a seated posture. On the table at the right stood an earthen statue of the God of War, a famous red-faced general, dressed in an ancient military uniform, holding a long-handled knife behind his back. A censer with a bundle of joss sticks sat on each table. There was a dish of fruit for Buddha and a dish of chicken for each of the two other gods. A cushion rested on the floor before each table.

Before the outbreak of the Pacific War, as Chief Wong bet on the horses, he had never failed to worship the God of Wealth at home and in the temples. But at the beginning of the War, after he betrayed his six former colleagues, he no longer prayed to the deity. People said that the God of Wealth would never bless murderers, and if any of them worshipped him, it might evoke his anger. Nevertheless, Chief Wong set up an altar for the god alongside with the altars for the two other deities in his present house. This way his family could still worship the god, but he never entered the room.

On the same floor Chief Wong set aside a larger room for the ancestral altar. At festivals such as the Ching Ming and the Chung Young, or on New Year's Day or special occasions such as the birthdays of the family members, he would worship his ancestors. He thought that his ancestors, especially his mother, would pardon his crimes and maybe even bless him no matter how bad he was.

'Most Honourable God,' prayed Chief Wong's wife on her knees one morning before the altar of the God of War, 'please keep the whole family from getting ill and being harmed by evil spirits... Also, Li-ling has ruined the happiness of our family. Please keep my husband from being infatuated with that witch...'

'Buddha,' beseeched Chief Wong's daughter-in-law quietly on her knees before the altar, 'please forgive Papa's past crimes and keep him from doing any further wrongs. Let the whole family live a peaceful and happy life...'

Fragrant smoke from the burning joss sticks filled the room.

Chief Wong stood outside the door as the wall clock struck eleven. 'Daughter-in-law, I want to talk to you,' he said.

The young Mrs Wong got up and approached him. 'Yes, Papa.'

'Tell the whole family I've just phoned to invite some guests to dinner tonight. Cooks and waitresses from Tai Tung Restaurant will arrive here about five.'

★

That evening in Chief Wong's living room, relatives and friends talked, sipped tea or nibbled melon seeds before eating a sumptuous dinner.

Chief Wong was fully occupied with a Japanese officer with a crew-cut, who looked about fifty, though much of his hair was white. He wore a one-star insignia on either side of the collar of his uniform. When Mr and Mrs So and their son arrived, Chief Wong broke off his conversation with the general to meet them at the entrance.

'I'm terribly sorry,' said Chief Wong. 'Only this morning I suddenly made the decision to invite all of you here for dinner tonight. It was too late to send out invitations, so I rang Mother-in-law.'

'Never mind,' responded Mrs So quickly.

'All of you are welcome, especially you, Father-in-law,' said Chief Wong cheerfully. 'This is your first visit.'

'Yes, it is, but I have a purpose for this visit.'

'What is it, please?' asked Chief Wong.

Staring at Chief Wong, Mr So said, 'I want to say it once and for all: I advise you to resign from your treacherous job as soon as—'

'Where's Mrs Wong?' interrupted Mrs So, elbowing her husband aside as Chief Wong turned red.

'She's... on the second floor,' he answered. 'She'll be coming down soon.'

'Where's Li-ling?' asked Mrs So quickly.

'She promised to be back before seven. She went to visit a former schoolmate on Cheungchau Island early this morning.'

'I see. What's the occasion tonight?'

'I have a surprise for you.' Chief Wong smiled. 'I'm sure all of you'll be greatly delighted, but I won't announce it until Li-ling returns.'

As the So family approached the old Japanese officer, he continued. 'First of all, I'd like you to meet General Tamura, who's interested in Chinese philosophy. This is Mr So, my second wife's father, who is well versed in the Chinese classics, his wife and their son, my little brother-in-law.'

After they exchanged greetings they sat down.

'Mr So, I admire Confucius and Mencius for their life-long devotion to improving human relations by preaching morality,' said the general in passable Chinese. 'But I'd think that China's slow progress in the past was due in no small degree to her placing too much emphasis on morality under the influence of Confucianism to the more or less neglect of law and science. These are two important factors for a strong industrial power.'

'General Tamura, look at the invention of destructive weapons as a result of advanced science and the ever-growing complexity of human relationships despite the comprehensiveness of modern law, domestic and inter-national. Without stressing morality as a complement to science and law, the world has been heading toward chaos. Only with emphasis on morality will the world be saved from final destruction.'

'Li-ling has arrived,' interjected Chief Wong before the discussion went any further.

When Li-ling saw her parents along with the hoards of guests, she stared with her mouth wide open. Chief Wong proudly brought her before the general.

'This is General Tamura,' said Chief Wong. 'May I present my second wife, daughter of Mr and Mrs So.'

'She's so young,' said the general. 'My two sons are older. And she's very beautiful. Be kind to her, Mr Wong.'

'That's why I've invited many guests for her sake.' Chief Wong clapped to attract everyone's attention.

Mrs Wong came downstairs. She stopped on the landing when she heard him proclaim: 'Gentlemen and ladies, I have the distinct pleasure of announcing that today my concubine will be promoted to the status of co-wife. She will henceforth be addressed as Mrs Wong, not Second Mrs Wong.'

There was a storm of applause, followed by congratula-tions offered to Li-ling by many of the guests. She gave a faint smile. And only after Chief Wong's two sons and daughter made faces at each other did his daughter-in-law follow suit.

Li-ling moved closer to her husband. 'Master, why didn't you tell me this beforehand?' she asked. 'You only told me to come back early this evening for a small dinner party.'

'I just wanted to surprise you. You've been unhappy since you joined my family, but aren't you happy now?'

'Even if I were happy with this status, would Mistress, Young Masters and Young Mistresses be happy?' she countered.

Chief Wong was stung by her reaction to his 'special favour'. 'I'm setting you in a higher position, yet you are very unappreciative. How can I withdraw my announcement?'

'Master, please, I prefer to remain what I am.'

Chief Wong grunted as the veins in his temples pulsated. 'Do you want me to lose face before this honourable general?'

Li-ling turned to the guests. 'I suppose most of you know this maxim: "Never do unto others what you would not want them to do unto you."' Then she dropped to her knees before Chief Wong.

Some guests around said that she was foolish while a few praised her, but most guests kept quiet about this.

'Bravo. That's what Confucius said,' declared the general, who then turned to Chief Wong. 'All people strive to seek position, power and wealth throughout their lives, many by unscrupulous means. This woman is unusual.'

'This will make me the laughing stock of Hong Kong,' said Chief Wong. 'I insist that Li-ling be promoted.'

'Husband,' whispered Mrs So, 'order Li-ling to accept this promotion. How extremely foolish she is!' Mr So ignored her.

His wife puffed out her cheeks. At last, she stepped forward and said: 'Li-ling, your husband is so nice to you and yet you're so ungrateful.'

'Yes, you should listen to your mother,' responded some guests.

But Li-ling remained on her knees and broke into tears, shaking her head.

'If you are disobedient, you are against filial piety,' hissed Mrs So.

The general stood up and said, 'Now, everyone, please calm down.' He then turned to Chief Wong. 'I'd like to suggest that this dinner be considered the celebration of my adopting Second Mrs Wong as a foster daughter. If both of you agree, Chief Wong, please announce it.'

'Gentlemen and ladies,' said Chief Wong with a smile, without waiting for Li-ling's response, 'I take pleasure in announcing that this banquet is to celebrate the adoption of my concubine by the Honourable General Tamura as his foster daughter.'

As this adoption is just a social convention without any legal implications involved, Li-ling thought, the guests understand that the general has used it as an excuse to assuage the awkward situation.

She stood up; her face relaxed.

Thunderous applause broke out when she got down on bended knees again, this time in front of the general. A maidservant handed her a cup of tea, which she promptly offered to him.

'Foster Father, please be seated and drink tea.'

'Second Mrs Wong,' said a lady guest with a smile, 'wipe away your tears. This is a happy occasion.'

Another lady handed a red packet to the general, who stuffed it with a pile of Japanese imperial notes.

'I'm giving this to my foster daughter for luck.'

'Thank you, Foster Father,' she said, kowtowing to him three times. He stood up and bowed to her in return.

As Mrs Wong saw this on the landing on her way downstairs, she turned around and hurried upstairs to the room of worship where she kowtowed deeply many times to the God of War. She left the room with a smile, but abruptly returned. She walked straight to the God of War and covered his eyes with her handkerchief. Next, she quickly kowtowed to the God of Wealth twice and to Buddha once.

After taking away the handkerchief from the God of War and whispering to him, 'Sorry' without looking at him, she left the room and started downstairs. Again she suddenly turned around, headed back up the stairs and went straight to the ancestral altar. She kowtowed to the Wong ancestors as deeply and as many times as she had done before the God of War.

After this, she went downstairs, greeting the guests in the living room with a broad smile.

Chapter Ten

One morning Li-ling was both surprised and elated with the arrival of a visitor.

'My dearest Miss Silva, how are you?'

'I'm quite well. And how are you, dear Li-ling? I haven't seen you since the outbreak of the war.'

After they clasped hands warmly, they sat side by side on a couch in the living room.

'Li-ling, two months ago I learned from friends that you'd been married to Chief Wong. Last night I wanted to contact you. Since the latest telephone directory published before the war contains your father's home number, but not Chief Wong's, I called your father.' Miss Silva paused before she continued in a hushed voice, 'He told me all about his arrest and your sacrifice. I feel sorry for you. Where are Mr and Mrs Wong?'

'He and his son have gone to work and she's on the second floor with her daughter-in-law and grandson.'

Miss Silva looked at her former student intently. 'How are you getting along with them?'

'Very well… Are you still living in the Green Mansion, Miss Silva?' Li-ling tried to sidestep the subject concerning her new family.

'Yes, with my family at weekends, but on workdays I live at the nurses' quarters of the former Queen Mary Hospital, now called the Shoho Hospital.'

'So you are a nurse now. I know you studied nursing before becoming a teacher.'

'Yes,' she shrugged. 'I can't earn a living teaching English any more.'

'Miss Silva,' Li-ling paused a while before she looked her former teacher in the eye, 'I'd like to tell you that Steve and I dated before the war, but we kept it secret from every one.'

'He didn't tell me that before the war either.'

'Two weeks before the outbreak of the war, somebody informed my father.'

Miss Silva's eyes widened. 'What happened?'

'My father beat me with a stick.'

The former teacher gasped. 'How could he do that? After your graduation, I met you only twice in the street, once with your father and stepmother, once with your schoolmates, each time only briefly. We didn't have a chance to talk.'

'That was true.'

'Li-ling, I must tell you about Steve's apartment. Four days after the fall of Hong Kong, the Japanese sealed it and listed his possessions inside as confiscated enemy property.'

'I know. Maisy Diaz, whose uncle once worked under Steve at the Hong Kong Land Company, told me so two days after it happened.'

'Do you mean Maisy, our number one school athlete?'

'Yes.'

'I remember her father is a Spaniard and her mother a Chinese, and Maisy can speak Chinese better than me.'

'Maisy sometimes helped arrange my dates with Steve through my maidservant.'

'Have you seen Steve since the Japanese took Hong Kong?'

'No. Before I was married, I went twice to Shamshuipo Camp to see him. When I handed the guards money, they just smiled. And as soon as they took it, they drove me away.'

'Li-ling, I went to the camp to see Steve once, and experienced the same setback. I learned all communications from the prison with the outside world are strictly forbidden, but I still don't understand why the Japanese prohibit even notes, food parcels or clothing.'

'They're suspicious that people might smuggle in war news, messages, poison, matches or knives. But what about you? How's your life?'

'I have barely enough to support my family,' sighed the teacher. 'Food is very expensive.'

'If you need help, I'll be glad to do what I can for you.'

Miss Silva's face flushed. 'Yes, I really need help, but not financially. I took the day off from work to see you for this purpose. Two days ago my nineteen-year-old half-brother and his Chinese gang broke into the warehouse of a textile factory which is under the control of the Japanese Government. They stole a large quantity of cotton yarn, but were caught by the police. Late last night I learned that they had been convicted. In ten days all the Chinese gang members will be executed by decapitation. My brother is to be shot to death because he isn't Chinese.' With tears in her eyes, Miss Silva struggled to regain her composure before continuing, 'My poor stepmother has been crying her eyes out. As far as I know, the Japanese gendarmerie is an organisation of both military police and intelligence and is also in control of the Hong Kong police.'

'Yes.'

'As your husband is the most influential Chinese working with the gendarmerie, I've come to seek your help.'

'I'll do my best. Please don't worry,' said Li-ling as she held Miss Silva's hands in hers. 'I'll phone my husband. Where's your brother being detained?'

'Central Police Station.'

Li-ling left the living room to make a phone call.

A short time later she returned. 'Miss Silva, we're supposed to go to the police station. My husband is sending his limousine for us.'

Upon their arrival at Central Police Station, the clerk asked Miss Silva to be seated in the waiting room while Li-ling was ushered into an office.

A portly Chinese officer rose. 'Good morning, Second Mrs Wong. Please be seated.'

'Good morning, Superintendent Bei.'

'I'll send for the Western convict.' The superintendent rubbed his bulbous nose. 'He stole government property, but fortunately it wasn't military supplies. If it had been, we wouldn't have a leg to stand on to set him free, not even for Chief Wong's sake.' He turned to a policeman. 'Bring the Western convict here.'

In a while, when two policemen dragged in a handcuffed youth, he stole a glance at Li-ling before he lowered his head. Dressed in a loose prison garment, he stood before her, his face unshaved and his hair in disarray.

'This is Michael Silva,' said one policeman.

As Li-ling looked at him, she instantly recognised him though he kept his head low. Her heart hammered uncontrollably when the memory of the rape flashed before her.

★

Both naked, Mike rolled over onto her in the bushes. She felt the full weight of his body crushing her. Roughly, he kissed her face again, his breath reeking of liquor before he moved his lips to her breast, sucking and biting mercilessly. In agony and fear, the strengthless Li-ling could only gasp for air.

★

'Second Mrs Wong, do you want me to set him free?' The superintendent's voice brought her back from her recollection.

She shook her head from side to side and took a deep breath. She never imagined that the brother of such a well-respected teacher as Miss Silva could be a rapist.

He signed his name 'Mike Young' in his blackmail letter, thought Li-ling. Perhaps that was why Steve pretended not to know me in Miss Silva's presence at the graduation. Steve was probably afraid that the teacher–pupil relationship between Miss Silva and me would be jeopardised if I learned that the harasser was her brother.

My teachers of Chinese classics taught me 'to treat an injury or insult with a grin' and my teachers of Christian religion, 'to love your enemies'. I can forgive a moderate injury or insult, but not my rapist!

'Second Mrs Wong, did you hear me?' asked the superintendent shrugging his shoulders with his hands raised. 'Do you want me to release him?'

'Superintendent Bei,' said Li-ling once she composed herself, 'a death sentence is too heavy for his crime. Could he be sentenced, say, to three or four years' imprisonment, which he deserves?'

'I'm sorry, this is a law specifically enacted by the Japanese during this wartime in Hong Kong. He is either guilty or not guilty of stealing government property. He must either be sentenced to death or set free. There's no middle course.'

Miss Silva is my good friend and former teacher and Michael is her brother, thought Li-ling. Yes, the sentence is too heavy. But this rapist should not get off without paying anything for his crime.

When Li-ling looked again at Michael Silva, she lost herself for a moment in another searing recollection of the nightmarish experience.

'Superintendent Bei, although death is too severe for his crime, I will not let him go free.'

'Then we'll execute him tomorrow at 6 a.m.'

'Why so soon after conviction? I've learned from the newspaper that execution should take place ten days after a conviction, according to the rule of the Japanese gendarmerie.'

'But it's lately been changed to two days due to food shortage.'

After all, it was entirely his own fault, she thought. I have no obligation to save his life. Finally she nodded.

'But Second Mrs Wong, it is you who asked for his release for the sake of your former teacher. Are you sure you've changed your mind?'

'Yes, Superintendent Bei.'

'Take him back to his cell,' he ordered. As the policemen took Michael out, still he did not raise his head.

The officer turned to her. 'What made you change your mind?'

'I've just recognised him as the one who sexually... harassed... my... schoolmate. I simply ask myself: why should we let this evil man go scot-free?'

'Yes, how right you are! The Japanese started this sacred war in order to wipe out all the Westerners and their influence from East Asia. Why should you help this particular bad Westerner?'

'Sorry for all the trouble I've put you to. Goodbye, and thank you.'

'It was no trouble. Give my best regards to Chief Wong. Goodbye.'

Li-ling returned to the waiting room. She turned to her former teacher and spoke in cold, clipped tones, 'Miss Silva, let's go. I can do nothing to save your brother.'

Miss Silva rose to her feet. 'But I don't understand,' she said, her face turning pale and her lips blue.

'He deserves the death penalty. He'll be executed tomorrow morning at six instead of ten days after the conviction. The rule's been changed.'

'Yes, he's committed a burglary, but isn't the death penalty too harsh?'

'It is a Japanese emergency law for wartime.'

'I think you could help if you wanted to. Have you tried hard enough?'

'No, I haven't tried.'

'Why?'

'Because he gave me the impression of a wicked man and he must be punished as such. That's all.'

'But you promised to help him.'

'Yes, but I've changed my mind.'

'Please, be merciful to him. He's young. He has a long life ahead of him.'

Li-ling paused for a moment. 'No!'

'He's my stepmother's only child,' Miss Silva sobbed. 'Since my father died, she has spoiled him. I know that you Chinese hold your teachers in high regard. I'm begging for your mercy. If my brother is released, he'll go to Macao to live with our uncle, an official of the Portuguese Colonial Government there. Mike won't be able to make trouble any more in Hong Kong. Please, Li-ling.'

Tears welled up in Li-ling's eyes. Her desire for revenge fought against her friendship and respect for Miss Silva. At last Li-ling said, 'Miss Silva, I'm sorry. I'll help you in anything – except this case.'

'But why? Why? I'll never ask you for any other favour.'

'No!' Li-ling shook her head firmly.

Miss Silva's shoulders drooped and she fell back into her seat.

'Why... Li-ling... you have changed... completely changed.' Then she straightened herself up in her chair and said loudly, 'Perhaps people change their nature when they become powerful. They drop their old friends. Now that you are the concubine of the most influential Chinese man in Hong Kong, you are no longer the Li-ling I once knew. You've broken your promise just like breaking a glass.'

Miss Silva abruptly stood up and pointed a finger at her former student and friend. 'You are a cold, marble statue – with no blood, no feelings, and no soul!' Then she stalked out of the room, face turning red.

Chapter Eleven

After Susan Silva left the waiting room, she asked for permission to see her brother. An officer led her into the reception room. Before long, two policemen brought in Michael, still in handcuffs.

'Michael Silva,' one of them said in English, 'you got ten minutes to talk with your sister.' Then he closed the door and stood outside with the other policeman.

When Michael saw his sister's expressionless face, his whole body stiffened like a stretched rope.

'Mike,' his sister said, 'Second Mrs Wong said you deserve the death penalty because you are evil.'

'Is that all she said about me?'

'Yes.'

'Then you don't know the reason why she turned our appeal down.'

Knitting her brows, Miss Silva said, 'No. The sudden change in her attitude without having a good reason, why? Why?'

'Susan, when you told me you wanted to ask Second Mrs Wong for aid, I... didn't tell you what I'd done to her because I was afraid you would change your mind. Now that she's suddenly withdrawn her help, you'll know the reason sooner or later. I want to... confess before I'm executed.'

'Confess?'

'I was crazy about her. About two years ago, I made advances to her in the street, and then Steve came along. He stopped me and we had a fight—'

'I'm ashamed of you!'

'I'm also ashamed of myself,' said Michael, lowering his head. 'And I have more to confess. Some time after she graduated, Miss So and Steve began to date in secret—'

'Yes, I know,' interrupted Susan. 'One month before the war I heard that from a fellow teacher, who'd seen them walking hand in hand in the New Territories. Now I understand the fight is the reason why Steve pretended to be a stranger to Li-ling at the graduation ceremony and why he kept their dates secret from me.' Susan heaved a sigh. 'Li-ling certainly hates you. But why did she go so far as to refuse to save your life? Like many Chinese, she used to ignore an ordinary transgression. Why has she become so callous now?'

'The night... before the war broke out,' stammered Michael, drops of perspiration beading on his face, 'after I heard a few honks from Robinson Road, I looked out the window. Soon I saw Steve and Miss So come out of the mansion. They kissed again and again in front of a truckload of soldiers waiting for Steve. I went completely mad and downed at least half a bottle of rum. After the truck left, she walked home. I followed her. I wanted her – she's so pretty...' His voice shook as he went on. 'I committed... a crime.'

'What? What did you say?'

'I... made love to her.' He spoke in a low hoarse voice, falling on his knees, 'though she struggled.'

Miss Silva pointed at him with a trembling finger. 'You... what? You! You... raped her?'

'Yes,' he finally admitted.

'You are worse than a beast!' she cried. 'How horrible! How could you do that? How could you?'

'I was wrong. It'd be useless for us to appeal to her again.' He choked. 'After my execution – but not before – please ask her to forgive me. Goodbye to you, and please say goodbye to Mummy for me.' He lowered his head and sobbed.

Susan Silva turned around abruptly and left without bidding her brother goodbye. She shook her head vigorously. I shouldn't have blamed Li-ling, she thought to herself.

★

That night at the Silva home in the Green Mansion, the dinner table had been set, but the food turned cold and remained untouched. The whole family usually enjoyed music during the evening, but that night the radio was silent. Instead, Susan and her stepmother sat on sofas, saying nothing, only weeping and sobbing. Though they were tired, they did not go to bed, because Susan knew that her stepmother, like her, would never be able to fall asleep that night.

Later, the elder woman suddenly cried out hysterically and hurled herself toward an open window. Before she could jump out, Susan darted forward, grabbing her around the waist and holding her back.

'He is my only son!' shouted Mrs Silva again and again, striving to free herself. 'It was all my fault.' At last she fell to the floor.

Susan helped her up, and steered her to the sofa. Then the younger woman swiftly poured a glass of wine. 'Please drink this to calm your nerves, Mama.'

Time ticked on, second by second.

★

'Li-ling, have you set the Westerner free?' asked Chief Wong when he came home late that night.

'No. I've changed my mind. He will be executed at 6 a.m..'

'Why?'

'Because I hate that Western rapist.'

He looked shattered. 'Then it is your teacher's brother who raped you?'

'Oh, no!' she said quickly. 'The sight of... any Western man reminds me of my rapist.'

'Poor Li-ling, that terrible impression can never be washed from your mind.'

Later, while Chief Wong lay asleep beside her, her mind still remained restless. I'm by no means a saint. Why should I regard such injury as rape as a trifle? Why should I forgive such an enemy as my rapist? Why should I be called a double fool?

But... how about Chief Wong? He's been raping me since he compelled me to marry him. If I'm tolerant of his many acts of rape through force of influence, why shouldn't I be tolerant, for Miss Silva's sake, of Michael's one act of violence? According to Papa, law can never be perfect.

The two forces continued to fight fiercely for hours on her mental battlefield. Though exhausted, she got up at 4 a.m. and turned on the light.

'Master, please get up,' she said. 'Time is running out. Please get up.'

'What? What?' Chief Wong opened his bleary eyes.

'I feel sorry for Miss Silva, because I've broken my promise to her. I want to spare her brother's life.'

'And that's why you looked so unsettled before we went to bed,' he said. 'All right! Let me ring Superintendent Bei to set Miss Silva's brother free, or he'll be executed in two hours. Will you be happy then?'

Li-ling nodded.

★

At last, footsteps approached the Silva home. Curious, Susan Silva went to the window and noticed the moonless, pre-dawn sky that featured only a few small stars.

Who's coming so late? she wondered. Li-ling to apologize? As the footsteps came nearer and nearer, they seemed familiar to Susan. The slow, even crunch, crunch, crunch matched those of her brother.

'No, it's my imagination,' she said aloud. 'It can't be Mike. Is his soul coming back to say goodbye?'

Now the silhouette of a man in the night was vaguely outlined by the starlit sky behind him.

'Mike!' she said. She struck her forehead repeatedly. 'Am I dreaming?' She wiped tears with the back of her hand.

'Oh Mummy, Mummy! It's Mike!' she cried.

Mrs Silva sprang to her feet from the sofa and rushed to the window.

That very morning Susan Silva telephoned Li-ling.

Chapter Twelve

That winter Mr So developed serious heart trouble and was confined to bed. One day after the herbal doctor left, several relatives and friends came to express their sympathy.

Mr So drank a bowl of hot medicated soup with Li-ling's help and said that he felt a little better. Then he waved everyone away but his daughter. Mrs So complained, but still he insisted.

He called Li-ling to his side and spoke, 'Wong took you as his concubine... by force of influence. He's killed many patriots. He shall be... executed by the Chinese Government after the war.'

'Papa, he makes many excuses for his actions. His father was an opium addict and died before he was born. He says at twelve he worked long hours in a factory. Later when his mother contracted tuberculosis, he took part in several violent robberies over several years to pay for her medical expenses and finally for her burial. Then he was imprisoned for fifteen years. Afterwards, he worked hard as a janitor in a Japanese firm for many years and learned the Japanese language, which enabled him to get a job in the National Intelligence Bureau a few years after Japan invaded Manchuria. But his colleagues looked down on him because he had no formal education, so he secretly attended night school. When the Japanese attacked Hong Kong, he sold his colleagues out. Of course, his unfortunate childhood can't be any justification for the crimes he's committed in later years.'

'We might say that Wong had a… modicum of filial piety for his mother. But, on the whole, he is utterly unfilial, for his treacherous acts have brought great… disgrace upon his ancestors.' Mr So coughed several times; Li-ling patted him on the back.

'Daughter,' he continued, 'you've suffered for all of us. We Chinese regard daughters as useless… but you've saved our family from ruin. You are like a son to me… nay, more than a son! I don't want to demand much more from you, but after I die…'

'No!' cried Li-ling, 'I don't want you to die!'

'My filial daughter, see to it… Chi-ching receives an education in a traditional school for at least… five years so that a solid foundation may be laid for his moral character… Then, send him to one of the few good modern schools where the moral aspect of education is also stressed. I don't want him to become a juvenile delinquent…'

He succumbed to a coughing fit. Li-ling brought him a cup of water. After taking a few sips, he resumed his talk.

'Also, on the day that Japan… surrenders, don't forget to place a substantial offering… at my joint tomb with your mother so that we may celebrate… to our hearts' content.'

She wiped her father's mouth with a handkerchief and said, 'I will remember.'

'Li-ling, before I… die… I… just tell you… my… mother and I and… you… also… fell victims to…' He suddenly stopped; his breathing was laboured.

'Papa! Papa! Please stop talking and rest,' urged Li-ling though she failed to understand what he meant.

In an instant her father lapsed into unconsciousness. Looking pale, she rushed out of the room to call back the doctor. One hour later, Mr So passed away. The whole family along with some relatives knelt before the body, each one weeping.

A few days after, a memorial service was held in a funeral parlour in Kowloon, where many pairs of scrolls, each with a eulogistic couplet written thereupon about the deceased, hung on the walls. Throughout the entire day Buddhist monks chanted, each beating time on a wooden skull-shaped block. As mourning relatives and friends came to bow three times before Mr So's portrait and his open casket, surrounded by wreaths, professional male mourners clad in white clothing shrieked, groaned, ruffled their hair and tore their clothes. Near the casket they sat on bamboo mats side by side with Mrs So, Li-ling, and her brother, who, all dressed in hempen clothes, cried bitterly.

Among the earliest visitors were Chief Wong, Sir William and their families. Each of them stayed a long time, mourning in sympathy. As General Tamura was leaving Hong Kong in two days, he was unable to come. Nevertheless, he had sent the So family a wreath for condolence, like all the other guests present.

The ritual lasted until midnight. Alone, the So family kept an overnight vigil beside the body.

The next morning a band of Chinese musicians in white uniforms, playing a dirge on Chinese clarinets and cymbals, led the funeral procession. The casket, covered with flowers and carried by eight bearers, followed. Then came the So family on foot, still in their mourning clothes. Next in line was Chief Wong's limousine, followed by Sir William's Rolls-Royce, which neither the British nor Japanese Hong Kong Governments had commandeered due to his unique position. Last were some pedicabs and rickshaws filled with relatives and friends of the So family. Before long Susan Silva alighted from her pedicab and joined Li-ling.

'Li-ling, take care of your health and don't cry too much,' said Miss Silva as they walked together in the procession.

'Miss Silva, please, ride in the pedicab. It'll take at least an hour for the procession to get to the Buddhist Cemetery.'

Both of them had to speak loud enough to cover the sound of the band ahead of them.

'No, I'd rather accompany you,' said Miss Silva. 'Besides, I have something confidential to talk to you about. I couldn't contact you yesterday due to work pressures, but I took a special leave of absence this morning.' Miss Silva moved her mouth close to Li-ling's ear. 'I saw Steve!'

Li-ling put her hand to her mouth.

'In the early hours yesterday morning, Steve and seven fellow inmates attempted an escape from the camp. They tried to go through a storm-drain nullah that led to the sea, where a junk was waiting near the coast to pick them up.'

'What went wrong?' gasped Li-ling.

'They were shot at, and five of them were wounded.'

Li-ling's vision darkened for a moment. 'Was Steve?'

'No, but later when he and two others jumped into the uncovered concrete nullah, which was thirty-feet deep and twenty-feet wide, he injured his right leg and arm, one of them his feet and another his back. Now all eight of them will be detained for treatment for some time in the Tung Wah Hospital in Kowloon before they are brought to trial. He'll have slim hope of being spared from execution!'

The word 'execution', struck Li-ling like a hammer. After she recovered, she asked, 'How'd you get the information about Steve's escape?'

'A few Chinese nurses who work in the Tung Wah Hospital have lately suffered from typhoid fever. I was transferred there to help for five days. I'll have to go back tomorrow to the Shoho Hospital. Yesterday morning at about eleven-thirty I saw Steve and a few other POWs under guard come in for treatment. He was so skinny, and his face so pale. I slipped into the waiting room to talk to him. Before we even opened our mouths, a gendarme guard rushed in, thrust his rifle butt against my stomach and pushed me away.'

'That brutal animal!' said Li-ling.

'During my lunch break I saw a single guard talking intently with an old Japanese woman, away from the entrance to the waiting room. I sneaked in again.'

'What happened?'

'After Steve talked about his escape, he said that he wanted to see you. I told him that this was a closely guarded hospital, and that even if you could manage to see him, you might be suspected of complicity in his attempt to escape.' Miss Silva cleared her throat before adding, 'Excuse me, but I knew then that you couldn't come without arousing your husband's suspicion. So I told Steve all about your involuntary marriage. I'm terribly sorry.'

'It doesn't matter, Miss Silva. In fact, I should thank you. Now that Steve has learned about my situation, he'll pardon my failure to visit him... even before his—' Li-ling choked. After she regained her composure, she asked, 'How did he feel?'

'He came to himself after a long while. He said that in any case, his days were numbered. When I said goodbye to him, in tears he wanted me to tell you that he would love you always and for ever.'

After the procession arrived at the So Family Tomb, there was a ritual in which a few Taoist monks chanted and rang small bells.

While workers lowered the casket into the grave, Li-ling, her stepmother and brother broke down, sobbing unrestrainably. As the coolies placed her father's casket alongside her birth mother's, Li-ling collapsed. Miss Silva lost no time in rubbing 'tiger balm' ointment onto her temples. After a while Li-ling recovered and got to her feet.

Ah Mei, Chief Wong's teenage daughter, and the old Mrs Wong then held on to Li-ling until the ritual was over.

After the guests left, Li-ling, her stepmother and brother stayed behind to kowtow to the late Mr and Mrs So, paying their last respects.

Chapter Thirteen

One afternoon Li-ling, dressed in a brown felt cheongsam, Chief Wong and Ah Fook took the limousine to Shamshuipo Camp.

'Li-ling, today is the first time I've seen you smile since your father died two weeks ago,' said Chief Wong.

'Of course I feel happy today, for I have a chance to take my revenge on my enemy.'

'Luckily, Lieutenant Colonel Genda, the commandant of the camp, is a very good friend of mine. He promised you a motor boat.'

'I'm also thankful I came across Mrs Mao.'

'It was lucky you met her. She lives near the Green and Blue Mansions, doesn't she?' asked Chief Wong.

'Yes. Before the outbreak of the war, twice Mrs Mao saw the Western villain loitering around that big banyan, teasing young girls who passed by. She's just a casual friend, and yet she went to the trouble of finding out the scoundrel's name and gathering as much information as possible about him from her neighbours. Once I see him, I'll be able to identify him.'

'We must invite Mrs Mao to dinner.'

'Certainly. Then I'll introduce her to you so that you may thank her in person. I should reward you too, for getting the commandant of this camp to check the list of the POWs here.'

Chief Wong smiled.

As they drew near the camp, they saw groups of young Western men clad in loose prisoners' uniforms of dark-brown cloth, each with an identity tag sewn on the left breast. Armed guards stood over them as they worked on road construction.

The limousine stopped at the entrance of the camp all surrounded by electrified barbed wire. Above, a flag of the Red Sun with its Red Rays flapped in the breeze. The gendarmes standing guard saluted Chief Wong. After the gates opened, they drove inside, past older male prisoners who were sweeping the open ground and cleaning the lanes and the outer walls of several buildings. Overlooking the camp from a central watchtower, guards with machine-guns observed the prisoners' moves.

As the limousine halted at the entrance of a two-storey building, the three got out. They were warmly greeted by a Japanese officer, a man of slight build with a small head like a snake and mousy eyes. His fleshy nose protruded far beyond his thin moustache. He showed his guests to a medium-size dining hall. Ah Fook carried a cylindrical crate made of bamboo strips he had taken from the boot of the limousine. It was over five feet long and about two feet in diameter.

On entering the hall, Chief Wong handed his host a large piece of heart-shaped jade, which the officer slipped into his pocket with a smile.

Scotch whisky, dishes of Japanese food and dim sum were served. The officer talked softly, barely moving his small mouth as he spoke. 'My dear friends, I'd like you to drink to your hearts' content with me today!'

'Sure, sure,' said Chief Wong in Japanese, 'we'll drink, but I'm sorry my wife doesn't. Lieutenant Colonel Genda, please excuse her.'

'Certainly. In Japan very few women drink.'

Genda downed two glasses of Scotch, one right after another.

'Oh my! Lieutenant Colonel Genda, you must have a great capacity for liquor,' said Li-ling in Japanese, too.

He smiled and she filled his glass with more whisky.

'You are General Tamura's foster daughter. He has an eye for the beautiful,' said the Japanese officer, glancing at her while he stroked his moustache.

'No, I'm not beautiful at all,' she said.

'You are too modest. I know both the Japanese and the Chinese are modest, not like those arrogant Westerners. When we first took Hong Kong, the British were still very lofty, thinking of their past glory of being mistress of the seas and their never-setting sun. But look at them now,' said Genda, pointing out the window at a number of older prisoners doing chores. 'They were lions before, but now they are sheep.' Chief Wong and the Japanese officer burst out laughing.

'Where are the women and children?' she asked.

'Inside the buildings. The women, who no longer have Chinese servants, have to scrub the floors and wash clothes themselves.'

The officer then turned to Chief Wong. 'You told me last week that a white man, now a prisoner here, assaulted your wife and that she wanted to take her own revenge. That's very good.'

Genda then turned to the two gendarmes standing by and gave an order, 'Fetch the prisoner's file from my desk for Second Mrs Wong.'

A gendarme left the room.

'As I told you the other day,' said Genda, 'he is one of the prisoners committed to trial in a few days on escape charges. Since he's to die soon by military means, you shouldn't lose any time in taking your revenge.'

'Lieutenant Colonel Genda, thank you very much for your help.' Li-ling smiled.

'It is my pleasure. We're friends. Our common enemies, the British and Americans, bullied us Asians for a long time. That's why Premier Tojo started this sacred war for the liberation of all Asians.'

Chief Wong raised his glass, saying, 'Long live His Majesty, Emperor Hirohito.'

'To his health,' said Genda, raising his glass.

'What's your attendant carrying?' asked Genda as he turned his attention to Ah Fook, who stood in a corner. Before Chief Wong could answer, the Japanese officer said, 'Oh, now I remember.' He tapped himself on the head. 'You mentioned a crate for pigs on the phone, didn't you?'

'Yes,' said Chief Wong. 'You told me you were curious about the crate and wanted to take a look at it first.'

'Ah, yes, you said that many years ago Kwangtung people used to punish a man guilty of rape by putting him inside such a crate and submerging it so that he would suffocate to death,' said the lieutenant colonel, touching the crate curiously. 'I heard of this custom from a Kwangtung friend of mine.'

'We call it the pig-crate punishment. My wife suggested she'd make the rascal suffer until he is near death. Then she'll bring him back here, to be executed later.'

'Second Mrs Wong, why don't you give him the maximum torture by submerging him and bringing him up as many times as possible until his body and spirit cracks? Have you ever seen a cat torture a mouse?'

'Lieutenant Colonel Genda, you are a genius,' she exclaimed.

'What fun! What excitement!' boomed the officer, roaring with laughter.

At that moment the gendarme came in with a file and handed it to Li-ling. She opened it and immediately pointed at the photo.

'Yes, it's all come back to me now, this is the one!' she cried.

'Bring him here,' ordered Genda.

The two gendarmes left.

'Let's share the fun and excitement today,' said Genda.

'You're welcome,' said Li-ling. 'Today I won't go back until I have taken revenge to my heart's content with your idea of maximum torture. But first, I'd like to take a short pleasure cruise in celebration of this happy occasion.'

'Second Mrs Wong, during our cruise, we'll spot the dirtiest and the most odious part of the sea along the coast for the punishment.'

'Bravo! Lieutenant Colonel Genda, you deserve another drink.' She filled his glass to the rim. The scarlet-faced officer emptied it in one gulp.

'Lieutenant Colonel,' said Chief Wong, 'I'd like to remind you that we are scheduled to attend a dinner party at 6 p.m. at the Ping On Restaurant. Have you forgotten?'

'Oh, yes,' said Genda, tapping his temple again. 'I was so excited that I forgot. The farewell party in honour of Colonel Nakaso. In that case, Second Mrs Wong, today you'll administer the punishment alone. Tomorrow, come again with Chief Wong and we'll play the game together. Arr! I'd rather enjoy the ingenious torture of a white man than any of the delicious food provided at tonight's dinner party.'

At this moment, two gendarmes dragged in a frail prisoner with his pale face downcast. However, his aquiline nose revealed that he was none other than Stephen! The sight of him broke her heart.

Li-ling slapped his face sharply. Before he could raise his head to look up, she slapped him again and both the Japanese officer and Chief Wong broke into laughter.

Eyes snapping with fury, Li-ling pointed her finger at him and screamed in Japanese, 'This is the man who raped me!'

Stephen looked blank.

'You beast!' she said in English. 'Your time is drawing near, but I won't let you lead a life of ease even on your last days... I want you to suffer the punishment a rapist should suffer according to our custom.'

Stephen's face flushed.

'Let's go now,' said Genda. They all walked out of the building.

'Ah Fook, bind this evil man's hands tightly behind his back,' ordered Li-ling in Chinese.

Ah Fook did so with a cord taken from his pocket. He and the two gendarmes shoved Stephen into the crate. After tying down the lid, the three men placed the crate in the boot of the limousine. All the men and Li-ling rode in two cars to the Shamshuipo Pier nearby.

As they arrived, a gendarme officer saluted them. Pointing to a motor boat flying a flag of the Red Sun with its Red Rays, he said, 'That is a gendarmerie patrol boat. According to a recent regulation, a patrol boat of this size shall not be in motion without at least three gendarmes on board.'

'Lieutenant Colonel Genda, will you give my attendant permission to help carry out the punishment aboard the boat?' asked Chief Wong.

'Certainly.'

Ah Fook and the two gendarmes carried the loaded crate to the boat and put it next to a junior gendarme officer who was seated at the helm.

Ah Fook then went back to fetch a large, heavy canvas bag and a reel of coarse rope from the limousine's boot.

The two gendarmes sat side by side on the bow while Ah Fook and Li-ling, with the bag and the rope beside them, were seated close to the crate.

As the officer started the motor, Li-ling waved to Chief Wong and Genda, both of whom waved back, smiling. The boat pulled away and headed northwest.

'Look at the canvas bag. It contains food and drinks... She's going on a joyful picnic,' said Chief Wong, grinning at the lieutenant colonel.

Chapter Fourteen

When the boat was still some distance offshore, Li-ling asked Ah Fook to take out a box of dim sum, a few soft drinks, a tin of Three-Five cigarettes and some drinking glasses out of the bag.

She then said in Japanese to the officer at the wheel, 'Before we start to punish this devil, we're going to take a pleasure cruise. Give me the helm. You join them on the bow and refresh yourselves with the drinks, food and cigarettes.'

The officer hesitated a moment and then asked, 'Madam, do you know how?'

'Certainly.'

'All right. I'll be pleased to turn over the helm to you.'

After Ah Fook had taken the drinks, food and cigarettes to the bow, the two gendarmes, each equipped with a rifle, and their officer, pistol strapped to his belt, all walked around nearby eating, drinking and smoking.

Looking at their flag fluttering in the wind and then at the setting sun sliding down the hills, the officer said to his two men in an arrogant tone, 'Our country, like the sun, is controlling the destiny of the world.' Then they toasted Emperor Hirohito of Japan.

As soon as Ah Fook saw a small deserted body of land called 'Ghost Island' by the fisherfolk, he turned to Li-ling and grinned. She secretly took a pistol from her handbag and a knife from her pocket. While the three gendarmes' attention was diverted from the crate, she cut the cord fastened to the lid, then the one that bound Stephen's hands.

'Jump overboard!' shouted Li-ling with military-like authority, pointing the pistol in the direction of the men on the bow. Blam! No sooner had Li-ling shot into the air and the flame spurted into the sky than Ah Fook and the two gendarmes dived into the water. However, the officer, who stood near the edge of the deck, hesitated.

'Jump overboard!' she shouted at him again as Stephen had just cleared the confines of the crate. Instead, the officer drew his pistol and fired. The bullet went wild. Stephen made his way to Li-ling and snatched the pistol from her hand. The officer shot once more, but this time Stephen returned fire. Still holding his gun, the officer fell backwards into the sea and never appeared again. In the meantime, Ah Fook and the two gendarmes swam towards 'Ghost Island'.

Beaming from ear to ear, Stephen stretched out his arms to Li-ling. But as he started towards her, he collapsed. She saw blood flowing from his right leg onto the deck and swiftly took cotton, bandages and iodine from the first-aid kit to dress his wound. But the bleeding continued and later Stephen lost consciousness. Eventually she brought the bleeding under control. 'Steve!' she cried again and again, desperately trying to revive him, but he lay there motionless.

When she finally looked up, she found that the boat was sailing in the direction of another island with a few motorboats moored to its pier, each flying a Japanese flag of the Red Sun with its Red Rays. There was also a platoon of Japanese sailors standing on the pier. Li-ling grabbed the blanket from the bag and quickly covered Stephen.

The Japanese officer in charge began to shout and signal her to bring the boat alongside the pier. Closer and closer the vessel approached.

The situation is hopeless, she thought. I have no pass and I can't ignore the order. If the Japanese come aboard, they'll discover Stephen. Then they'll take us back to Hong Kong to be executed.

Her fear increased. Her heart pounded. She took a few deep breaths to gain her composure. After tying the boat to the pier, she slowly mounted the concrete steps, looking calm though her heartbeat accelerated.

After she reached the top step, the officer cursed her as she walked nonchalantly toward him. When she stood before him, she took a piece of hard paper out of her handbag and held it close to his face before he snatched it. Li-ling could see many eyebrows raised. She could tell that all the sailors were wondering how this strange young woman could have the courage to defy their officer.

It was a photograph of Li-ling standing with a white-haired Japanese officer. His hand was on her arm. He wore an insignia of one star on either side of the collar of his uniform. The officer immediately stood at attention, his eyes and mouth open wide.

'Is this General Tamura?' he asked meekly.

'Turn the picture over,' she ordered.

The officer turned it over and saw the following words in Japanese:

To my dearest foster daughter, Li-ling

With Love,
Hideo Tamura

'I'm terribly sorry,' said the officer in a faint voice. 'Madam, would you please come to our office and have some tea? You look tired.' He then gave the photo back to her.

'No,' she said in a cold tone. 'I want to take refreshment on my boat.'

'Certainly, madam! May I ask where you're going?'

'I'm going back to Shamshuipo Pier. I was on a pleasure cruise alone, but I got lost.'

'You must go that way.' The officer pointed southeasterly.

Before long, Li-ling was back in her boat with a box of six Japanese red-bean cakes and a bottle of soda. Although her palms were wet with perspiration, she sat down on the deck, eating the cakes and drinking the beverage in an intentionally leisurely manner. Only after she had finished eating and had wiped her mouth clean with a handkerchief did she start the engine. Before she turned the motor boat in a southeasterly direction, she waved to the wide-eyed sailors.

The night was closing in fast. When the boat was far enough from the island, she reversed her course. The little craft, with two lovers eloping in a way she had never imagined, was soon swallowed up by the darkness.

Chapter Fifteen

Early in the next morning, under the cover of a few evergreen willows with their slender hanging branches and crescent-shaped leaves, Li-ling anchored the boat in a stream near the south coast of Kwangtung Province. The air was thick with the smell of seaweed. Soon she heard Stephen moan in a low voice.

'Oh, my Steve,' she cried out.

Li-ling's heart sang after they had narrowly escaped the devilish claws of King Yen, the Chinese God of Death. She knew that each had as much to tell the other as the Yellow River had unlimited water to flow into the sea. And yet she did not know where or how to begin. She realised that Stephen had the same feeling. They looked at each other but could not see, for tears of joy flooded their eyes. They then indulged in long, sensuous kisses.

'Steve, after I married the Chinese traitor, I was heartbroken. I thought I'd lose you for ever.' Li-ling wiped away his tears, then hers.

'Li-ling, after I was caught escaping from the camp,' said Stephen slowly, 'I thought I'd never see you again.'

They kissed each other again and again as if to make up for their separation.

'What happened, dear Li-ling, after I lost consciousness?' asked Stephen at last.

She told him. When she mentioned the sudden change of attitude shown by the Japanese officer from pride to humility, he laughed.

'You must have worked out an elaborate scheme for all this,' said Stephen. 'I thank you very much.'

'After Miss Silva told me about you, I contacted Mr Liu for advice to plan our escape.'

'Who's Mr Liu?'

'The Chinese in uniform who tied you up.'

'Now I remember. He tied the cord loosely around my wrists.'

'He's Chief Wong's bodyguard and, at the same time, the leader of the Hong Kong underground workers of Free China. He knows Japanese very well, but he speaks pidgin Japanese to fool the enemy. He's quite resourceful, but sometimes deliberately acts clumsy and says silly little things. He stammers in front of others, but to me he speaks normally since he revealed his status to me as an underground worker. That's why he's nicknamed "Ah Fook" which means "the fool" in Cantonese slang. People like to call him by his nickname.'

'He doesn't mind being called that?'

'No. This way no one suspects his involvement in dangerous and complicated espionage.'

They laughed, and she continued with her story.

'I saved the lives of his underground colleagues in Hong Kong, so he was grateful to me. At several secret meetings he showed me how to fire a pistol. He drew maps for me indicating escape routes. He gave me addresses of his fellow workers on our way to the stronghold where the Guerrilla Headquarters of Kwangtung Province is located. He also taught me to perform in his intelligence world of special signs, signals and codes.'

'For example.'

'I remember an important signal: leaving a handkerchief on the floor would mean, "Danger – you'll be under immediate arrest!" This is for spring only, for another season, the same warning would require a different signal.'

'Li-ling, although you were brought up as a traditional Chinese girl confined to your home, your judgement, determination and courage are far superior to many men's.' Stephen gazed at her with sparkling eyes.

'Women can be just as astute, determined and courageous as men. But I still have a lot to learn. If you hadn't been quick enough to snatch my pistol and shoot that officer, both of us might have been killed.'

'You were a little hesitant in pulling the trigger. Remember, in an emergency there is no room for so-called kindness. You must kill!'

'Anyway, I owe you my life.'

'I too, owe you mine.'

Li-ling helped Stephen walk ashore. At last she sat him on the shore under a mallow tree with its many leaves resembling hearts.

She went back to the boat and took out an old, torn leather briefcase from her canvas bag and put the first-aid kit in its place. After returning to the shore with the bag containing the kit, she went back to the boat and steered it to midstream. The briefcase contained a hammer and a spike. She drove the spike through the bottom of the boat, which sank with the briefcase and the tools. Then she swam ashore and changed before she went back to Stephen.

Now Li-ling and Stephen sat together under the mallow. Before she let him drink a bottle of soda and eat a bean cake, she took out the first-aid kit, dressed his wound and covered it with a new bandage.

'Here's a present for you,' she said after he had finished eating. She produced a blue wool sweater from the bag. 'It took me two months to knit this for your birthday, but I never got to give it to you because the war broke out.'

He slipped it over his light-brown hair. 'Thank you very much. It is beautiful!'

With it on, Stephen looked healthier. She was certain that once he gained back the weight he had lost, it would fit him perfectly, for she had created it to accommodate a mass of biceps and a muscular chest and back.

She paused for a while before saying, 'I had to accuse you of assaulting me because I had to convince Chief Wong and the Japanese commandant to have you punished. The villain was in reality—'

'Mike!' interposed Stephen, whose expression blackened. 'Miss Silva told me about it at the hospital. She said that since the rapist was her brother and the victim was my lover, she shouldn't hide the crime from me.'

'Steve, she didn't tell me that she'd told you about my ordeal. Perhaps she thought that I wouldn't want you to know, but my mind wouldn't rest as long as I hid it from you.'

He caressed her smooth cheek. 'Li-ling, don't worry. It was not your fault. Miss Silva asked for my forgiveness. I said no! I will take revenge on Mike some day.' Stephen spoke the last two sentences in a loud, shrill voice; the veins of his temples stood out and the pupils of his eyes dilated, frightening Li-ling. 'Why on earth did you save him from being executed?'

'Then, Steve, why don't you take vengeance on Chief Wong, too? He raped me legally for about a year after a marriage ceremony he forced on me. The harm done to me by Michael was comparatively a trifle.'

'But Miss Silva told me that Chief Wong saved your father's life, so you married him, even as a concubine.'

'He threatened to have my father beheaded unless I married him, though he had no evidence whatsoever against my father as a Chungking agent.'

'Wong and Mike took a hard slap at your self-esteem as well as mine. I'll be in torment until I can take vengeance on them.'

'Steve, in the last analysis, your arch-enemies, as well as mine, are the Japanese warlords who started this war. In the 1937 Nanking Massacre alone, about four hundred innocent Chinese were killed, and countless women raped. Can we have our revenge on all of our enemies? What about Hitler's and Mussolini's gangs, now still slaughtering people in Europe and Africa? It's only natural for you to want to avenge me. But what would be the use?' Then she looked serious and added nervously, 'Steve, now I'm a woman... with blemishes, can you still love me as much as before?'

'To me, my dear Li-ling, you are still an intact pearl, as bright and spotless as your soul and heart.'

Her face radiated colour and tears welled up in her eyes.

'How was your life in the camp?' she asked after a moment of silence.

'Terrible! Three months ago, two of my fellow prisoners were charged with "not looking respectful enough in front of a senior Japanese officer" who came to inspect us. I defended them, but all three of us were flogged. I still have some scars in my back. I can tell you scores of such cases one by one.'

Li-ling placed her fingertips on his lips. 'Tell me later when we have plenty of time. Steve, we're still in the occupied area and our destination is far away. I'll go to the city of Sheungtak and ask for help from the underground. According to Mr Liu, it's normally a nine- or ten-day walk from here and back. I'll try my best to be back in seven or eight days.'

'But you haven't had enough rest yet.'

'It can't be helped. Poor Steve, you'll have no shelter and little food and drink. You have a fever and your wound is still serious.'

'What you've done for me will keep my spirit strong enough to withstand any suffering,' said Stephen sincerely. 'I'll never feel lonely as long as you are with me.'

'Steve, what do you mean? I'll be away from you for quite a few days.'

'But I'll have this to remind me of you,' he said, pointing at his sweater. They both laughed.

'Here's a pistol for your protection.' She placed it on his lap.

From her canvas bag she took a large piece of cloth and some old clothing, along with some daily necessities. After shedding her cheongsam, she donned a woman labourer's old jacket and pants made of coarse dark-blue cloth, padded with cotton over her slip. She took off her high-heeled shoes, got some cryptograms and two capsules of microfilm from the hollowed heels and put on a pair of rubber shoes. Finally she tucked her hair into a coarse, light-brown kerchief.

She put her leather handbag, cheongsam and high-heeled shoes into the canvas bag, and left it with Stephen. Then she placed the other items on the piece of cloth and tied the two pairs of diagonal corners to make a cloth pack.

'Why don't you use the bag?' asked Stephen.

'Too heavy and large for travelling. Besides, country-women use such a cloth pack. Steve, there are cakes, tins of meat, bottles of water and drink, the first-aid kit and some daily necessities left for you in the bag.'

'You haven't taken any food and drink yet. You need to eat and drink something before you leave, my love.'

'I want to leave you as much food and drink as possible.'

Stephen shook his head.

'Steve,' she sighed, 'we're lucky to be together after so long a separation. Yet, we have to part again after so short a meeting.'

He cradled her oval face in his palms and kissed her again and again before they said goodbye.

Chapter Sixteen

Disguised as a labourer, Li-ling spent the entire day travelling on the muddy paths that lined the countryside. The sight of people digging in the earth for roots to eat moved her. She took her meals at wayside stalls. Late at night, she found a small, old two-storey inn in a town, where the innkeeper, a fat woman, showed her upstairs to a room furnished only with a bed, two chairs, a table and a dim, flickering oil lamp. There was a small adjoining bathroom.

When Li-ling paid for the room, the woman took hold of her hand before she could withdraw it.

'Your skin is so tender and smooth; your face white and clean. Are you a lady or a labourer?'

Li-ling pulled her hand away without answering.

After the fat woman left, Li-ling closed the door. She quickly washed her hands and face and brushed her teeth. She was so exhausted that she lay down on the bed without removing her clothes and fell asleep without turning off the lamp.

At midnight, she was awakened by noises outside her door. She thought it must be either a rat or a cat.

Suddenly she noticed an iron rod poking slowly through a crack in the wooden door. She sprang to her feet. To her horror, she heard some men whispering.

'Who's there?' she cried out. But there was no response.

Suddenly someone began forcing the door, the noise becoming louder and louder. She quickly grabbed her cloth pack and jumped onto the window sill. Before starting to climb down, she saw someone moving in the dark street below. She stopped short.

She remembered that Kwangtung was notorious for kidnapping as well as robbery, especially during wartime.

What if I'm kidnapped? Who'll pay my ransom? Surely Steve will starve to death. Maybe I should never have saved him in Hong Kong, only to let him linger to death on the shore here.

In sheer despair, she jumped back inside, giving herself entirely to fate when something dropped out of her pack onto the wooden floor with a thud. She looked around in the dim light. It was the pistol! She picked it up quickly.

Steve always cares about me before himself, she thought as she fired two shots out of the window. Outside the door, the footsteps retreated. Silence followed. But then she heard footsteps again.

'I have a gun!' she warned. 'Who's out there?'

'The innkeeper. Look at my door! What happened?'

'Some thugs tried to break in,' replied Li-ling, one hand opening the door and the other holding her pistol.

'Where are they now? And why do you have a gun?'

'Look at this!' she cried, picking up an old, strange-looking tobacco pipe near the door. Pointing to a room not far away, she said, 'Before I moved in, I saw one of the men standing near that room smoking this pipe.'

'Did you see them trying to break down the door?' asked the innkeeper.

'They were outside. How could I see them?'

'I can't help you if you can't identify them.'

Suspicious of everyone around, Li-ling sneaked out of the inn before dawn. She disappeared into the darkness and continued her journey.

When she came to a slushy path, she picked up some mud, spattered her clothes, face and hands and dug her fingers deep into it to dirty her fingernails.

During the early morning hours, she safely passed two gendarmerie stations. In the first large town, the gendarmes were talking with each other, not paying attention to pedestrians passing by. At the second, no gendarmes were in sight.

Some time after noon Li-ling had to stop at the centrally located gendarmerie station in a populated city. Ahead of her in line were two boys in their late teens, dressed in school uniforms, each carrying a heavy trunk. The two gendarmes, one tall and the other short, searched them and their trunks thoroughly.

Throughout the rummage Li-ling was worried about her pistol, cryptograms and microfilm she kept in her pack though she composed herself the best she could.

Now it was Li-ling's turn. When the tall gendarme looked at her with slit eyes and pointed to her pack, she felt her palms get wet with perspiration, for she understood that it was an order for her to unknot it for a search. Instead of complying, she sneezed, pinched her nostrils between forefinger and thumb and blew her nose before she wiped her saliva-smeared hand on her pants. The short gendarme lost no time waving her through. Li-ling's mind smiled.

With light steps, she continued on her journey. And before long, her concern over her beloved Steve became foremost in her mind again.

How will Steve protect himself against wild animals? Ah Fook said that in Kwangtung Province some tigers roamed about in the hills and mountains. Although Steve is near the coast, who can be sure that tigers never wander there?

She remembered a true story that about twenty years before, in the New Territories, two children claimed they'd seen a tiger rambling in the hills. Nobody believed them, but eventually the tiger killed two policemen before it was shot dead.

Just before Li-ling left Hong Kong, people had told her that starving parents exchanged their babies for food. She wondered if starving people would kill Steve as imported food. She thought of her loved one, no safer than a small, helpless animal living alone in the wilderness, at the mercy of nature.

On arrival at a big town the following afternoon, she smiled when she saw a sign above the open iron gate at the entrance to a garden that read: 'Buddhist Temple'.

As she stepped inside the garden, she saw a number of peepul trees, each about twenty feet tall, planted on both sides of a concrete path leading to the temple. Their large heart-shaped leaves with long, narrow tips and long, flexible stalks caused them to clatter in the wind. The walls of the temple were built of orange bricks. Green tiles covered the double concave roofs with pointed corners. After taking a short walk on the path, Li-ling stepped over the protruding door sill and entered the big hall. The inside was shrouded by wisps of light-blue smoke.

Without hesitating, she knelt by the side of two country women on their knees before the altar of the statue of the seated Buddha.

'Oh! Most Honourable Buddha,' she prayed silently, 'please protect my British friend, Stephen Jones, who's now lying on the shore of a stream southwest of Sunlik. He's completely helpless... ill, wounded, thirsty and starving. Great Britain is an ally of China in this war. Stephen is our friend now. Merciful Buddha, please keep wild animals, Japanese, Chinese traitors and evil spirits away from this good man. I will do good deeds throughout my life to repay your kindness...'

After she had kowtowed to Buddha and donated some money to a monk, she walked much faster, with a spring in her steps.

At night she reached a village where there was only one inn, but she passed it by. She walked on throughout the night and the following day, passing a number of villages and small towns. It was strange to her that she did not feel tired. In the evening she arrived at the city of Sheungtak, where she passed another gendarmerie station without encountering any trouble. Later, she found the street and the number of the house she sought – a bungalow. To her surprise, the sign hanging above the thick wooden gate read: 'The Eternal Life Coffin Shop'.

She knocked at the gate. After some time she heard a man's voice from inside: 'We close at five. It's now six. Come back tomorrow.'

'I'm not a customer. I'm visiting someone,' said Li-ling.

'Come back tomorrow,' said the voice, sounding irritated.

Li-ling gave the coded knocks that Ah Fook had taught her: five knocks with the fist and seven quick ones with the knuckles.

'Who is it?' An eye peeped through the narrow space along the edge of the gate.

'I'm a woman, named Lam Ju-di,' said Li-ling. 'I'm here to see Mr Lo Bing-yau, please.'

'Miss Lam, there's no employee bearing that name. Perhaps he worked here before. I've worked here for one month only,' said the voice.

'But I have a message for him. Tell him that his cousin, who's come from Hong Kong, is ill. He's recuperating at a good friend's house at 109 Chungshan Road, first floor, Canton. That's all.'

'Miss Lam, please come in,' said a middle-aged man dressed in labourer's coarse clothing as he opened the gate and extended his hand. While they were traversing the large courtyard, he said, 'Miss Lam, please call me Shing, my present name; Lo Bing-yau is a former one. Sorry I didn't know who you were until you mentioned Hong Kong 109. I have communicated with him twice before, but never met him in person. My code number is Kwangtung 278.'

'Don't apologize, Mr Shing.' Li-ling smiled. 'HK 109 told me to contact KT 278. I'm very glad to meet you.'

'So am I, Miss Lam.'

Mr Shing showed Li-ling to a small room. After he switched on the light, she saw a bed, a table and a chair. There was a small adjacent bathroom with a wooden bathtub.

'This is one of the two vacant rooms reserved for visitors,' said Mr Shing.

'Here's something from HK 109,' she said, handing Mr Shing the cryptograms and two capsules of microfilm.

'This may be useful information that will help us against our enemies. We thank you heartily.'

'Please, I should thank HK 109 and all of you for helping me, too.'

'Miss Lam, are you hungry? Do you want something to eat?'

'No, thanks. I took my supper at a stall an hour ago.'

Mr Shing handed her a cup of water and took the cryptograms and film to another room. There he instructed two of his fellow underground workers to decipher the messages and develop and print the film. Then he returned to Li-ling's quarters.

She told him about the events that had led up to her arrival in Kwangtung with Stephen, their objective now being to get to the Kwangtung Guerrilla Headquarters.

'It was a miraculous escape. You are braver than most men. Where's Mr Jones now?'

'I left him hidden under a tree on the shore of a stream, about five miles southwest of Sunlik.' She pulled a map from her pack and pointed at the spot.

'It'll be a tremendous task getting him to the guerrilla stronghold. I'm afraid we can't help.' Mr Shing left with a creased forehead.

Li-ling paced back and forth. What if they refuse to help? she worried. Then Steve will die. 'Heaven, please help Steve,' she prayed.

'Miss Lam,' said Mr Shing after he came back, 'we just learned from the decoded message that you saved the lives of sixteen underground workers; very noble of you. As for your friend, Britain is our ally. Therefore, no matter how great the risk, we'll do our best to help.'

Li-ling smiled. 'Thank you very much. By the way, yours is a coffin shop. Where are the coffins?'

'Our factory is in the rear of this bungalow and we have dozens of low-quality coffins in the store for sale to poor people.'

'This business is a very clever front for underground workers. I admire all of you.'

Mr Shing bowed. 'Please go to bed now. We'll act early tomorrow morning.'

'Goodnight,' said Li-ling yawning.

'I must warn you to stay fully dressed while you sleep. We have tunnels under the garden behind. We can escape through them in an emergency. Goodnight.'

Chapter Seventeen

The next morning when loud knocks at the door awakened Li-ling, her heart pounded. She sprang to her feet, snatched her pistol, and turned it towards the door. 'Who's out there?'

'Shing. Good morning, Miss Lam.'

She breathed a sigh of relief and lowered her pistol. Smiling, she opened the door. 'Good morning, Mr Shing. I'm very sorry.'

'Never mind, Miss Lam. Did you think I was a robber?' They both laughed. 'We'll bring a bucket of hot water and breakfast to you soon. We shall expect you in the courtyard in an hour.'

'Thanks. I'll be there.'

'By the way, it's true that Japanese gendarmes seldom search pedestrians and their luggage for weapons at their stations as they did at the beginning of the occupation. Now they only search when they get suspicious. As to your pistol—'

'That's why I've been able to carry it with me all the way here,' she interjected.

'Miss Lam, sometimes a pistol is useful in self-defence, but you can't avoid passing gendarmerie stations in occupied areas. What if the gendarmes halt you for a random check?'

Li-ling recalled the scene which had happened only the day before, so she handed him her pistol. 'I've sewn gold pieces and jewels in my cotton-padded jacket for emergencies,' she said. 'What if the gendarmes find them?'

'Nowadays in big cities they don't seize valuables, but in small towns some may.' Then he left.

Later, after she had brushed her teeth and washed her face, Li-ling took off her clothes before the full-length mirror in the bathroom. She could not help smiling at the contrast between her white body and her dirty, sun-darkened face, neck and hands, which she likened to a difference as great as day and night. She took a bath and sang during every minute of it. Afterwards she ate two bowls of rice gruel, a piece of salty bean curd and a small dish of soybean sprouts for breakfast.

At 8 a.m., she went to the courtyard, where she saw a large unpainted coffin made of rough wood near the gate. Mr Shing, another middle-aged man and several young men, also dressed as labourers, were standing around.

'Who died?' she enquired, coming forward.

'Nobody,' said Mr Shing with a smile. 'See the two robes on top of the coffin? Your English friend will lie inside as a dead man, wearing the large burial robe. One of our men wearing the hempen mourning robe will act as a close relative of the "deceased". Four men will carry the loaded coffin for about two and a half days to a cemetery with "the relative". There, your friend will come out a "live" man. Then one of my men will escort you both for a few more days to the guerrilla stronghold.'

'After the coffin has been sealed, my friend will surely find it difficult to breathe,' said Li-ling.

'Don't worry. There are a few cracks in the edges of the three side planks at the bottom that allow air flow, and a hidden hole of the fourth for transmission of water, food and medicine.'

'Amazing! Mr Shing, did you just now prepare this coffin or is it ready to hand?'

'Last year, the governor of Kwungtung of the Wang regime came to inspect this area. We made arrangements to assassinate him. Our man killed him, but was shot to death by his bodyguards. We had already made this large coffin to smuggle our stout assassin to the cemetery from which he could escape to the guerrilla stronghold. Since he was killed, we've kept the coffin and the robes.'

'I am sorry for him!'

'These are my colleagues,' said Mr Shing, 'Mr Pao, the escort leader, whom we call Old Pao, and four young men, Ah Kwok, Poon Pan, Yung Yan and Ah Bing. This is Miss Lam.' Li-ling shook hands with each of them.

'Miss Lam, there'll be no problem for a few days on the first trip with an empty coffin,' continued Mr Shing. 'Throughout the next trip to the cemetery when your friend is lying inside the coffin, you must keep a distance from our men, especially near any gendarmerie station. In case of an emergency, they, though unarmed, may make a surprise attack with their poles on the gendarmes. If our men succeed in subduing the Japs, follow them wherever they go.'

'What if they're captured?' asked the wide-eyed Li-ling.

'They won't be. They'll take their own lives rather than be arrested.'

'What should I do then?'

'If that happens, return to inform us immediately.'

'What if Mr Jones is captured?'

'Captives either reveal the truth to the enemy at the expense of our country or are tortured to death,' explained Mr Shing. 'Here are two capsules of cyanide, one for you, the other for your friend.'

'We don't want to be arrested either.'

'Besides our coffin business, we have become professional coffin bearers, so to speak, for the past several years. Under cover, so far we have been able to gather intelligence and also smuggle munitions, medical supplies and important documents hidden in dead bodies to the cemetery successfully. From there guerrillas in disguise can take them to the stronghold. Should your friend want anything, all my colleagues can speak some English.'

The five men said goodbye to Mr Shing before they set off. The four young ones carried the coffin tied to poles put on their shoulders. Old Pao slipped into the hempen robe and brought up the rear. Having smeared her dark face and hands with mud, Li-ling followed them some distance behind, carrying her cloth pack.

The underground workers and Li-ling took their meals at stalls, occasionally rested by the roadside and slept in small inns while the empty coffin was parked in the streets. She talked to them only when she was certain no one was around. The coffin was left unexamined at the few gendarmerie stations in the two cities along the way. Throughout the nights it was placed outside the inn compounds, which were surrounded by bamboo hedges.

After five days' journey, they found Stephen fast asleep in the bushes. He looked pale and thin. His food, drink and medicine had all run out. Li-ling wept.

Ah Bing, an orderly, woke Stephen up with Li-ling's help.

Stephen slowly opened his eyes, and once they focused, he smiled. Still, he was so weak that he could hardly utter a word.

The orderly removed the dirty bandage from the wounded leg. 'The wound isn't very bad,' he told her. 'The bullet went clear through. But as you can see, it's still infected.'

Ah Bing took Stephen's pulse, and afterwards, cleaned the wound. He applied iodine, replaced the bandage and gave him a pill to take with water.

Li-ling provided a bottle of soda and a tin of fish for Stephen. The food and drink seemed to revive him.

'How long have you been without food and water?' she asked.

'About a day and a half.'

'Poor Steve, I'm sorry we couldn't get back earlier.'

Suddenly she noticed bruises and abrasions on his face, neck and hands, some smeared with blood. 'Steve, what happened?'

'Look there!' He shuddered, pointing to a pile of branches and leaves some distance away. 'In wartime everything is unpredictable. Underneath that pile you'll see something unfortunate!'

All the underground workers went over to remove the branches and leaves. They uncovered the corpse of a lanky old man. Ah Kwok jumped back. On closer inspection, they found bruises and abrasions on the face and hands and deep, bloody finger imprints on the neck.

Someone cried, 'He must have been strangled to death!'

Turning to Stephen, Ah Kwok stammered, 'You... you...' He stopped, perspiration beading on his forehead.

'You what?' asked Old Pao while all the others kept silent awaiting Ah Kwok's answer.

'You murderer!' exploded Ah Kwok. 'You foreign devil! This is the body of my uncle, my late mother's cousin.' Then he turned to the body. 'My poor uncle! When alive you couldn't afford to get married and now you've died a tragic death.'

Chapter Eighteen

'I couldn't keep from killing him,' said Stephen to Ah Kwok.

Ah Kwok darted at Stephen with a raised fist. But before he could strike, Old Pao charged at him and pushed him to the ground, shouting, 'Stop! Don't be crazy!'

Ah Kwok got to his feet, gasping, 'He's no better than the Japs. If I had a gun, I'd shoot him right here and now!'

'Calm down,' said Old Pao. 'Let Mr Jones explain.'

'This man... discovered me earlier this morning while he was collecting firewood,' said Stephen. 'I tried to explain who I was, but he just stood there and stared at me. I gestured for water and food. He came closer. I thought he understood, so I grabbed his arm to help me sit up; but he shouted and tried to run away. We struggled, hitting and scratching each other over and over. I told him to stop shouting, but he continued. So I held on to his neck until I was exhausted. I just wanted to keep him quiet. I never meant to kill him. I'm sorry.' Stephen looked exhausted.

Li-ling shuddered.

'Let's go,' said Ah Kwok. 'Leave this cold-blooded foreigner to die here. He's killed an innocent countryman of ours simply because my uncle was frightened and didn't understand English.'

Li-ling's face turned pale.

'I suggest the coffin be carried back with my uncle in it and that the foreign devil be left here to his own fate,' said Ah Kwok.

No one raised any objections.

While Old Pao prised up the nails from the coffin, Poon Pan and Yung Yan silently put the burial robe on the corpse. After the lid was slid aside, they laid the body in the coffin.

Li-ling wondered how she was going to save Stephen's life.

'Stop, please!' she suddenly shouted, thinking of the Grand old Man in the Moonlight – the Chinese God of Love. 'Suppose that man had been set free, how could you be sure that he wouldn't have spread the news about Mr Jones until the Japanese and their Chinese lackeys heard it?'

'You're talking nonsense,' said Ah Kwok.

'I mean, if the Japanese and their lackeys had heard the news, who knows, they might have ambushed and caught us by now.'

She could see reason struggling with sentiment on the faces of the other underground workers. It was as though the wind was dispersing dark clouds.

'He killed in self-defence, not only for himself, but also for all of us,' argued Poon Pan.

'After all, Britain is our ally,' said Yung Yan.

'Ah Kwok, don't be nervous,' said Old Pao. 'This is war! Now, Poon Pan and Yung Yan, take the body out of the coffin, remove the burial robe from it and let our English friend wear it,' ordered Old Pao.

He then turned to Stephen, saying, 'You must eat and drink very little for the next two or three days so that you may suppress the call of nature as much as possible. If you cough, you must cover your mouth. You'll have to suffer the pain of your wound in silence. Remember, "Lack of patience upsets great plans!"'

'I think that I can endure any suffering,' said Stephen with a laugh.

'We've carried coffins for years as our profession. Some gendarmes in this area are familiar with our faces. So don't worry, Mr Jones.'

Poon Pan and Yung Yan helped Stephen put on the burial robe and get into the coffin.

'Mr Pao,' said Li-ling, 'I've brought a handbag, a cheongsam and a pair of high-heeled shoes with me. Shall I discard them?'

'Of course. If the Japs find them, they'll get suspicious.'

Li-ling took all of her daily necessities and her labourer's dark-gray summer suit out of the canvas bag and placed them in the cloth pack. She then covered the bag containing the handbag, the cheongsam and the high-heeled shoes with mud and branches, with the help of her companions.

'Hey, we can't leave my uncle here to be eaten by birds, animals and insects,' protested Ah Kwok.

'But we can't stay here any longer to dig a grave, or we'll run the risk of being discovered,' said Old Pao. 'I'm sorry.'

'Then I insist we carry my uncle in the same coffin with the foreigner to the cemetery. The main problem is whether the Japs'll open the coffin. If they do, there'll be no difference in risk whether they discover a live Englishman or one plus a dead body.'

Old Pao, whose English was the best, scratched his head before he explained Ah Kwok's suggestion to Stephen.

'I don't mind that,' said Stephen, getting out of the coffin. 'In fact, I'd feel guilty if we left the body of this innocent man unburied.'

'Poon Pan and Yung Yan,' said Old Pao, 'take off Mr Jones's burial robe and put it back on the dead body before you lay it in the coffin.'

Old Pao then turned to Stephen. 'You'll have to lie side by side with the body. The odour will be difficult, but it'll only be for two or three days.'

'Never mind. I'll endure it,' said Stephen with a grin, stepping into the coffin.

Old Pao turned to Ah Kwok. 'After we arrive at the cemetery you can bury your uncle there.' He then took off the mourner's robe and handed it to Ah Kwok.

Eyes veiled with tears, Ah Kwok nodded.

'Miss Lam,' Old Pao told Li-ling, 'upon reaching the cemetery, our English friend will get out of the coffin. The manager and the janitor are our men and will offer help. Then Ah Bing alone will lead both of you for a few hours through some small villages to the mountainous district. Once there you'll climb and walk through the brush for three days or so before reaching the Guerrilla Stronghold.'

'We heartily thank all of you, Mr Pao,' said Li-ling.

She turned to Stephen, who was now lying beside the dead body, and said, 'Poor Steve, you have already suffered enough. Now you'll go through more fire and water than human patience can withstand.'

Stephen gazed into her eyes with a smile.

Old Pao hammered a few nails into the edges of the coffin lid to seal it.

Four underground workers carried the coffin with Ah Kwok following as a mourner. When no one was around, the underground workers passed water, food and pills to Stephen through the hole.

For two days of this trip, the coffin and its bearers were ignored at each gendarmerie station they passed. The first night the coffin remained in the street, quite close to the inn. Li-ling got up twice and carefully checked from afar to make sure her dear one was all right. She did not go near the coffin to cheer him up so as not to arouse suspicion.

On the second night, they stayed in an inn in a big town. The proprietor would not permit the coffin to be placed too close to the inn compound. So it had to be placed on a piece of muddy ground some two hundred yards away.

★

Li-ling got up before dawn to cheer Stephen up in the coffin. As she was talking to him, two teenage boys approached on tiptoe. They were each dressed in unbuttoned Chinese jackets, one wearing a cap perched over his right eyebrow and the other with his cap turned backwards.

Step by step, they drew nearer and nearer. She did not notice them until they were about twenty feet away. She abruptly stopped talking to Stephen in mid-sentence.

The two boys started to walk toward her quickly. She clenched her jaw.

'Hello, pretty, talking to a ghost, eh?' said the older boy with a cunning smile, stretching his hand to tweak Li-ling's chin.

'Yes,' said Li-ling, knowing it would be useless to deny it.

'Ha, ha! Could the ghost hear what you said?' asked the younger one.

'Why not?'

'Who are you speaking to?' asked the older boy.

'The ghost of my late husband.'

'What were you talking about? About love? With a dead body? Why not make love with a live man like me?' The older boy winked at his younger friend.

'I prayed to him for health and peace for our family,' said Li-ling, striving to look calm despite her fear.

The older boy hit the coffin with his fist. 'Money,' he shouted.

Li-ling lost no time in handing a pile of banknotes to him.

Upon glancing at it, he threw it onto the coffin and said, 'This is an insult.' He spat onto the ground. 'With your hundreds of these devalued dollars we could only take a few meals in a low-class restaurant. Give us your jewels!'

'I'm a poor farm labourer,' said Li-ling. 'How could I have jewels?'

The older boy winked at his companion, who went behind Li-ling and held her arms.

'What do you want?' asked Li-ling.

'You must take off your clothes to prove that,' the taller boy said with a grin as he started to unbutton her clothes.

She screamed and pulled back, then all of a sudden a flurry of strange, inhuman shrieks were emitted from the coffin. The white-faced boys let Li-ling loose, and stared at each other wide-eyed before they bolted without looking back, leaving the pile of money on the coffin.

'The two rascals are gone,' said Li-ling at last. 'Steve, they thought you were an angry ghost and might snap their souls from their bodies. You were very smart indeed.'

'Li-ling, when you screamed, I thought they'd rape you. I could hardly control myself. I made strange noises, taking the chance that these country people were superstitious.'

They both laughed.

Chapter Nineteen

Shortly after noon on the third day of transporting the loaded coffin, the underground workers stopped at the last gendarmerie station with Li-ling some distance behind. The two gendarmes, one fat and the other thin, searched the coffin bearers.

Just as they were ready to set off, the thin gendarme pointed at the coffin and commanded in Japanese, 'Open it for examination!'

Understanding what he meant, the bearers stopped. Li-ling knew they must be apprehensive, but they did not show it.

Old Pao grabbed his claw hammer and turned to his men. 'Stand back, all of you. You know how infectious this "cholera" is.'

His co-workers stood back and watched in silence with their brows drawn together.

Old Pao put a cloth to his nose and mouth with one hand and began to slowly prise the nails from the coffin with the other.

The fat gendarme spoke. 'Let them go, we've seen enough.'

'Don't trust them,' said the thin one, standing near the coffin. 'You know how cunning these Chinese are. They could be fooling us.'

'Well, then,' said the fat gendarme, 'you go ahead and check the coffin yourself. I'm going to stand back here with these men.'

Old Pao continued to prise up the coffin nails. A few minutes later he slid aside the coffin lid. A great smell shot into the air.

The skinny gendarme turned his face and began to cough. 'Wait here,' he said. He then quickly walked back to the station. 'Cholera?' he mumbled.

Old Pao stood back away from the coffin, still covering his nose and mouth with the cloth.

The thin gendarme came out with an iron rod. Covering his nose and mouth with his handkerchief, he took a quick look into the coffin before he turned his face away from the coffin. Then he beat the corpse with the rod and then poked it around the inside perimeter of the coffin rapidly with an extended arm.

As long as Li-ling saw this from a distance, she felt her soul depart from her body. She worried about Stephen. Could he be seriously hurt?

After finishing, the thin gendarme gasped to Old Pao, 'All you Chinese *bagayarou*, go!'

After Old Pao closed the lid and secured it, he spoke to the gendarme in Japanese. 'You'd better discard that rod.'

'Get out of here,' shouted the gendarme, throwing the rod at them.

When Li-ling came to the station later, the thin gendarme searched her cloth pack and her body. She was glad that Mr Shing had taken her pistol before she left his coffin shop and was relieved when the Japanese failed to detect her valuables hidden in her winter clothes.

Li-ling did not join the underground until they were far away from the station.

'Steve, did you get hurt?' she asked once she had caught up.

'No. When I heard the nails being prised off the lid, I pulled the robe over me and edged my way under the body as much as I could. Luckily it protected me except for two strikes through the robe.' Stephen laughed through his clenched teeth.

'You outsmarted the Japanese!'

★

In the mid-afternoon when the party arrived at the cemetery, all the visitors had gone. The manager, the janitor and his wife greeted them warmly.

After Old Pao prised the nails off the lid of the coffin with the hammer, the hosts helped Stephen get out and showed him to the restroom. Later, the janitor's wife fetched a box of medical supplies and Ah Bing ministered to Stephen's wounds and gave him an antibiotic shot. Though he looked better, he was nevertheless stiff after lying in the coffin for so many days. Ah Bing massaged Stephen's back, then his limbs, for half an hour.

Before long, they held a quiet burial ceremony for Ah Kwok's uncle.

'Li-ling,' sighed Stephen after the ceremony, 'while I was "dead" in the coffin, I had brought nothing with me – no power, no position, no wealth. It is the same with a dictator, a warlord, a king or a billionaire at his death.'

'Here's a pistol for you,' said old Pao to Li-ling. 'Mr Shing ordered me to get this from the cemetery manager in exchange for the one he took from you.'

'Yes, I remember,' said Li-ling. 'But I don't want it.'

'But you need it for your safety beyond here. Although there are no gendarmes to search you in that no man's land, wild animals may attack you.'

Li-ling took the pistol.

Ah Kwok approached Stephen and said, 'Thank you for allowing my uncle's body to lie with you in the coffin.' They shook hands.

While Ah Bing stayed behind, all the other underground workers said goodbye to Li-ling and Stephen, who thanked them heartily.

Stephen looked like a wild man with his weedy beard and his smelly body. He needed a shave and a bath very badly. Water had to be carried from a distant stream, and only one bucket of water remained with a few bottles of boiled water for drinking. Therefore he was given the privilege of using the only bucket of water available. By the time he finished his bath and shave, night was upon them.

Ah Bing, Li-ling and Stephen continued their journey.

Part Three

Chapter One

As Stephen could not keep up with them, Li-ling and Ah Bing slowed their pace. For hours they passed several small villages under cover of darkness before they reached the mountainous district. Now they sometimes faced steep elevations, which they climbed with difficulty. When the terrain flattened out, they walked through thick brush. Stephen needed his companions' help especially when they ascended and had to rest on occasion. The janitor's wife had given them rice cakes and water for their meals. At night they slept under the trees, covered with blankets provided by the manager.

The next morning while Ah Bing was still fast asleep, Li-ling and Stephen woke up to find two men pointing pistols at them. They got up slowly and raised their hands with eyes wide open. Must be robbers, Li-ling thought.

The men then woke Ah Bing.

Wiping his bleary eyes with the back of his hand, he called out, 'Blockheads.'

Li-ling shuddered, worrying that they might shoot. Instead, they left with grins on their faces.

'"Blockheads" is the latest password; those two men are sentinels for the guerrillas,' explained Ah Bing in English.

Li-ling and Stephen burst into laughter.

Late in the afternoon after a strenuous walk, they fell asleep for some time until Stephen awoke. He was alarmed to see the hood of a cobra emerge from behind Li-ling's head. He slowly moved his hand toward the covered pistol lying by her side and shot at the snake twice before killing it. After that incident, the group decided to take turns standing guard any time they rested.

The third night, during Ah Bing's turn on duty, he heard a noise on the hillside above. He fired a number of shots in that direction until they heard a tiger roar and run away.

The fourth morning they arrived at their destination – the Guerrilla Headquarters of Kwangtung Province. To Li-ling and Stephen, it was a new atmosphere, a new sky, a new land, a new people – a new life!

★

The guerrillas immediately took Stephen to a clinic housed in a hut, where his wound was dressed and the infection looked after. Li-ling was freed from anxiety when told that gangrene had not set in and that Stephen's recovery looked promising.

The headquarters, situated in a stronghold, covered a wide area of mountains, valleys and woods. Many canvas tents, pitched here and there, stood along with some wood huts among the trees. These structures, as well as the gun emplacements, the parks for military supplies and the magazines were all camouflaged with leaves and branches. Several man-made caves and underground tunnels were dotted about the area. The guerrillas hid in these during occasional aerial bombing and artillery shelling by the Japanese.

Some of the guerrillas wore ragged uniforms; others shabby clothes. The Chinese Air Force and the US 14th Corps, recently reorganised from General Chennault's Flying Tigers Squadron, stationed in Free China, some-times airdropped buckets of water, food, ordnance, munitions, medicine, canvas, tools and even cigarettes into the stronghold. There were few doctors, nurses and orderlies. Amid thousands of men there were only nineteen women – all nurses.

The guerrillas' lives were hard, and they were constantly under rigid training, yet their morale was high. Spirits soared after the outbreak of the Pacific War, with the United States and Great Britain fighting side by side with China against their common enemy. Patriotic people and groups of soldiers who deserted the puppet regime of Wang Ching-wei joined them from time to time.

Although the Sino-Japanese War was in full swing in other parts of China and Burma, there seemed to be a lull in this area except for occasional skirmishes outside the periphery of the stronghold. Only at the very outset of the Pacific War were Chinese regular troops and guerrillas ordered to ease Japanese pressures on Hong Kong by launching a few surprise attacks at strategic points in the south of Kwangtung.

After a few days' rest in the stronghold, Ah Bing said goodbye to Li-ling and Stephen. They thanked him heartily and Li-ling cried with gratitude.

Three weeks after their arrival at the guerrilla stronghold, Stephen could walk normally. Then he was assigned to the artillery unit to give further training to the gunners. In addition, he also served in the engineering corps as a consultant. Li-ling had been working as an assistant nurse since her arrival.

Although Great Britain and the United States were China's allies, right from their arrival at the stronghold, Li-ling noticed that some of the guerrillas stared at her and Stephen.

'Miss So,' asked one man in Chinese with a grin, 'how could a chicken marry a duck?' Li-ling kept quiet. The man walked away with his companions, who burst into laughter.

'What did he say to you?' asked Stephen. 'I don't understand Chinese.'

Li-ling shrugged her shoulders. 'Oh, nothing,' she said. 'Forget about it.'

Stephen's nostrils flared, and he kicked a rock. 'Tell me the truth,' he said, 'or I'll get him to tell.'

'All right,' she said. Then she reluctantly told Stephen what the man had said.

Stephen's eyes looked as if they would pop out of their sockets. He turned, ran after the men and caught them up. He grabbed the speaker by the shoulder from behind and spun him around so hard that the man fell to the ground. He jumped at him but suddenly halted and turned around. He went back to Li-ling.

'I'd have given him a good beating but suddenly—'

'You remembered the saying about grave matters being taken as trifles and trifles as nothing,' interrupted Li-ling.

Stephen gave a slight smile.

At another time, a guerrilla approached Li-ling and said, 'You seem to have a taste for game more than poultry.' Then he walked away.

Stephen wanted her to translate the remark for him. After he heard it, he only shook his head.

However, most of the guerrillas gave little thought to the mixed relationship.

After work and on their off-duty days, Li-ling and Stephen often joined them in recreational activities, such as playing Chinese chess or bouncing a shuttlecock off the foot. They would talk, sing, laugh and joke with the guerrillas. Gradually they even gained the favour of many of those who had been prejudiced against them.

When Li-ling and Stephen were alone, they listened to the singing orioles and the humming of the cicadas; they watched the activities of the ants and the nesting of the birds. In summer, they admired the wild tutcheria trees with their large glossy leaves and white flowers. In winter, they smelled the sweet fragrance of the blossoming flowers of the wild litsea trees. In the evenings, they rejoiced in looking at the changing colours of the clouds painted by the rays of the setting sun. At night, they enjoyed gazing at the moon and the twinkling stars. They gave thanks for every moment they spent together.

Over the passage of time Stephen's colour gradually returned, and his body became a mass of rippling muscles again.

'Steve,' she said as they sat alone on a rock one moonlit night a few months later, 'this place is much smaller than Hong Kong, and yet we are free.' She caressed his cheek with her hand and placed a feather-light kiss on his lips.

'Li-ling,' he said, still wearing the same POW's clothing which he had worn in Hong Kong, 'here there's no worry about money, taxes, inflation, social status, jobs, investments, and whatnot. I think I'm beginning to understand what the Chinese are after when they seek "peace of mind".' He put his arms around her waist and pulled her against him. She rested her head on his shoulder.

A little later she pointed to the labourer's dark-gray summer suit that she wore. 'Here women don't worry about dresses, hairstyles, and make-up.'

'Here we are like brothers and sisters in a big family, aiming with confidence at only one single purpose, the defeat of the Japanese. This is the first time I've ever experienced real happiness.' He stroked her dark hair. 'I wish this could go on for ever.'

They kissed and tugged at each other playfully until they tumbled to the ground where they held on to each other, laughing joyfully.

Chapter Two

A little more than a year and a half after Li-ling and Stephen arrived at the stronghold, General Ting, Commander of the Kwangtung guerrillas, became ill. Li-ling cared for him during the morning shift in the hut which served as both his office and bedroom for that time. One day just before noon, after the general had taken some medication, a guerrilla entered the hut, saluted, and delivered a report. The general sat up and read it. Then he looked at the calendar on his desk, which indicated 1st May, 1944. A photo of Generalissimo Chiang Kai-shek, Head of State of China and that of Mao Tse-tung, Chairman of the Communist Party were beside it.

After dismissing the guerrilla, the general sighed.

'General Ting, what is wrong?' asked Li-ling.

He handed her the report. 'It's a long story, but it's all here on this intelligence report regarding Japanese munitions. You may read it.'

> *Report 301*
> *26/04/44*
> *0100 hours*
> *K. T. 175*

Reliable: Japanese convoy 20 military trucks (not 15 as stated in 25/04/44 Report 300) of munitions will travel from Chingyeung on Peng Min-yuen Road, and pass through

Peng Village noon 02/05/44 (same date and time as Report 300) to Taiping.

'As you know,' said the general, 'eight months ago, twelve hundred soldiers defected from the Wang Ching-wei Regime and joined us. We expended about a quarter of our ammunition during the three-day battle to rout the Japanese troops, who pursued the defectors. Since then, the bulk of our airdrops have been food instead of munitions. Two months ago, two large magazines of ours were drenched during a storm and about two thirds of our ammunition was destroyed. Therefore, we are running very low though the deserters have brought some Japanese arms and ammo with them. It goes without saying that the Japanese must have learned about our plight through intelligence.'

'Where is Peng Village?' asked Li-ling.

'It's twenty-five small wooden houses situated on a large plateau.' General Ting showed her a map. 'Rectangular in shape, it's located at the mid-level of one mountain among a range of many, some twenty miles east of this stronghold. Normally, it takes ten hours to walk from here to the village through the brush of the high country. Above the plateau is another, about one twentieth its size and square in shape, called Peng Family Tombs, where General Peng Min-yuen of the Southern Sung dynasty in the twelfth century was secretly buried with eleven other members of his family.'

The general coughed several times; Li-ling poured him a cup of warm water.

'Was General Peng a close associate of the historical hero, General Yo Fei, who won many victories over the Chin invaders from the north?' queried Li-ling.

'Yes. After General Yo Fei was executed on a trumped-up charge, General Peng fled here with his family, the present Kwangtung Province, then a far-off desert district. They settled secretly on the lower plateau for scores of years to avoid persecution. As time went by, General Peng and his family passed away one by one and were buried on the upper plateau. Later their descendants moved elsewhere.'

'General Ting, when was this historical secret discovered?'

'A few years after the Republic of China was established in 1911,' he said. 'In order to pay a high tribute to this patriotic hero, the Kwangtung Government repaired the tombs on the upper plateau, constructed a small temple named after him in the village on the lower plateau and erected a flight of about five hundred stone steps, leading from the village to the tombs.' The general took a few sips of water before he went on. 'The Kwangtung Government also built the two-lane Peng Min-yuen Road from the city of Chingyeung winding north-westward up the range of mountains. It passes through Peng Village and then southwest down the range to end at the city of Taiping, all along the natural contours. As a result, a score of families settled in Peng Village to sell souvenirs to tourists who visited the temple and tombs until the Japanese invaded Kwangtung in 1938.'

'General Ting, why don't the Japanese use the much shorter old road built from Chingyeung to Taiping which is entirely on level land?'

'Because it has been bombed three times during the past two months and is severely damaged,' gasped the general, pointing to the map. 'Until two months ago the Japanese sent only a couple of truckloads of ordnance and ammunition every two months on the old road. But this time they are using the long-distanced, roundabout Peng Min-yuen Road to transport an unheard-of number of twenty truckloads!'

'Why so many?'

She handed another cup of water to the general, who drank it before continuing.

'Undoubtedly the Japanese will soon launch a major attack. They can assemble a force of as many as five thousand men from the vicinity in a few days. Against the Japanese with their abundant supplies of ammunition plus their superiority in weapons, our four thousand men with our shortage of ammunition and inferior arms couldn't hold out long despite our geographical advantages. Eventually we'd be entirely annihilated.'

'What will you do, General Ting?'

'We've laid out two plans. Under Plan A, we'd send thirty men by cover of night to Peng Family Tombs. They'd hide there until tomorrow noon, when they'd go down the stone steps and make a surprise on the Japanese convoy passing the village. After blowing up all the trucks with munitions, our men would make a hasty retreat. Even if we suffered casualties, the attack would be worth while – at least the Japanese wouldn't be able to make a major drive against us until they could again replenish a great deal of their munitions.'

'Why only thirty men?' asked Li-ling.

'On the upper plateau behind each of the twelve tombs stands a big old tree. Only two or three men can hide behind each tree.'

'General Ting, if you blow up the twenty truckloads of munitions passing the village, wouldn't you also kill all the villagers and burn down all the houses?'

'Of course. When we found out we couldn't warn the villagers to leave in advance, we gave up Plan A. Now we have been concentrating on Plan B to seize the munitions. As long as we're in possession of a large amount of arms and ammunition, it'll be much more difficult for the Japanese to make a major assault on us.'

'Isn't it much more difficult to seize munitions than to destroy them?' she asked.

'Certainly. Under Plan B, we'd send the same number of men to hide in Peng Family Tombs. But we're concerned about all that could go wrong with this second plan.'

Li-ling frowned as General Ting continued, extending his index finger, 'First, when the convoy passes by the village, we must induce as many Japanese soldiers as possible to get away from the trucks. Second, we must ambush them elsewhere. Third, we must kill any of the Japanese soldiers left with the trucks so that none of them are able to blow up the munitions before we can seize them.

'Fourth, a Japanese patrol car from Chingyeung or Taiping passes through the village eight or nine times a day at irregular intervals. We must block their approach to the village before we make our escape with the captured goods.

'Fifth, Japanese sentinels are posted along the edges of the south side of the mountains. As soon as they detect anything suspicious, they'll alert the Japanese garrisons in Taiping, who're able to get to the village within three hours by car. Before they arrive, we must be able to get away safely with hundreds of boxes of guns and ammo.'

'Sounds complicated. Is it?' asked Li-ling.

The general's features darkened. 'Since we received the first intelligence report the night before last, we've solved the third, fourth and fifth problems, but we haven't been able to find answers to the first and second ones – to induce as many Japanese as possible away from the trucks and ambush them.'

'Then should we give up Plan B as well?'

'This afternoon,' he wheezed, 'we'll call an emergency meeting to make the final decision.' Then the general coughed.

Li-ling helped him sit up and patted him on the back before he continued, 'Miss So, all of this is confidential, but you may consult Lieutenant Jones during your lunch hour to see if he can solve the first two problems. Thus is the Chinese saying: "It is beneficial to gather opinions from different sources." As a foreigner, he may have some unique suggestions. You can show him the map and then report back to me at 1400 hours today, please.'

★

Not far away from General Ting's hut, there was a kitchen, one of two score in the stronghold. At noon smoke rose from the chimney and the aroma of inviting food drifted out of the windows to the two lines of guerrillas waiting to be served.

'How's General Ting?' asked Stephen as he and Li-ling moved through the line.

'He's still ill, but he'll recover soon,' she said. 'He wants me to talk to you about something.'

They each got a bowl of yams and some vegetables, then went to a tree far away from the crowd.

Throughout lunch in the shade of the tree, Li-ling whispered to Stephen the details of General Ting's two military plans and pointed out the key spots on the map. At last, she asked him whether he could make any suggestions about Plan B.

After giving the matter some thought, Stephen shook his head. 'No. I'm afraid not.'

Li-ling looked at her watch. 'I must report to General Ting at 2 p.m. Are you sure?'

'Yes, I'm sure. Li-ling, I love you. I love you very much, I love you for ever! Goodbye.'

Knitting her brows, she said, 'Steve, what's the matter with you? I love you, too. See you later.'

As she walked away, she seemed to hear Steve sobbing. But when she turned around, she saw only his back as he was leaving in the opposite direction. No reason why he should weep, she thought.

*

Li-ling could only lunch and sup with Stephen occasionally, but was able to see him every evening. When she went to see him at his tent that night, his tent-mates informed her that he was attending a meeting at the office of the engineering corps. She returned to her hut and waited for him until 10 p.m. when the oil lamp in the hut had to be turned out. She had a difficult time falling asleep.

It must be urgent, as the engineering corps has rarely had meetings run so late, she thought. Finally, sleep came.

*

At about 10.45 a.m. the following day an open-top patrol car with four Japanese soldiers, which had headed northwest-ward up Peng Min-yuen Road, stopped at the bottom of the flight of the stone steps in Peng Village. In the hot sunlight, the wind was quiet, the white clouds sleepy and the leaves idle. Even the birds moved their wings slowly in flight.

There a woman was hanging out clothes on an open ground; a man was scattering corn around for the chickens in front of his hut; two boys were watering a paddy field, two girls were fertilising a vegetable garden and a few children were playing 'hide-and-seek' near the temple. One of the soldiers scanned the mountains nearby with binoculars. At 11 a.m. the car left the village and proceeded southwestward down the road.

Fifteen minutes later, a white man with light-brown hair, dressed in a dirty khaki shirt and trousers and holding a pistol, suddenly appeared at the doorway of the house nearest to the junction of the road and the bottom of the stone steps. The man was Stephen Jones!

The white-haired couple in the house raised their hands immediately. Since the Japanese had taken the south of Kwangtung Province in 1938, not a single white man had ever been seen in this occupied area.

The house consisted of a medium-sized room with a double bed and some wooden furniture, a small kitchen on the left and a small bathroom on the right beyond. A hedge of bamboo surrounded the backyard.

Stephen wavered a little as he walked into the room. 'If you… cooperate, you need not be afraid,' he said.

The couple lowered their hands.

'What do you want?' asked the old man in English.

'We parachuted out and landed too far from the guerrilla stronghold. We've gone thirsty and hungry for one day. We need water and food.'

The old woman went to the kitchen to fetch him a bowl of lukewarm water. Stephen emptied it with one gulp and asked for two more bowls.

'Have you got buckets?' asked Stephen.

'Yes,' said the man. 'Please come to the kitchen.'

'We want at least ten buckets of boiled water and two of cooked rice. In a few hours many of my fellow airmen are coming to fetch them.'

'But we only have five,' said the man, pointing to three buckets full of water and two empty ones in a corner. 'We have built a very small pool for storing rain on the mountainside, quite a distance from here.'

'Then we'll take four buckets of boiled water and one of cooked rice for the time being.'

The man used an axe to cut firewood into narrow strips in the backyard. Then the woman boiled water and cooked rice in the kitchen.

'How is it that you speak English?' asked Stephen.

'My wife and I can speak some Japanese, too. For twenty years we earned our living by selling souvenirs to English-speaking and some Japanese tourists until war broke out here about five and a half years ago.'

As soon as the woman cooked the rice and added soy sauce, Stephen sat on a chair and devoured two bowls. Afterwards, no longer did he falter when he walked back to the bedroom. He put a US twenty-dollar bill on the table. He then lit a 'Lucky Strike' cigarette, and placed the pack on top of the money.

A few minutes past noon, the woman had boiled eight pots of water and filled one of the two empty buckets to the rim. She had also cooked two pots of rice and put all of it into the other one.

The roar of motor vehicles suddenly sounded as they came up the road from the southeast.

When the man looked out the windows with a small telescope, his face turned pale. 'How come so many Japanese trucks?' he shouted. Then he told Stephen, 'You must leave right away!'

After Stephen took a look with the telescope, he turned a deaf ear to the man.

The woman came out of the kitchen and said, 'One bucket almost full of boiled water and one partly filled with cooked rice are ready. Mr American, please, go away before it is too late.'

'I must hide here until I get all the water and rice we need.'

'No! If the Japanese find you here, they will chop off our heads,' cried the man, 'unless we tip them off beforehand.'

Stephen again ignored them. They turned red.

Looking through the windows one by one with the telescope, they saw a long row of trucks approaching, each with two soldiers seated in the front, an open-top car with five soldiers taking the lead and another open-top car with the same number of soldiers bringing up the rear. As the rumbling grew louder, the couple looked more and more apprehensive.

A few minutes later, when the lead car was about fifty yards from the house, Stephen ran to the kitchen. He took the bucket of boiled water and the one of cooked rice, and headed for the door.

'Mr American, you crazy!' said the man.

Finally, Stephen raced out the door.

'He should have left earlier,' said the woman.

'Never mind that,' said the man. 'Now we should be concerned about how to clear ourselves of suspicion.'

Stephen rushed across the road toward the stone steps. The soldier driving and the officer seated beside him in the vanguard car took a quick look at each other with their eyes wide open before the officer shouted 'Halt!' in Japanese, drawing his pistol.

Chapter Three

No sooner had the officer fired and the bullet whizzed by the white man's head with light-brown hair than Stephen abruptly dropped the two buckets and spilled the contents before he fled. He imagined himself as a male spider who had just completed his mission and was now fleeing from the deadly grasp of the black widow. However, the officer did not fire a second shot.

'Lieutenant Ono,' said the driver, 'you could've killed him. Now he's gotten away, probably in the direction of the guerrilla base. He's definitely an American airman.'

The officer grinned. 'That's the reason I want to keep him alive,' he said. 'Do you think I showed mercy to the enemy?'

The driver said nothing.

By this time Stephen had reached the steps. Now he ran up them as fast as he could. As soon as the lead car pulled up in front of the house, all the occupants jumped out and the old man emerged.

'Japanese big brothers,' he said in their language, 'please understand I am not at all anti-Japanese. Let me—'

'Why did an American come out of your house?' interjected Lieutenant Ono in a shrill voice, grabbing the trembling man by the collar. 'Did you hide him?'

'No! No!' said the old villager, shaking his head vigorously. 'He entered my house with a pistol about an hour ago.'

'Why did he stay so long? Tell me everything or you will be beheaded.' The lieutenant released his hold of the man's collar.

He gave an account, gesturing wildly.

'Are you sure the American asked for ten buckets of water and two of rice?' asked the officer. 'How could he carry away so many buckets at one time?'

'He said that many of his fellows were coming down to fetch them.'

The man then handed the Japanese officer the pack of cigarettes and the twenty-dollar bill left by the 'American'. After slipping them into his pocket, the officer let him go. The lieutenant blew a whistle and instantly all the soldiers left their vehicles and assembled in front of him.

'We've just seen a white man running away from us with buckets of water and rice taken from the old man,' said the lieutenant. 'There're probably a number of American airmen who've bailed out and are now up there in the mountains.' He pointed to Peng Family Tombs above. 'I want to catch them alive before they join the guerrillas. They're hungry and thirsty and surely know we outnumber them. They'll likely surrender to save their lives. As you all know, the Wang Ching-wei Government has recently announced a reward of one hundred taels of gold for capturing an American alive and fifty taels for a dead one. We can look forward to sharing hundreds of taels among us—'

He was interrupted by a loud cheer.

'Get going,' ordered the lieutenant. 'Six drivers are to stay behind and take care of the trucks.'

Forty-odd soldiers hastily rushed to the steps, carrying rifles and four light machine-guns. For a few minutes they climbed the steps in pairs with the lieutenant bringing up the rear.

'Spread out?' asked one of the gasping soldiers, who had just reached Peng Family Tombs.

'Who cares? We're exhausted,' said another.

'Why are we worried about a few hungry and thirsty American dandies?' asked a third soldier, triggering laughter on the part of his fellows.

'Spread out, you damned fools!' shouted Lieutenant Ono, the last man to step onto the tomb ground. 'Are your heads all muddled with the thought of gold?'

Before the soldiers could obey his orders, more than twenty guerrillas and Stephen suddenly burst into view from behind the big trunks and fired at the Japanese soldiers. Stephen and Lieutenant Fan each carried a light machine-gun; the rest, rifles. Within two minutes, many of the Japanese soldiers lay in pools of blood, most of them dead, others wounded. Lieutenant Ono and a few soldiers escaped death and quickly retreated.

As they descended, guerrillas emerged from piles of branches and leaves bordering the steps and fired at them. These Japanese were soon dispatched. The one-sided battle lasted only a few minutes.

In the meantime, as the four Japanese soldiers, who had left the village in a patrol car earlier, were spiralling down the mountains, they heard the gunfire. They immediately turned around and headed back at full speed.

The six Japanese drivers left behind to guard the trucks heard the shots, but did not see the fighting. Concerned, they all gathered at the bottom of the stone steps and waited for the return of their comrades. Soon they saw four of their fellow soldiers rushing down the steps.

The one in front shouted jubilantly: 'Long live Emperor Hirohito! We've killed a few and captured many Americans.'

'Long live Emperor Hirohito!' responded the six drivers joyfully.

These four 'Japanese' soldiers fired at the six drivers, killing them all.

Of the four guerrillas wearing Japanese uniforms in disguise, three said to their leader who had shouted to the Japanese, 'Bravo! Corporal Chau!' They gave him a 'V' sign which he answered with a wide smile. They hoisted him above their shoulders and walked around the trucks, happily singing 'The March of the Guerrillas'. They were followed by a handful of excited teenage boys who had dared to come out of their houses once the fighting was over.

'Look!' screamed Corporal Chau suddenly. 'A Japanese patrol car's coming!' He pointed to the southeast. He jumped to the ground as his comrades stared. He gave them orders.

'Stay here and let me handle the situation alone.' Then he dashed past the long line of trucks of the convoy parked on the sloping road and got into the last one.

He could not start the engine because there was no key inserted in the ignition, so he released the handbrake and let the truck roll down the sloping road, pushing the rearguard car along with it. As the two vehicles moved, they gained momentum. Corporal Chau was about to jump out of the truck when the pair of vehicles began to swerve. Instead he stayed in to steer.

Before the patrol car in which the Japanese rode could dodge the collision, the truck and the rearguard car collided with it, triggering a series of loud explosions. The three vehicles, engulfed in flames, rolled off the mountainside and careened scores of yards into the jagged rocks below.

As soon as they witnessed the heroic death of Corporal Chau, the three guerrillas disguised as Japanese soldiers like him buried their faces in their hands.

The day brought death to three guerrillas and injury to seven. Forty-six Japanese soldiers were killed and four seriously wounded. Two guerrilla orderlies treated all the wounded.

While a few of the guerrillas were collecting uniforms, weapons and ammunition from the dead Japanese soldiers, the rest unloaded the heavy boxes of munitions from the trucks with the help of some of the villagers, including the old man who had given rice and water to Stephen.

After the guerrillas emptied the first four trucks, they drove the vehicles southwestward down the road on a mission of blocking the traffic. Then they emptied another four trucks, and they too drove the vehicles, but to the southeast, downward on a similar mission.

By 1 p.m. the returning Japanese patrol car, which had heard the gunfire, was forced to halt before a roadblock of three badly damaged trucks, some ten miles from the village. The four soldiers found it impossible to remove the obstacle.

At about 2 p.m. almost all the unloading had been finished when one guerrilla said to another, 'Lieutenant Fan, I doubt if we'll be able to carry these hundreds of heavy munition boxes home. Besides, the Japanese in Taiping will get here in an hour; they must have been alerted by the sentinels who had detected the gunfire two hours ago.'

'Don't worry.' Lieutenant Fan smiled. Suddenly they heard voices from the west shout, 'We're coming!'

About two hundred guerrillas had been proceeding through the thick brush toward the village with Captain Hon in the lead. These reinforcements had been sent to carry home the boxes.

During the previous night they had started from the stronghold later than the thirty guerrillas who had been assigned to take a direct role in the combat. They stopped at a place about two hours' walk from the village on a mountain where tall trees offered covering. They hid there until they heard the first gunfire at noon. They did not leave the shelter of the trees earlier, so as not to be observed in broad daylight by Japanese sentinels stationed on the edges of the south side of the mountains.

These guerrilla reserves including a few doctors and orderlies brought stretchers and medical supplies in addition to ropes, big bamboo baskets and thick branches, which would be used to carry the munition boxes. Within twenty minutes they had tied hundreds of these securely into the baskets.

Captain Hon, standing alongside with Lieutenant Jones and Lieutenant Fan, ordered all the guerrillas to face the southeast where the explosion had spread the remains of Corporal Chau down the mountainside, and to stand at attention for three minutes to pay their farewell respects to the young hero. Many of them wept.

Now they travelled back from Peng Village, singing the national anthem. Stephen, carried on stout shoulders, and the wounded guerrillas, lying on stretchers, were at the head of the column. The dead bodies of the guerrillas, except that of Corporal Chau and the injured Japanese soldiers, all lying on stretchers, were in the rear. Two village boys in their late teens volunteered to join the guerrillas.

Meanwhile, ten men were assigned to blow up the empty trucks left in the village. Upon completion, they hurried to catch up with their comrades.

Chapter Four

The next morning it was another nurse's turn to tend to General Ting. The whole day long Li-ling was on duty, nursing the sick and the wounded as usual; she had no chance to hear or think any more about the Japanese convoy.

After supper that day, Li-ling was eager to see Stephen. She went to his tent but was told that he was attending another meeting at the office of the engineering corps.

'Again?' asked Li-ling. 'Did he sleep here last night?'

'No,' answered one of Stephen's tent-mates, but then a chorus of 'Yes' echoed throughout the tent.

She took a ten-minute walk to the hut which housed the office of the engineers. Finding it completely dark, she shook her head, and went to see General Ting.

When Li-ling came into his hut, General Ting was talking with an officer and a nurse, all seated. After Li-ling exchanged greetings with them, she asked: 'General Ting, how are you today?'

'I feel much better. Thank you and Mrs Sung for nursing me and Colonel Long for accompanying me.' The general took a look at all of them, who responded with smiles.

'Don't mention it,' said Li-ling. 'General Ting, may I ask you a question?'

'Go ahead.'

'Did you order Lieutenant Jones to act as a decoy for the Japanese?'

'Oh, I see that you're as clever as he,' commented the general, 'though you thought of it one day later.'

'Miss So, we didn't order or even request Lieutenant Jones to do anything,' interjected Colonel Long.

'Let her read the letter,' said the general. The colonel took a letter from the drawer and handed it to Li-ling, who opened it with a pair of scissors.

'Miss So, be seated and read,' said the colonel.

1st May, 1944

My dearest Li-ling,

By the time you read this letter tomorrow, we'll have either succeeded or failed in our mission. God only knows. If I am killed and the mission succeeds, my death will be worth while. But, please, Li-ling, I want you to know what's been on my mind if I never see you again.

After you told me about the Japanese convoy of munitions, I hit upon a plan. Some time after we parted, I went to see General Ting while he was meeting with Colonel Long and three other officers directly involved in the planned operation. To my surprise, I learned that since the night before last they had been making preparations for the same kind of plan as mine in which I'd act as a decoy to lure the enemy into an ambush. They designated it 'Operation Rice Bowl'. They needed a decoy and they thought I would be the best choice. But why General Ting didn't assign me the task until I volunteered, I don't know.

They then guided me through the steps necessary for my part in the operation.

I wrote this letter after the meeting adjourned at 5 p.m. I asked the general to hand it to you the following day.

Since many Chinese, especially you, my dearest Li-ling, have risked their lives to save mine, why shouldn't I risk my life to save yours and the lives of the whole contingent of guerrillas in return?

I have no desire to become a hero, but since I've not had the chance to show my love for you the way you've expressed yours for me, this may be the only opportunity.

Very likely I'll be killed tomorrow. But if you know that I am doing this because of my undying love for you, you shouldn't grieve too much. The universe may vanish some day, but my love for you will never never end!

Goodbye, my dearest Li-ling and send my best wishes to all my fellow guerrillas.

My love for ever,
Steve

After she read the letter, she realized that Steve had been unable to control his emotion the previous day. It was because he knew he would never see her again as he volunteered to take the life-and-death risk of decoying the Japanese. Li-ling felt grateful for the way Stephen had sublimated his love for her by demonstrating his love for her country, but she feared for his life. She suddenly trembled and then slumped in the chair. Mrs Sung helped her drink a cup of water.

'Mrs Sung,' said General Ting with watchful concern, 'please help Miss So back to her quarters and let her rest. It's 9.30 p.m. We can do nothing now but await the return of our men in a few hours. We'll all hope for the best.'

'General Ting,' said Li-ling, recovering, 'thank you, I'm all right now. I'd like you to answer one more question: why didn't you request or even order Lieutenant Jones to act as a decoy?'

The general asked Colonel Long to explain on his behalf.

'Miss So,' said Colonel Long, 'as soon as we received the first intelligence report about the Japanese munitions, we held a meeting. We decided "Operation Rice Bowl" was the only alternative. We all agreed, except General Ting, to request Lieutenant Jones to act as a decoy. As he was white, he was the only choice. However, General Ting said that Lieutenant Jones was a former British POW, under our protection, but not under our command. And although he was working here voluntarily, it'd be unethical to request him to die in such a very dangerous mission. General Ting emphasised that this was a matter of principle.' Colonel Long cleared his throat before continuing, 'But General Ting also said, "Judging from Lieutenant Jones's past history, he'll probably devise a plan similar to ours because he is quite clever. He'll certainly offer help of his own accord because he has a strong sense of justice. Don't worry."'

Li-ling remembered that when she and Steve arrived at the guerrilla stronghold, the intelligence corps had made detailed inquiries about Stephen's and her past and their relationship.

'Miss So, when you came here yesterday to report to General Ting that Lieutenant Jones hadn't made any suggestions,' went on Colonel Long, 'General Ting was somewhat disappointed. However, he still held out hope that Lieutenant Jones would eventually come to offer help. But when the meeting scheduled for 2.15 p.m. commenced, he still hadn't shown up.

'At this critical moment the three officers and I asked General Ting to change his mind. But he remained adamant. "I still believe that he will eventually come," he said. "Wait five minutes more."

'After the time passed, General Ting finally yielded. "However," he emphasised, "it should be strictly a polite request."

'Overwhelmed with joy,' added Colonel Long, 'I rushed out of the hut to contact Lieutenant Jones, and bumped into a man who was approaching the hut. It was he – Lieutenant

Jones! I was dumbstruck. As soon as he came in, he offered himself as a decoy to the Japanese. You can imagine how elated we were! I saw tears of joy and gratitude well in General Ting's eyes. What a man of foresight!'

The general smiled.

'General Ting, was it a coincidence that while I was on duty here yesterday morning, a guerrilla submitted that second report to you?' asked Li-ling with a bitter smile.

'No. I am terribly sorry,' he said. 'I received it the night before last. We wanted it to be resubmitted in your presence the following morning so that I—'

'Could ask "you" to consult Lieutenant Jones,' finished Li-ling.

Silence reigned in the hut while her expression turned wry, to the embarrassment of all present, especially General Ting.

General Ting is hypocritical and cunning, she thought. Although at first he refused to ask Steve to undertake this extremely dangerous job, he tried to use me to trap Steve into volunteering. What if Steve dies? Then all my efforts to save his life will have been in vain and General Ting will be freed of any blame!

But… once I did think that Ah Fook had also set a trap for me. Are these two men alike in their thought patterns? However… whether they set a trap or not, both did so from patriotic motives.

'General Ting,' said Li-ling, 'never mind. I apologize for my discourtesy. Goodnight.' After the general, Colonel Long and Mrs Sung shook hands with Li-ling, she left.

As she returned to her hut, she worried again that Steve might have been killed in this dangerous mission. She turned restlessly in bed long after the oil lamp was turned off.

All of a sudden a strange thought flashed through her mind. General Peng Min-yuen, the historical patriotic hero, lying in Peng Family Tombs, surely must have helped the guerrillas kill all the Japanese. With his spiritual power, how could he stand by with folded arms and watch the Japanese kill his fellow patriots and Steve, their fighting comrade?

Soothed, she fell asleep.

Chapter Five

Two months later General Ting held a ceremony in front of the flag proudly displayed of the Blue Sky, White Sun and Red Earth. A small military band played the national anthem while General Ting, representing the Chinese Government of Chungking, conferred the rank of major and pinned the badge on Lieutenant Jones, and the rank of captain and the emblem on Lieutenant Fan. He also handed the insignia of the posthumous rank of second lieutenant to the late Corporal Chau's cousin, an orderly, for keeping. While General Ting eulogised the bravery of the three officers, he expressed grief for the wounded and the dead and gave proper awards.

At last he said, 'Without the spirit of sacrifice on the part of Major Jones, a national of our British ally, "Operation Rice Bowl" would not have been possible and greater importance would not have been attached to our guerrilla forces.'

Airdrops began coming more frequently and on a larger scale than ever before, bringing in a steady flow of food and supplies, especially munitions. A recent item of supply was military uniforms. Now at least half of the officers, including Stephen, were dressed in the same gray uniforms that replaced the old ones or their shabby clothes. To Li-ling, Stephen looked the handsome hero. Each time the Allied planes circled in low sweeps dropping supplies, the guerrillas cheered and shouted: 'Long live China' and 'Long live the Allies!' Li-ling felt that their voices were about to crack the sky.

Two gruelling years had passed since Li-ling and Steve arrived at the stronghold, yet she felt that their love had made them ten years younger.

'Li-ling, I have a surprise for you. This afternoon General Ting suggested that you and I have our wedding here!' said Stephen as they strolled through the woods that evening.

'He must have been joking. He belongs to a conservative generation.'

'He admitted that at first he didn't like mixed marriages. And then there's the matter of giving us permission to get married at the barracks, which is against the rules. But he promised to act as witness at our wedding and to present us with a small tent for our bridal chamber on behalf of the whole contingent when more canvas is available.'

'Oh, dear Steve,' she said, her eyes flashing, 'I am the happiest woman in the world. When I was young, I thought that when I got married, I'd be dressed in traditional bridal clothes, and sit in a colourful, decorated, bridal palanquin with eight bearers. Many relatives and friends, all nicely dressed, would attend the ceremony, but now I don't care.'

'My dear Li-ling, I may be the poorest bridegroom in the world. I have neither a ring to give my bride, nor money to pay for a simple dinner for my guests. Yet I am the luckiest man in the world.' He tilted her chin back gently and kissed her.

That night, she slept soundly in a bunk in her hut.

★

Led by a procession of soldiers who were playing 'The March of the Guerrillas' on trumpets, Li-ling rode down the hill in a plain sedan chair with no overhead cover carried by two bearers. She was dressed in a jacket and skirt made of red coarse cloth and wore a bamboo ring of flowers on her head. Stephen, dressed in a long blue Chinese gown and black waistcoat, both made of coarse cloth, waited at the edge of the woods for her.

When the sedan chair arrived, Stephen helped her out amid the firing of blanks from machine-guns and rifles, like the sound of exploding firecrackers. When the band played the wedding march at the same fast pace of a military tune, the couple walked in rhythm toward General Ting. Dressed in his new uniform, he shouted, in front of hundreds of guerrillas:

'As witness at the wedding, I hereby declare Major Stephen Jones and Miss So Li-ling husband and wife.'

Then Stephen and Li-ling bowed to each other. The guerrillas cheered.

The couple walked hand in hand to the bridal chamber – a small tent. Above the door hung a piece of red wood with the Chinese character written in black ink meaning 'double happiness', a traditional symbol of marriage. Stephen carried his bride inside.

Beside the small tent, round tables were set with good food and excellent wine by smartly dressed waiters. As the guerrillas saw this and smelled the odours which wafted over to them by the breeze, they licked their lips and rushed forward as if to charge the enemy. Frightened by these shabbily dressed men who were scrambling like starving people during a famine, the waiters ran away. The tables, the dishes of food and the bottles of wine vanished with them. The guerrillas burst into laughter, and pretended to eat and drink to their hearts' content with imaginary chopsticks and spoons, slurping loudly.

Stephen and Li-ling came out of the tent hand in hand and approached them.

'We're sorry, we don't have food and drinks for our guests on such an occasion,' they both said.

'Plenty! Plenty!' shouted some of the guerrillas, wiping their mouths with the backs of their hands.

'We're full,' shouted others, tapping their stomachs.

'As Commander of the Kwangtung Guerrillas, I propose a toast to the new couple,' said General Ting. He, too, drank an imaginary glass of wine, and all of the guerrillas followed suit.

★

Li-ling woke up from her dream smiling. It was like a Peking opera, she thought, where the movements and gestures of the actors and actresses and the properties and background are symbolic. She smiled.

★

One day alone in her hut, Li-ling was tearfully reading a creased note when she heard Stephen call her. She hastily put the note into a drawer, dried her tears and then opened the door.

'Li-ling, what's the matter?' asked Stephen.

'Nothing.'

'There must be.'

'I was crying.'

'Why? We recently received an airdrop of canvas. General Ting's just promised to pitch a tent for our wedding next month. Now you should smile.'

'Oh, dear Steve, he told me so this morning. I was so happy that I couldn't help crying. I'm looking forward to that day when I become the number one wife of the man I love.' Li-ling tried to look as cheerful as possible.

★

At dawn the following day, everyone was awakened by a trumpet sounding an emergency, followed by noises in the woods. Later, hundreds of unfamiliar men and about two hundred guerrillas of the local contingent, most in torn and ragged uniforms or clothes, staggered down the hills from the northwestern corner of the stronghold. In their wake, about one hundred moderately wounded were being carried piggyback and about fifty seriously wounded or ill were being carried on stretchers.

A few hundred underground workers under the leadership of General Ting now received them. Some helped carry the wounded or sick; others brought bottles of water. The doctors, nurses and orderlies stood by to administer medical care.

General Ting walked back with a scraggly-bearded uniformed officer who looked to be middle-aged. As they passed Li-ling, she was tending a wounded guerrilla on a stretcher. The officer stared at her for quite a while, but General Ting was too occupied with his own conversation to notice.

That night the seriously wounded and sick were accommodated in some of the huts specifically evacuated for them, while others rested in the tents along with the local contingent.

★

Two evenings later Li-ling and Stephen walked hand in hand through the woods.

'Li-ling, the medical corps has done a tremendous job under trying circumstances. You must be very tired after these two gruelling days.'

'Yes, but without everyone's cooperation, we couldn't have done the job properly. Steve, I'm afraid that we can't get married right away. We haven't even got enough canvas for pitching tents for General Chang's men, to say nothing of a tent for our bridal chamber.'

'How do you feel about that?' said Stephen as he sat down on a rock and motioned Li-ling to sit beside him.

'Well, as long as we love each other, I'll be happy. Indeed, I regard this place as our Shangri-La.'

Chapter Six

The next morning when Li-ling left her hut for breakfast, a man dressed in a ragged uniform approached her.

'Miss So, I'm General Chang's orderly. He wishes to see you.'

Frowning, Li-ling asked, 'What does he want to see me for?'

'I don't know. Please come with me.'

He showed her into a hut where the scraggly bearded general rose to meet her.

The general looked over at the orderly. 'Leave us now.' Then he turned to Li-ling. 'Please sit down.'

'Thank you, General Chang.' Li-ling pulled up a chair for herself.

The general poured two glasses of water. Li-ling took one and thanked him.

He paused for a moment before asking, 'Is your father Mr So Wing-on?'

Li-ling's eyes opened wide before she answered. 'Yes. He passed away about two years ago.' She pointed to the blue woollen flower she wore in her hair. 'I'll wear it for one more year to express my mourning according to custom.'

'I'm sorry. He died of a heart attack, didn't he?'

'How did you know?'

'Your mother was a distant cousin of mine.'

Li-ling's face brightened. 'Oh! You must be Uncle… Yan-ping! Mama mentioned you a couple of times. After she died, we received your condolence telegram. I'm sorry I didn't recognise you. Twelve years ago I saw your photo with Auntie. You were clean-shaven and were dressed in smart Western-style clothing. I thought you were a civilian officer of the Chinese Government.'

The general sat down. 'Well, your mother sent me a photo when I was in China. In it, you were with your father, two mothers and baby brother. It looked like you were in your early teens at the time. When I got here three days ago, I noticed you because you favoured your father. Yesterday General Ting told me everything about you. He was glad I had found my niece here!' The general took a sip of water. 'I was a few years younger than your mother. We played together as children. The last time I saw her was twenty-four years ago. As a soldier I've been on the move in China since the Japanese invasion of Manchuria about thirteen years ago.'

'And I must tell you, Uncle, everyone says General Chang Yuk-ying is a hero. But I didn't know it was you.'

'I've changed my name to my wife's maiden name, so that I might remember her all the time and avenge her.'

'Why?'

'Your aunt and your eight-year-old cousin were tragically killed in a Japanese random air raid on Chungking five years ago.'

Li-ling covered her face with both hands, bent her head and cried. It took a long while for her to collect herself. After she took a sip of water, she said, 'Oh, Uncle, I'm so sorry.'

'Never mind. I have re-channelled my grief into efforts to get revenge on the Japanese. In December 1941, I led my regiment to attack occupied Canton in order to ease Japanese pressure on Hong Kong. After several severe battles, my regiment was completely surrounded. I surrendered with my men.'

'How come?' Li-ling said before she cupped her hand over her mouth.

'I pretended to collaborate with the Japanese,' continued the general, 'when all the Chinese accused me of betraying my country. But I could only reveal my plan to two of my close subordinates. For that entire year, I often wept during the night.' The general cleared his throat before going on: 'When the time was right, I told my other subordinates about my plan, and we killed a score of traitors as well as ten so-called Japanese advisers assigned to keep watch over us. We made a surprise attack on the Japanese garrison while the guerrillas came down the mountains to assault them from the other side. Although we suffered some casualties, we killed and wounded five hundred Japanese before joining forces with the guerrillas to retreat to the mountains. I was promoted to major general and appointed commander of the thousand-strong joint forces there by the Chungking Government.'

'Congratulations! Uncle, you must have been very happy then, regaining your reputation.'

The general nodded slightly. 'Afterwards, we had skirmishes with the Japanese on and off for more than two years. Two months ago, we were surrounded. At last we broke through in different directions, but a few days ago I ran into an ambush with a few hundred of my men. Luckily, the men of your contingent came to our rescue in time. But now, Li-ling, let me hear about your family. How are your second mother and your brother?'

'They're being treated badly by my husband in Hong Kong. I learned this from a note smuggled here to me by an underground worker in Hong Kong.'

'General Ting told me you were forced to marry the traitor Wong. The system of concubinage was abolished in China many years ago, though not in Hong Kong. Anyway, Wong will be executed after the war.' The general paused with a smile. 'You helped an English prisoner of war escape. I couldn't believe that you, just a young girl, could be more courageous than many men.'

Li-ling inclined her head in a small bow. 'I don't deserve your praise.'

'How's your English friend? I admire his heroic role in "Operation Rice Bowl". I heard that the two of you are going to be married.'

'Yes, Uncle.'

He grinned. 'Congratulations to you both.'

'Thank you very much. I see you don't have the prejudice against Westerners that Papa had. Papa must have had some Western blood in him, but why did he dislike Westerners so much? Uncle, on his death bed his exact words were, "My mother and I and you also fell victims to—" Then he stopped short and lapsed into a coma. An hour later, he passed away. I still don't understand what he meant. My parents never talked to me about my paternal ancestry.'

General Chang sighed deeply. 'In fact, your grandfather was English, so was your father, and so are you, according to Chinese custom.'

Li-ling froze. 'What?'

'Your grandfather was actually Mr Shepherd, not Dr So. Mr Shepherd was of pure English descent. Your grand-mother was pure Chinese. He loved her, and promised to marry her, but later when he knew that he'd be transferred from the Hong Kong Government to the British Foreign Ministry in London, he changed his mind. Then your grandma became pregnant, so he duped her by arranging a fake marriage during a short stay in Japan. Finally, he deserted her and returned to London to marry an English-woman.'

'But if he loved Grandma, why didn't he marry her?'

'Probably such marriage would have adversely affected his diplomatic career. Soon your grandmother gave birth to your father. A few years later she lost her sanity and was placed to the care of an asylum while your father was sent to Shartin Orphanage.'

'Poor Grandma and Papa!'

'After two years in the asylum, your grandmother was discharged. But she grieved so much that she made your father, then an eight-year-old child, kneel before Buddha in a monastery and swear that neither he nor any of his offspring would ever marry a Westerner. The following year she passed away.' He stroked his beard.

Li-ling's jaw drooped open before she said, 'Now I understand why my father beat me when he learned of my dates with an Englishman.'

'It's also clear that your father felt remorse for having done that. Can you guess the last word he wanted to say before he lapsed into a coma?'

After a pause, Li-ling asked, 'Was it "racism"?'

'Right you are!' said the general, striking the table for emphasis. 'Your grandfather wronged your grandmother, then your father and even you, though indirectly – all because of racism. In other words, your father wished to tell you that he no longer harboured any racial prejudice.'

She widened her eyes. 'Uncle, how would he feel about my marriage with a Westerner if he were alive?'

'Certainly, no problem.'

Her eyes sparkled. Her uncle's conclusion relieved the sense of guilt she had felt as 'an unfilial daughter'. 'Why'd Papa change his mind?'

Silence prevailed before the general replied, 'Maybe your father was deeply touched by your personal sacrifice to save his life.'

'Uncle, perhaps because Great Britain and the United States, which have exploited China for so long like the other imperialistic powers, have now become our allies and have given up their privileges in China.'

'Probably for both reasons.'

'Papa was more adverse to Western culture and more inclined to retain Chinese traditions than the educated Chinese in general. I didn't know why until I learned from you today about his parents.'

'It's also probably because of his education at the Chinese Department of the Central University in Nanking.'

'What happened to Papa after Grandma's death?'

'He continued to receive traditional education in the orphanage. For several years he came first in his class in all of his subjects as well as conduct. Dr So, a member of the board of directors of that orphanage, adopted your father despite his Western blood. Dr So practised traditional Chinese medicine and had no son of his own.'

'No wonder the portrait placed alongside my paternal grandma's on the altar table was that of Dr So instead of Mr Shepherd. Papa must have taken the family name of So in memory of the doctor.'

'Yes.'

'Since the Chinese at that time were so anti-Western, did Mama's family disapprove of her marriage to Papa because he had Western blood?'

'There was no problem because your maternal grand-parents passed away before your mother met your father.'

'Did you agree to Mama's marriage at that time?'

'Yes. I have a broader outlook on life. But some of her relatives and friends didn't turn up at the wedding ceremony held in Canton. They remained cold towards the couple until some years later when they learned of your father's kindness towards her. It was strange that when your father knew the objections to his marriage to your mother had arisen from racism on the part of her relatives, he laid the blame not on them but on his own father. He hated his Western blood. His bitterness turned into, should I say, an obsession?'

'Poor Papa!'

'I understand from General Ting that you'll be married soon. Since our men arrived, there's no more canvas left for pitching a tent for your bridal chamber. I'm sorry. As soon as the situation here is back to normal, we'll erect a new tent for you.'

'Thank you very much. I'd like to introduce my English friend to you tonight.'

'Fine. Until tonight, Li-ling.'

Chapter Seven

For a few days after the arrival of a few hundred battered guerrillas at the stronghold, the local contingent was busy tending the wounded and sick. Then normal activities gradually resumed.

One month later, in the mid-morning when the sun was warm and the wind was calm, Stephen and Li-ling were invited to General Ting's hut.

'Good morning, Major Jones,' said the general in English. 'In the name of the Chinese Government, I'd like to thank you again for your heroic actions in "Operation Rice Bowl". This operation has provided us with sufficient arms and ammo to greatly enhance our combat strength.'

'Actually, some of the thanks should go to Li-ling,' said Stephen. 'Without her I wouldn't have been here in the first place.'

'Of course, we heartily thank both of you. Today I'd like to give both of you some good news.'

'Follow me.' He motioned them to come along. The three left the hut.

After passing by a few tents, they stopped at a small one made of new canvas. Above the entrance hung a wooden sign with a large Chinese character meaning "double happiness" written in black ink.

'As a marriage without a wedding chamber can't be called a marriage,' said the general, 'we've pitched this tent for you. As any place without a double bed can't be called a wedding chamber, the engineering corps has designed one with artistic carvings and will deliver it in four days. And the nurses will sew a bridal dress in six days. Then you can get married in a week.'

Li-ling clapped her hands and danced around. Then Stephen scooped her up in his arms and spun her as both of them laughed.

'General Ting, thank you very much,' said Li-ling and Stephen in unison.

'Don't thank me. Let's get back to my office and I'll show you something.'

Inside the hut, General Ting opened a drawer, took out a thick stack of papers and handed it to Li-ling. 'These are all petitions submitted to me in the months following "Operation Rice Bowl". We would have pitched a tent earlier, but there was not enough canvas until last week when we got supplies.'

As Li-ling translated some of the more interesting petitions for Stephen, her voice broke with emotion.

'"We love Major Jones and Li-ling and beg you to give special permission for them to get married." "Please allow Major Jones and Li-ling to be married. We want them to be happy." "In our long war with Japan, we haven't seen a wedding. We want to see one for Major Jones and Li-ling to be held here." "We want to see Li-ling dressed in bridal clothing." "Stephen and Li-ling's marriage will bring luck to us."'

Tears streamed down Li-ling's cheeks. She looked up to see Stephen's eyes watering as well before they returned to their work.

★

Late in the afternoon, unexpectedly, the skies clouded darker and darker and the cold wind howled louder and louder. On the open ground outside General Ting's hut, he stood with Colonel Long, Matron Chau and two teenage guerrillas, all looking serious. In front of them stood the nurses and about one hundred guerrillas, all of whom looked anxious. The men wore their winter clothing or uniforms, some tattered; all the women except Li-ling had put on old, shabby, Western overcoats.

'Is something wrong?' Stephen asked Li-ling.

She nodded.

General Ting gestured to the assembly to keep quiet, then said, 'Before I tell you the reason why I've convened this emergency meeting, I'd like to explain the war situation.

'Since the outbreak of the Pacific War Japan has been sending troops to various countries in Southeast Asia.' He pointed to a map hanging on a bamboo pole behind him. 'But since early 1944, their land routes in all the occupied southern parts of China and their sea routes south of the China coast have been seriously threatened by Allied planes taking off from airbases in Free China.'

Li-ling interpreted for Stephen.

General Ting lit a cigarette and inhaled deeply before he went on.

'Therefore, large numbers of Japanese troops have launched offensives in the past months to take as many cities, especially with airbases, in Free China as possible as their initial objective. One month ago they went farther inland to occupy Luichow, Kweilin and Tushan, three strategic cities in the southwest of China.' The general again pointed to the map.

Li-ling's and Stephen's brows furrowed.

'Three weeks ago,' continued the general, 'intelligence told us that three crack units of Japanese reinforcements began to be dispatched from Manchuria to these three cities for further invasion towards Kweiyang and Chungking in the north, and towards Kunming and the Burma Road in the west, which the Japanese secretly call the "Double General Assault". This time their ultimate objective would be to exterminate Free China once for all!'

The general caught his breath. 'In the past we've been instructed to avoid confrontation with any large Japanese force in case the Japanese made a major assault on this stronghold. We'd split into small units to operate elsewhere in order to preserve our strength. Only when the Allies launched a major counter-offensive would we guerrillas engage actively in harassing the enemy troops in the rear. But three hours ago I received a new instruction from General Yu, dated three days ago, as follows:

> *General Ting,*
> *Five days ago the most powerful unit of the Japanese reinforcements suddenly turned due south towards your stronghold instead of moving directly to join the so-called Double General Assault as the three units had done in the past twenty days. Its mechanised vanguard reached Ningchin yesterday. It's clear that this advance force along with the Japanese troops stationed in the vicinity will surround your stronghold in four or five days. Then the main force of the unit will soon arrive to finish you off in a few days.*
>
> *As the general war situation has changed, you should shift from guerrilla warfare to position warfare. I hereby order you to make the maximum use of our topographical advantages to engage the large number of enemy troops as long as possible, regardless of casualties. We must delay the Double General Assault.*

'As a result of this new order,' continued General Ting after reading the instruction, 'I've held a meeting with my assistants and we have unanimously decided to evacuate all the nurses early tomorrow morning.'

Li-ling and Stephen both clenched their fists.

'General Ting,' begged Li-ling, 'could I stay here to help? You need nurses badly.'

'No,' said General Ting. 'If this stronghold falls to the Japanese, any women captured will suffer greatly. Major Jones and Miss So, I'm very sorry that your marriage must be cancelled.'

'I am grateful to all of the guerrillas for not discriminating against me as a "foreign devil",' responded Stephen, 'but treating me as a member of this great family. The love shown by the whole contingent is a great consolation to us even though we can't get married at present.'

'In Hong Kong, many of my friends and relatives would disagree with my wedding to a Westerner,' stated Li-ling. 'But here, every unit has petitioned to arrange a marriage ceremony for us.'

Li-ling and Stephen held each other's hands tightly.

The general turned to the nurses and said, 'All you White Angels, assemble here at six o'clock tomorrow morning. Our respected Matron Chau, a native of this district, will lead you to Peng Village as your first lap on the way to Free China.' He glanced at the two young men beside him and added, 'Lone-lone and Bee-bee are from Peng Village. Right now they'll travel throughout the night and tell the villagers to make preparations for your arrival tomorrow evening.'

Everyone applauded the young men, who waved to the meeting as they left.

'White Angels,' continued General Ting, 'after you've passed through several towns down Peng Min-yuen Road and reached Hanglang on land level, you'll head northeast all the way to the city of Fungping. There Matron Chau will get somebody to lead you to Free China. She will say a few words to you before the meeting's dismissed.'

'All you White Angels,' said Matron Chau, glancing at her watch, 'take your supper now. Then pack up and go to bed early. You'll have a strenuous journey with hand luggage, starting tomorrow. Goodnight.'

Li-ling and Stephen said nothing. As they walked away to join a line for supper, Stephen wiped away the tears from Li-ling's eyes and gently caressed her cheek with his hand.

'After supper,' said Li-ling, 'I must say goodbye to my uncle in person.'

★

Early the following morning, it snowed heavily. Twenty nurses turned up in front of General Ting's hut. About two hundred guerrillas who had been specially attended to by the nurses were present to say goodbye. Hot yam gruel was served to everyone. Li-ling and Stephen each held a bowl and slipped behind a nearby tree. For a long while they simply looked into each other's eyes with the warm glow of love. In her mind it seemed to melt all the white snowflakes into tears.

'Dear Li-ling, even if I died now, I wouldn't complain of my fate. I feel that the past two years have been the happiest time of my life.'

'Recently we've heard on the radio that the Allies have won battles on many fronts in Asia and Europe. Though we've had some temporary setbacks in the China Theatre, I strongly believe that in the near future you'll be able to come to see me at Chungking Municipal Hospital.'

'I will. Godspeed.'

'Godspeed.'

General Ting, General Chang and Colonel Long now arrived and shook hands with the departing nurses.

'Where have you put the taels of gold I gave you last night?' General Chang asked Li-ling, when she approached him.

'I've sewn them into my padded jacket,' she said, pointing to the labourer's dark-blue clothes in which she was dressed.

'I bought them because depreciated bank notes were too bulky to keep,' said General Chang. 'If you need money, sell them. I'll keep a few taels of gold for myself in case of emergency. This may be the last place I live to see. Goodbye, Li-ling.'

'Uncle, you won't die.' Though tears blurred her vision, she put on an optimistic front. 'I hope we'll meet in Chungking after the war. Uncle, take good care of yourself. Goodbye!'

The guerrillas formed a line to wave goodbye.

The crickets are chirping a dirge for our departure, she felt. And sorrow is flowing like endless streams in the hearts of all the people.

Li-ling's legs felt heavy. She dragged along with her cloth pack, turning to look back again and again. She considered the snow flakes cruel, for they fell more heavily, blocking her view of Stephen. To her this precious moment seemed to be her last chance to imprint his image upon her mind for the rest of her life.

Chapter Eight

Matron Chau's party of nurses under the escort of two squads of guerrillas ordered to protect them from being attacked by wild animals, walked eastward through the brush in the snowy mountains. At times they rested, ate rice cakes and drank water. It took them twelve hours, two more hours than it normally took the guerrillas alone to get to the village. Because Lone-lone and Bee-bee had notified the villagers to prepare for the nurses' arrival, they readily provided all of them except Li-ling with labourers' old jackets and pants, cloth kerchiefs, rubber shoes and cloth packs, in addition to a hot supper and warm beds.

The following morning Li-ling showed the nurses how to darken their faces and dirty their fingernails in order to complement their disguise. Since the nurses could not get their hair permed in the stronghold, they had straight hair, adding to the labourer's look. Before they departed, they thanked all the villagers and the two squads of guerrillas.

The nurses walked southeastward in groups of twos and threes down Peng Min-yuen Road. Although it snowed high in the mountains, rain fell at the lower levels. Fortunately, the rain stopped by night, allowing them to reach a small town on a lower plateau, where they stayed at a small inn for the night.

After another day's walk, they reached the bottom of the mountain on the east side. During the next twelve days, the nurses headed north, passing through a number of towns and cities smoothly, except for once when a group of three nurses and their cloth packs were searched at a gendarmerie station in a city.

From the fifteenth day onwards, five of the nurses suffered from malaria one by one at an inn. While their peers recuperated, the rest of the nurses were stranded. It took nine days for all the sick to recover before the party could continue their travel.

On the twenty-fourth morning of their journey, they awakened in an inn to find that a downpour had flooded the district. They had no choice but to stay there for another week.

'As the saying goes,' said one nurse, 'misfortune never comes singly.'

It was then that they talked about missing their fellow patriots at the stronghold. Li-ling worried about Stephen especially.

After the flood receded, the nurses continued. On the thirty-fourth day they arrived at the city of Fungping, where they checked into a small hotel.

'You all rest in your rooms,' said Matron Chau, 'while I pay a visit to a relative nearby. After I come back, probably in two hours, I'll take you to dinner.'

The nurses were so tired that many of them dropped onto the beds and dozed off immediately.

Matron Chau came back about two hours later. She lost no time in taking her colleagues to a small restaurant on a side street nearby. A gentleman of medium build welcomed them at the entrance where a 'Closed' sign hung. They entered the only dining hall of the restaurant where there were nine square tables, each with four chairs. On the walls there were red banners with the names of dishes written out in Chinese. All the people sat except the gentleman and Matron Chau.

'My dear fellow colleagues,' said Matron Chau, 'this is Mr Hui, the manager, and also a cousin of mine. I've told him about our life and the present situation in the strong-hold, and he's just contacted a defector of the Wang Regime. He'll send two men to our hotel tomorrow at daybreak to guide us for two days before we can safely cross the border from Japanese-occupied territory into Free China.' She added, 'Mr Hui is so generous that he'll treat us to dinner.'

The nurses applauded.

'This meagre dinner is nothing,' said Mr Hui, 'as compared with my respect for your great sacrifice and for your contribution toward our country. I sincerely wish China as well as all of you good luck. White Angels, in this restaurant, you can speak as freely as you like, for the two waiters and the cook are our men. Dinner will be served soon.'

He and Matron Chau then sat at a table together with two other nurses.

The first course was tofu soup, followed by chicken and pork delicacies, which the nurses had not tasted for years. Disregarding table manners, they devoured the food, chewing noisily.

'We're like people in a famine,' said Li-ling, triggering laughter from her colleagues.

While they were enjoying their meal, they heard shouts of 'Important news! Special issue!' from outside the restaurant.

'We haven't read a newspaper for a long time,' said one of the nurses excitedly. Li-ling hurried out to buy a copy.

She staggered back to the restaurant. As soon as she stepped into the hall, she dropped to the floor.

After two nurses lifted her up and placed her on a chair, one of them wiped her face with a towel and the other retrieved the paper and shouted, 'Oh, Heaven!'

She then read aloud:

Guerrilla Base Taken
Two Generals Killed

One month ago, the Japanese Imperial Army laid siege to the so-called stronghold of the Chinese Guerrilla Headquarters of Kwangtung and demanded an unconditional surrender, but the guerrillas refused to comply. Then our army launched an attack with the support of the Japanese Imperial Air Force. After thirty days of fierce fighting, the Imperial Army killed most of the guerrillas and wounded the rest before taking the base at three o'clock this morning.

General Ting Shiu-ping and General Chang Yuk-ying were killed.

Li-ling and her fellow nurses wept.

'Please take care of Miss So,' said Mr Hui as he was ready to leave the room. 'I'll try to get confirmation. The Japanese always exaggerate their victories. You go on with your meal.'

Two hours later, Mr Hui returned. Li-ling was sitting up now, her face pale.

'The guerrillas put up a heroic fight for a month before the fall of the stronghold,' said Mr Hui. 'Two days before the fall, owing to a severe shortage of ammunition, Colonel Long led one thousand men to the northeast and Lieutenant Colonel Shaw led about the same number of men toward the northwest in their breakthroughs of the enemy encirclement. They were both ambushed. Three quarters of them were killed, wounded or captured. All in all, both sides suffered heavy casualties. This newspaper, which only publishes news favourable to the Japanese, fails to mention the loss of many Japanese planes during the dogfights with the Allied air force.'

'Mr Hui,' asked Matron Chau, 'what happened to General Ting, General Chang and Major Jones?'

'Major Jones? The only foreigner? He was killed in combat two days before the fall of the stronghold and both General Ting and General Chang were killed when the stronghold fell.' Mr Hui's eyes were moist. 'Our men working with the Wang Government got confirmation from the Japanese.'

With eyes red and a voice that was breaking, Li-ling said, 'Did Heaven play a… trick on me? Why didn't Heaven let us… die together? Only a little more than a month ago I saw them all lively and happy – my dear Steve, my uncle, General Ting and many of my patriotic comrades-in-arms, but now they've become ghosts.'

'Let's go back to the hotel early so that Miss So may rest,' suggested Matron Chau.

'Thank you all for looking after me,' said Li-ling a while later. 'I'm all right now, but I'll bid you goodbye tomorrow morning and go back to Hong Kong.'

'Why?' asked two nurses in unison.

'When I joined the guerrillas, I left my stepmother and brother behind—'

'Hong Kong to you is like a tiger,' interrupted a nurse. 'You've escaped from its mouth. Why do you want to jump back into it?'

'As you know, my family is being punished as my scapegoats. I'll be disloyal if I abandon them. At first I didn't intend to go back because of my promise to meet Steve in Chungking, but now he's dead, I'm going back to Hong Kong to take my mother and brother to safety.'

'But you'll face the death penalty!' said another nurse.

'I must take the risk,' said Li-ling. 'What else can I do? It'll take me a few days to go from here to Waishing, where I can travel by sampan to Canton on the first lap of my journey.'

Despite the nurses' pleas, Li-ling was adamant.

Now sweet red-bean gruel was served as dessert, but nobody wanted to eat.

After they went back to the hotel, they were so tired that they went to bed early. Li-ling remained awake all night long, thinking of her Steve while sorrow wetted her pillow through and through.

★

As Li-ling left early next morning, she hugged each of her nineteen fellow nurses, all in tears as if they were sisters of the same family.

On the first day of her lone journey, Li-ling ordered a dish of *chow mein* at a sidewalk food stall in a town. She did not even pick up the chopsticks before she paid the bill and left.

Another day after Li-ling had enquired the way of a man on the street, she said, 'Thank you, Steve. Goodbye.'

Looking stunned, the man said, 'How'd you know my Christian name?'

Li-ling blushed and hurriedly left.

When she missed Steve, she would recite in tears the famous couplet quoted in Chinese literature, 'The silkworm produces cocoons of fibre until it dies; the candle sheds tears until it turns ashes.'

As Li-ling ate less and less and grieved over her Steve more and more, her clothes became looser and looser.

A few days later she arrived at occupied Canton, the capital of Kwangtung.

Part Four

Chapter One

A little more than a month later, Li-ling disembarked from a fishing junk onto a beach of Hong Kong Island in the early afternoon with a mixture of anger, anxiety and joy. In labourer's dark-gray summer clothes and with dirty face and hands, she walked through the slums, carrying her cloth pack. She saw some ruins and rubble here and there, and noticed people looking even thinner in their shabby clothes than those in occupied Kwangtung. At last she knocked at the door of a wooden shack on the hillside. A thin boy of nine or ten opened it.

'I'm a friend of Mrs Chen. May I come in?' asked Li-ling.

'She's my aunt,' said the boy. 'She's living at the So house.'

'Are any adults in?'

'No, but my sister's coming back from her factory soon. Please come in.'

On entering the house, Li-ling found the living room very clean, though small, with a wooden table and two wooden chairs in the middle, and a rattan chair in one corner.

The boy went into the kitchen. After he brought a cup of water for Li-ling, he asked, 'Is Auntie your maid?'

'No, she isn't. I'm just a labourer.'

The boy went into the adjacent room, brought a photo back and held it in front of Li-ling. It showed Li-ling in her early teens with Chi-ching. As she looked at it, a flood of memories surging through her, she paid little attention to what the boy was muttering.

'You are Second Mrs Wong; you are also Miss So Li-ling. At the door I didn't recognize you, but now I do. You shouldn't have told a lie. Do you know that your tongue will be cut off when you are in hell after you die?'

There was the sound of a key unlocking the front door.

'Elder Sister Mui's back!' shouted the boy.

A girl in her late teens stepped in. Her eyes grew round at the sight of Li-ling.

'Second Mrs Wong,' said the girl, 'I almost failed to recognise you. How do you do? We've heard a lot about you from Auntie. My name's Ah Mui. This is my little brother, Ah Dee.'

Li-ling smiled. 'Why have you come back from work so early?' she asked. 'It is only 12.30.'

'Due to lack of raw materials,' said Ah Mui, 'we work only half a day.'

'Is your income enough to cover the high cost of living?'

'Barely.'

'Does Ah Dee go to school?'

'No. Most of the teachers have left Hong Kong. I teach him Chinese for two hours every day. Second Mrs Wong, why did you come back to Hong Kong? It is extremely dangerous for you.'

'A long, long story. I'll tell you later.' Li-ling's jaw tensed as she spoke. 'Now I need your help urgently. I want to see two people today. First, please call Mr Liu Kwong-ming, nicknamed Ah Fook, Chief Wong's bodyguard. As today is Saturday, he should be at Chief Wong's home in the afternoon. He is a trustworthy friend of mine. Just tell him you're a friend of Miss Liu Oi-ping, one of my secret pseudonyms, and that I'm seriously ill. Because he's my so-called cousin, he'll certainly come here to see me as soon as possible. Second, please call Chen Ma, your aunt to come here, too.'

'Chief Wong's men are living at So's house,' said Ah Mui. 'They listen to every telephone call, incoming and outgoing, on an extension. Shall I tell Auntie that Ah Dee is seriously ill so that she may use this excuse to leave right away?'

'No, no, no!' screamed Ah Dee, turning red. 'I'm all right. Why do you want to lie about me?'

Li-ling winked at Ah Mui, who then quickly said, 'Ah Dee, I'm sorry. I'll use any excuse except that you're ill. I promise. Is that all right?' asked Ah Mui, raising her right arm.

Ah Dee nodded, but still looked displeased while Li-ling handed Ah Mui a piece of paper with Chief Wong's, also Ah Fook's, telephone number.

'Second Mrs Wong, you look tired. Please rest on my bed inside,' offered Ah Mui, pointing to the adjacent bedroom.

'No, my clothes are dirty,' said Li-ling pointing to her clothes. 'I'd rather rest on the rattan chair.'

'I'll make the calls in a nearby restaurant and be back in thirty minutes. Then I'll cook lunch.' Ah Mui turned to Ah Dee. 'Don't disturb Second Mrs Wong. Go take a nap in the bedroom.'

After Ah Mui left, Li-ling took her dark-blue padded jacket and a sewing kit from her cloth pack. She opened the edge of the jacket with a pair of scissors, and slipped her hand inside through the opening. She took out three small cloth packages and put them on the table, then she carefully sewed up the opening of the jacket and put it and the kit with its contents back into the pack before she settled into the rattan chair.

Later when Ah Mui came back, she saw that Li-ling was asleep, so she went straight into the kitchen.

At about three o'clock when Chen Ma opened the door and came in, the boy shouted, 'Auntie,' wakening Li-ling. Ah Mui came out of the kitchen to greet her aunt.

'Young Mistress!' Chen Ma looked shattered at the sight of Li-ling. 'How are you? How did you get so dark?'

'I've lived most of the daytime in the sun for the past two years.'

'Why'd you come back?'

'Steve and I fled to the guerrilla stronghold in Kwangtung. Before the Japanese besieged it more than two months ago, all the women were evacuated. Afterwards many guerrillas including Steve were killed. Where else should I go?'

Chen Ma's eyes filled with tears. 'Poor Mr Jones!'

'How are Mama and Chi-ching?'

'Young Mistress, over six months ago, Chief Wong sent his wife's second cousin and three of his men to live on the ground floor of the So house. Since then these men drink day and night and even invite whores to stay overnight. When Mistress goes out, one of the men goes with her on the pretence of protecting her. Mistress and Young Master live alone, and relatives and friends try their best to avoid them. Even Sir William doesn't dare call her. Only Miss Silva, who returned from Macao, comes to the house to keep Mistress company. Miss Silva is Portuguese; Chief Wong's men haven't yet caused her any trouble.'

'Chen Ma, what's Miss Silva doing in Macao?' asked Li-ling.

'A year and a half ago she moved to Macao with her stepmother. Her uncle got her a job in the Portuguese Government there as an education officer. She recently came here on vacation for a few weeks to see a few friends and former students.'

'I have some bad news,' added Chen Ma. 'A few months ago, both the Blue and Green Mansions were bombed and burned down.

'Oh, no!' cried Li-ling. Silence prevailed for the next few minutes.

'A year ago, Japanese Hong Kong Government became aware that the big houses in which Japan's high-ranking officers lived, especially in the Peak District, might attract the attention of Chinese and American planes. It ordered all the residents of the two old mansions to move out and let its Japanese officers move in secretly. As a result of an air raid, quite a number of them were either killed or wounded.'

'Chen Ma, has Young Mama been able to make ends meet?'

'Mistress sold most of her jewels to buy food. Luckily, the price of jewellery is quite high.'

'Second Mrs Wong,' said Ah Mui, 'I've called Mr Liu Kwong-ming, Ah Fook. He's coming soon.'

'I've seen Ah Fook many times,' said Chen Ma, 'but we've never talked. People say he's a traitor.'

'No, Chen Ma. He is an underground worker.'

Chen Ma appeared transfixed.

'He sent a note to me in the guerrilla stronghold a few months ago,' added Li-ling, 'telling me that Lieutenant Colonel Genda and Chief Wong had been mistreating my stepmother and brother.'

Ah Mui went to the kitchen and brought out a big bowl of yam gruel. She put it on the table. 'Second Mrs Wong, you must be very hungry. Please eat.'

'Ah Mui, how can we welcome Young Mistress with this food?' asked Chen Ma. She then dragged Ah Mui by the sleeve into the bedroom. 'Pawn my ring and buy some rice, roasted pork, and sauced chicken for her lunch,' whispered

Chen Ma to her niece, taking a small, thin gold ring out of the inner pocket of her jacket.

Li-ling had opened the door and saw what was happening.

'No. Chen Ma, please. I ate yams instead of rice and meat in the guerrilla stronghold.' Li-ling then told them to come back to the living room and made Chen Ma put back her ring. 'Chen Ma, we are grateful to you. Since the outbreak of the war, you've continued to work for my family and received little pay. All the other servants left Hong Kong one by one. Here are three taels of gold for you.' Li-ling took one of the three packages from the table and handed it to her. 'If you sell them one by one, they'll last you a long time. Your niece and nephew look undernourished.'

'No,' said Chen Ma. 'My niece can afford to buy meat for Ah Dee and herself on occasion.'

Looking stern, Ah Dee interposed, 'That is a lie! We have not tasted meat or even rice for years. Auntie, you always teach me to be honest.'

Chen Ma's face turned expressionless.

'There you are, Chen Ma,' said Li-ling. 'Please accept it.' She handed the package to Chen Ma, who still declined. Then Li-ling patted Ah Dee on the back and said, 'Ah Dee, I'm sorry I lied about my identity. You are an honest boy.' She handed the three taels to him.

'Thank you, Second Mrs Wong,' he said.

After she whispered a few words to Ah Mui, Li-ling sat at the table, took up the bowl and ate the gruel while Ah Mui and the youngster took their meal in the kitchen.

By the time Li-ling finished, Ah Fook arrived, still in his uniform. They greeted one another warmly. After Ah Mui and Ah Dee came out of the kitchen, Li-ling made polite introductions for all.

Li-ling told them about her escape with Stephen to the guerrilla stronghold and their happy life together there. When she got to Stephen's feat in 'Operation Rice Bowl', they all clapped. But when she mentioned the fall of the stronghold and the heroic deaths of the many guerrillas, including Stephen, all looked sad.

'The Japanese planned to take the stronghold within a few days,' said Ah Fook. 'They'd never expected that the ill-equipped guerrillas could have held out for an entire month, diverting their large force from joining their imminent Double General Assault in the southwest of China. The delay gave the Allied powers much more time to consolidate their defences and deploy additional troops there. The latest news came through intelligence that the Japanese advances on the two fronts have since been completely checked and the enemy has suffered heavy casualties.'

They all applauded.

'Young Mistress,' asked Chen Ma, 'Why did it take you so long to get home from Canton?'

'Because it took me the first twenty days just to find a woman guide. After we came to a village near the China–Hong Kong border, we crossed a range of hills for one whole day and night before I alone swam across the Shumchun River and sneaked into the New Territories. Then I had to evade Japanese border controls once there. After this I had to walk to Kowloon and pass a few gendarmerie stations. I was afraid to take a ferry from Tsimshatsui Pier, so I boarded a fishing boat to come here.'

'Young Mistress, until now I've never imagined that a woman could do all that you did. I am very proud of you!'

'Chen Ma, you ought to be proud of yourself too, because it is you who brought me up.'

They all smiled.

'Anyway, Ah Fook,' stated Li-ling, 'thank you very much for helping Steve and me in our escape. Although he's dead now, he told me that his two years with me in the guerrilla stronghold had been the happiest in his life. And mine, too.'

'Second Mrs Wong,' said Ah Fook, looking straight into her eyes, 'you must leave Hong Kong immediately. You are on the "Most Wanted Civilians" list with a handsome reward for your arrest. Your picture and description are posted at all main traffic centres. Hong Kong is very small, so you can't hide.'

'Young Mistress, you can hide here,' said Chen Ma.

Ah Fook shook his head. 'No, no! The Japanese and their lackeys are planning to comb houses in all the districts for anti-Japanese elements in the near future. If they find Second Mrs Wong here, you and Ah Mui will be in great trouble.' He then turned to Li-ling. 'You must escape to Macao instantly... without your mother and brother. I can arrange to have a fishing boat at Stanley Bay ready for you any time.'

'But... but... how can I leave without them when they are in distress? I must see Wong to get them released.'

'Second Mrs Wong, please don't. Once you step into his house, you'll never be able to get away. Do you know that he killed Bella?'

'Oh, my Heaven, but he loved that dog so much.'

'Yes. But a few days after your escape, at the peak of his rage, he shot her to death for breaking one of his favourite vases.'

'Ah Fook, I don't understand. Bella saved him in mid-February from an assassination attempt one month before I joined the Wong family.'

'Our intelligence organisation plotted this murder. Afterwards Chief Wong was afraid of further attempts on his life, so he looked for a bodyguard until he got me in early April. Second Mrs Wong, last year the chief got another Alsatian. He named her Bella, too. Three months ago she scratched the corner of his eye when he hugged her, but he didn't punish her.'

'What made him change so?' asked Li-ling.

'Since the landing of the Allied forces in Normandy last June, he's not been so hard on people suspected of anti-Japanese activities. I don't think he'll turn you over to the Japs if you go back, but he will continue to keep you at home as his concubine.'

'If Wong's changed, why's he gone so far as to place guards at my home?'

'It might be a trap Genda and Wong have both deliberately set for you, though they may have had different motives. They must have been quite sure that you, well known for your filial qualities, would come back to rescue your family. And they were right. But if you refuse to remain his concubine, Second Mrs Wong, he won't hesitate to turn you over to the Japs. I wrote to you about your stepmother and brother because I'd promised to do so, but I also warned you not to come back. I beg you, don't go to see Wong.'

'Ah Fook, I'm sorry.'

He shook his head, then turned to Chen Ma. 'Please, persuade her to change her mind before it's too late.'

'Young Mistress, I'll tell you about your stepmother,' said Chen Ma, blushing. 'She always blames you for ruining the reputation of the So family because you ran away, especially with a Westerner. She doesn't love you, so why do you want to die for her? After all, Wong's men only give her trouble, but her life is not in danger at all. For your own life, please listen to Mr Ah Fook.'

'But I owe her the same filial regard as my own mother,' argued Li-ling.

Chen Ma shook her head.

Ah Fook stood up and said, 'I must report to Wong for duty right away.'

'Ah Fook,' said Li-ling, 'when I escaped from Hong Kong, you gave me gold. I sold a few taels for my expenses on my journey, but when I evacuated the guerrilla stronghold, my uncle gave me a lot more. After giving my guide ten taels, I have three taels left for you.' Li-ling took one package from the table and handed it to him.

'No, absolutely not!' he said. 'I gave you the gold as a present. I'll never be able to repay you for saving my life and those of my colleagues. Besides, you may need it in case of emergency.'

'Thank you, Ah Fook. I don't need money here. Instead, you need it badly for your job.'

As she insisted, he took it and thanked her.

When he passed Ah Dee, he stopped. 'Ah Dee, for the safety of all of us, don't ever tell anyone about our visit.'

'Don't worry, Mr Ah Fook,' said Ah Mui. 'Second Mrs Wong has already told me to explain to him why he must keep her visit secret. I did so while we were eating our lunch in the kitchen. Now he also understands why he must keep your visit secret, too.' Ah Dee nodded.

Ah Fook said goodbye to all of them. Ah Mui opened the door and saw no one about.

'Young Mistress,' said Chen Ma some time after Ah Fook left, 'I'll go now. I must cook supper for Mistress and Young Master. Are you leaving too?'

'Yes,' said Li-ling, 'but for safety's sake we must leave separately. Here's a package of a few jewels of my own I've not sold. Give it to Mama and Chi-ching.' Li-ling took the last package from the table and handed it to Chen Ma.

Chen Ma raised her eyebrows. 'Young Mistress, won't you keep it for future use?'

Li-ling shook her head vigorously.

Chen Ma tightened her lips, nodded her head and took the package. 'Very well,' she said, tears streaming down her cheeks. 'Young Mistress, please take good care of yourself.'

Then Chen Ma said goodbye and left with the jewels in her inner jacket pocket.

★

Some time later, Ah Mui took the same precaution for Li-ling as for Ah Fook before she departed. Li-ling walked by a few small wooden shacks on the hillside before she came upon a middle-aged man and woman. The woman glanced at her. After a few seconds the woman suddenly stopped.

'Did you notice that the labourer we just passed slightly resemble a wanted person in a photo posted in main traffic centres?' said the woman to the man, 'At first I didn't think much about it, but on second thought, this labourer may just be So Li-ling, Second Mrs Wong, in disguise. I remember that Chen Ma, Ah Mui's aunt, was So Li-ling's long-time maid. Miss So could have just left after hiding at Ah Mui's house.'

'Let's follow her,' said the man grinning. 'We can report to the police and have her arrested.'

Li-ling walked as fast as she could down the nearest sloping muddy path leading to a street, then to a main road streaked with tram tracks.

After following her breathlessly on the main road, the couple spotted two patrolling policemen emerging from a side street behind Li-ling. The couple started to walk even faster, getting closer and closer to the uniformed men. But when they were about twenty feet away from them, the woman abruptly halted and held the man back.

'Stop!' she gasped. 'I'm not quite sure she is So Li-ling, for this woman's very dark. According to the description given, So Li-ling is white. On second thought, as she is wanted in Hong Kong, there is no reason for her to come back. Therefore, we must be sure.'

The two policemen turned into another side street. The couple saw the young woman waiting alone at a tram stop.

'Here's our chance to take a closer look at her,' said the woman. 'We'll sit opposite her in the tram. Besides, I'll make a lame excuse to shake hands with her.' She smiled.

After a pause, his eyes sparkled. 'Now I understand.'

Li-ling noticed the couple as they approached the stop. How could they catch up with me unless they, too, walked as fast as I did? she reasoned.

When the tram arrived, the door opened in front of Li-ling; the couple stood behind her. She turned with a smile and motioned to them to board first. As the man got on, he said, 'thank you.' As soon as the woman set foot on the tram, Li-ling waved to the conductor, signifying that she was not going to board. The tram pulled away.

'I thought she showed respect to elderly people like us, but now I know why,' said the man.

Nodding a few times, the woman said, 'She must be the wanted So Li-ling.'

'We should've reported her to the policemen just now. It was all your fault.'

'I'm sorry.'

'Since she's now on the alert, it'll be difficult for us to trail her again. How about reporting to the Japanese Gendarmerie Main Headquarters right away that So Li-ling has been to Ah Mui's house?'

'Not so easy. Ah Mui's not dumb. What if she flatly denies it?' She paused. 'Don't worry, my husband, I can get confirmation from somebody easily and report to the Gendarmerie Main Headquarters today.'

'From who?'

'I'll tell you when we get home,' she said with a wink.

Chapter Two

The wall clock struck six in Chief Wong's first-floor family room. Li-ling, still dressed as a labourer, was offered a cup of tea by Ping-tsai.

'Second Mrs Wong, why did you come back?' asked the maidservant softly.

'My English friend was killed in action in Kwangtung. Where else could I go?'

As she spoke, a young, strongly built subordinate of Chief Wong's came upstairs saying: 'Second Mrs Wong, Chief Wong said over the phone he'd be back soon.'

'Thank you, Ah Hall,' said Li-ling. 'Why did Mistress, Young Master and Young Mistresses leave for Macao?'

'Allied planes have been raiding Hong Kong frequently. Chief Wong wanted them to move to the Portuguese colony for safety. He felt so lonely that he invited me to stay here.'

Ah Hall had just phoned Chief Wong at a friend's luxurious villa. In the living room he and three friends were playing mahjong, each with a flashily dressed, heavily made-up woman seated beside him. A strange mixture of smoke, perfume and the smell of liquor filled the air along with the clicking sounds of the tiles. Holding the phone and sipping brandy, Chief Wong choked and dropped his glass when he heard of Li-ling's return, but he poured another before he left.

On his way home, Chief Wong thought, Li-ling may no longer be attractive after living a rough life with the guerrillas. If that's the case I'll avoid trouble by handing her over to the Japanese right away. Of course, if she's still beautiful and cooperative...

★

In the meantime, Ah Dee, who was writing at his desk, set the writing brush down on his ink slab, and answered the door.

'Ah Dee,' said a short skinny boy at the doorway, 'my mother invites you to our house to eat rice gruel with beef.'

'No, Ah Park,' said Ah Dee, forcing a smile. 'My elder sister will give me a good scolding if I haven't finished my homework today. How about tomorrow?'

'No. Tomorrow's Sunday; there won't be any more gruel left.'

'Well, all right. I haven't tasted rice and meat for a long time.' Ah Dee hurried out of the shack to join his friend.

They passed by a few small wooden shacks on a muddy path before reaching Ah Park's. As they entered the small living room, Ah Dee was greeted by the woman who had trailed Li-ling earlier that afternoon.

'Ah Dee,' she said, 'you are a good boy. I've prepared a delicacy especially for you.' She went into the kitchen and brought out a bowl of hot rice gruel with beef. He sat at the table and deeply inhaled the aroma before quickly emptying the bowl with a spoon.

'Very delicious. Thank you, Auntie Faw.' The little guest licked his lips.

'How about playing a game of chess with me?' asked Ah Park. 'Last time I lost to you, this time I want to win.'

'No. Elder Sister Mui's coming back soon. I'd better leave now.'

'Don't worry, Ah Dee,' said Mrs Faw. 'After all, a chess game doesn't take long.'

After the woman cleaned the table and took the empty bowl to the kitchen, Ah Park put a paper Chinese chessboard on the table. The two boys sat opposite each other and put the pieces in place. The woman came back and took a seat at the table between them to watch. The boys moved the pieces alternately. After three minutes, Ah Dee proclaimed checkmate.

When he stood up and was ready to say goodbye, she said, 'Ah Dee, stay a while. Please, listen. You'd be a great general to defeat the Japanese because a great general is always a good chess player.'

He smiled and returned to his seat.

'Ah Dee, have you heard about General Yo Fay, who beat back the enemy?' asked Mrs Faw.

'Yes. Several teachers have told us the hero's story,' said Ah Dee, glancing at Ah Park, who nodded his approval.

'More than two years ago in Hong Kong there was a brave Chinese woman who killed a Japanese officer and helped a British prisoner of war escape,' said the woman. 'Her name was So Li-ling. Have you heard of her?'

'Yes.'

'I admire her. Do you?'

'Certainly.'

'Have you seen her?'

Ah Dee hesitated. He opened his mouth, but uttered no sound. As Mrs Faw realised that Ah Mui must have warned her brother to keep quiet about Miss So, she did not press the issue, remembering the maxim: 'More haste, less success'.

'Ah Dee, how about another bowl of gruel?'

He nodded with a smile. Mrs Faw brought another bowl. She then turned to Ah Park. 'Son, I want to be alone with Ah Dee. Go to the bedroom and keep Papa company.'

'Ah Dee, are we good neighbours?' she asked.

'Yes, for many years,' he said, with his mouth half full.

'Should we trust each other?'

'Certainly.'

'Should we tell lies to each other?'

'No one should ever tell lies.'

'Now, let's come back to So Li-ling. What an anti-Japanese heroine!' she sighed.

Ah Dee only raised his left thumb to express his agreement and continued to eat.

'Ah Dee, be honest. Is she beautiful?'

'But… but Elder Sister Mui told me not to tell others anything about anyone.'

'Did she tell you not to tell others about So Li-ling, too? I just want to satisfy my curiosity. Why would I let evil men harm this patriotic heroine?'

Ah Dee stared at her and continued chewing.

'Ah Dee, you are ungrateful. You won't even give me a yes or no after you've eaten two bowls of my delicious gruel.'

'All right. I'll tell you.'

'Good,' she said with a smile, eagerly waiting for him to speak.

'But let me finish the bowl first.'

'No. You can tell me while you're eating.'

'All right, but you must keep the matter secret.'

'Sure, sure.'

'I want you to swear that your tongue will be cut off in hell after you die if you don't keep it secret. If you don't swear, I won't tell you.'

'All right.' She stood up.

'Raise your hand.'

Mrs Faw raised her right hand and said, 'I swear that—' A series of knocks at the door stopped her.

She hurried to open it. Ah Mui stood in the doorway. Ah Dee spilled half of the remaining gruel on the floor before he dashed to join his sister.

'Sorry, Auntie Faw. Ah Dee must have been nervous when he saw me,' said Ah Mui. 'He hasn't finished his homework.' She seized her brother's hand and left.

While the grumbling Mrs Faw cleaned up the mess with a wet towel, her husband and son came out of the bedroom.

'I heard your conversation,' said Mr Faw. 'We've lost an award of twenty taels of gold.' He paused to cough before adding, 'Since the outbreak of the war, we've very seldom smelled meat; since the Japanese no longer rationed rice, we've very seldom tasted it. Now it seems that we may never be able to afford them again.'

'Mama, what's the matter?' asked Ah Park.

'Shut up!' she said.

★

As Ah Mui and her brother walked home together, she asked, 'Ah Dee, did Auntie Faw ask you if you'd seen Miss So?'

'Yes, she did.'

'Did you say yes or just nod?'

'No, I did neither.'

'Good Boy. Did you say, "I've never seen her in my life", as I told you?'

'No.'

'Why?' asked his sister, clenching her fists. 'After all, it is only a white lie. I've told you what a white lie meant.'

'Yes, I remember, but I don't want to tell even a white lie!'

'Why?'

'Because a white lie is also a lie.'

'Then what happened?'

'Auntie Faw continued to press me to tell her about Miss So. She said I was... ungrateful. I refused, then a thought came to my mind.'

'What thought?'

'If I broke my promise to you and told her the fact, my promise would... become a lie. Then I would suffer in hell.'

'You were right.'

'But at last I gave up because I'd eaten two bowls of her delicious gruel.'

'What?' shouted the sombre-faced Ah Mui.

'I promised her that I'd tell her about Miss So Li-ling if she'd... swear to keep it a secret.'

'Did she swear?' asked Ah Mui, raising her eyebrows.

'Before she had the chance,' Ah Dee paused to clear his throat and then went on, 'you came and she stopped swearing. Since she didn't swear, I didn't tell her the fact. Therefore, I didn't... lie to her, nor to you either.'

Smiling, Ah Mui stroked her brother's head in a circular motion when she said, 'You are stubborn, but you have a... logical... mind.'

Chapter Three

As soon as he arrived home, Chief Wong rushed upstairs with Ah Fook close behind.

'Li-ling,' gasped Chief Wong, seeing her in the family room. At first sight of her, he felt that she looked like an unattractive country girl, very dark and without any make-up, wearing labourers' clothing. But at a closer look he noticed her natural beauty. His bones suddenly melted with a burning desire and his heartbeat accelerated.

I must sleep with her tonight, he thought. I'll smell her fleshy breasts and taste her smooth body. But now I must be nice and gentle.

'Li-ling,' he said, still breathing hard, 'for a long time, we thought you were hiding on one of the numerous small islands of Hong Kong. Later I was surprised to hear a rumour that you and your English friend had escaped to the guerrilla base in Kwangtung. A few hundred POWs attempted to escape during the first few months of the Japanese occupation, but not many of them succeeded. How were you and your Western friend able to travel as far as the guerrilla base without being detected?'

'That's a long, long story,' she said coldly. 'I have no obligation to give you an account.'

'Two months ago when the news came that the guerrilla base had been taken by the Japanese, I thought both of you had been killed.'

She sat rigid. 'Before the siege, all the women were evacuated.'

'Oh, I see. Where's your friend now?'

'He was killed there.'

'Of course. Almost all the guerrillas were exterminated, including two generals,' said Chief Wong with a gloating smile. 'Your friend was lucky. He should have been executed long before. Those prisoners who attempted to escape with him were all executed a few days after you left.'

Li-ling's eyes blazed. 'My reason for coming back is to help my mother and brother whom you've treated so badly.'

'It's not my fault. It's Lieutenant Colonel Genda, who's put pressure on me.'

'Now I beg you to let Mama, Chi-ching and Chen Ma go to Macao with Miss Silva tonight.' To Chief Wong it sounded like an order, not a plea.

'The Portuguese lady who has visited your mother recently?' he asked.

'Yes. She lives in Macao, but she's now here on vacation.'

'But it was her brother, who victimised you, wasn't it?'

'Yes. How did you know?'

'Because when Superintendent Bei brought her brother before you at the police station, you suddenly retracted the help which you'd promised. Besides, later that evening I asked you why, and you said in a slip of the tongue: "Because I hate the Western rapist." I didn't bother to think through the matter until two months later when you escaped with the alleged rapist, who turned out to be your lover. Then I concluded that the rapist must have been Miss Silva's brother. It's unfortunate that when I sent my men to look for him, he'd already left for Macao. By the way, since Miss Silva is your rapist's sister, how could you trust her?'

'Though he is bad, on the contrary, she is good-hearted.'

'You and your lover lived a hard life with the guerrillas, didn't you?'

'Yes, but we were very happy.'

Chief Wong lit a cigarette, looking her up one side and down the other. 'Well, Li-ling, let bygones be bygones. I'll give your family a handsome allowance every month... secretly, of course. What's there for you to worry about? You must remain in hiding in my house, so the Japanese won't arrest you and chop off your head.'

'I don't know how long the war will drag on. Chi-ching is ten years old now. I want him to study in a modern school in Macao, but with a disciplined environment. In Hong Kong, no such school exists any longer. Besides, Macao is free from war. There, Miss Silva will take care of my family, too.'

Chief Wong looked at his watch. 'Tonight? It's 6.30 already. The last steamship leaves in two hours. How about tomorrow? We'll have more time to think of a safer plan.'

'But tomorrow, or even in the next moment, you or circumstances may change.' Li-ling gazed steadily at him.

'Li-ling, I won't change. I've always been concerned about your happiness. Didn't I try to promote you to the status of co-wife? Didn't I treat you well? Haven't I forgiven you for all the harm you've done to me?'

'Harm I've done to you?' she snapped. 'Have you lost favour with your Japanese bosses because I helped a POW escape?'

'No, thanks to the many friends I have among the Japanese officers, but I've lost face.'

He paused and gave her a beady stare. 'Li-ling, I am entirely obsessed with you.'

'I won't be happy until you let my family leave for Macao tonight.'

'All right,' he said after some hesitation, 'if you don't mind the risk. Ah Fook, see them off at the pier for the last steamship for Macao tonight. Don't forget Miss Silva. Tell my men to continue to stay in the So house to avoid suspicion on the part of Lieutenant Colonel Genda.' Chief

Wong took a sip of tea from a cup offered by Ah Fook. 'I'll put through a call to Lieutenant Yamada, a good friend of mine, head of the gendarmes stationed at the pier,' added Chief Wong. 'I'll tell him that Mrs So is the wife of my collateral relative, Mr Chung Pui-lam and Chung Chi-ching is their son, and ask him to issue special passes for them and Chen Ma. Use my limousine and report back to me as soon as you've completed your mission. This is strictly confidential. Now go.'

Once Ah Fook had left, Chief Wong went to his bedroom and used the telephone.

After some time Chief Wong said from the doorway, 'Li-ling, I've phoned. Look at your dirty face. Let's take a bath now so that we may go to bed early... You must be very tired.'

'I won't take a bath until my family has reached Macao safely.'

'Then I'll have my bath first. Now come in and rest on the sofa.'

★

At his quarters, Mariko, dressed in pyjamas, sat on a sofa in his living room. He glanced at his watch periodically. Finally there was a knock at the door; his aide hurried to open it. A young gendarme officer came in. He saluted Mariko, handed him an envelope and announced:

'Colonel Mariko, this is Colonel Takasugi's telegram which just arrived from Canton, as I told you over the phone.'

Mariko seated himself at his desk and opened the envelope. As he read the telegram, his hands shook. After about a minute, he looked up.

'Second Lieutenant Kobi, you may resume your duty now.'

Kobi left.

The colonel dismissed his aide, went into the kitchen and poured himself a glass of wine. He gulped it down and then poured another.

★

When Chief Wong finished his bath, his maid brought him his supper. He said to her, 'Ping-tsai, send for Ah Hall.'

'Yes, Master.'

He turned to Li-ling. 'Since my principal wife and all the children left, I take my meals in my bedroom. Li-ling, you must be hungry. Eat something.'

She shook her head.

'Li-ling, you miss your family, don't you?'

She nodded.

'Don't be sad. Let's enjoy life tonight,' he said with a grin. 'After the war is over, you'll see them again.'

While he ate, there was a soft rap at the door.

'Chief, what can I do for you?' said a man's voice.

'Ah Hall,' said Chief Wong, 'order all my men and maids to keep Second Mrs Wong's return a top secret and do not let her leave my house without my permission.'

'Yes, Chief. Goodnight.'

'I'm sorry,' said Chief Wong to Li-ling. 'I did it for your safety as well as mine.'

After he finished eating, he went to the bathroom to clean his teeth. He brushed them so hard that he broke the handle of the toothbrush.

'Li-ling,' he said with lust in his eyes after he came back to the bedroom, 'I've longed for you just as a piece of dry farm land longs for rain.'

He stretched his arms and was ready to kiss her when they heard a knock at the door.

'Who is it?' shouted Chief Wong.

'Ping-tsai. I want to take away the dishes and clean the table.'

'Come in,' he sighed.

She put the bowls and dishes on a silver tray and cleaned the table with a wet towel. She closed the door as she left.

Chief Wong was about to embrace Li-ling again when he heard another knock.

'Ping-tsai, again?' he shouted.

'Yes, I want to take out your clothes for laundering. Sorry.'

'Take them tomorrow! If you disturb me again, I'll fuck your mother!'

Then he swept Li-ling into his arms and kissed her face and neck feverishly before she could push him away.

'How many women have you slept with?'

Before he opened his mouth, the telephone jangled in his ears. Only after it rang a number of times did he go slowly to a corner of the room to pick up the receiver. He said rudely, 'Hello, what the hell are you calling at this late hour for?'

Suddenly he changed to Japanese and spoke softly, 'I'm very sorry. I didn't know it was you, Colonel Mariko.' Chief Wong stopped and listened to the voice on the other end before saying, 'Please hold. Let me tell my maid to leave the room first.'

He covered the mouthpiece of the receiver with his hand and turned to Li-ling. 'Get out!'

Li-ling took a fast step out of the room and barely closed the door. She stood by the door with her ear to the opening.

Chief Wong waited for a while before he went on, 'Very sorry for the delay. Did you say the telegram stated that... he is the head of the Hong Kong branch? Are you sure that's his name? I never thought of that even in my... wildest dreams.

'Colonel Mariko, please, give the names and addresses of the ten others. Let me jot them down on paper.

'Ah Fook's coming back soon...' Chief Wong again stopped and listened to his boss for some time while he jotted down the names and addresses. Then he placed the piece of paper beside the telephone.

'All right,' he continued, 'tonight I'll extract additional names and addresses of his fellow workers from him. You are right. If we transfer him to the headquarters now, the news may leak out and all his men will escape. Certainly, I'll keep all the people in my house from contacting anyone outside.'

He listened for a while and then continued, 'You are right. Tonight I'll need a lot of time, patience and tact to interrogate this cunning man. I'll torture him as I see fit... Don't worry. I have three men, Ah Hall and my two strong watchmen, to help me. Leave the matter to me and rest easy. I'll let you know the result before deciding where to go from there. Goodnight and pleasant dreams.'

No sooner had Chief Wong hung up than he rushed out of the room. When he saw Li-ling standing quite a distance from the door, he relaxed and motioned her in.

After they got back to the room, Li-ling set the door ajar. She lost no time in seizing his pistol from his holster on the table and pointing it at him!

Chapter Four

'If you shout, I'll fire!' snapped Li-ling. 'Hold up your hands and back away.'

Chief Wong's jaw drooped, and he raised his hands halfway.

'When Ah Fook comes back,' she warned, 'don't order your men to arrest him.'

'Are you out of your mind, Li-ling?' asked Chief Wong through clenched teeth. 'Now drop the pistol and I'll keep this a secret. You'll never get out of this house. You'll eventually be caught and beheaded. Please, Li-ling.'

'Don't move. For my country I am not afraid of death.'

'I am not afraid of death, either,' he said with a wicked grin. 'I've killed many people. I'll be charged in China with treason and executed after Japan is defeated. Anyway, death to me is only a matter of time.'

As he moved slowly toward the bell button, Li-ling ordered, 'Move back to the bed or I'll shoot!' She pulled back the hammer. Chief Wong did as she ordered. However, when Li-ling sneezed and her attention was somewhat distracted, Chief Wong suddenly dashed to the bell button. Before he could touch it, Ah Fook unexpectedly burst into the room and stabbed him twice in the chest with a dagger. Chief Wong went down.

'I've seen your spring signal on the floor in front of the door. Thank you for your timely warning,' Ah Fook said, pulling a handkerchief out of his pocket and handing it back to Li-ling.

She quickly gave him the list of names and their addresses and told him everything while Chief Wong moaned a few times. Looking at it, Ah Fook said, 'Now I must tip off all my co-workers, even though they are not on the list, as soon as possible, but not here. The phone may be tapped. Lately the Japanese haven't trusted any Chinese. Anyway, I can get only those of my co-workers who can get to the Stanley Bay to join us by midnight at the latest. Then we'll all set out in a boat and reach a secure place by 1.30 a.m.'

Li-ling flung her left hand in the air. 'I can't get out of this house. Wong gave special orders to his men. Never mind me. I'll try to cover this up until my mother and brother arrive at Macao and all of you get away from Stanley Bay safely.'

'You'll be glad that your family, Chen Ma and Miss Silva have left and will safely arrive at Macao by midnight.'

'Thank you.'

As he lay sprawled on the floor, Chief Wong's eyes half opened for an instant, fluttered and then closed again.

'Miss So, you'll sacrifice your life to save ours for the second time. We are grateful to you. How can I go away without you? There's only one way to save your life.'

'How?'

'I'll – set this house on fire!'

Li-ling's tongue became paralysed before she stammered, 'What about Chief Wong?'

'Let him burn. Why should we care about him? All these years members of the British Army Aid Group and even innocent civilians have died at his hands, let alone our underground workers. Miss So, we'll take advantage of the chaos as the fire burns. I'll change my clothes; you're already in labourer's clothing. I have a cycle ready, and we'll ride together. Who would recognise us in the streets at night?'

'But the fire might spread and kill innocent people.'

'It's a risk we have to take. Mind you, Miss So, this is your last chance!'

'No, no, no! I would rather die than let people take the risk.'

'Then I must kill Wong in order to make sure he's finished,' said Ah Fook, getting his dagger ready again.

'No need. In case of emergency I'll shoot him to keep his mouth shut before I kill myself.'

After a pause Ah Fook said, 'I can only hope that you'll have the good fortune of getting to Stanley Bay before midnight.'

'I don't think I can make it.'

Ah Fook took a small cloth package out of his pocket and then said, 'Mrs So declined your present.'

'Is she still angry with me?' she asked with a bitter smile.

Ah Fook smiled and shook his head. 'By no means. On the contrary, this time your stepmother is concerned for you.'

'How come?'

Ah Fook shook the package as it made tinkling sounds in his hand. 'Just imagine, she's a greedy woman, yet she would not accept your jewels even in this difficult time.' He then handed the package to Li-ling.

She shook her head. 'I still don't understand.'

'All this time your stepmother thought that you'd deserted her and your brother and would never come back. Today she was deeply moved, even to the point of tears, that you sacrificed your life to come back to get her and Chi-ching out of what she termed "the prison home". She said that though she had barely enough jewels left for her and Chi-ching, she would not take away yours which could be useful to you. She added that Chi-ching has missed you, and they look forward to a reunion with you as soon as possible.'

Tears welling up in her eyes, Li-ling felt the warmth of the package she was holding as if it were the friendly hand stretched out to her by her stepmother. Consequently, Li-ling put it in her handbag.

Ah Fook shook hands with her. 'I'm sure that after the war is over, both the Chinese and British Governments will decorate you and Major Jones with high honours. Goodbye.'

By the time he reached the staircase, his eyes were misty. He turned around and saluted her before he left.

★

In the meantime, Chief Wong remained on the floor bleeding.

This man deserves one thousand deaths, Li-ling thought as she watched. Why should I lend him a hand?

As time went on, the pool of red blood became larger and larger, and her heart gradually softened.

As he opened his eyes, Chief Wong said faintly, 'Water, water!'

Li-ling recalled what her father had said on his deathbed about Wong, 'He's utterly immoral except for one merit – he had a modicum of filial piety for his mother...'

This man has been duly punished, she concluded. Confucians advise people not to go to extremes.

Li-ling put the pistol on the table. She then brought him a glass of water and helped him drink. She fetched the first-aid box. Because his pyjamas and undershirt were drenched in blood, she cut them away with a pair of scissors. She cleaned the stab wounds with a piece of cotton soaked in alcohol and tried to stop the bleeding. Then she carefully applied iodine and bandaged them.

Although she helped Chief Wong get to his feet and walk over to the bed, he staggered. When they were near the table, he suddenly shook off her hold, moved a few steps and grabbed the pistol from the table. He turned around and aimed it at her. She gasped. However, he was weak and dropped to his knees, but he still held the pistol.

'Despite Miss Kwan's accusation,' he said slowly, 'until today I've never suspected Ah Fook and you were... collaborators. Now I also understand why he saved my life during that... assassination attempt. Both of you should have been beheaded a long time ago. What have you to say?'

'Kill me,' said Li-ling calmly as she recalled the scene in which her father had chosen death rather than cooperate with the Japanese.

'No, I... can't,' stammered Chief Wong, releasing the pistol. He pressed his hand to his heart and said, 'I feel a pang here whenever... I recall the scene in which I killed my beautiful and brave... Bella. Li-ling, for vengeance, I might have... shot you the way I shot her on the spur of the moment. But I was suddenly... moved by the concern you showed me. This brought back Bella's death scene. Throughout my partial consciousness, I still... heard your conversation, though not very clearly.' He coughed severely before he went on.

'Li-ling, without... taking my limousine, you... could never get to your destination in time. Press the button.'

Sobbing, she nodded.

He resumed in a weak voice, 'Three days after the outbreak of the Pacific War... two of Britain's great warships were sunk. Believing that the war would drag on for many years, I joined the Japanese... However, since then my peace of mind has been disturbed, though subconsciously at first, because I was—'

'Conscience-stricken,' she interrupted.

'No, not at all. Even... as a child I cursed Heaven for my ill fate and swore that I'd use whatever means needed to make up for what I'd been deprived of. That is money, money, and plenty of money!'

'Then what's disturbed your peace of mind?' she asked.

'Because even at the beginning of the war, I was well aware… the day of Japan's defeat would come despite its remoteness. Toward the end of 1942, when Japan and its Axis… partners were checked in their advances, I began to sense… the war would come to an end much sooner than I'd expected.' Chief Wong paused to rest before he continued. His voice grew weaker with each word he uttered hereafter.

'I've gradually needed… more and more stimulants – to excite and resuscitate my mind… just like Genda's sadistic ones. But mine are women, women and plenty of women. Although I've slept with many beautiful women, none of them compared with you favourably in virtue… You declined my promotion of you to co-wife, and you've never accepted my valuable presents.'

Chief Wong wiped his nose with the back of his hand.

'Don't think a wicked man doesn't respect' – he almost choked – 'virtuous people. I respect them more because I lack what they possess, just as an ugly man' – he coughed – 'respects beautiful women all the more.'

'You treat women as if they were machines to satisfy your desire,' said Li-ling.

'Yes, but you are an exception. Sometimes I think I should be content with my lot as long as… I can merely appreciate your looks, your manner, your smile and frown… your tears…without even touching you. Yet I've never been able – to win the affections of the only woman I've ever really loved. What would be the use… even if I keep you here… until the war's over.'

They heard a knock at the door.

'Ah Hall, is that you?' he asked.

'Chief, I can't hear you. Please speak louder.'

'Ah Hall, wake up the chauffeur and tell him to get... the car ready... for Second Mrs Wong,' he said louder.

'Chief Wong,' asked Ah Hall, 'are you sure? You gave orders not to let Second Mrs Wong leave the house.'

Li-ling's face turned pale.

After a pause, Chief Wong said, 'For safety reasons... she should stay at a friend's house... for a few days.'

Li-ling's colour returned.

'Chief Wong,' asked Ah Hall, 'Is there anything wrong? Are you all right?'

Li-ling froze. She wanted to say, 'Chief Wong is very tired,' but remained silent.

'I'm all right... only tired and maybe I drank too much,' said Chief Wong.

'Goodnight, Chief Wong, Second Mrs Wong.' Ah Hall left.

Li-ling sighed quietly.

'Li-ling,' said Chief Wong in a lower voice, 'though I've lived in wealth and power, I haven't been happy... because I've had no peace of mind.' He paused to breathe deeply. 'Now I am happy. I'm dying before the pitying eyes of a lovely woman I love... not the contemptuous eyes of thousands of people pointing... accusing fingers at me... a traitor while I'm paraded on my way to the... firing squad. I've had many, many such nightmares.'

As Chief Wong gasped for air, Li-ling patted him on the back.

'On her deathbed my mother told me to make up for my crimes by doing good deeds. Although Ah Fook is my number one enemy, he is a... great spy and I admire him. For your sake as well as for my country which I owe... blood debts, I'll save all your lives.' He spat blood onto the floor. 'In fact,' he went on, 'I don't want to live any longer. If I wanted to live on, I could call Ah Hall to send for a doctor. But then all my efforts to help you... your family and the underground workers... would be fruitless.'

'You're in agony,' she said. 'What can I do for you?'

'Hurry, Li-ling. Go... before it's... too late. Take... pistol... in case...'

She bent down, attempting to assist him to the bed, but he motioned her to leave.

'Goodbye.' Li-ling left with his pistol in her handbag, tears rolling down her cheeks.

Chapter Five

Once Li-ling boarded the limousine, she ordered the chauffeur to drive her to the town of Stanley at the southernmost part of Hong Kong Island.

'Second Mrs Wong, we missed you. How are you?' asked the chauffeur.

'I'm fine, Ah Kung. How are you and your big family?'

'They're all very well. Second Mrs Wong, why did you come back? It's dangerous!'

'I came to persuade Chief Wong to make arrangements for my mother and brother to leave Hong Kong. I can't go with them because I'd be recognised. Chief Wong wants me to hide at a friend's house at Stanley for the time being.'

The limousine, flying a Japanese pennant, headed toward Stanley. On the way she looked back several times to see if any car was following. They passed by several stations, where the gendarmes stood at attention.

*

An Austin motorcar emerged from Stanley Internment Camp.

'Where to, Lieutenant Colonel Genda?' asked the driver, a non-commissioned gendarme officer.

'To meet my girl in the Wanchai *Consolation House*,' answered the officer from the back.

'Yim-fun? You could get better-looking girls than her.'

'Perhaps, but she's the most masochistic,' Lieutenant Colonel Genda said, and then quickly added, 'I mean... she's nice... very nice.'

The Austin now drove from Stanley northward while Chief Wong's limousine headed in the opposite direction. There was little motor traffic anywhere in wartime Hong Kong, to say nothing of this hilly area, on which they were travelling, especially at night. As time went on, both cars got closer and closer to each other and finally arrived on the same two-laned road.

One lane of a section of the road between the two approaching cars was closed for repair and the other remained open for traffic. Two Chinese workers stood at either end of the section, each with a large gas lamp hanging on a scaffold with a 'stop' sign under it.

As the Austin arrived at the south end of the section a little earlier than the limousine reached the north end, the workers signalled the Austin to go through the open lane and the limousine to wait.

In the bright light of the lamp when the Austin passed the stationary limousine at the north end of the section, Lieutenant Colonel Genda and his chauffeur on the one side and Li-ling and Ah Kung on the other glanced at each other through the open windows of the cars. For a second, Li-ling felt as if an ice cube had slipped down her back. She recognized Lieutenant Colonel Genda, but he did not seem to identify her.

After the Austin passed the limousine and continued its northbound journey, the limousine travelled south in the open lane.

'Ah Kung, did Lieutenant Colonel Genda and his chauffeur see us?' asked Li-ling.

'Yes, they must have. Second Mrs Wong, this time you'll surely get caught.'

'You're right. I must give myself up, but we can't turn around here in this only one narrow lane.'

'Yes, Second Mrs Wong,' said Ah Kung, looking pleased as he continued to drive.

After the limousine had passed the south end of the section, Ah Kung made a U-turn in two lanes and waited for the workers' signal before heading back north in the open lane. He said to her, 'I agree that you should turn yourself in.'

Li-ling was quiet and thoughtful.

★

Lieutenant Colonel Genda frowned for a long time before he turned to his chauffeur.

'Corporal Nishio, did you see whose car that was?'

'Certainly, it was Chief Wong's. I recognized his chauffeur, Ah Kung, too.'

'Did you notice who else was inside?'

'Yes, a maidservant in the back seat.'

'How did you know she was a maidservant?'

'She was dressed in labourer's clothing.'

After musing a while, the lieutenant colonel snapped his fingers and said, 'Then she mustn't have been a servant. Thank you for reminding me of her clothing.'

'Why?'

'As a maidservant, she should've been sitting beside the chauffeur,' said Genda, stroking his thin moustache. 'Several months ago, I pressed Chief Wong to keep the So family isolated from their relatives and friends, expecting Second Mrs Wong to come back to Hong Kong to see her mother and brother. Ha, ha, she's fallen into my trap!' He coughed before he said, puzzled, 'But I just don't understand why Chief Wong let her travel in his car at this late hour to Stanley, nay, perhaps Stanley Bay.'

'Nor do I.'

'There must be something fishy. Was she Second Mrs Wong in disguise?'

'Yes, something's strange.'

'Corporal Nishio,' he suddenly shouted some moments later, 'make a U-turn right away. We must catch her!'

'Why a U-turn?' asked the corporal, continuing to drive onwards. 'Lieutenant Colonel Genda, if we continue to go north, we can get to the nearest gendarmerie station within five minutes. There, we can call the Stanley Headquarters to order all stations in the vicinity to set up roadblocks and all patrol boats to blockade Stanley Bay. Then Second Mrs Wong and her gang can't get away. But if we go south, it'll take us at least ten minutes to get to the nearest station.'

'Shut up! Turn around and get going at full speed,' shouted Genda.

Nishio obeyed and the car turned around and went south.

★

After the limousine reversed its direction and returned to the north end of the road section under repair, Li-ling told her chauffeur, 'Please stop.'

Ah Kung shrugged his shoulders and pulled over. 'Why?' he asked.

'Get out, please, and let me drive,' said Li-ling.

Ah Kung remained seated. 'You don't know how.'

'Of course, I do. My English friend taught me.'

'What do you intend to do?'

'At first I intended to join the underground workers who are leaving Stanley Bay in a boat instead of hiding at a friend's house as I told you. But since Lieutenant Colonel Genda saw us here so late at night, he will suspect that I am planning to escape with the help of underground workers in a boat, of course. However, I must save them from being caught by preventing him from reporting to a gendarmerie station for a blockade of the bay.'

'I don't understand why at first Chief Wong gave us orders not to let you leave the house, but later changed his mind. What's the matter with him?'

'No time to explain now. You'll find out.'

'Second Mrs Wong, you love our country, I agree, but are you out of your mind? There's no hope of success! You'll kill yourself!'

'Yes. I attempted suicide once before, but that was for myself. This time it is for a great cause... for my country as well as my friends. I'll try... like a kamikaze.' Her tone was firm.

'Second Mrs Wong, with your foster father's influence, you won't die. The war will be over soon. You have a good future. Why do you want to die for those underground workers? Why don't you let them take the risks for their jobs? If you don't listen to me, I may be beheaded as an accomplice. I have to support my wife, my six children and my old mother. Please, pity me, Second Mrs Wong.' Ah Kung remained riveted to his seat.

'Here's a package of eight pieces of jewellery,' she said, putting it on his lap. Then all of a sudden she poked the muzzle of Chief Wong's pistol into the back of his neck, shouting, 'Take the package and get out quickly or I'll shoot! Run away or you'll get involved.'

As the hazy-eyed Ah Kung hastily got out with the package, Li-ling took his place behind the wheel. Looking fidgety, he walked very fast in the opposite direction toward Stanley. She drove north at full speed, regardless of her own safety when the lives of many underground workers were at stake. The trees that lined the road seemed to be flying over her head.

★

'Lieutenant Colonel Genda, may I ask why you didn't mind a five-minute delay in alerting the gendarmerie station?' asked the corporal, driving the Austin at full speed.

'Surely we can catch them before they can get to the bay.'

'But why all this trouble? Why don't you let the other gendarmes do the job?'

'Vengeance! If Second Mrs Wong is arrested by the gendarmes, she'll be sentenced to death, but her sentence will definitely be commuted to life imprisonment.'

'Why?'

'Second Mrs Wong is General Tamura's foster daughter. Unfortunately, he returned to Hong Kong last week after serving about two and a half years in Burma. Moreover, her sentence may be further commuted if we win the war. Certainly she'll be freed if we lose.' He cleared his throat. 'Since she escaped with a POW in my custody about two and a half years ago, all my peers have been promoted, but I still remain a commandant, merely transferred from Shamshuipo POW Camp in Kowloon to Stanley Internment Camp on Hong Kong Island.'

'Now I understand your feelings.'

'Even a death sentence won't be sufficient compensation, to say nothing of a mere imprisonment. I want to take the law into my own hands!' Genda curled his lips.

'How?'

'First, I'll shoot her chauffeur to death in order to frighten her. Then I'll wound her, but not to the point of making her lose consciousness. I want to hear her cry and watch her agonised face while she's bleeding to death. Of course I'll fire at both of them from behind so that it looks like they were fired on while escaping.'

'Why fire on them from behind?'

'That way we'll avoid General Tamura's possible suspicion of my revenge on her.'

'You're very clever indeed.'

Although the Austin was going at full speed, Genda kept repeating, 'Faster! Faster!'

★

After the limousine and the Austin had each reversed its direction, they travelled towards each other again, still on the same road.

'In an emergency such as this, there's no place for so-called kindness – you must kill!' Li-ling seemed to hear Stephen's voice when she saw the Austin getting closer and closer.

'Stephen,' she murmured, 'I'll be joining you soon!'

She decided to swerve right into the Austin's path and slam headlong into it.

But this critical moment suddenly reminded Li-ling of the Confucian idea of benevolence and the Christian commandment of 'Thou shalt not kill.' In an instant she subconsciously felt as if it would require a great deal of strength to make the veer; she only moved the wheel slightly. In the meantime, when corporal Nishio saw the limousine swerve toward his Austin, he tried to pull to the left, but it was too late. The two cars bumped and bounced off each other. The Austin crashed against a tree, then rolled down the hillside. It finally settled upside down on a small plateau, some fifteen yards below. The two Japanese lay unconscious inside the Austin. The limousine hit an iron pole and crumpled. Its big size and weight kept it from overturning, but Li-ling too was knocked unconscious.

About two hours later, the two Japanese regained consciousness. Pinned by the entangled wreck, there was little room for them to move. It took considerable strength for them to yank off the shards of broken glass and strips of twisted metal and leather before they made their way clear enough to squeeze through one crushed door opening.

When they got out of the Austin, they found that they had sustained serious bruises and bleeding cuts. Nevertheless, they shook hands, each with a broad smile. Together they painstakingly climbed the hillside to the road. Genda ran breathlessly toward the limousine, pistol in hand, Nishio following him.

Since she came to herself, Li-ling had attempted to remove the twisted steering wheel pinned against her bosom, but her efforts were in vain. She too had suffered bruises and bleeding cuts. Her head hurt; her strength had run out.

The two Japanese officers came to the limousine. As soon as the corporal caught sight of a pistol and a cloth pack on the seat beside Li-ling, he grabbed them. After Lieutenant Colonel Genda stared at her for a moment, a look of exultation swept over his face.

'Where's the chauffeur, Second Mrs Wong?' he sneered.

'I didn't want him to get involved in my personal business.'

'You never dreamed that you'd... fall into my trap,' he said bowing deeply to Li-ling with a cold laugh, showing his buck teeth. 'You'll be treated fairly now.'

Li-ling looked blank. Blood dripped down her face from cuts on her forehead, but she did not care. The two Japanese worked hard to pull the twisted wheel away and finally extricated her.

'Now walk down the hillside,' ordered Genda, readying his pistol. Just as Li-ling began to move, lights suddenly emanated from the north, then a moment later from the south of the road in the midst of the darkness. With their mouths wide open, the three of them saw the lights getting brighter and brighter as two motor cars raced toward them.

Finally the cars halted beside them. Several gendarmes jumped out along with Ah Kung.

'Lieutenant Colonel Genda,' said a gendarme saluting him, 'I am Corporal Shindo, reporting to you. Thanks to the information given by Chief Wong's chauffeur at my station twelve minutes ago, we immediately phoned the Stanley Headquarters and nearby stations. Then we rushed here.'

Lieutenant Colonel Genda looked blank.

When Li-ling's eyes met Ah Kung's, he quickly turned his scarlet face away. Then she glanced at her watch. It was almost two o'clock. She relaxed, for she knew that her family had already arrived in Macao and that Ah Fook and his men must have reached safety by this time. Now she felt some blood running down her face, so she wiped it with her handkerchief.

She was shoved into the back seat of one car between Genda and Nishio while Ah Kung and the other gendarmes boarded the other. Both cars headed towards downtown Hong Kong Island.

Chapter Six

From the early hours throughout the day, in her prisoner's loose dark-brown jacket and pants, Li-ling sat on a canvas bed in a cell inside the Japanese Gendarmerie Main Headquarters. Meals were brought in regularly, but she did not eat. She recalled happy moments she had shared with her loved ones, especially Stephen.

Since Steve and Papa are dead and young Mama and Chiching are under the care of the reliable Miss Silva in Macao, thought Li-ling, there's not much to worry about. It doesn't matter to me if I die.

Though she could not sleep at night, she remained calm, waiting for her final fate.

In the cool dawn the following morning, a Japanese prison officer, wearing a black leather patch over his left eye, unlocked the door of the cell and handcuffed her hands behind her. Then he led her outside to board a waiting covered van with about twenty male and two female prisoners, all in handcuffs, already inside. The van started, two smaller open ones full of Japanese gendarmes following. An hour later, they reached a large piece of open ground.

The prisoners were ordered out and lined up at intervals a few feet apart. Their handcuffs were removed and each prisoner was handed a pick and a shovel and ordered to dig his own grave. Tears mixed with sweat as they toiled under the unblinking eyes of the gendarmes, who held rifles with fixed bayonets. When the prisoners did not work fast enough, they were prodded with rifle butts. Afterwards, the gendarmes ordered them to turn their collars down and kneel at the edge of the holes. Their hands were bound with ropes behind their backs, and their eyes blindfolded with strips of coarse cloth.

Some prisoners shrieked defiance, some cried hysterically, and a few, including Li-ling, remained calm. She prayed to Heaven for the next life when she could meet Steve again. She imagined that their souls would transmigrate into a pair of butterflies flying freely side by side, or a pair of larks singing merrily together. She wished their love would remain as long as the universe.

As if in an abattoir, one by one the prisoners' heads were slashed from their bodies by a single blow of the sabre. Blood spurted from their severed arteries. The heads rolled into the pits. The gendarmes kicked the mutilated carcasses into the graves and buried them with the earth the prisoners had just dug out.

As an executioner approached Li-ling with his bloody sabre, she shouted, 'Long live China! Down with Japanese imperialism!'

Just as the killer readied his sabre for the strike, an open-top car roared up and skidded to a stop. The prison officer with the eye patch shrieked, 'Stop! Stop!' then jumped out of the car. He rushed toward the executioner, shaking a document.

As the butcher read it, he murmured, 'How could General Tamura spare the life of such a notorious woman?'

Li-ling's hands were unfastened and the blindfold removed. Standing on death's doorstep one moment and her miraculous release the next had made her completely numb. To her, there was no demarcation line between life and death, just as there appears no horizon between the sea and the sky when they are the same hue. The prison officer drove her back to the Gendarmerie Main Headquarters.

★

Sitting alone in a room at the Gendarmerie Main Headquarters, General Tamura looked at a Japanese newspaper lying on the table in front of him. The headline read: 'Germany Surrenders – Japan Fights On.'

He knew that the United States Navy and Marines had earlier taken the Philippines and Okinawa, and that the Chinese and British troops had lately occupied Burma.

My country has been losing everything it has gained so far, he thought. What do personal promotions, prestige, power and wealth matter now?

About an hour later, on arrival at the Main Headquarters, the officer with the eyepatch told Li-ling, 'Lieutenant General Tamura will see you now.' He showed her into the room. She noticed that her foster father now had two stars on either side of his uniform collar.

The officer submitted a stack of documents to the general, who put them on the table. He motioned the officer to leave, then invited Li-ling to sit across the table from him.

'Li-ling,' asked General Tamura in Japanese, looking at a document before him, 'do you understand the great offences that you have committed against the Imperial Empire of Japan which were read to you yesterday afternoon?'

Li-ling nodded.

'Under the practice of your country,' continued the general, but in a mild tone, 'you'd be decorated. But unfortunately you are under our jurisdiction. Therefore, you shall be sentenced to life imprisonment. If you'd been caught a few months earlier or if the governor hadn't come back in time from Canton early this morning for me to ask him to commute your death sentence, you couldn't have been saved from execution. You are very lucky, indeed.

'After Chief Wong learned of your arrest at 3 a.m. yesterday, he called and talked to me for about fifteen minutes. With his last breath he told me everything about you, laying blame on himself alone. I was greatly shocked at his confession that you'd married him as a concubine in order to save your father's life. It's clear that his motive was to elicit my sympathy so that I would seek mercy on your behalf.'

The general took a few sips of water from a glass before going on. 'I appreciate the essence of the famous Chinese saying: "When a bird is dying, its chirp is sad; when a man is dying, his word is good."'

'When Chief Wong told me about your elopement as soon as I returned to Hong Kong last week, I then wondered why you had married him even as a concubine while still having a lover. Since Chief Wong didn't explain and I was too busy, I didn't bother to ask him to elaborate on his personal business. I didn't understand the whole truth until he confessed before his death.'

He wiped his mouth with a handkerchief, then continued.

'Chief Wong said it was ironic that as Head of the Chinese Intelligence Section of the Japanese Gendarmerie Main Headquarters in Hong Kong, he'd completely trusted Ah Fook for almost three years – the man who turned out to be the leader of the counterpart intelligence. As a proud man, Chief Wong hinted that he'd rather die than face his colleagues and the people when he became the laughing stock of Hong Kong.

'I tried to comfort him by saying that he was not to blame, for it was the then Lieutenant Colonel Soken, now General Soken, who had strongly recommended Ah Fook to him in the first place.' The general coughed before he resumed. 'Knowing that Chief Wong was seriously wounded, I asked him to send for a doctor. But he flatly refused. He seemed to have lost interest in life. At last he dropped the receiver and kept silent. Later I found out he was dead.' The general shook his head.

'I've studied Confucianism, and find you, my foster daughter, are the epitome of all the traditional virtues of 'a Chinese woman: filial piety, kindness, forgiveness, devotion to one lover and loyalty to friends. And yet, you also have the judgement, determination, ability and courage of a modern woman, nay, a strong-willed man. You are not only beautiful, but also the embodiment of the highest character of the East and the West I've ever known.'

'Thank you,' whispered Li-ling, her head bending low.

'After I graduated from Japan Military Academy,' he went on, 'I tried very hard to realize my ambition... to become the commander-in-chief of the entire Japanese army. Each promotion made me very happy, but only for a short while. Then I waited anxiously for the next.

'Your outlook on life, as indicated by your unselfish behaviour the day I first met you, has gradually broadened mine. Since then I've been free of unnecessary stress and at peace with myself with or without promotion, like a Taoist or a Buddhist. For this I'm grateful to you.'

The general cleared his throat before resuming, 'One evening at a dinner party, when you asked me to influence the governor to increase the rice ration for the Chinese people, you braved the wrath of my colleagues. Although I looked displeased, I admired your courage and virtue.

'Were you as happy the two years that you were with your English friend as Chief Wong said?'

Choking with sobs, Li-ling could not speak, but slumped on her knees in front of the general and nodded repeatedly.

'I'm glad,' he said, walking to the door. 'Goodbye, Foster Daughter.'

Chapter Seven

About three months later on 6th August, 1945, Hong Kong time, the first atomic bomb dropped on Hiroshima; on 9th August, on Nagasaki.

On 15th August the Emperor of Japan read the imperial prescript during a nationwide broadcast from Tokyo. He ordered his subjects to lay down their arms and surrender peacefully. The war in Asia and the Pacific ended – bringing the final conclusion to World War II.

Instead of rifles, grenades, artillery, mines and bombs, firecrackers exploded in celebration. Shops and offices suspended business. Beggars stopped begging; scavengers took a holiday. Theatres and restaurants were crowded with people as if admission and food were free. The occasion was more exciting and exhilarating than Chinese New Year's Day. After weeping for three years and eight months, Hong Kong finally smiled.

At noon on the same day, the Japanese Government of Hong Kong issued a special order to the wardens of all the civilian prisons to release the inmates irrespective of the length of their sentences due to a 'lack of funds'.

In a women's prison in Kowloon, Li-ling and her fellow inmates exchanged addresses. Then she changed from her prisoner's dark-brown uniform into her suit of labourer's dark-gray clothes.

'Miss So, don't forget to send me an invitation to your wedding,' said a middle-aged woman as they packed.

'What wedding?' asked a young woman, shaking her head.

The older one whispered to her. The younger one then said, 'Miss So, don't forget me.'

Li-ling bade farewell to them and left with her cloth pack.

'Why is she so foolish?' asked the younger woman, looking puzzled.

Pausing between each word, the older woman said with a smile, 'This is love!'

★

As her country and she were freed, Li-ling greeted everyone she met in the streets with a smile.

Suddenly, a three-wheeled pedicab stopped beside the kerb near her. 'Second Mrs Wong,' shouted the coolie, sitting on the saddle-like seat, 'how are you?'

'Ah Kung!' cried the jolted Li-ling, 'I'm fine! How are you?'

'Where're you going?'

'To Buddhist Cemetery.'

'So far away. Please get on.'

'No. I can't afford the fare. Thank you.'

'Never mind. The ride for you is free. After all, I only have this vehicle because of you.'

'Me? Why?'

'Do you remember that you gave me a package of jewels when we parted? I bought this vehicle and paid my mother's medical fees with your valuables.'

'I'm glad you made good use of it.' Li-ling climbed on.

'I should thank you for your gift to help my family through this difficult time.'

The pedicab started its journey. On the streets most of the vehicles were operated by manpower. When a truck filled with Japanese soldiers passed by, adults shouted at them and children threw stones at them, but they ignored it.

Li-ling heard a pedestrian say, 'They were lions, but now they are sheep.' She smiled.

'Second Mrs Wong,' said Ah Kung, 'I apologize for having double-crossed you.'

'No need. I understand. Otherwise the Japanese would have accused you of helping me escape or abstaining from informing them of my attempt to kill Genda beforehand.'

'It took me two hours to walk to the gendarme station to report on you. I knew very well that by that time you would have already confronted Genda.'

'In fact, I should thank you instead,' explained Li-ling. 'If the gendarmes had not arrived at the scene in time, the sadistic Genda would have tortured me.'

The pedicab turned into another street. 'Ah Kung, do many people know that I've come back to Hong Kong?'

'No. After your miraculous escape with your English friend, you became a legend and the Japanese lost face. Later, after you came back and helped Ah Fook escape, the Japanese didn't want another heroic story to get around. As soon as you were arrested, the Japanese gendarmes warned Chief Wong's subordinates and domestic servants to cover up your return and ordered us to tell people that Chief Wong had gone to Macao to see his family. His body was secretly buried somewhere.'

'Did you think I was executed?'

'At first, yes. But a few days later, I met Ah Hall. He told me secretly that your death sentence had been changed to life imprisonment. I was happy to hear that.'

'Ah Kung, please stop at the nearest restaurant for food offerings and a grocery store for incense sticks for my late parents.'

'Do you need money, Second Mrs Wong? I can give you some.'

'No, thank you.'

★

It took them more than one and a half hours to get to her destination because of the numerous pedestrians on the streets.

At the So Family Tombs with the help of Ah Kung, Li-ling lit a bundle of incense sticks with a match and inserted them into the marble censer standing in front of the upright marble gravestone. She could not hold back her tears when she saw her father's portrait alongside her birth mother's, both inscribed on porcelain plates inlaid on the gravestones. She opened three cardboard boxes respectively containing soy sauce chicken, barbecued pork and crispy duck, already cut into pieces, and took the apples and bananas out of a paper bag. She placed all the food in front of the censer, then knelt three times, each time making three kowtows before this temporary altar.

Before she stood up, she said, 'Papa and Old Mama, I'm happy to tell you that Japan surrendered today. We are a free country again. Chief Wong was killed a few months ago. We are sure that all traitors will soon be punished.

'Young Mama and Chi-ching are in Macao under the care of my former teacher, Miss Silva.

'Please celebrate to your hearts' content with these offerings on this happy day.'

Ah Kung then bowed deeply three times to the two portraits.

Li-ling and he shared the meat and fruit with four skinny children who had just come to beg for food. They all used toothpicks to lift the meat into their mouths. The children devoured the food in no time.

Eyes wet, Li-ling sighed quietly, 'Poor Steve, when and where can I find your body and get you a grave so that your soul may rest in peace?'

Chapter Eight

On hearing Emperor Hirohito's broadcast, Japanese commandants and guards of all the POW and intern camps hurriedly vacated when it was rumoured that their inmates would seek revenge.

At 3 p.m. that day a Rolls-Royce flying a Union Jack and two loaded trucks entered the guardless Shamshuipo POW Camp. Sir William, dressed in Western clothing, got out of the car and was greeted by the English camp officer at the general office building. They headed for the microphone before an assembly of the former prisoners of war, who were either standing or sitting on the open ground.

'Gentlemen,' said the officer before the microphone, 'we take pleasure in announcing that Sir William Wen, the former number one non-official member of the Executive Council of our Hong Kong Government – not the Japanese Hong Kong Government...' Sounds of laughter from the audience cut off his speech. He held his hand up, signalling for silence before he continued, '...has sent us a truckload of presents.'

Applause broke out.

'I'd like to add that Sir William has also recently rendered valuable service in expediting delivery of food parcels and medical supplies to all the POWs from the International Red Cross,' the officer continued. 'I now thank him heartily on behalf of all of us for his concern for our well-being and for his gifts, which we so badly need. Now may I invite Sir William to speak to us.'

Loud applause greeted Sir William. He addressed the meeting in English:

'Major Boon, thank you very much for your compliments. Gentlemen, I do feel highly honoured to have an opportunity to speak to you on such an historic day as this. You should be proud of your part in creating such a great day in history for the cause of world peace with your blood and sweat. You did fight bravely for us in Hong Kong for eighteen days three years and eight months ago, and you have suffered in this small hell ever since. When we Chinese heard that many of you died of malnutrition, disease and harsh treatment, we grieved. We're sorry that we couldn't even express concern for your plight, nor could we show our respect for your service in the defence of Hong Kong until today.'

Sir William wiped some tears from his eyes with his handkerchief before he went on. 'Now that the war is over, as the representative of the Chinese Chamber of Commerce, of which I am the honorary president, I have hereby brought a small gift for each of you in order to show our appreciation. We have a saying: 'A gift may be of small value, but the thoughtfulness behind it is immense. We sincerely hope that you will enjoy a life of freedom and peace you most deserve. May God bless you all.'

Applause broke out again. Then Major Boon led Sir William on a tour of the camp.

Sir William chatted with the sick and the disabled, one by one, some of whom were lying in their bunks. He enquired about their past sufferings at the hands of the Japanese, their present health condition and future plans.

When Sir William stopped beside a man, he noticed two distinct jagged scars on his left cheek and his half-empty left sleeve. The man was asleep on his right side in a bunk, his face towards the wall.

'Major Boon, where did this soldier get wounded?'

'Sir William, he is an officer. About two and a half years ago, he attempted to escape with a few fellow prisoners, but they were caught, and he got wounded. However, some time before the trial date, he made another escape, this one quite miraculous, with a Chinese girl. Later, they joined the Free China guerrillas somewhere in Kwangtung Province.'

'Then how did he get back here?'

'When the Japs attacked the guerrilla stronghold a few months ago, he was seriously wounded and then captured. Afterwards, the Japanese treated his wounds in a hospital in Canton and subsequently returned him to this camp only four days ago.'

'What was the girl's name?'

'He didn't tell me her name.' Major Boon turned to the only one of his room-mates present. 'Do you know, Jackie?'

Jack shook his head.

'Where is she now?' asked Sir William.

'She left the guerrilla stronghold with the nurses for Chungking before the Japanese attack,' said Major Boon, 'according to the officer.'

'Could the girl's name be Li-ling So? Her father was a good friend of mine.'

'What makes you think of that?'

'Because Miss So helped a British officer, then a prisoner of war, escape with her from Hong Kong about two and a half years ago,' said the knight. 'What's this officer's name, please?'

'Stephen Jones,' said the major.

'Then why didn't the Japanese punish him for his escape?'

'According to him, the Japs realized by then that they'd lose the war soon.'

'Since I have to hurry to another POW camp, I'm afraid I have no time to talk with him even if he wakes up now. Major Boon, I am very concerned about Miss So's fate.

Now that the war is just over, I'll be very busy. Would you mind if I call on this officer, who may be Miss So's friend, in two or three days for a long chat?'

'By that time we all may have moved out.'

'Then would you give me his address and telephone number?'

'I have no record of these. Soon after the Japanese took Hong Kong, they transferred all the officers and their files here to the Argyle Street Camp except six officers, including me, to help run this camp. Steve took the identity of a dead private in order to remain behind, so he could escape from here, which is near the coast.'

The major turned to Jack, 'Do you know?'

Jack shook his head.

'After Steve awakes, Jackie, get me his address and telephone number so that I may mail them to Sir William.'

'Yes, Sir.'

Major Boon and Jack saw Sir William off at the entrance of the camp.

★

After they left, Stephen awoke.

He said to himself quietly, 'Dearest Li-ling, keep believing that I'm dead. Marry a Chinese man, so your relatives and friends won't discriminate. I hope that you and he will love each other, so that he may heal the wounds of your heart. But at the same time never forget me – your first love. Then I'll be more than satisfied despite our permanent separation. Goodbye, Li-ling, God bless you!'

Thin and rather pale, Stephen arose. While he put on his POW clothing, Jack came back and handed him a paper parcel and a bottle of Watson's orange drink, saying, 'You didn't attend Sir William's speech. On behalf of the

Chinese Chamber of Commerce he gave each of us a present.'

Inside the parcel Stephen found a ten-dollar note issued by the Hong Kong and Shanghai Banking Corporation, a towel, a pack of tissue paper, a small bar of soap, a toothbrush, a small tube of toothpaste, a comb, a safety razor and two Chinese egg cakes.

He took out the tattered, shrunken sweater which Liling had knitted for him from his fully packed, torn leather suitcase and stuffed the parcel and then the bottle of drink inside. Though there was little space left for the sweater, he put it over the bottle and, with Jack's help, crammed it into the suitcase so tightly that he could barely press the metal catches to close it.

'I was too tired to attend,' said Stephen.

'You're always sleepy,' said Jack, 'but once you get some nutrition, your strength will return.'

'I packed this morning. I should have been home now, but Major Boon ordered us to stay for Sir William's visit.'

'Steve, after he delivered his speech, Sir William came here on a tour of inspection while you were still sleeping. He suspected that the girl you escaped with might be his good friend's daughter... a Miss So.'

'Jackie, how did Sir William know this?' asked Stephen, banging his fist on the table. 'I told you to keep my escape a secret from any Chinese, didn't I?'

'It was Major Boon, not me, who mentioned your name and the escape. In fact, you've told us little about the girl. We didn't even know her name until Sir William told us. He asked Major Boon to get your phone number and address so that he may contact you later.'

'No. I don't want to see him.'

Jack shook his head and left the room.

Then Stephen recalled what he had told Jack two days before.

★

'Jackie, look at me,' Stephen had said in suppressed torture, holding a mirror. Then he threw it to the floor, shattering the glass and scattering the tiny pieces everywhere. 'My sweetheart is so beautiful.'

'But you can get an artificial arm fixed and your scars refined,' said Jack.

'These physical imperfections can't be completely rectified in spite of modern technology. I'll still be ugly and crippled.' Stephen shook his head.

'Steve, you are an engineer. The loss of a left forearm only affects a blue-collar worker; a deformed face, an entertainer. Why do you worry so?'

'Although my girlfriend is devoted to me, her family, relatives and friends strongly object to her marrying a Westerner, to say nothing of a scarred and disabled one. I don't want her to suffer for the rest of her life.'

'Then will she be happy, the rest of her life without you?'

'Since she's been wanted by the gendarmes and the police of Hong Kong, she's stayed in Chungking. Now that the war is over, she'll come back here. I hope that she'll marry a young Chinese man from a decent family, so they'll live happily ever after. She probably thinks that I was killed, as were most of the guerrillas.'

'Steve, how's it that you've survived your disaster? When you briefly told Major Boon about your escape and your life in the guerrilla stronghold in his office the day of your arrival four days ago, I was not there, so I don't know as much about you as he does.'

'Two days before the fall of the stronghold, General Ting, Commander of the Guerrillas, told me to join Colonel Long's men in an attempt to break through the enemy lines to return to Free China. Unfortunately, a few hours before he was to lead the breakthrough, some guerrillas and I were firing at a squad of enemy advancing up the mountain when a grenade exploded within two feet of our howitzer, killing two of our men and wounding me. When my forearm was amputated, I lost a lot of blood with no transfusion. I lost consciousness for three days, and each day I was left for dead.'

'What then?'

'I regained consciousness one day after the stronghold fell.' After a pause, Stephen sighed. 'General Chang was killed and General Ting committed suicide just before the stronghold was overrun.'

'What a tragedy!'

'This was told to me by one of the two hundred and fifty seriously wounded guerrillas who, like me, were captured by the Japanese. About two hundred of them died on the following days. The fifty or so survivors were sent to hospitals in nearby towns. I was lucky. Two wounded Japanese officers and I were sent by ambulance on a two-day trip to the well-equipped Canton Military Hospital. I rested there for a few months under proper medical care but still without a transfusion. Then I was brought here in a Japanese motor boat.'

'What are your plans for the future?'

'I'll go back to my parents in Dublin, the sooner the better before my sweetheart comes looking for me in Hong Kong or even in London,' said Stephen grimly.

★

'Steve,' said Jack, after he came back into the room, 'now the situation's different. Since Sir William knows you're in Hong Kong, he'll surely tell Miss So about you after she comes back from Chungking. How could you be so cruel as to separate from her for good?'

'Wouldn't it be cruel to her, too, if I married her?'

Jack shook his head with a bitter smile.

'Jack, when are you moving out?'

'Many of us will have to remain here for a few days before our old barracks are ready. After supper we're going to take a tour of the outside world and enjoy our first day of liberty.'

After Stephen said goodbye to Jack and a number of other fellow inmates, he left the 'Hell' as they termed it with his suitcase.

In the streets, Stephen walked slowly and rested periodically by sitting on the pavement. Some pedestrians raised their fingers to show a 'V' sign; others came up to him and saluted. He smiled in return.

At last, when he reached the Tsimshatsui Ferry Pier, the clock hanging over the entrance to the ferry building struck five. He boarded a ferry to cross the harbour from Kowloon to Hong Kong Island. Aboard, many of the passengers, including some ex-POWs and ex-internees, sang and drank.

After disembarking on Hong Kong Island, he caught sight of a Union Jack flying over the roof of a building in the distance – the first one he had seen for the past three years and eight months.

It has never looked so beautiful before, he thought. Tears streamed down his cheeks as he stood at attention. He stared up at it for a long time and saluted before he left.

He walked homewards, going slowly up the sloping Garden Road. When he reached the cable-tram terminal, a pedestrian told him that the service had been suspended for some time. So he continued his journey to the Mid-Levels District on foot.

Stephen now walked westward along the level Robinson Road. As he thought about his home, he smiled. But he reeled with shock when he saw the two skeleton structures – all that remained of the Green and Blue Mansions. He walked up the sloping path leading to where his apartment house used to be and sat on the ground in front of the debris.

Greatly moved, he recalled how Li-ling had visited him for the first time and said, 'Good morning' instead of 'Good afternoon'; how they had joked and laughed; how they had cried; how they had hugged and kissed; how he had called her name again and again when he had not seen her for three or four days.

Finally he got up and walked down the path.

Where shall I go to find shelter for the night? Can't stay in a hotel, no money.

He remembered that when Li-ling and he separated at the guerrilla stronghold, she had given him four taels of gold for emergency. But when he woke from his unconscious state, he found that his Free China's badge, the gold and his Omega watch were all missing.

He had no alternative but to go back to Shamshuipo Camp. But after quite a while, he turned around and walked in the opposite direction. He wondered whether the So house was still intact. After going some distance, he caught sight of the same big banyan with its ever-green halo bearing many slender supporting trunks, each with its own crown of dense foliage. He recalled how he had first met his Li-ling there. Like an old film, his memory played in his mind.

★

Dressed in an old brown suit, Stephen stepped out of his car. He stared at Mike. Then he turned his gaze to Li-ling. 'You look familiar, a St Mary's girl from this neighbourhood?'

Clasping her hands in front of her, she looked straight into her Stephen's blue eyes. 'Please tell him to stop bothering me.'

With his eyebrows raised, Stephen turned to Michael. 'Come on, leave her alone.'

Dropping his hands to his side, Michael said, 'Steve, all I want is a date – just a date.'

Stephen shrugged. 'The young lady doesn't seem interested. You can't force her.'

Michael's eyes turned to fire. 'This is none of your business, Steve. Besides, she's only a half-breed.'

Li-ling tried to walk away, but Michael grabbed her arm.

Stephen ran up and pulled her free.

*

On his way again, Stephen walked slowly. It took him fifteen minutes to get to the So house. It stood there intact. Out of curiosity he looked through the lattice of the iron gate at the overgrown weeds all over the garden. No one appeared to be home. He turned and left.

I can't make the long journey back to the camp before I take some rest, he thought, yawning.

Chapter Nine

Li-ling and Ah Kung still chatted and played with the children. When it was time to leave, she kowtowed three times to pay her last respects to her parents.

As Li-ling reached Tsimshatsui Pier, the clock hanging over the entrance to the ferry building struck six. She bade farewell to Ah Kung and crossed the harbour on the ferry. After she disembarked on Hong Kong Island, she walked home up the sloping Garden Road, then westward along Robinson Road.

When she arrived at the skeleton structures of the two mansions, she broke down and cried. She recalled how Steve had taught her to dance, swim, drive a motor car, and operate a motor boat and how she had written his name again and again whenever she missed him.

She continued homewards. As she passed the big banyan, she remembered a past scene.

*

Throwing a quick punch that caught Steve off guard, Michael knocked him to the ground and snapped, 'Damn you!'

Rising swiftly, Steve swung and connected squarely with Michael's jaw. Now the two men were locked in a fierce fight. Fists, feet and elbows exchanged quickly, bruises and abrasions on their faces.

Her heart still pounding, Li-ling half ran and half walked away quite a distance before she turned to look back. She saw that the evil man seemed to be winning.

★

At last Li-ling arrived at her home about two and a half years after her escape. Her house was still standing, but the garden was a mess. She pushed open the gate and entered the garden. The house was locked. She rang the bell over and over, but received no response. All the curtains were lowered; no gleam of light showed through the windows.

Suddenly, she pictured in her mind the well-decorated living room all lit up! Li-ling saw through the curtains the many smiling guests who, one by one, offered the So family – her father, birth mother, second mother carrying a baby in her arms and a girl in her early teens – the same wishes, 'May you have many, many sons and countless, countless grandsons and great-grandsons to come!'

'If only sons and no daughters,' protested the young girl, 'in future, how could the sons marry wives to beget grandsons and great-grandsons?'

The whole room roared with laughter. Li-ling's father nodded with a smile while her second mother's face twisted.

After quite a while when she still stood in front of her dark home, in tears Li-ling smiled at her recollection of the occasion of her younger brother's first-year birthday party when she was twelve years old.

She now decided to go to Sir William's house in the Peak District for the night instead of going back to the women's prison which was so far. Soon after, she met an old servant of a neighbour, who looked shocked. He told her that a number of Wong's men who had lived at the So house had hurriedly moved out after the surrender of their Japanese masters that morning.

She said goodbye and walked further west past a few houses before she reached the stone steps which were a short cut to Conduit Road leading to the Peak District. After she got to the top of the flight, she was greatly touched when she found that all the beautiful Hong Kong orchid trees planted around the pavilion had been cut down during the war. As she recalled that she and Steve had chased each other several times among them with their rounded, double-lobed leaves and purplish-red flowers, she broke into tears once more.

She saw a Western man dressed in POW clothing sitting on the circular bench at the table in the centre of the pavilion. He was asleep, forehead resting on his right forearm on the table. When she came closer, she noticed two distinct scars on the left side of his face and his half-empty left sleeve. She felt a pain in her heart when she thought that this man must have fought and suffered for Hong Kong.

On the table she saw an empty bottle of drink and some cake crumbs. On the bench to his right was an old worn suitcase partly covered with a folded-up old blue woollen sweater.

She continued on her way. After she stepped onto Conduit Road and proceeded to the Peak District, the cool wind blew, bringing a chill up her spine. She recalled another scene from her past.

★

Still unclothed, Li-ling curled up into a tight little ball, sobbing. Her entire body ached with fevered agony; a tearing pain burned in her groin. Blood trickled down her nape and also down the lower part of her body. Exhausted, she trembled and her teeth chattered. She began to sneeze and cough severely.

★

That poor soldier may catch cold while he's asleep, she thought. Why didn't I cover him with his sweater? It's still summer, but the air's cool, especially in this district, as night approaches. By the look of him he had gone hungry and suffered malnutrition. As a citizen, I have an obligation to prevent this war hero from getting ill on this very first day of peace. She walked back to the pavilion.

She picked up the sweater from the suitcase. The colour had faded; one sleeve was missing; a few ragged ends hung down from the shoulder. Looking closer at the sweater, she shouted, involuntarily, 'It is so similar to Steve's!' She spread it over the stranger's back.

Stephen awakened. He opened his left eye and squinted at Li-ling – his dearest love. His whole body began to quiver uncontrollably, but he did not turn his head.

Li-ling blushed. 'I'm very sorry to have awakened you. I was afraid that you might catch a chill.' Fearing that he might misunderstand her intention, she added, 'I had a good English friend, Mr Stephen Jones of the No. 1 Battery of the Hong Kong Volunteer Defence Corps. He was once a prisoner at Shamshuipo POW Camp. Did you know him? Have you heard of him? He was a hero, but now he's dead. I knitted a sweater for him, just like this one.'

Stephen shook his head slightly without raising it, then closed his left eye.

While she was talking to the soldier, Li-ling noticed tears falling drop by drop onto the table.

After she said goodbye, she added, 'If I hurt you, I'm terribly sorry.'

He did not respond.

She walked away while questions continued to plague her, one after another.

If Steve was killed in combat, how could that be him?

Why did he shed tears? Has he lost his home like Steve? Does he grieve over the death of his loved one like me?

Why did he ignore me? Perhaps he didn't want to face strangers, but any wounded soldier should feel proud.

Many sweaters are made of blue wool and fashioned in a cable-stitch pattern. What's so strange about the similarity?

Can this man possibly be Steve? Did he want to hide his identity from me because he didn't want me to pity him? Nonsense!

After all, Steve is dead. Mr Shek confirmed that he'd been killed in combat. It is only wishful thinking that this man is Steve.

Again she recalled an incident.

*

In the New Territories Stephen and Li-ling saw a marching band of musicians dressed in flame-red jackets and pants, playing Chinese clarinets, gongs and cymbals. A beautifully decorated enclosed bridal palanquin carried by four bearers followed. When the procession stopped at the open entrance to a large hut, firecrackers were set off to welcome the bride. The young girl wearing a gorgeous wedding dress and a colourful headdress with strands of beads hanging over her face stepped out of the palanquin. A crowd gathered around as the *tai kum* helped her into the hut. From the entrance they saw many guests inside, dressed in new clothes, looking very happy and showing much interest in an easel which stood beside the bride. It held the picture of a young man. She kowtowed before the altar of the bridegroom's ancestors. When an old couple took their seats in front of the altar, she kowtowed to them also. Throughout the ceremony, monks standing beside the altar table chanted and chimed small bells.

★

Li-ling proceeded along Conduit Road for some time, puzzling over the questions in her mind.

As to the sweater, since it is so worn and even one sleeve is gone, why does the man still keep it? Is it something special to him? Perhaps he keeps it as a souvenir of his war experience.

'Li-ling, are you out of your mind?' she asked herself out loud. 'Forget the whole thing. You'll never again meet Steve on this earth except in your dreams.'

As she walked on, suddenly she remembered something else.

★

Stephen and Li-ling had been on the shore of a stream near the south coast of Kwangtung – the first place of hiding on their escape route from Hong Kong.

'What you've done for me will keep my spirit strong enough to withstand any suffering. I'll never feel lonely again as long as you are with me,' said Stephen to Li-ling when they were seated side by side, leaning against an evergreen seacoast mallow with its heart-shaped leaves.

'Steve, what do you mean? I'll be away from you for quite a few days.'

'But I'll have this to remind me of you,' he said, pointing at the new sweater he wore. They both laughed.

★

Now Li-ling abruptly dropped her pack and dashed back breathlessly. Though she fought for each breath, she ran faster and faster. While she was still some distance away from the pavilion, she seemed to hear someone call her name.

It's merely my imagination, she thought.

When she looked up, she saw the crippled man rushing toward her from afar. As they met, they embraced. Their tears of joy blended. Their souls united.

After experiencing so much suffering and facing death so many times in the old world of war and hatred, she felt that they were about to enter the new world of peace and love.

Acknowledgements

Thanks are due, in great measure, to the following who gave good advice on my novel: the Right Reverend S K Cheung, Mr C H Haye, Mr N C Chau, Dr C H Wen, Prof S I Hsiung, Mrs Elaine Bierhauer, Mr Hank Reinecke, Mr Boyd Simmons, Mrs Christine Rossi, Mrs Shirley Mossman, Mr Michael Maher, Mr Jim Murphy, Mrs Elizabeth Lee, Mrs Cathy Bowling, Mr Art Cardenas, Mr Al Vezzetti, Mr John Jacobsen, Mrs Dolores Cullen, Mr Wayne Hearne, Mrs Ginny Benson, Mrs Linda and Mr Wayne Howell, Mrs Emily Christenson and Mrs Eleanor Wash.

Thanks are also due, in no small degree, to the following who made a general comment on my work: Su Law, Mr Lee Chen, Mr Min Chen, Miss Josephine Wai, Ms Josephine Lo, Miss May Poon, Miss Carol Shen, Mr Fletcher Day and Mr T C Li.

Nineteen of the above are either former or present members of the San Dimas Writer's Workshop.

Résumé

Mr Henry Kwun Chen's career has varied. In the late 1940s to 1950, working as a merchant with his two siblings, he ran his family's enterprises in Shanghai: an exchange bank, a stock company, a pharmacy, a clinical laboratory and an X-ray centre. From 1950 to 1980 he worked as an educationist in Hong Kong, becoming a teacher, a senior inspector of schools, the officer-in-charge of the Chinese Language Teaching Centre and Principal of Christ College. Since 1981, he has devoted some time to writing as a hobby in the United States.